For Jay, who fixes things when I break them.

"WERE YOU AND VICTOR HAPPY?"

"Let's see." Setting aside her glass, Sandra crossed her feet, clasping her hands behind her head. "Did I think I was happy? Absolutely. Did I love Victor?"

Mike regretted asking her about him. She was reciting the questions with the same unsettling cadence of a cross-examination.

She moved her hands to her lap. "With every bit of my heart," she said, and he was disconcerted to hear a tremor of tears in her voice. She cleared her throat. "Did Victor love me? Ah, now there's a puzzle. Can you ever know what's in another person's heart?"

Christ, what was she saying? That Victor hadn't loved her? "What do you think now?"

"That I don't know a thing."

Leaning forward, Mike brushed a lock of hair away from her cheek. Just to see if it felt as silky as it looked. It did.

She gasped softly and pulled back. "Mike—"

"Shh," he said. "I won't hurt you."

"Yes, you will." She studied him intently, considering. "But I think it might not matter."

SPECIAL READING GROUP GUIDE INSIDE

ALSO BY SUSAN WIGGS

The You I Never Knew

SUSAN WIGGS

Passing Through Paradise

GRAND CENTRAL
PUBLISHING

NEW YORK   BOSTON

This book is a work of fiction. Names, characters, places, and incidents are the product of the author's imagination or are used fictitiously. Any resemblance to actual events, locales, or persons, living or dead, is coincidental.

Grand Central Publishing
Hachette Book Group USA
237 Park Avenue
New York, NY 10017
Visit our Web site at www.HachetteBookGroupUSA.com

Grand Central Publishing is a division of Hachette Book Group USA, Inc.
The Grand Central Publishing name and logo is a trademark of Hachette Book Group USA, Inc.

Printed in the United States of America

First Printing: February 2002
First Special Price Edition: July 2008

10 9 8 7 6 5 4 3 2 1

Life and death do not wait for legal action.

—Daphne du Maurier

Passing Through Paradise

Chapter 1

Ten Tortures for Courtney Procter

1. *Tell her she's finally growing into her face.*
2. *Organize a boycott of her show's sponsors.*
3. *Send her a silicon recall notice.*
4. *Get a convict to mail her fan letters from prison.*
5. *Tell everyone who she used to date—and why he dumped her.*

" . . . officially ruled an accident, but the sleepy coastal town of Paradise still holds one woman responsible for the tragedy that took prominent politician Victor Winslow—his beautiful young widow, Sandra. Despite last night's ruling by the state medical examiner, unsettling questions persist."

The bluish image flickered as the camera tightened its shot on the blond TV reporter. "Witnesses who last saw State Senator Winslow alive on the night of February ninth have testified that he was engaged in a heated argument with his wife. An anonymous caller reported that the Winslows' car was traveling at a high rate of speed when it spun out of control on Sequonset Bridge and plunged into the Sound.

"Investigators later discovered a bullet embedded in the car's dashboard. Traces of the victim's blood were detected on Mrs. Winslow's clothing.

"None of this was sufficient to satisfy the state's burden of proof that a murder occurred, but *this* reporter promises to investigate further the trail leading to the late Senator Winslow's wife, the sole beneficiary of a large life insurance policy . . .

"And so Sandra Winslow, known locally as the Black Widow of Blue Moon Beach, is left with only her conscience for company. This is Courtney Procter, WRIQ News."

Sandra Winslow set down her journal and pen. Picking up the remote control, she aimed it at the morning newscaster's taut, surgically enhanced face. "Bang," she said, pressing the OFF button. "You're dead. What part of 'ruled an accident' didn't you get, Courtney Proctologist?"

She stood and walked to the broad, bow-front window, with her arms wrapped around the emptiness inside her. She savored a fragile sense of triumph—finally, the accident ruling had come through—but the local news report left the door open for trouble. No matter what the ME ruled, there were those who would always hold her responsible.

A harsh wind, on the leading edge of the coming storm, flattened the clacking dune grasses and churned the waters of the Sound into a froth. A handcrafted suncatcher in the shape of a bird vibrated against the windowpane, stirring memories she couldn't escape.

Sandra felt so far away from the person she'd once been, and not just because she'd moved into the old beach house after being released from the hospital. Only a year ago, she'd sat at the head table of the Newport Marina ballroom, wearing a pink knitted suit with black trim and matching shoes, her gloved hands folded in her lap. With his trademark panache, her husband held forth from the podium, speaking with compelling eloquence of his commitment to the citizens who had just elected him to a second term. He'd spoken of service and gratitude and family. And love. When Victor spoke of love, he could make even the most jaded heart believe.

He'd singled Sandra out as his steady anchor in the shifting seas of politics. His family and friends surrounded her in a warm cocoon of affection, as if she were truly one of them. After the speech, she sipped coffee, shared small talk and smiles, held other women's babies and stood proudly at the side of her famous husband.

The man who was missing, and now presumed dead.

She stared out the window, tucking ink-smudged hands into the back pockets of her jeans.

For Sandra, there was no "presumed" about Victor's death. She knew.

The wounded morning sky, as lackluster as midwinter itself, grew duller rather than brighter with the coming day. Looking out over the gray-shadowed beach, she felt a piercing loneliness, so sharp and cold that she flinched and hugged the oversized sweater tighter around her.

Victor's sweater.

She shut her eyes and inhaled with a shudder of emotion. It still smelled of him. Faintly spicy and clean and tinged with . . . him. Just him.

Damn Victor. How could he have done this, told her those things and then died on her? One minute you love someone, she thought, you believe you're tied to him forever, the next minute fate cuts you loose. And all the disillusionment and shattered hopes had nowhere to go.

She picked up the notebook again, flipped the page and read over her notes for the story she was working on. Her editor had already granted a sixty-day extension, and she was coming to the end of the second deadline. If she didn't turn in the manuscript soon, she'd have to repay the money they'd advanced her to write the novel in the first place.

The money—modest sum that it was—had been spent long ago on luxuries such as groceries and legal fees. Even though she'd never been charged with a crime, she had incurred an amazing sum of attorneys' fees. Now, at last, she would be entitled to the life insurance settlement.

The idea of profiting from Victor's death made her feel queasy. But she had to do something, had to pick up her life and figure out a way to go on. It was torture for her to live in Paradise, among the people who had adored her husband. Sometimes she even went up the road to Wakefield to run errands simply because she didn't want to encounter anyone who had known Victor.

The trouble was, everyone knew Victor. Thanks to his family name and the swift incandescence of his political career, followed by his spectacular demise, the whole state knew him now. Sandra would have to go somewhere far away to escape his shadow.

And now, finally, she had a chance to do that. Something unexpected was happening inside her. She was free, unattached. She had nothing to hold her now—not Victor's political calendar, certainly not any social obligations. A soaring sense of freedom rose like a raft of birds from a marsh.

Now that the death investigation was finally over, she edged toward a decision that had been hovering in her mind for months. She could fix up the place, sell it, hit the road. Her destination didn't seem to matter as much as the urge to run.

She picked up a flyer she'd found on a community bulletin board outside the post office. "Paradise Construction—Restoration and Remodeling. Bonded and Insured. References." Grabbing the phone before she could change her mind, she dialed the number and got—not surprisingly—a voice-mail message.

Sandra hesitated, not sure what to say. Her house was in a state of extreme disrepair. She needed a specialist. She settled for leaving the address and phone number.

Outside, gale-force winds tore at the wild sea roses under the window. Thorns scratched across the wavy, sleet-smeared glass pane. No wonder ships lost their way in these waters; she could barely detect the slow blink of the Point Judith lighthouse in the distance.

The bone-deep, icy cold of the winter storm reached invisible fingers through the cracks and chinks in the old house. Shivering, she picked up a log for the woodstove. It was the last one in the bin. The stove door opened with a rusty yawn, and she laid the log on the embers. Aiming the bellows, she pumped away until the glowing heart of the coals reddened and then burst into little tongues of flame licking along the underside of the log. Not so long ago, she hadn't known the first thing about heating with a woodstove. Now it was as routine as brushing her teeth.

As the blaze took hold, she adjusted the vents and picked up her journal again.

Ten Advantages to Being Poor

1. You learn to build fires for warmth.
2. You can tell phone solicitors to—

Who was she kidding? She'd never come up with ten. Setting aside the messy notebook, she glared at the small, furious fire.

She felt like the Little Match Girl, burning up her whole supply of matches. Hans Christian Andersen's heroine had been at her wits' end, her survival in question. Sandra imagined herself with no heat, the last bit of firewood gone, curled into a fetal position in front of the stove. Who would find her there? She imagined weathered bones being discovered years in the future, when her memory was no more than a scandalous blot on the history of the town and some developer hired a wrecking crew to demolish the ancient house and replace it with a high-rise of oceanfront condos.

She wondered if other people had these thoughts when they ran out of firewood.

Some of the local teenagers earned money by splitting and stacking wood for the summer people, who liked to build bonfires on the beach for clam bakes. But despite the new ruling, Sandra was pretty certain she wouldn't find anyone willing to split wood for her, not in this town.

The icy wind crescendoed, howling under the eaves of the old beach house, entering through the cracks, making a mockery of the tepid heat from the last stick of wood in the stove.

The big house had been in her father's family for generations, built more than a century ago as a summer retreat. Ever since, the old place had sat abandoned and neglected, like a bleached skull at the edge of nowhere. Although the house wasn't insulated for winter visitors, Sandra had no choice but to live here now.

At least she had a roof over her head. But her husband was dead and no matter what the truth was, everyone blamed her. She held secrets in her heart that she would take to the grave.

Staring out the rain-lashed window again, she tried not to feel the cold drilling into her bones. The storm had pummeled the dead tangles of brier in the field beside her house. On the beach, the wrack line lay thick with whatever flotsam the waves had driven home. A delicate rime of frost silvered everything—the dunes, the rocks, the windows of the house she couldn't afford to heat.

Heat. This was getting ridiculous.

She put on a heavy plaid coat, stuffed her feet into gumboots and headed outside. The rain had slacked off, but the wind blew sharply across the property. As she crossed the driveway toward the garage and shed, a flutter of paper at the side of the road caught her eye.

When the rumors had started, she used to find the occasional roll of toilet paper hurled from a car, draping the overgrown hedge by her mailbox. She ought to be used to the humiliation by now, but she wasn't.

Hers was a typical rural mailbox, poking out from a hedge of wild roses—nothing special, not even marked with a name. Just the house number.

The small metal box lay torn to bits in the ditch beside the road. The crooked red signal flag lay in the middle of the pavement, pointing south. The galvanized steel housing had been reduced to twisted wreckage—a plane crash in miniature.

"My God," Sandra said through chattering teeth. "Now what?"

Firecrackers; probably some local kid's cherry bomb or M-80. Why hadn't she heard them? Maybe last night's storm had drowned out the noise, or perhaps she'd mistaken the sound for a car backfiring.

Driven by the bitter wind, the mail rolled and tumbled

along the ditch and roadside. She recognized the cover of a lingerie catalog she never ordered from, a sheaf of oil-change coupons she would forget to use until they expired, and the daily credit card solicitation. Even when the whole world was against you, the credit card companies still wanted you to shop.

Kicking the debris around with the toe of her boot, she recognized a telltale scrap of pale blue and picked it up. The paper was the color of a check from her literary agency. Sure enough, there had been a check in the box.

When Victor was alive, her modest earnings had been a rather gratifying bonus. Now that he was gone, the money meant survival.

She suspected the vandals didn't give a rat's ass about her survival. People still thought she was the Black Widow.

Sandra crushed the paper in her hand. Enough. She'd had enough. Something cracked inside her and slowly broke apart like an iceberg shoving up against a rock.

Enough.

At the lean-to by the garage, she glared at the stack of fat, seasoned logs. Flinging the torn check aside, she grabbed the maul from its hook, used her foot to roll a log onto the colorless grass and set it upright. She brought the blade of the maul down squarely into the heart of the log, splitting it apart. The pith of the wood was pale, slightly moist, fragrant with a clean scent. Setting up each broken half, she split them one after another, a little surprised by her deadly accuracy with the maul. Finally she picked up each split quarter and tossed it into the rusty wheelbarrow to take back to the house.

She moved on to the next log, and then the next, whaling away with a sense of purpose as hot and clean as new fire. She had no notion of time passing, though the stack of quartered firewood in the wheelbarrow grew steadily. She was like a machine, pulling out a log, splitting it, splitting it again until sweat mingled with the tears pouring down her face.

Chapter 2

*M*ike Malloy pulled his pickup truck off the road a few yards short of the address the woman had left on his voice mail. He spotted a rural mailbox post—without the mailbox. The house number had been destroyed along with the box, but then he saw it stenciled on the road by the volunteer fire department.

The old Babcock place? That had to be a mistake. Punching buttons on his cell phone, he listened to the message again. *"I need some work done on my house at 18707 Curlew Drive. Please call Sandra at (401) 555-4006."*

Holy crap. It was *that* Sandra. Victor's widow. Resting his forearms on the steering wheel, Mike studied the old, isolated place. He'd been aware of the house for years, but never realized it belonged to the woman all of Paradise loved to hate. He figured he knew what had happened to the mailbox. Local kids went joyriding along the bumpy coastal roads, and many a night's entertainment involved the smashing of mailboxes. Mike himself had committed his share of mayhem back when they were all teenagers. Victor seldom joined them on those outings—even then, he seemed to have an innate preoccupation with keeping his nose clean.

The usual method was to vandalize boxes at random, but Mike sensed that this one had been done in with a special malice.

The citizens of Victor Winslow's home district were mad as hell.

Mike let the old oil-hungry engine idle as he sat thinking about the gossip and rumors storming through Paradise. Though he'd only been back a few weeks, he'd heard a dozen versions of last year's tragedy. All the stories pointed the finger at Victor's enigmatic widow.

He glanced at the area map lying open on the bench seat of the truck. It was a remote spot, a green punctuation mark on the edge of the vast blue Atlantic, but apparently not remote enough to keep Sandra Winslow out of the media's limelight.

No one had lived in the big old Victorian beyond the hedgerow in years. When they were kids, Mike and Victor used to come here and pelt rocks from their slingshots at the Babcock place, which had been occupied only in the summer. The two boys had been inseparable, spending summers on the beach and winters skating on Frog Pond. When they were twelve years old, they'd become blood brothers in a solemn ceremony involving a dull Boy Scout knife, a campfire at Horseneck Cove and some chanted Latin phrases read from the back of a dollar bill.

A lifetime had passed since that star-filled night, but he could still remember the way the waves, with curling

phosphorous lips, had lifted, translucent against the moon-
light, then slid up along the sand in the hissing rhythm that
had been the theme music of their boyhood.

They'd lost touch, as best friends often do, when
adulthood had intruded like an incurable disease.

And now this.

Victor was dead and Mike was scrambling to regroup
after being nailed in a vicious divorce.

Which, given what had happened to Victor, didn't
seem quite so bad.

He figured it was no coincidence that, only a day after
the ruling, Sandra Winslow was ready to spend money.
Knowing Victor, he'd probably carried a hefty life insurance policy.

"So what do I do now, Vic?" Mike said aloud, his
breath fogging the windshield of the truck. But he already
knew. He needed the work.

Mike Malloy used to be at the top of his game. In Newport, he'd owned a construction firm that specialized in historical restoration. But the divorce had broken that apart
along with everything else. Now he was trying to recover,
starting small again with light construction, remodeling,
pretty much anything that needed doing. He never expected to find himself starting over at this point in his life.

This time of year, a decent project was hard to come
by. A few summer people might contract for repair work
on their empty vacation houses; the weather did its part by
ripping off shingles, blowing in windows, flooding base-
ments. A long-term job would be perfect right now.

He drummed his fingers on the steering wheel, put the
old Dodge in gear and turned into Sandra Winslow's driveway.

The place looked as bereft as a toy left out in the rain.
It was a Carpenter Gothic built in typical 1880s style, tall

and narrow with a steeply pitched gable roof edged by lacy bargeboards. Pointed arches framed the windows, and a one-storey porch wrapped around three sides of the first floor.

Even in a state of neglect, the structure exuded an airy delicacy. This was clearly a summer place, designed and situated to make the most of sea breezes blowing in from the water. The only provision for winter seemed to be the fieldstone chimney at one end.

The gray siding hadn't seen a coat of paint in decades, he guessed, and the roof had sprouted moss, lichens and poison ivy. The sagging front entrance sullenly greeted visitors, and a rooftop widow's walk was bordered by a row of broken railings.

Even so, Mike detected a subtle, uncontrived charm in the board and batten trim, the bay and oriel windows, the steep cross gables hand-hewn a century ago. But like the house, the original appeal had been warped and weathered. Shutters that had probably been functional half a century ago hung crooked from rusty hinges. At least one had plummeted into an overgrown lilac bush.

The place was a disaster. People who wanted to slap the Winslow woman behind bars ought to see it. Maybe there was a sort of purgatory for people who got away with murder. Maybe it looked something like this.

Except his trained eye kept going to the soaring lines of the house, the unself-conscious grace of the scrollwork trim, and the drama of the setting—a private half acre at the edge of the dunes, facing the broadest view the state had to offer.

The landscaping had run wild, and the lawn consisted of a dead trampled area circling the house like a tattered skirt. Ancient wild roses bordered the verges, some reaching as high as the first storey of the house. Wind and cold had long since stripped the leaves from the snarl of bushes, leaving bald rosehips behind.

Mike killed the engine. When he got out of the truck, he heard a rhythmic thunk from the vicinity of the garage, long ago converted from a carriage house.

Someone was chopping wood. He walked around behind the garage to see who it was.

From the rhythm of the chopping, he expected someone large. Experienced. He'd split his share of wood and knew it wasn't exactly high tea.

At first he didn't recognize Sandra Winslow. He'd seen her only in pictures, and he was fairly certain she didn't dress this way for the press. Faded jeans and an oversized plaid hunting jacket. Some of her brown hair was caught into a messy ponytail; her feet were stuffed into cracked rubber boots. Her face was chapped from wind and cold.

Split logs lay scattered around her, littering the ground like small corpses. Oblivious, she kept chopping away with single-minded purpose, lifting the maul high overhead and burying it in the wood, then giving it an expert twist as she wrenched it out for another blow. She paused once and made a small, surprised sound in her throat. Then she stooped down to watch a tiny brown field mouse dart to safety behind the woodpile.

She took the next log from the opposite end of the pile, away from the mouse. She lifted the maul to swing it again.

"Excuse me," he said.

She stopped in midswing and turned to face him, angling the ax across her chest. She looked dangerous—red-cheeked and wild-eyed, full of deadly fury.

"Who are you?" she asked.

"My name's Mike Malloy." He paused to see if that meant anything to her. Had Victor ever mentioned him?

Probably not, judging by her guarded expression and her next question: "Wh-what do you want?"

Loaded question, and she must've known it. He'd come looking for work, and found the woman accused of killing Victor Winslow.

He held out a business card. "I'm a contractor. You left me a message a while ago."

"I didn't realize you'd reply in person." Her gaze flicked at the house. "So. I'm in the market for some repairs."

"Starting with the mailbox," he said.

She looked away, and he figured he'd said the wrong thing.

"The place is a wreck." She leaned the maul against the side of the building. "This is not news to me. I don't need some drive-by handyman to tell me so."

Handyman. Mike wasn't insulted. He wished things could be that simple.

"I haven't told you much of anything yet. Ma'am." He didn't like her. After only a few moments, he could tell she was difficult, combative, holding up anger and distrust like a riot shield.

This was a stupid waste of time, Mike decided. He put the business card in the wheelbarrow with the split wood, anchoring it with a log. "Anyway, that's how to reach me if you decide you need me." Without looking at her again, he turned and walked toward his truck.

He was just about to get in and drive off—relieved, already thinking about the next business call—when she yelled out, "Wait."

He turned back and saw her standing there with the card in her hand. "Just what is it you do?"

"I fix things."

"What kind of things?"

"Tell me what's wrong, and I'll fix it."

For some reason, that seemed to strike her as funny, but not in a pleasant way. A harsh, staccato note of laughter burst from her and then died. "As a matter of fact, I've decided to sell the place."

Mike hid his surprise. Homes like this rarely came on the market. In spite of its barely livable condition, a house on Blue Moon Beach was a potential gold mine.

"In that case, you do need me. There's no way this place would pass inspection. When did you decide to sell?"

She glared at the wreckage of her mailbox. "About twenty minutes ago."

She was not exactly a barrel of laughs.

Mike shut the door of his truck and said, "Tell you what. Why don't we have a look around the place, Miss—?" It was risky, pretending he didn't know who she was, but he figured if he played dumb, she'd quit acting so edgy.

"Sandra Babcock Winslow," she said, stuffing the card in her pocket. She watched his face with a probing stare, but Mike didn't give any indication that he recognized the name. He'd deal with her on a need-to-know basis. Over the years, he'd worked with dozens of clients and hadn't felt obliged to tell them about his past or his personal life. If he let on that he'd known Victor, she might order him off the premises.

She walked toward the edge of the yard, where a tumble of bracken fern and brier formed a natural barrier between the property and the dunes. Crushed by the blight of winter, the gentle terrain of the yard was worn hard and smooth.

A strong wind blew Sandra Winslow's brown hair every which way, partially obscuring a face that was both impatient and haunted. "The house dates back to 1886," she said. "My great-grandfather, Harold Babcock, built it as a summer place. At one time, the family planned to re-store it."

This didn't surprise Mike—the house was a diamond in the rough, and he saw what the place could be. In New-port, knowing how to treat historic houses had been the key to his success. He had a knack for peeling back the lay-ers of time, for correcting misguided modernizations, for excavating the intent of the original builder.

The house on Blue Moon Beach had an old home's way of stirring a sense of nostalgia, the kind that pierced through cynicism and disappointment and the heaviness of years. Just for a moment, he imagined the Babcock house restored, handsome as a clipper ship, the garden in bloom, a rope swing suspended from the gnarled hickory tree, kids playing in the yard.

Mike told himself he ought to view the house for what it was—run-down, neglected, blighted by rot, infested with bad karma by its cranky resident.

And yet . . .

"Well?" she asked.

"Perfect candidate for restoration," he said, his words true and unequivocal. "Even though it's in lousy condition now, the structure and workmanship are outstanding."

She laughed again, that bitter note. "You have a wild imagination, Malloy."

"A good eye," he said, annoyed by her sarcasm. "I won't fool you—the place needs work, but I'm guessing it's got strong bones. The roof itself might be okay, too, under all the plant life."

"Trust me, it's not okay." She led the way to the en-closed sunroom, which faced the endless water.

Without thinking, he picked up an armload of split wood.

"You don't have to do that," she said.

"No charge," he replied, then followed Victor's widow. The Black Widow of Blue Moon Beach—wasn't that what the local press called her?

She stood at the door to her house and held it open. "'Step into my parlor,'" she said, a touch of irony in her voice.

"'Said the Spider to the Fly,'" he finished for her, entering the house.

She flipped her hair out of her face. "Oh, you know that little rhyme?" She seemed surprised. People always were; they expected workmen to be illiterate, ignorant even of nonsense poems.

"I sounded out the words," he said.

She pulled off her rubber boots and left them by the door. "You must have children, then."

He nodded. The fact that he had kids defined him entirely now. "A boy and a girl."

"That's nice." Her expression relaxed a little. It was the first hint of softness he'd seen in her. She really did seem to think it was nice that he had kids.

Mike wondered why there weren't any little Winslows running around. Victor had really liked children, he recalled. He'd been a swim instructor at the YMCA in Newport when they were in high school. Each summer, he'd given sailing lessons at First Beach.

It was just as well there weren't any children, Mike realized. What kind of kid needed to grow up hearing that his mother had killed his father?

He set the wood in a stack by the door.

She didn't thank him, but pointed to a corner of the ceiling. "That's what I meant about the roof," she said.

Streaks of mildew stained the ceiling and wall. "Fixable," he said. "I'd have to take a closer look."

She folded her arms in front of her. "I never said—"

"Neither did I," he interrupted. "I'm just looking."

"You must have a lot of time on your hands."

"Yeah, well, it's the slow season." He strolled into the next room, a tall narrow kitchen with ancient linoleum rubbed bare in places, an old scrubbed pine table and a big cast-iron sink. Stuck to the window with a suction cup was a bird made of colored glass. The humming refrigerator bore a collection of cartoon-character magnets, scrawled notes and lists. The room smelled faintly of spices and dish soap. "This is original cabinetry work," he commented. "Nice, but it's got the worst paint job I've ever seen."

She ran a hand over a cabinet door, thickly coated with glossy seafoam green. "One of my great-aunts, I think." She winced and turned her hand over, studying her palm. A row of livid blisters, some broken, covered the base of her fingers.

"You should wear gloves when you chop wood," he said.

"Uh-huh."

Without thinking, he took hold of her wrist. She reacted instantly, trying to pull away.

"You need to clean this up," he said, leading her over to the sink and turning on the cold water. He felt strangely aware of the fragile bones of her wrist, the smooth, delicate skin in his grip. She had bluish ink stains on her fingers.

He stuck her hand under the stream of cool water. It probably stung, but she didn't flinch. "Let's see the other hand," he said.

More blisters. He made her rinse that one, too, and while she did, he got a couple of paper towels to pat them dry. He cradled her hand in his, palm up, making a nest of his own hand around hers. "Do you have a first-aid kit around here somewhere?"

"This is not a major medical emergency," she said.

"If you don't cover up these open blisters, they could get infected."

"Whatever." She rummaged around in the cabinet under the sink and produced an ancient Girl Scout kit. Poking through it, he found a roll of gauze and tape, and a bottle of Mercurochrome so ancient its cap was rusted.

"You're not coming near me with that stuff. I was traumatized by it as a kid."

He pitched it into the trash can under the sink. "Probably toxic by now anyway." Taking her hand, he wrapped the gauze and loosely taped it in place.

As he tended to the other hand, she held up the first, turning it this way and that. "Now I know you're a dad. Good field dressing," she said, flexing her fist. "I look like a prizefighter."

It sounded a little incongruous coming from someone her size, and he almost smiled. "Wear gloves the next time you chop wood."

"Good plan."

"So how long have you lived here?"

She leaned against the counter. "Less than a year. The house has been in the family forever, though. But nobody's done much for it lately." She pushed away from the counter and led him into the next room, a big sitting area with a sagging sofa facing the woodstove, set into the fieldstone hearth. A panoramic bow-front window with cushions on the sill framed a stunning view. More books than he'd ever seen outside a library lined the shelves flanking the fireplace, and there were still more books in the library alcove adjacent to the parlor.

"The floors creak," she said, demonstrating in her

sock feet and opening a door as she passed it. "Basement leaks. All the windows rattle, and so does the banister. God knows what shape the attic's in. I dumped a lot of moving boxes there and haven't been up since."

She headed upstairs, wiggling the railing like a loose tooth. The second storey had a laundry chute, a shotgun hall running the length of the house, a bathroom and three bedrooms, two of them completely empty except for a draping of cobwebs. The third had a bank of windows facing the sea and an old four-poster bed of dark, scarred walnut, the traditional sheaves of rice carved into the posters. It hadn't been made up, and she didn't seem to care. A limp stuffed bear, the garish sort given away as carnival prizes, lay amid the tangled blankets. Paperback novels were stacked haphazardly on the nightstand, along with a prescription pill bottle, a spiral notebook and a pen. A faint, flowery smell—a woman smell—hung in the air. He wished he hadn't noticed that.

The atmosphere had the transitional feel of a seedy hotel room. But again, as he had in the yard, he looked past the peeling wallpaper and dingy woodwork, and saw a room transformed, the bed angled for a view of the sunrise over the water, prisms in the leaded windows casting rainbows on the walls.

"So that's about it," she said, brushing past him as she walked out of the room.

She smelled of shampoo and sea air and something else, something lonely, maybe. In the hallway, she indicated a pair of doors. "The linen closet, and stairs to the attic."

He went to have a look, picking his way around battered luggage and cardboard cartons, haphazardly stacked, some of them labeled in a scrawl of Magic Marker.

"Just move the boxes if they're in your way," she called after him. "Did the roof leak?"

"I don't think so." The dormer windows were so dingy they barely let in enough light to see. The frames showed a powdery brown dusting of rot. Reaching up, he tugged the string to turn on a bare lightbulb. The roof beams and supports, hand-milled a century ago, had the sturdiness of ship's timbers. Batting away cobwebs, he shut off the light and went downstairs.

She stood in the cavernous, sparsely furnished parlor, her back to the stove, her bandaged hands unconsciously reaching for the heat. "Well?" she asked.

"What do you want to do with the house?"

"I told you, I intend to sell it," she said. "Which means getting it fixed up, obviously. I'd never find a buyer for the place in this condition."

If he had the money, Mike would buy it from her as is, on the spot. The place was that appealing to him—an old Victorian summer place on the beach. But most people didn't want to spend good money for a never-ending home improvement project. And Mike didn't have the cash—good or otherwise.

"So what's your price?" she asked.

The woman didn't mince words, he'd give her that. "Depends on what you want."

She laughed again without humor. "What are my options?"

"A full historical restoration or just buffing up?"

"Whatever will get me the sale." She sounded weary and a little annoyed, but not at him.

"That would be plan A—the full restoration in compliance with guidelines from the National Register of Historic Residences."

"That matters?" she asked.

"Money in the bank. You'd get top dollar for a restored and certified vintage home, and it'd sell quickly. This is a rare place—the location and the house itself. If you slapped on some paint, fixed the wiring and plumbing, trimmed the hedges and did the roof and floors, it'd pass inspection, but you'd lose any chance of certification from the National Register."

"And *that* matters?" she repeated, her voice sharp with sarcasm.

"You'd end up waiting longer for the right buyer, and you'd get a lot less."

"I'm used to getting less than I expect," she muttered.

"That chip on your shoulder will come in handy if we need to knock out any walls."

"Fine," she said, "then I'll hang on to it."

She stared at him, and maybe it was a trick of the light, but he had the weirdest feeling of recognition. He could see softness hidden behind the caustic facade. He saw the woman who'd saved a mouse in the woodpile, who collected refrigerator magnets and read herself to sleep at night. She was no longer a scandalous figure on the local news, thin and somber behind dark glasses as her lawyer hustled her to the car. She was totally different in person. She had enormous eyes, sort of brown, sort of gold, soft around the edges in direct contradiction to her prickly attitude.

He'd seen the occasional photo of her and Victor in *Rhode Island Monthly*. The Winslows had been the state's resident royalty, newsworthy down to the way they parted their hair. The society pages always showed her smiling up at Victor, maybe laughing. And something about seeing her now pierced Mike with a feeling of sadness.

"What can you do for me, Mr. Malloy?" she asked quietly, the sarcasm gone.

There was a world of meaning in that question.

He hesitated, trying to figure out what he expected to come of this—besides a business contract. He wanted to make sense of the senseless, maybe, even though he knew it was futile. He now had a close-up view of the Black Widow of Blue Moon Beach.

She made a terrible first impression, but their short meeting had convinced Mike of two things. First, the woman was holding something in. And second, regardless of her reputation, she was his best prospect in an otherwise bleak season.

If he worked on her house, the Winslow family—Victor's parents, who had once treated Mike as a second son—would probably regard him as a traitor. Or maybe not. Business was business, and they might be glad to see the last of their daughter-in-law. Fixing up her house would speed the process.

"I'll work up a couple of proposals," he said. "One for a full restoration, and the other for cosmetic surgery."

"They both sound expensive."

"Anything you spend comes off your gain on the house when it sells, so you end up reporting a lesser amount to the IRS."

"All right." She plucked at the bandage around her hand, flashed those bourbon-colored eyes at him. "I'd like that. I'd like to see a proposal."

"I'll get it for you in the next couple of days," he promised.

"Okay." She went over to a desk equipped with a laptop computer, a printer and stacks of paper. Mike idly picked up a framed photograph of her as a girl with tanned legs and bare feet, sitting on a porch swing with a man and a woman. From the sunlit dunes in the background, he could tell the picture had been taken at Blue Moon Beach.

"Your folks?" he asked.

"Yeah." She didn't elaborate.

They looked ordinary, unremarkable and kind. You never really knew how your kids would turn out, he thought.

"So you can call with your bid anytime," she said. "I'm usually . . . home."

She stood close enough for him to catch another whiff of that womanly smell, part perfume, part chemistry. A phantom heat shimmered between them, and Mike tried to scowl away the sensation. Not her, he told himself. Not her.

In his line of work, he'd had his share of come-ons from bored young wives of rich Newporters, left alone in their vintage houses. But the interest had always been one-sided, because he held himself to a strict policy of business only.

Yet he couldn't avoid a quick memory of the mussed bed upstairs, and he was all too aware that Sandra Winslow lived here by herself, more lonely than bored. And regardless of her past, she wasn't anybody's wife now.

Chapter 3

Journal Entry—January 5—Saturday

Ten Things to Do Before Selling the House

49. *Take Granddaddy Babcock's steamer trunk to Mom and Dad.*
50. *Figure out where I buried my coin collection in the yard back in 1972.*
51. *Check references on Malloy.*

Malloy. Michael Patrick Malloy, according to his business card. Looking back at her overgrown list, Sandra realized his name had come up at least a dozen times, and she hadn't even hired him yet. He preoccupied her, kept tugging at her thoughts, and she didn't understand why.

There certainly wasn't anything personal between them, yet he reminded her sharply of how much she missed simple human contact. He was a handyman, she needed her house fixed, end of story. Nothing unusual about that. She'd hired fix-it men before, and had never found herself fantasizing about the plumber or the Roto-Rooter man.

But there was something about the way Malloy had appeared, timing his arrival at her most lunatic moment. A knight in a rusty pickup truck, a tape measure in a holster at his hip. She didn't want to think about what she would have done if he hadn't shown up just then, but it was not overly dramatic to imagine he'd saved her from doing something desperate and stupid.

Not that it would matter to him. He had been completely businesslike, walking from room to room, scribbling notes on a clipboard. Except he didn't look like any businessman she'd ever known, in his Boston Red Sox cap, work boots and faded jeans. His hair was a little too long, his attitude too—

A sudden pounding made her jump out of her seat, spilling her pen and notebook to the floor.

She glanced at the door. It was broad daylight, she told herself, not the middle of the night. Still, she couldn't keep from reaching for the fire poker next to the stove. Advancing toward the front door, she wished she could see through the sidelight, but a while back, it had been broken by a thrown rock and boarded up.

Her fingers tightened on the brass handle of the poker and her breath came in quick gasps, inducing a brief dizziness. Given the threats and harassment she'd endured since Victor's death, she had learned to respect and fear every bump and thump in the night. Or day.

This is supposed to be over, she wanted to scream. It was an accident, damn it. But her lawyer had warned her that the ruling wouldn't end her troubles. She'd learned to trust what he said.

The knock sounded again. Louder, more insistent. Taking a deep breath, Sandra cracked open the door. The safety chain drew taut across the narrow gap. When she saw who it was, her knees turned warm and watery with relief. Thrusting the fire poker in the umbrella stand, she pressed the door shut, disengaged the chain and opened the door.

The winter wind slung knife blades of penetrating cold into the drafty old house. Light-headed with relief, Sandra stepped aside to let her visitor in and quickly shut the door.

She hadn't been expecting her mother to make the drive from Providence, but somehow she wasn't surprised to see her. "Come on in, Mom," she said. "Come over by the fire, where it's warm."

"Hello, sweetie. I brought you an afghan." She held out a crinkly plastic bag.

Sandra gave her a quick, tight hug. "Another Dorrie Babcock original. You spoil me."

"No, I knit like the wind." Afghans were her specialty. She took up knitting in one of many attempts to quit smoking, and then she'd become one of those rare individuals capable of smoking and knitting simultaneously. "And where were you yesterday? I really wish you'd get an answering machine. I think you're the only person on the planet who doesn't have one."

Actually, Sandra did have one. She put it away soon after the accident—as soon as the anonymous messages started coming. "Sorry, Mom. You must've called while I was working outside. Chopping wood." She held out her bandaged hands.

"For heaven's sake." Dorrie smiled briefly before taking off her hat, then bent to unclasp the same plastic, shoe-shaped boots she'd worn for the past thirty-something years. As always, her hair was sculpted into lacquered dark swirls that, thanks to Miss Clairol, had not changed in decades, and only the deepening lines of character in her strong face betrayed her age.

"So," her mother said, hanging her coat on the hall tree. "Things are better, yes?"

"Much," she said. Aside from the fact that her mailbox was blown up and her house was falling down, everything was just peachy. But she forbade herself to complain to her mother. Throughout the ordeal, she'd done her best to shield her parents from the worst of the fallout—the constant hounding, the phone calls, the whispers and the doubts.

Lord knew, Dorrie and Lou Babcock had put up with enough trouble from her when she was young.

A framed picture of the three of them stood on the end of the desk. It had been taken when Sandra was about eleven. Her mother leaned against her father, hugging his arm while he grinned down at her. Sandra held her father's hand, not quite smiling. She hadn't smiled much when she was a kid.

"I'll go make tea," Sandra said. She was a creature of habit. When company came, be it her mother or a party official, she fixed tea in cool weather and lemonade when it was warm. As she measured a spoonful of loose leaves into a chipped stoneware pot, she reflected that it felt strange to do something as normal as making tea when nothing was normal anymore. But that was the nature of life; everything didn't simply stop and hang suspended at the top of the Ferris wheel while you sorted out your problems. Everything kept turning. Everything kept going.

"How were the roads?" she called from the kitchen.

"Icy. But traffic wasn't bad."

"Mom, you know I'm always glad to see you. But you didn't have to come," she said, carrying the teapot into the living room. Sandra pictured her driving the Grand Marquis down from Providence over slippery roads. "I love having you visit, but I can't expect you to come running every time the local news pounds another nail into my coffin. Since Victor died, I've been teaching myself to cope on my own."

"Of course you have, dear."

"At the very least, you should've had Dad drive you." Picking up the large copper kettle from the plate on the stove, she poured boiling water into the pot, then set the lid on it to brew.

"I'm fine driving myself. Perfectly fine."

Sandra set out the sugar bowl and filled the cream pitcher. Putting everything on a tray, she carried it into the parlor.

"That's lovely," her mother said, patting the sofa beside her. She sent Sandra a warm smile.

Sandra sank down next to her mother and leaned her head on Dorrie's shoulder, inhaling the faint, comforting scent of Keri lotion, Aqua Net and cigarettes. "Sorry about the lecture, Mom. Thanks for coming, really."

Dorrie patted her knee and then leaned forward to pour tea through a strainer into their cups. "How are you?" she asked, then predictably answered her own question. "You're too thin."

"I'm fine, Mom." With ritualistic precision, Sandra measured sugar and milk into her cup. The lighthouse foghorn let out a long, mournful blast that rattled the windows.

Sandra shivered at the sound. Turning sideways on the sofa, she tucked her feet under her, sipped her tea and said, "So I guess you saw the news."

Her mother's gaze remained fixed on the tempered glass door of the woodstove, and the dancing flames within were reflected in the lenses of her glasses.

"What did you think of the broadcast?" Sandra prodded.

Dorrie turned her head to look at Sandra, blinking as

though she had just awakened. "I'm sorry," she said. "What was that?"

Sandra hesitated. Lately her mother had seemed a bit distracted. Was it the mess with Victor, or something else? Perhaps her mother was getting hard of hearing, or maybe something worse was going on. The thought made Sandra's blood run cold, but she didn't dare broach the topic with her mother. Dorrie tended to get defensive about medical matters.

"I was just wondering what you thought of the news," Sandra said. "You did see *Providence Daybreak*, didn't you? Courtney Procter. I swear, she was gloating all through the story. I could hear it in her voice." Sandra pulled her knees up to her chest and stretched her sweater over them. "How does it feel, being the mother of the Black Widow of Blue Moon Beach?"

Dorrie laced her fingers together, squeezing hard. Probably craving a cigarette. "That woman is a clown. The whole news show is made up of sensational garbage."

"That's why she gets such good ratings. What makes me crazy is that people around here believe her."

Dorrie took a thoughtful sip of her tea and set down her cup. "When something this bad happens, folks need to blame somebody. Or else they have to accept that God can be cruel. And you ought to know that no Winslow from the beginning of time could ever think such a thing."

Sandra pictured Victor's parents, heartbreaking in their dignity as they sat listening to the medical examiner. Their son was officially and legally dead, even though there was no body to make the conclusion real. He had died in an accident—that was the part they didn't accept. Accidents simply didn't happen to people like Victor.

"You always understood the Winslows better than I ever did," Sandra observed.

"Maybe so." Dorrie brushed her hand over Sandra's head in an old, familiar gesture. "Relax, honey. The investigation is over. What happened was a terrible accident. You're finally free to grieve for your husband."

Sandra propped her chin on top of her drawn-up knees. Freedom to grieve was not what she needed right now. She pressed her jaws together to keep from blurting out the latest incident of vandalism. Someone had spray-painted the letters *O.J.* on the side of the garage. Though she didn't sense any physical danger, the vicious implication of the act still shook her. But she was more angry than scared. She'd applied that anger to scrubbing off the graffiti, taking most of the paint with it. If that was grieving, she was getting good at it.

She poured herself more tea, willing her nerves to calm. She used to think there was no problem so enormous that sharing a cup of tea with her mother couldn't fix it. Now she had found that problem, and it was a whopper. And yet, just for these few moments, warmed by the intimacy of a shared cup of tea, she found it easier to breathe.

"Hey, Mom," she said, "what would you think if I sold the house?"

Her mother's eyebrows lifted behind her glasses. "You're going to leave here?"

"I have to face facts. Now that Victor's gone, it's time for me to pick up the pieces and put together some sort of life for myself. Somewhere else. Somewhere far from here."

Her mother studied her intently. It might have been a trick of the light, but Sandra sensed something more than the usual wisdom and compassion in her mother's face. There was sadness, too. A sort of surrender.

"Maybe you're right, dear. Your grandparents left the house to you, free and clear. It's your decision."

"This place has been in the family forever. Do you think Dad would be upset?"

"The only thing that upsets him is making bogey when he's shooting for par. Honestly, he hasn't thought about this place in years." She glanced around the room. "You'll have to get some work done before listing it. Hire someone."

"I think I already have." Sandra felt an odd little quiver inside, thinking of Malloy. On some level, she suspected she might be inviting more into her life than a simple contract with a handyman. "A . . . guy stopped by yesterday and looked around. He's going to put together a proposal. I didn't have the heart to tell him I'm broke."

"That's temporary. Victor's life insurance belongs to you, and it's high time you received it." She ran her hand over the threadbare arm of the old sofa.

"My lawyer's handling that." She didn't add that after deducting legal fees and paying off the debts from Victor's latest campaign, she'd barely have enough to cover the restoration work, but she was determined. She couldn't stay here, walled off from the world, no matter how much she loved the wild shores of Blue Moon Beach. What had happened that night, what was said in the car, had changed her life. But she couldn't let it destroy her. Thanks to the painfully drawn-out process of the inquest, she'd been obliged to stay in town. With the proceedings behind her, she was free to go at last.

"So you want to leave Paradise." Her mother gazed out the window at the wide winter sky. "You always seemed so at-home here. This was the place where . . . I thought you found what you were looking for."

"I did, but my only link was Victor. That's become clear enough since the accident. Other than my hairdresser—who's from Texas—these people were Victor's friends, Victor's constituents. I always thought of this house as my sanctuary, but it's not anymore."

"Will you return to Providence, then?" her mother asked.

To Providence, not *home*. Sandra thought it was an odd way to phrase it. She shook her head. "That doesn't seem far enough." She couldn't imagine passing the State House, seeing its alabaster dome glaring down at her like an accusing eye. Never again would she be able to stroll along the brick-paved streets of the state capital without remembering the way they used to be . . . the lie they used to live.

"To be honest, I haven't thought that far ahead," she said. "And you know, I've never even tried being on my own. I married Victor right out of college. But I need to figure out who I am when I'm by myself."

"Believe me, it's not too late to learn to live without a man."

There was a heaviness to Dorrie's words that puzzled Sandra. She waited, but her mother didn't elaborate.

"You'll be fine, Sandra. I know you will. The important things are still intact—your good health, your youth, your writing career."

Sandra felt a rush of sentiment. "You and Dad always believed in me, even when I was a basket case."

"You were never a basket case."

"Oh, Mom. I was. You know I was."

"Sandra, that was all so long ago. You don't still think about it, do you?"

Every time I open my mouth to speak, she thought. But she wouldn't admit it to her mother. Lord knew, Dorrie had struggled with the problem every bit as much as Sandra had. Dorrie felt a mother's pain and frustration and helplessness. For years, she'd sat up at night, listening to her daughter cry behind closed doors.

Lou and Dorrie Babcock had raised a daughter who stuttered—not just the occasional slip of the tongue, but a strangling, devastating affliction that threw a shroud of silence over Sandra.

With a wave of gratitude, she remembered all the years of patience and repetition, her mother sitting with her for hours flashing word cards at her, and her father staying up late with her to work on diaphragm and breathing exercises. It wasn't until high school that Sandra had actually trusted herself to speak more than a few words to anyone outside her family, and then did so only when she had to.

She'd always suspected that she was the only girl ever to make it through St. Cloud High School without having a single friend. She was the original invisible girl, as colorless and nondescript as a manila file folder. The funny thing was, she hadn't minded her isolation all that much. She liked books and reading, not boys and cars. The adventures in her mind were infinitely more vivid and exciting than any prom date or homecoming game.

Or so she told herself, firmly and repeatedly, until she believed it.

"I'm fine now," she assured her mother, "and I'm going to be fine." Leaning forward, she gave her a hug, grateful for the familiar softness of her shoulder.

Dorrie patted Sandra's knee. Her hand had thin, almost translucent skin and a sprinkling of spots that for a moment made it look like the hand of a stranger. Sandra couldn't bring herself to see her mother as old. When she shut her eyes, she could still feel that hand gently brushing the hair out of her face, or cupping a palmful of sunflower seeds to feed the winter cardinals, or flashing deftly across a row of knitting.

"Maybe we should all move to Florida," she declared, speaking over the thin whistle of the wind. "These New England winters are just too brutal."

Dorrie leaned down and picked up her pocketbook. "Actually, dear, I have other plans." She handed Sandra a colorful envelope.

"What's this?" She took out a printed ticket. " 'Cruise to a New You'?"

Her mother's face shone in a way Sandra hadn't seen in a long time. "Three months in the Caribbean and South America aboard the *Artemisia*."

"Sounds heavenly." Sandra scanned the itinerary—Nassau, Coco Cay, Montego Bay, a dozen others—each adventure related in lush, overblown prose. Sandra paged through a glossy brochure depicting sugar-white beaches, palm trees nodding lazily in the tropical breeze, sunshine . . . *escape*. She checked the departure date. "You're flying to Fort Lauderdale tomorrow night?"

Dorrie nodded. "I didn't want to leave before . . . well, you know."

"Before you found out whether or not I was going to be indicted for murder."

"I was totally confident in the investigation. What kind of mother would I be if I thought they'd find probable cause? But I wanted to be here for you. In fact, you should come with me. What do you say?"

Sandra felt a flare of interest, but quickly doused it. "You know I have to stay here, Mom. Because of the house." Forcing a smile, she handed back the brochures. "What an adventure."

"I've got my passport, my bikini and my Zyban tablets all packed."

"Zyban tablets?"

"A prescription for quitting smoking. I'm going to

cruise to a new me, I guess," her mother said, tucking the ticket away in her purse. "Quitting smoking. That'd be new."

"Twelve weeks. That's a long time. And a lot of money," Sandra said.

Her usually frugal mother lifted her shoulders in an elaborate shrug. "It's an investment in myself. I'm going to take Spanish lessons, learn to play blackjack, dance the macarena, get a new hairstyle, new makeup . . . new everything." Dorrie lifted her teacup. "To adventure," she said, touching her cup to Sandra's.

"To adventure."

Dorrie stood up. "Would you like to take a walk?"

Sandra sent a knowing look at her mother's voluminous purse. "I guess you haven't started the tablets yet."

"Exactly."

While her mother went outside to light up, Sandra grabbed her jacket from a hook by the mudroom door, jammed on a hat and gloves and hurried out. Dorrie headed north on the lonely gray beach, walking along the uneven wrack line where seaweed and debris flung up by the North Atlantic lay in a thick, untidy chain. In the summer, tourists came out early to scout for unbroken shells and bits of opaque beach glass, tumbled by the waves. In winter, the treasures lay unclaimed by foragers, and the sea would take them back.

Weathered ridges of sand rippled in motionless waves from the beach. The damp, yielding surface slowed Sandra as it shifted beneath her. Dorrie kept her gaze trained straight ahead at the big craggy point crowned by the lighthouse. The icy wind was making her eyes tear up; the moisture blew back against her temples and dried there, leaving a faint film of salty white.

"I won't miss the winter," Dorrie said, tugging her coat closer around her.

"I'll miss *you*," Sandra said, but quickly added, "This is going to be fabulous. You and Dad must be so excited."

"Your father's not going."

Sandra frowned, certain the howl of the wind had made her hear wrong. "Did you just say Dad's not—"

Her mother nodded.

Sandra nearly stumbled over a clump of seaweed. "I can't believe you're taking a cruise by yourself."

Dorrie gave a strange laugh. "I can't believe it, either."

"Dad didn't want to go?"

Her mother hesitated. "After thirty-five years of business travel, he's not interested. Getting him to go anywhere is like prying a snail off a rock."

"You've never been away from Dad before."

"He's been away from me."

"That was different. It was business. Talk to him, Mom. Convince him to go with you on the cruise. The two of you would have such a great time."

"He's not coming." Dorrie's voice was firm but expressionless.

"How can you be sure he wouldn't want to? He's never been fond of traveling, but I bet he'd love—"

"Sandra, I need to tell you something." Dorrie stopped walking and found a seat on a pale driftwood log. The black scar of a dead bonfire marred the sand in front of the log, and old beer bottles lay strewn in the salt grass. "Sit down." She patted the spot beside her. "I've been trying to find a way to bring this up, but I'm not doing a very good job."

Sandra felt a cold, hard squeezing in her chest, her throat. She sensed something different about her mother—it was subtle, but perhaps her eyes gleamed brighter; her hands moved nervously, clenching and unclenching. It was so unlike her practical, plan-ahead mother to book a lengthy cruise, a dream vacation, or to plan anything at the spur of the moment. Dorrie never used to spend money on frivolities. It was the sort of thing people did when they won the lottery . . . or learned they only had six months to live. "Mom?" Sandra's voice broke as she sank down beside her. "Mom, are you sick?"

Dorrie shook her head with a hint of impatience. Dropping her cigarette butt in the sand, she buried it with her heel. "Don't be silly. I'm healthy as a moose. If I look a little peaked lately, it's probably from everything that's been going on."

The past year had been hard on her parents, Sandra reflected guiltily. "Then the cruise sounds like the perfect escape. But Dad probably needs to get away just as badly as you do." She forced bright enthusiasm into her tone. "Would you like me to talk to him?"

Dorrie braced the heels of her hands on the log, leaned back and stared straight out to sea. "I'm going alone, dear. You see, I've left your father. I've been staying at Aunt Wanda's in Woonsocket the past couple of weeks."

A dull buzz of shock hummed in Sandra's head. "I don't understand."

"We're getting a divorce."

Sandra shook her head as though she had water in her ears. *Divorce*. The word sounded odd, foreign, something she didn't recognize, the name of an exotic food she would never dare to taste. It was just too bizarre. She couldn't wrap her mind around it. Divorce was not something that happened in her family, or in Victor's, either. But most especially, it didn't happen to her own parents, who had been married thirty-six years.

Agitated, she got to her feet. "Mom, no—"

"This decision was a long time coming." Her mother's voice was dispassionate as she went on. "I won't pretend it was easy, but it's the only solution I can see. Your father and I want you to know that we both love you—"

"Oh, come on, Mom." Stooping, Sandra picked up a rock and flung it as far as she could, not looking to see where it landed, not caring. "That sounds so . . . *rehearsed*. It's the sort of thing people say to seven-year-olds. Couples who are getting divorced like to pretend it doesn't affect their kids. But you know what? Even a seven-year-old knows the truth. It still hurts. It always hurts."

"Life hurts," Dorrie said. "So far, no one's found a cure for that. We all have to deal with it in our own way."

"The way you are? By running out on Dad?"

"Just because I'm the one leaving doesn't mean I'm the one doing the running out." Dorrie stood and started walking again.

With panic knocking in her chest, Sandra fell in step with her. "I wish you would tell me what went wrong. And why you believe it can't be fixed."

Dorrie stuffed her hands in the pockets of her old car coat. The camel wool garment appeared with the regularity of the seasons, unwrapped from the dry cleaner's moth-proofing each November, then retired to the basement each March. Sandra's mother didn't even change her coat, and here she was wanting to change her whole life.

"Sandra," she said, "a thirty-six-year marriage doesn't end simply because some*thing* went wrong. It's just that there were too many years during which nothing went right. The difference between then and now is that I've finally decided to do something about it." Dorrie veered around a foamy wave that came rolling toward them. "You see, your father and I always had this vision of our lifestyle once he retired. The trouble was, we never compared notes. I assumed we would do things together—learn a new language, see the world, take dancing lessons, go to a ceramics class, try new adventures. It was so obvious to me that I naturally assumed your father was on the same page."

"So what was Dad's vision?"

Dorrie made a little explosive sound of disgust. "Golf or fishing every day with his buddies, while I continue doing all the housework, all the errands, all the groceries, all the cooking, all the bills. Same as I always have. So he gets to retire, and I'm in for life without parole."

"You two should be able to work it out." Sandra couldn't believe how frightening this felt to her. It was a blow in the dark, another loss, another death. Something vital had vanished from her life, and she could never get it back again. "Get him to help more around the house."

"I've tried. He's hopeless."

"Then learn to play golf so you can go with him."

"I've tried that, too. *I'm* hopeless."

"This is not rocket science, Mom. People who love each other should—"

"Maybe that's just it," Dorrie said, pulling up the hood of her coat. "Maybe, somewhere in the middle of all those years, the love got lost."

Her mother's words made Sandra feel a deep and aching sadness. Love couldn't be that way, she thought. It just couldn't fail like that. Then she remembered Victor, and her conviction faltered. Maybe secrets haunted her parents' marriage, too. Who could really know someone else's intimate relationship?

Sandra stared at the restless sea, glossy gray beneath a brooding sky. The whole world was sliding out from beneath her feet, and she had no idea how to pull it all back into its proper place. She was beginning to question her own judgment about everything. The foundation of her family was crumbling. Things she believed to be true turned out to be lies.

"You can't let this happen, Mom," she said, raising her voice above the wind. "You and Dad have to try harder, go to counseling, work this out—"

"We're not characters in one of your books, dear," Dorrie said gently. She slipped her arm around Sandra. "I'm so sorry. But this is my life, or what's left of it. I have to take this step. It's really happening, and nothing you say or do will stop it."

Sandra saw pieces of her life like bits of colored glass through a kaleidoscope—scattered and splintered, constantly changing. "How long have you been planning this?" she asked.

"It's been a long time coming, but we wanted to wait until the business with Victor was over before telling you. Now we've all got to move on."

The wind whipped up gritty dervishes of sand on the beach and battered at the dune grasses. Another storm was coming in fast. Sandra tasted it with each breath she took, felt its heaviness pressing at her.

Dorrie started back toward the house. "It's cold out here, and I have things to do." She put her gloved hand on Sandra's arm. "I have a plane to catch."

Sandra turned to the house, the falling-down house she was so eager to sell, and walked beside her mother in silence. Above the dunes, the big Victorian hunched like a shorebird in a storm. Overgrown sea roses and lilacs nearly obscured the bow-front window, and the gray, weathered siding matched the drabness of the thunderheads rolling down from the north to wallop the coast with another winter assault.

The place had stood for more than a hundred years.

Now it teetered on the verge of collapse. Mike Malloy—a regular guy who drove a pickup truck and fixed things—claimed he could restore it, and suddenly that promise meant everything to her.

Chapter 4

*T*he storm struck when Mike was fifty feet off the ground, clinging to the catwalk on the Point Judith Light. The winter barrage chugged like a locomotive, hurling all its energy at the old brownstone tower. Wind and stinging sleet lashed at his shoulders and back as he struggled with a sheet of marine plywood. It caught the wind like a kite in a gale, pitching and thrusting him to the edge of the catwalk.

Archie Glover had called from the Coast Guard station to report that one of the windows had blown out, putting the room-sized, antique French lantern at risk. He needed help, right away.

Mike jammed his leg against the iron rail to keep from going over. From inside the beacon, Archie shouted something, but Mike couldn't hear. Wishing he'd taken time to strap on safety gear, he wrestled the plywood against the broken window, bits of glass grinding beneath his boots.

With numb, slippery hands, he screwed a series of stout iron clamps in place and hoped the temporary repair would hold until the weather cleared.

Archie held open the door, and Mike shoved himself inside to the relative quiet of the beacon. He wiped a sodden sleeve across his cold-stung face. "When I said I was looking for restoration work, this wasn't quite what I had in mind."

"For a minute there, I was afraid we'd lost you." Archie headed down the spiral staircase. "There's coffee on."

"No, thanks," Mike said, his teeth chattering. "I'd better be getting back."

Archie handed him a check. "Keep this high and dry."

Leaving the lighthouse, Mike drove along the debris-littered road to the marina. The storm skirled to the south, leaving a restless, tossing sea in its wake. A single light burned in the harbormaster's office and others glimmered from some of the larger fishing vessels, but the docks were all deserted.

Mike still didn't think of the boat as "home," but since he'd come back to Paradise, he'd been living aboard the cabin trawler *Fat Chance*, docked with the fishing fleet at the tiny port.

Beamy but well appointed, the boat became Mike's when his father retired to Florida. Years ago, Mike and Angela used to spend nearly every summer weekend aboard, taking leisurely runs out to Block Island, anchoring in private coves, fixing soup and crackers for dinner and making love to the hushed rhythm of the waves. Angela hadn't set foot on the boat in a long, long time.

Zeke leaped to greet him when he boarded and stepped

into the main saloon. He paused to scratch the dog behind the ears, then headed for a quick, scalding shower in a bathroom so compact he could barely stand up straight or turn around.

When Mike emerged from the bunk in dry clothes, Zeke thumped his tail, eager to go out for his usual evening rounds of the Paradise docks. "All right, all right," Mike muttered, pulling on a jacket.

His gaze fell to the pages of notes and sketches on the chart table, which now housed a computer and printer as well as his father's sea charts. At the top of his stack was one of innumerable letters from Loretta Schott, his divorce attorney. The family court judge had doubts about a guy who lived on a boat.

Some people believed he was "living the dream"— he'd restored the forty-two-foot boat to a pristine live-aboard with an office, a snug galley, two staterooms and two baths. But without the kids, it was a ghost ship, adrift on unremembered dreams—now his only dream was to stay connected to the kids.

The custody evaluator assigned to his case wasn't into living the dream. Even though the kids were wild about the boat, the court-appointed evaluator gave the *Fat Chance* only temporary approval. Mike had until the start of the new school year to find a permanent residence. According to Loretta, he'd get better evaluations if he settled down in a proper house.

Frustrated, he'd stayed up late last night, putting his thoughts together about the Babcock place. Earlier today, he had replaced her mailbox. It had only taken him about five minutes and he hadn't even honked his horn to get her attention. He figured she'd know who had fixed it for her.

Part of him wished he could tell the Winslow woman he wasn't interested in her house, but another part wanted to tackle the challenge of a one-of-a-kind restoration. Besides, it was his best prospect for a long-term job. He studied the sea chart beside the computer, his eye going to the spidery lines marking the coast.

He traced his finger from the port of Paradise to Blue Moon Beach. Six nautical miles. North by northeast. Maybe his luck was about to change.

"Let's go, Zeke."

The dog scrambled to the sliding-glass door and bolted the moment Mike cracked it open. Zeke vaulted ahead, leaping through the cockpit deck and onto the creaking dock, sniffing like crazy. Like he hoped to find something different in a place that never changed.

Mike followed more slowly and stood in the hushed aftermath of the storm, listening to the hiss of the sea and the restless crying of gulls, watching the twilight glitter on the gale-churned water.

And thinking about Sandra Winslow again.

Who the hell was she, and why had Victor married her? He never made a random choice in his life, and he rarely made mistakes. That was supposed to be Mike's specialty. But a year ago, Victor had wound up dead and Mike lived alone now, his only company a poodle with a bad haircut.

The air held the sort of chill found only at the brittle edge of the New England coast. Mike turned up the collar of his parka and shoved his hands deeper into his pockets.

"Hey, Mike."

He turned to see Lenny Carmichael coming toward him on the dock. A flat fisherman's cap made Lenny seem even shorter and squatter than he was, so that he resembled a railroad spike someone had hit with a hammer. He moved with the ambling gait of a man who was never far from the sea. And he wasn't. His father was a lobster fisherman;

Lenny had joined the family business as soon as he was old enough to drop out of school.

"Hey." Mike nodded his head. "What do you know?"

"I heard you were up at the lighthouse, fixing a broken window."

Privacy, Mike reflected, was in short supply in Paradise. "Yep," he said. "Hell of a way to spend the afternoon."

"We missed you at Schillers. Archie bought everyone a round in your honor. You should have been there. You're off to a good start, Mikey. There was never any doubt."

Mike thought it strange that people still held a high opinion of him, even after all these years.

"Gloria sent you this." Lenny set down a loosely closed cardboard box. "She made too much, like always." He spoke with the flat, elongated Rhode Island accent the locals all tried to lose if they wanted to get somewhere in life. Lenny, of course, didn't want to go anywhere. Neither did Gloria. She liked feeding people. Especially guys who'd been dumped by their wives.

Mike knew what he'd find in the box. A big, boiled lobster worth seventy-five bucks in a Manhattan restaurant, a couple of dinner rolls, potatoes swimming in butter. At first, Mike had been embarrassed by Gloria's charity. To be honest, it had pissed him off. But a pissed-off guy could never intimidate Gloria Carmichael. She was married to Lenny, after all.

"Be sure to thank her," Mike said. "She doesn't have to keep feeding me, though."

"I'll tell her thanks, but not the other," Lenny said. "She was just saying she's sick of looking at the rotten railing of our front porch. I bet she'll be calling you soon."

"Tell her I don't accept cash, checks or credit cards. Only food."

"She'll love that. What can I say? My old lady likes cooking better than sex."

"Maybe that's why the restaurant's such a hit," Mike suggested. A couple of years back, Gloria had opened a summer shack up at Point Judith, selling lobster rolls and egg salad sandwiches to tourists from Boston and New York.

"I'd rather have the sex," Lenny grumbled.

"I hear you, buddy. I hear you."

"So," Lenny went on, "things are going okay for you."

Considering the lightning speed of the local gossip network, Mike decided he'd best let his old friend know what he was up to. "I got a lead on a big job off Ocean Road. On Curlew." He pretended the idle comment had just occurred to him. "I'm putting in a bid to restore the old Babcock place."

"The Winslow woman's house, you mean?" Lenny gave a low whistle. "She didn't waste any time, spending her husband's money."

"There's no deal yet," Mike said.

"Gloria'd tell you to milk her for all she's worth."

"What's Gloria got against Sandra Winslow?"

"The woman's young, good-looking and she got away with murder. What's not to hate?" Lenny spread his hands. "The wife's been following that scandal like a soap opera, on account of it's local. Say, didn't you used to be really tight with Victor Winslow?"

"When we were kids. We lost touch." Mike remembered how he'd been back then, filled with pride that he was actually going off to college, the first of his family to do so. He felt as though someone had taken the shrink-wrap off his ambitions, at last. For two years he had soared, playing football, making the grade, dating the head cheerleader, devouring life like a giant submarine sand-wich, all for him.

Then came the tackle that had ripped his right knee into separate parts, the dismissal from the team, three surg-eries . . . and finally Angela. The head cheerleader had shown up in his hospital room, brandishing a small white stick with a pink plus sign on one end. Pregnant. He had to quit school, get a job and marry her.

"So what's the Black Widow of Blue Moon Beach like, up close and personal?" Lenny asked.

Mike studied the line of bobbing fishing vessels, their skeletal arms raised against the darkening sky. "I don't know, and I don't want to know. Her house needs fixing, and I need the work." He knew he wouldn't tell Lenny that she'd been crying when he met her, that she looked amaz-ing in blue jeans and rubber boots, that her voice was soft and husky and that she never once smiled.

"Gloria still thinks she's guilty as mortal sin." Lenny bumped the toe of his shoe against an iron cleat. "I mean, the car went right off the bridge, for chrissake. The dame got herself out, not a scratch on her. Meanwhile, he's shark bait."

"Maybe when the car was sinking, she only had time to get herself out."

"She claims she doesn't remember squat about the wreck. Selective amnesia, if you ask me."

"You don't believe her?"

"Hell, nobody believes her."

"Then why the accident ruling? Why not charge her?"

"I guess that shyster lawyer from Newport fixed things." He took out an old burl pipe and tucked tobacco into the bowl. "I just feel sorry as hell for the guy's family. Really nice folks, the Winslows. They didn't deserve this."

Mike felt a twinge of guilt when he thought of Victor's

parents. Ronald Winslow had returned from Vietnam with a purple heart and a crushed spinal cord. Challenged rather than defeated by his disability, he'd graduated with honors from Harvard Divinity School and had become pastor of the largest Protestant church in southern Rhode Island.

He'd married Winifred van Deusen for love, though it was a great convenience that she came with a large, inherited fortune. They'd doted on their only child, putting all their dreams into Victor.

The thought of losing a child made Mike's blood run cold.

He'd better pay the Winslows a call, tell them he was planning to work on Sandra's house. He wanted the job, needed it, but he owed it to the family to let them know.

Lenny lit his pipe, shielding the lighter with his cupped hand. Zeke came skittering along the dock, something disgusting held in his jaws, dripping down his untrimmed chin whiskers. He dropped it at Mike's feet. Today's catch was a clump of black mussels strung together with a tough beard of seaweed. Mike kicked it over the edge of the dock and into the water.

Lenny puffed on his pipe. "When are you going to get a real dog, Mike?"

"I didn't pick him. I'm just the sucker that wound up with him. Anyway, the kids are nuts about Zeke."

"I guess you're stuck with him, then."

"Yeah." Mike acknowledged that Mary Margaret and Kevin were his whole world, the reason he got up in the morning, the reason he took the next breath of air.

His immediate reaction to the divorce had been to secure his rights as a father. He'd spent pretty much all he had, fighting for time with the kids. But in the end, Angela dictated the visitation schedule. Married to a wealthy Newport restaurateur, repped by the hottest family law firm money could buy, she won it all—the house, the kids, her father's stake in the construction firm. Mike had been granted limited visitation with the kids, and for now, his home was the old trawler his father used to take out fishing. Angela's money and the right lawyer could tip the scales of justice, so that a mother's indiscretion was considered insignificant, and the environment less harmful to his children than sleeping on a pair of bunks on his boat.

"So the Babcock job's going to keep you busy?" Lenny asked.

"Maybe," said Mike, "if she likes my proposal."

"She better be damned grateful you're willing to help her at all."

"I can't be picky about where the work comes from, not right now."

Lenny tapped the bowl of his pipe on the heel of his shoe. "I better be going. Got to get an early start in the morning. See you around, Mikey."

"See you." Mike whistled through his teeth, and Zeke came running. It was warm in the galley of the trawler; at least that was what Mike told himself. He tried not to burn too much propane for heat. Except when the kids were with him. He'd set his own hair on fire if it would keep his kids warm.

Chapter 5

Ten Things to Eat Without Cooking

1. *Carrot and celery sticks with nonfat ranch dressing.*
2. *A Macintosh apple.*
3. *A slice of melba toast.*
4. *A cup of nonfat cottage cheese.*
5. *A handful of dry-roasted peanuts.*
6. *Popcorn with no butter or salt.*
7. *Popcorn with a ton of butter and salt.*
8. *A bag of deep-fried pork rinds.*
9. *A quart of Cherry Garcia ice cream.*
10. *A pound of Godiva chocolate.*

The blisters were healing. At twilight, Sandra stood over the kitchen sink, unraveled gauze trailing from her wrists as she inspected her palms. She was washing her hands when she heard a truck roll up.

A FedEx. Running very late.

It could mean anything. The ordeal of the past year had taught her to expect the worst.

Hurrying to the front door, she signed for the flat, nearly weightless envelope and thanked the bored-looking driver, who seemed relieved to have reached his last stop of the day.

Zipping through the seal, she opened the parcel to find a long, perforated business check from Claggett, Banks, Saunders & Lefkowitz, the firm she'd engaged after Victor's death. The memo on the check stub noted succinctly that this was the first payment from the insurance settlement, less the firm's fee for obtaining it. The insurance company had, of course, termed Sandra's claim fraudulent because Victor's body was never recovered. But the ME's ruling of death, based on brutally clear circumstantial evidence, had brought the situation to a grim conclusion.

She stared, unblinking, at the check in her hand. So this was it. Victor's life, reduced to a dollar amount.

An unsettled feeling stirred in her chest. Setting the check on the hall table, she stepped out onto the porch, into the cold evening. She walked down to the yard, haunted now by shadows of deepest indigo and by a breeze that still held the muscle of the afternoon storm.

She'd come to love the wild, isolated coast, the stark views and the clean-washed smell in the aftermath of a storm. Could she ever find a place like this again? Running her thumb along the peeling paint of the porch rail, she tried not to allow her heart to ache over having to go, but regrets kept pounding at her, relentless as the waves. She'd spent the past year trying not to feel anything, and the effort was beginning to exhaust her. It's just a stupid old falling-down house, she told herself. She should feel glad she was getting rid of it.

"Ah, Victor," she said to the searching wind. "I wish you could give me a sign. Tell me what to do." One of the hardest things about being alone was that there was no one to toss things around with, no one to consult. She was on her own, rafting through unknown waters, and hadn't a clue about whether or not she was choosing the right course.

Heading to the shed to get more firewood, she glanced toward the road and stopped in her tracks. Then, with inborn caution, she walked to the side of the road.

There, atop a square post next to the ditch, was a new mailbox of galvanized steel, with the address stuck on in reflective numbers.

Malloy, she thought. When had he fixed this? He really was a drive-by handyman.

Chilled by the night air, she hurried back inside and fed another log to the iron stove. Then she settled on the sofa to go through the mail. It was the usual assortment of junk solicitations and bills. NRA stuff again. Why were they always after her? She supposed because Victor had been so firmly in favor of gun control. Setting aside the mail, she picked up the phone to let her lawyer know the check had arrived. Although he'd not been her favorite person, Milton Banks had been her advocate through the entire investigation, and when the ruling had come down Thursday afternoon, he'd been ebullient.

When his voice mail clicked on, she started speaking, only to be interrupted by Milton himself, live and in-person.

"So you got it. Ha! Are we quick or what?" he demanded in a working-class Boston accent. "You can rest easy for now."

So can you, she thought, considering the size of the firm's fee.

"I won't be resting," she said. "I have plans."

He hesitated. "What kind of plans?"

"I'm going to fix up this house, sell it and get the heck out of Dodge."

"Christ, Sandra, you ought to know better."

"What do you mean?"

"If you take off now, it'll look like you're fleeing."

"I am." She curled the phone cord around her index finger.

He was quiet for a moment. "Look, I told you, the ruling's only the first battle. Just because they didn't find probable cause doesn't mean you're home free."

A chill touched the base of her spine. "But I am. Home. And free."

"Of course you are," he said quickly. "But what's your hurry? Stick around. Do it on your own, so the court doesn't order you to."

"I've stuck around for a year, Milton." The icy apprehension slid through her and tightened in her gut.

"I warned you about this months ago. Regardless of what the ME found, there's going to be a civil suit. The Winslows' attorneys have been researching their case for months."

Irritation pushed through her fear. Milton had warned her to expect trouble, but she put it out of her mind. The idea that her in-laws would sue her shouldn't come as a surprise—nothing should. The unbelievable had already happened. "How do you know it'll even materialize?"

She could hear the long pause of an inhale while Milton lit a cigarette, then exhaled into the receiver. "Because I'm a good lawyer. They've been in pre-suit prep forever, poking around for leads. Dollars to donuts they're getting ready to file as we speak. Mark my words—they want somebody to go down, Sandra, and you're the one. You were in the driver's seat that night. Sorry to say, they've got options—negligent, careless, reckless—they might even try to pin 'intentional' on you. So brace yourself."

She pressed her teeth together until her jaw ached, holding in a scream. Unwinding the phone cord, she drummed her fingers on the receiver. The old affliction strangled her, and it took several seconds of breathing exercises before she could force her next words out. "The place needs a lot of work, so we've got some time," she informed Milton. "But believe me, the minute it's fixed, I'm out of here, lawsuit or no lawsuit."

"Just relax, kiddo. No judge will let this go to trial on such flimsy evidence. They'll have to find something a lot more compelling than they've uncovered so far."

Sandra gripped the receiver so hard that her healing blisters stung. There was plenty of evidence to find, and if it came to light, she was toast.

Chapter 6

Journal Entry—January 6—Sunday

10 Things to Do on a Sunday Morning

1. The NYT crossword puzzle.
2. Make pancakes in the shape of lawyers.
3. Go to church.

Sandra stared at item number three, and her heart sped up. Could she? Did she dare?

Until she actually wrote the words, she didn't realize that the outrageous idea had been hovering at the edge of her mind, pulling at her even as she tried to push it away.

When Victor was alive, Sunday mornings had taken on the mantle of ritual. As the pastor's son and a public figure himself, her husband treated worship as something more than a spiritual activity. Each Sunday, he rose early and dressed with meticulous care. He always looked perfect, slender and handsome as a plaster saint as he guided her to a box pew with an engraved brass plaque commemorating the first Winslows of Rhode Island.

Now she was alone, still reeling from the shock of her

mother's announcement and from Milton's warning about a lawsuit.

She had the sensation of hovering on a precipice, about to plunge over the edge. She'd been a recluse for far too long, keeping to herself while the locals gossiped. Although Sandra had never been a fighter, some small, insistent voice inside kept nagging, nudging, telling her to barge unafraid into the life she wanted. She'd done nothing wrong, nothing but lose her husband under tragic circumstances, yet she kept feeling as though she owed the world an apology.

Ye are cursed with a curse: for ye have robbed me, even this whole nation.

No more, she thought, suddenly awash with the cleansing heat of defiance. It was time to quit acting guilty.

Cursed is the one who perverts the justice due the stranger, the fatherless and widow.

She paced up and down as the decision firmed in her mind. She had to stop torturing herself with uncertainties. She had to get out, do something.

Picking up the insurance check, she firmly endorsed it to Old Somerset Church. As she did, a lightness swept through her, as if someone had lifted a rock off her chest. Then, filled with defiant energy, she tried on and discarded several outfits, finally choosing a navy knit suit with matching shoes—subdued but stylish. Winifred Winslow, whose friends from boarding school still called her "Winky," had approved it for a DAR luncheon, one of many lessons on being the wife of a politician.

Sandra did her makeup and hair with anxious attention, wishing she could find a way to mask the pallor in her cheeks and the hollow look of having lost too much weight too quickly.

The drive to town should have calmed her nerves, but

with each mile, tension knotted tighter in her stomach. The road formed a brittle ridge of shale and granite along the coast, curving around to the main part of town. Winter-bare trees etched the stark landscape, as thin and straight as gouges made with a knife against a canvas of amber meadow grass. Frost hid in shadowed pockets of the fields and clung to the undersides of tumbled boulders at the shoulder of the road. Out on the water, fishing boats plowed through the gunstock-gray ocean, and scavenging gulls circled over the skeletal arms of the raised nets.

Sandra flexed her gloved hands on the steering wheel. For weeks after the accident, she'd been afraid to drive. Panic would gather in her chest, squeezing her lungs until she could hardly breathe. She forced herself to get in the car, go through the motions, focus on her destination. But the nightmare endured.

Fragments of memory haunted her even now; she could still see the slick black ice of the road and the glare of another car's headlights in the rearview mirror. She could still hear the whine of tires hydroplaning across the bridge deck. Her ears rang with the explosion of impact, followed by the vicious hiss of the airbag detonating.

With a will, she pushed the past away and tried to relax her grip on the wheel. Painted wooden signs, weathered by the ceaseless battering of sea winds and slashing rain, marked the boundary of the township. Paradise was a true hometown, with sidewalks and tree-lined lanes, snug houses wrapped by porches, a grid of streets leading to the business area of neat shopfronts arranged around a faux-colonial community center. A drive-through donut shop, Gloria's Shrimp Shack and the Twisted Scissors Barber Shop formed a truncated strip mall near the waterfront.

Slowing to a cautious twenty-five miles per hour, she passed the town commons, an oblong green space with a pond in the middle. In the next block . . . She told herself not to look, but couldn't help it. She studied the Winslow estate, an eighteenth-century mansion in the middle of a pristine lawn. Less than a mile from that was the handsome but less ostentatious converted carriage house that had been the Winslows' wedding gift to her and Victor.

All her life, Sandra had looked for a place to belong and finally, in Paradise at Victor's side, she'd found it. When she lost him, she lost more than a husband. She lost her home, her community, her place in the world. She needed to find that again. The question was, how could she do it without Victor?

They had lived in the eye of the community, an up-and-coming state senator and his quiet new wife. Now the residence housed a small family, and changes were apparent—new lace curtains that, Sandra thought, compromised the clean lines of the upstairs dormer windows. A little red tricycle on the front walk caused her chest to ache with an old, familiar yearning. She had wanted children, but Victor kept putting it off.

Thinking back on those tense, late-night discussions, she realized how skillful he'd been, finding a reason to wait each time she broached the subject. First he had to settle his campaign budget. Attend to his mother, who had suffered—and survived—breast cancer. Win the election and raise funds for the next race. Position himself to climb the ladder to politics at the national level.

Anything but the truth.

She pulled her outdated Plymouth Arrow into a parking space at the church. The tower clock rang half past, and she let out a sigh of relief. She'd wanted to arrive early and approach the Winslows in private. Although it was tempting to make her gesture before the entire congregation, she couldn't bring herself to do something so manipulative and disingenuous.

It was the sort of thing Victor would have done. But then again, it would have worked for Victor.

Drawing the strap of her purse over her shoulder, she slammed the car door. Self-conscious after her long absence, she recalled her first visit here, when she was the outsider, the unknown quantity, an object of scrutiny. In some ways, that had never changed, but eventually she'd meshed with the intricately woven pattern of church and town; she'd been comfortable here, much the same way she'd been comfortable with Victor.

But even in the most connected moments, she sometimes felt like a fraud—she'd never been particularly religious and some aspects of the church scene felt false to a person of her dark imagination. Yet her duties as Victor's wife had included volunteering in the children's Sunday school, and secretly she thought leading a chirping chorus of "This Little Light of Mine" offered more grace than her father-in-law's thundering sermons.

Tucking her coat around her, she headed for the rear of the church and a wide door marked "Pastor's Office." She didn't have long to wait. Within a few moments, the Winslows' van turned into the rear lot and glided into the spot reserved for the pastor. They didn't appear to see her at first as they went through the routine of disembarking from the van.

After thirty years of living as a paraplegic, Ronald Winslow managed with easy grace. His wife neither pitied nor babied him; to Sandra's knowledge, she never had. They always looked completely natural together, as dignified as any blue-blooded New England couple of a certain age. The bond of their love was a subtle but tangible thing—he effortlessly adjusted the electric glide of his chair to her pace as they crossed the parking lot. The sight of them had a special poignance for Sandra now. The thought that her parents would never be together like that again burned her like a brand.

The knot in her stomach tightened, but she forced herself to walk toward the access ramp leading to the office.

"What are you doing here?" Her father-in-law's blunt question stopped her.

With the chill wind lashing at her cheeks, she faced him squarely. *Ten Really Bad Ideas for a Sunday Morning...* Her notion of coming here, which had filled her with hope an hour ago, now seemed the height of foolishness.

"Hello, Ronald," she said, feeling their stares like chisels. "Hello, Winifred."

Victor's mother didn't even look at her. The outline of her turned-away face spoke more eloquently than any words. Her small, delicate nostrils emitted twin puffs of frozen air. Winifred, who had taught her how to plan a benefit dinner and give a speech to the League of Women Voters, acted like a stranger now.

Sandra heard the faint whine of a ship's whistle in the harbor, the plaintive cry of a winter curlew overhead. No other sound intruded. Somehow, she found her voice. "I'm here because I want this to be over," she said. "It was an accident. You were there for the ruling. You heard."

It had been torture, sitting across the aisle from them, their sadness a dead weight, their censure pure poison.

"We heard the ruling." Ronald moved the chair slightly in front of his wife as if to protect her. "That doesn't mean we heard the truth. You were in the driver's seat. You survived, and Victor died."

Grief had ravaged this man's noble face, so like the face of his only son. Shadows of sleeplessness were carved beneath his eyes; his cheeks looked ruddy, the way they did when he ate too much on Thanksgiving during the football games. A vital piece of this man was missing, and Sandra knew there was no way he'd ever get it back.

Victor had been their miracle baby, their only child—prayed for, desperately wanted, born against all medical odds to a man whose disability should have prevented conception at all. They raised him as their ultimate work-in-progress, mapping out a perfect life for their golden boy. He measured up in all ways but one—the woman he'd chosen to marry.

When Victor introduced her to his parents just three weeks after their first date—if you could call it a date—the Winslows had been gracious and unfailingly polite, but couldn't quite mask the disappointment in their eyes. The words they would never, ever speak aloud hung like a fog in the air: *Why her? She's a nobody, and so young. We had such hopes for you. . . .*

Later, Victor confessed that they'd spent years pushing him toward the daughter of their closest friends, a woman who was beautiful, ambitious, pedigreed and well connected. A woman who had carried a torch for Victor ever since they'd met at a church picnic as teenagers. Her name was Courtney Procter.

After watching the WRIQ reports, Sandra knew for certain that Courtney had never forgiven her.

"You know I'd never harm Victor." Thrusting her hand in her pocket, she closed her fist around the check. "You know me, Ronald," she went on, struggling to keep her tone even, her voice free of hesitation. "I didn't do anything wrong."

"No one ever knew you, Sandra," Winifred said, finally speaking out in a cold lash of anger. "You never let them."

Sandra thrust the check at Ronald. "This is the first

part of the life insurance settlement. I'm donating it to the church." The pale green slip of paper dropped into his lap.

He brushed it away as though it were a live coal, and it fluttered to the bare pavement. "You can't buy absolution with your profits from Victor's death."

"I'm not trying to buy anything. I don't need to, because I didn't do anything wrong—except, as you said, survive." She held his gaze, and recognized the hurt buried in his eyes. "I miss him, too. I miss him every day, just as you do. That's what this is about."

"You're trying to buy your way out of trouble, and it won't work."

"Stop." Winifred put a hand on her husband's arm. "We don't have to listen to any more of this." With that, she turned, making her way up the ramp. Stone-faced, Reverend Winslow angled his electric-powered chair and followed his wife.

The Winslows were beyond comfort and apparently, beyond reason.

Sandra gripped the railing, started after them, then stopped. She stared down at the check, tumbling like a leaf along the pavement. A slow burn of anger swept through her. Her hand slipped down the iron railing as she stepped backward once, twice. Then, with shoulders squared and chin held high, she retrieved the check, turned away from the church and hurried toward her car.

The front doors of the sandy brick church now stood open to the day. She could see the glow of candles within, and the spice of fresh flower arrangements wafted from the sanctuary. The subtle, murmuring notes of the organist warming up for the processional rode the morning breeze.

But it was a false welcome, she knew that now. She wanted to kick herself for her own stupidity. She should have listened to Milton. Of course they wouldn't change their minds simply because of the ruling.

Enough, then, she told herself, slamming the car door on the belly-deep sound of the church bells tolling. It would never be over. Especially not now. Everything was just starting now. Her hand closed around the check in her coat pocket. By declining her money, they were making her decision about the house much easier.

Yet it didn't feel easy. These people wanted her humiliated, banished, ruined. They probably wanted her to burn in hell. A hundred times, she had been tempted to reveal the whole truth about that night, but she always fought the impulse. The truth would only add bitterness to their grief, and no explanation would bring Victor back to life.

Despite their anger at her, Sandra felt protective of Victor's grieving parents. They'd been so proud of Victor. They missed him so much. Ever since his death, she'd shielded them from something only she knew. She told herself it was because she respected their grief—but maybe in her heart she was also engaged in a silent bargain: I'll spare you the truth about your son if you'll forgive me for my role in his death.

She tried to decide if she felt differently now. They'd drawn the lines of battle, and a dark urge stirred inside her. She was tempted with every nerve in her body to blurt out how wrong they were about everything, how they never really knew their own son. But she didn't want to be the one to end their dreams, to turn cherished memories to bitter disillusionment.

She wasn't being a martyr, wasn't being noble, keeping her silence. She was simply being pragmatic. To end her silence at this point would do more harm than good. Because the truth was, during his last moments on earth, her husband had given her a reason to want him dead.

Chapter 7

*F*or lapsed Catholics and divorced dads, there was nothing as lonely as a Sunday. Mike drove through the streets where he'd spent his boyhood, a dull ache pressing at his chest. You don't get any second chances in life, he reflected. If you don't get it right the first time, you can't just start over from scratch. But that was just what he was trying to do.

On the seat beside him, Zeke sat at full attention, ears pricked and tongue lolling. Every few seconds, the dog indulged the occasional need to bark.

Before the divorce, Mike used to take his kids to mass at St. John's, and after catechism class they'd drive up to the beach, or just hang around the house, shooting baskets or riding bikes. It had been easy to believe those days would never end, easy for both him and Angela to pretend they didn't see the end coming.

His head and heart were crammed with memories, but they were fragmented—Mary Margaret's first step. Kevin's first communion. Trips to Florida to see his folks. As for the day-to-day stuff, it was all a blur, like the landscape smearing past when you sped down the Interstate. He had buried himself in work, chasing down jobs, building up a clientele with single-minded, manic energy.

And for what? So Angela could get a new car every year. So he could upgrade his boat. Join a country club. Send the kids to private school.

He knew why. He wanted the best for his kids, but he had never fully understood what that meant. He'd always felt like a failure, getting booted off the team and having his scholarship yanked, quitting his degree program to start a business. Everyone admired him; he'd become one of the biggest contractors in Newport, and for years, that had defined him. Time passed at warp speed. Then one morning he woke up, looked at his wife and saw a stranger.

A stranger who wanted a divorce.

She'd "met" someone.

Mike shook off the thought of his ex-wife. Today he had something else to think about—a long-overdue condolence call to Victor Winslow's family.

He drove even slower, pissed at himself for putting this off. He and Victor had been best friends, and no matter how many years had passed, he owed the family a visit to express his shock and grief and genuine sorrow. Now he had the added burden of a confession to make. He was putting in a bid to restore Sandra Winslow's old house at Blue Moon Beach.

In the church parking lot of Old Somerset Church, a woman hurried away from the building, fast, like she had to go throw up or something.

Mike pulled off to the side of the road and watched

her. Dark coat flapping in the wind. Shiny brown hair. *Sandra Winslow*. What the hell was she doing here?

She got into her car and slammed the door. For a minute, she sat there with the heels of her hands resting on the steering wheel and her head down. The morning light haloed the fragile, unguarded lines of her face.

Mike tried to dismiss the unsettling image of her. The house, not the woman, concerned him, he told himself, easing up on the brake pedal. Just then, Zeke decided to bark. Son of a bitch had a loud bark.

Her head lifted, and she looked straight at Mike.

Busted.

Shit, he thought. Shit shit shit. Peeling out now would look rude. He couldn't afford to be rude to a potential client, even Sandra Winslow.

He raised one hand in a half wave. She rolled down the car window. At a loss, Mike slapped the truck in park and got out, telling Zeke to stay. He walked across the parking lot. "Car trouble?" he asked.

"No."

He glanced at the church. "They let you out early for good behavior?"

"Something like that." She grimaced. "I changed my mind about church today."

She was a real charmer, he thought. Yet there was something in the way she held herself that made her look as though she could break at the slightest pressure. She was about to cry, he realized uncomfortably, focusing on the dangerous brightness in her eyes. He shouldn't care— he didn't care—but he heard himself say, "I was just going to go for a cup of coffee. You want to join me?"

She flexed her hands on the steering wheel. "All right. Where?"

"Follow me." Mike kicked himself all the way back to

his truck. He led the way to the drive-through donut stand, and she waited in her car while he ordered the coffee and two donuts. No big deal, he told himself. He'd give her a cup of coffee, then find the Winslows when church let out.

At the end of the road, he pulled over and got out. A dock jutted from the seawall where a little fleet of quohog skiffs bobbed. To the side of the wall, a sandy slope led down to the water. Zeke exploded from the truck as if shot from a cannon. The dog raced flat-out over the sand, kicking up a spray before disappearing over a tumble of wave-gouged rocks.

Carrying the coffee in a cardboard tray, Mike motioned for Sandra to join him. She followed him through the empty breezeway of the abandoned concession stand. In summer, the place swarmed with families and students on vacation, but now the wind howled through the shadowy passageway, spitting them out on the other side, where there was nothing but ocean, sand and sky.

He set the tray on a concrete picnic table. "There's cream and sugar in the bag with the donuts."

Sandra sent him a funny little look. "Thanks," she said, prying the lid off the coffee. She added cream, then poured in at least three packets of sugar. She seemed a little steadier now, he observed. A decent guy would probably ask her what was wrong, why she'd been in such a hurry to leave the church . . . but Mike didn't want to know. He'd spent his entire marriage trying to figure out a woman, and he'd failed. He wasn't about to try to understand Sandra. Though he barely knew her, he suspected she was a hell of a lot more complex than his ex-wife could ever be. But his mind kept coming back to the idea. With Angela, no matter what he did, he hadn't been able to fill the empty spaces inside her. Whereas with Sandra, that could be his key role—he'd known it instinctively the first time he'd met her, and the feeling only grew stronger with each passing moment. It was a strange and unwelcome notion, and he hoped it would go away.

Stooping, he picked up a length of driftwood and flung it for Zeke, who sped off in pursuit.

She blew gently on her coffee, then took a sip. "Is he any particular breed of dog?"

"Poodle, but don't tell him that."

"What's his name?"

"Zeke."

"Of course. What else would you name a poodle?" Her smile was genuine, reaching her eyes this time. Big brown eyes, long lashes. It was a hell of a smile, even better than he'd pictured it. "I bet your kids love him."

"Yeah." He was glad he had Zeke, though the dog was ridiculous even without the haircut. He missed his kids so bad that he almost said something to Sandra Winslow.

The separation and divorce had stripped him bare by layers. He'd looked around one day and realized he had nothing but his boat, his truck, tools and equipment he couldn't stand to part with and a cell phone with an overdue bill. He was slowly crawling out of the hole, rebuilding his business, but some days he felt as though he were standing still.

Zeke had nosed his way into Mike's life through a back door Mike hadn't yet barricaded against sentiment. He'd been at the quarry up in Waverley, picking out flagstones for a patio he was building in Point Judith. In the office, he'd encountered a foreman glaring down into a dilapidated cardboard box. The guy explained that his wife's French poodle had whelped, all the pups had been sold and for the life of him he couldn't give away the runt of the litter. Conformation problems, coloration problems, a whole litany of complaints. This one was for the pound.

Mike had peered into the box at the little white ball of fluff, and that back door had cracked open just enough to let in the furball, worms and all. He was in denial about the breed, even though it was printed clearly on the AKC papers. He figured if he never clipped Zeke's hair, he'd eventually forget he was a poodle.

"I'm glad I ran into you," Sandra Winslow said. "There's something I need to explain."

Great, he thought. Here it comes. She'd changed her mind about the job. "Yeah?"

"It's about my late husband, Victor Winslow. You've heard of him, haven't you?"

"Sure. Everyone has." Mike didn't elaborate.

She looked straight out to sea, tiny wisps of hair blowing around her face. "Last February, he and I were involved in an accident." Her hand trembled, and she set down her cup. "The medical examiner officially ruled it an accidental death. But there are still some people who think the worst of me." She took a deep breath and stuffed her hands into her coat pockets. "Anyway, I thought you should know that before you do business with me."

"Did you think I'd change my mind?"

"I don't know, Malloy. I don't know you."

He helped himself to a donut and offered her one. "You're the client, I'm the contractor. I'm interested in your house, not your reputation."

She hesitated, then took the donut from him. "Thanks. I skipped breakfast this morning." They ate in silence, watching the waves rush up to shore. Sandra chewed slowly, her nose and cheeks growing pink in the cold wind. She looked totally different from the wild-eyed woman he'd encountered at the woodpile. She had the strangest effect on him—he was emotionally broke, and had nothing to offer in that department. Yet something about her brought back all the things he missed about being connected, having a family. He resented her for that, and at the same time, he was drawn to that very aspect of her.

"How are your hands?" he asked.

"Healing," she replied, showing him. "Thanks. And thanks for the mailbox. I assume you're the one who replaced it."

"Yep. No problem. I'll get that proposal to you soon."

"Good. Well." She dusted the crumbs from her hands. "I'll look forward to that. I'd better be going now."

They walked together to their cars, and Mike thought maybe her step was a little lighter. He felt guilty, playing dumb when Gloria Carmichael had been filling him in on all the Winslow gossip. But he figured the less personal he got with this woman, the better.

Out of habit, he held open her car door for her, then stood back while she pulled away. He whistled for Zeke, and within seconds the dog streaked to the truck and sprang up in a single perfectly aimed leap.

Mike headed back to the church and sat with his pickup truck idling roughly in the cold morning air. After a while, the church bells rang and people streamed from the building. They walked in little family clusters, toddlers holding on to their parents' hands and swinging their feet up in the air, old people leaning on each other as they made their way to their cars.

An electric-powered wheelchair emerged from the main entrance. Reverend Ronald Winslow shook hands with the departing parishioners, his gently smiling wife beside him.

Mike continued to wait, the chill slipping into the cab of the truck, until the last of the worshipers had left. Then he got out, cautioning Zeke to stay put.

The Winslows were headed for their van when he caught up with them. "Mr. and Mrs. Winslow?"

They stopped, eyeing him curiously. Up close, he could see how much they had changed. They both looked smaller, diminished by their loss. Ronald's thick hair had turned snow-white; Winifred's navy coat hung loosely on her thin frame.

"I'm Michael Malloy," he said. "Mike. I used to be friends with your son Victor, years ago when we were kids."

Ronald Winslow frowned, but his wife's face immediately softened. "Michael. Of course," she said, holding out both gloved hands. Mike took them awkwardly, held on for a brief squeeze. In his mind's eye, he imagined he could still see the mom in Stuart plaid skirt and navy-blue cardigan who used to bake cookies after school, who showed up at every class play or swim meet or choir recital Victor was in.

"I remember you perfectly, Michael," Winifred said. "The two of you met at swim team tryouts, didn't you? Was it in the third grade?"

"You have a good memory," Mike said. He could still picture the two of them, skinny and pasty in their Speedos, eyeing each other across the lane lines. He and Victor had been unlikely companions. Victor had worn the mantle of privilege, the son of a well-respected pastor and an old-money debutante. Mike's father was a commercial fisherman, his mother a dyer at Cranston Print Works. To a couple of small-town boys in school, class differences didn't matter. But out in the real world, they had. A lot.

"Michael played quarterback on the high school football squad," Winifred said, resting her slim hand on her husband's shoulder. "I'm sure you remember that."

The older man grinned as he made the connection. "You're right. Been a while."

"It sure has."

Mike couldn't think of a decent way to broach the topic, so he came right out with it. "Listen, I should have called or visited sooner, but I haven't been back in the area long." He didn't elaborate; he wanted to get this over with. "I can't tell you how sorry I am about Victor."

Ronald Winslow's grin disappeared, as Mike had known it would. The older man's hands trembled, and he pressed them together. Desperation and confusion haunted his eyes, and Mike realized he was no longer the self-assured war hero and leading citizen. Ronald had survived Vietnam, but losing Victor proved to be a disability he couldn't surmount.

"Thank you." Winifred took out a pair of dark glasses and quickly put them on. "He was the most precious thing in our lives. This is everyone's loss."

"Of course. When I heard he'd been elected to the General Assembly, it didn't surprise me a bit."

Winifred smiled with heartbreaking pride, still clinging to Ronald's shoulder. "Why don't you come back to the house for coffee, Michael? We'd love to hear what you've been up to."

Great, he thought. First Sandra, now this. He should have gone fishing this morning. "Thanks. Nice of you to offer."

He followed them, his truck coughing in the wake of their specially equipped van as it glided through town with the dignified pace of a parade float. The Winslows lived in a big colonial with a yard like a golf course. The long front porch, painted a dazzling white, looked as though it had undergone cosmetic dentistry. He recognized the hickory tree where he and Victor had once suspended a rope swing.

The iron gate leading to the salt marsh behind the house had rusted to a mild greenish color. Beyond the marsh lay the long waterfront; Mike and Victor used to claim they could see all the way to Block Island, and vowed to swim there one day, just to show it could be done.

The van slid to a halt under a projecting side portico, and Mike stopped his truck behind it. The van door opened, and the wheelchair platform lowered with an electronic whir.

"Recognize any of this?" Winifred asked.

"All of it. I have a lot of great memories of this place."

The genuine delight in her expression made him glad he'd come after all. Of course, he hadn't brought up the topic of working for Sandra yet.

"Let's go inside where it's warm, then."

As he walked away from the truck, Zeke let out a howl of outrage and pushed his fuzzy face against the windshield.

"Sorry about my dog. If he bothers you—"

"No bother at all," Ronald said. "He'll settle down once he knows we're not going to kidnap you."

When Mike stepped into the big, bright kitchen, more memories showered over him. With a clarity he hadn't expected, he recalled the welcoming warmth of this place as he and Victor sipped hot chocolate after a day of sledding. In the summer, they used to track beach sand across the polished tile floor, and ransack the freezer for ice cream bars.

With controlled, precise movements, Winifred poured coffee, and the three of them sat in the big front room, decorated with furniture that had been in the family forever. Although the antiques were priceless, the Winslows didn't keep them as status symbols but as reminders: *This is who we are.* Winifred's needlepoint glasses case rested on a side table in the same spot it had decades before, alongside a leather-bound volume of Proust. Yet despite the elegant presence of signed paintings, Irish crystal and museum-quality colonial antiques, an emptiness haunted the beautiful room.

"You look absolutely wonderful," Winifred said, her eyes shining with a fierce maternal hunger. In her gray flannel skirt, crisp white blouse and flat shoes, she appeared unchanged—except that her face reflected unbearable loss. "So . . . so grown-up."

"Adulthood tends to do that to a guy."

Ronald tipped cream into his coffee. "I wish you and Victor had kept up. You two were quite a pair, as I recall."

"I wish we'd stayed in touch, too." Mike stared at his big hands, resting on his knees. "I figured we'd run into each other one day. I shouldn't have left it up to chance."

Winifred gazed at a display of sterling silver framed photographs on the table beside her. Victor was the subject of each one—skiing, sailing, grinning into the camera as he won some award or other. She shut her eyes, visibly battling a grief Mike could only imagine. "I wish Victor could be here. He always thought so highly of you, Michael. The two of you were like brothers."

"Look, Mrs. Winslow," he said, "I didn't mean to come here and make you feel bad—"

Ronald cleared his throat. "Your coming here is a blessing," he said. "Tell us what you've done with yourself. Last we knew, you got a football scholarship to URI."

"That's right."

"I remember how proud your folks were. You boys had that big clam bake to celebrate."

Mike could conjure up every moment of that summer night. He and some of the guys had helped themselves to a case of beer from his parents' basement and built a bonfire on Scarborough Beach. Sweating brown bottles of Narragansett in hand, they'd sat against the driftwood logs and stared up at the stars. Thanks to the beer, the night sky had spun gently as though they were watching it from the deck of a ship.

He could still picture the bonfire, the laughing faces of his friends, the crazy promises that they'd never lose touch, the feeling that the whole world was waiting for him. Everything had seemed bright and new, the future golden, the world opening up like a giant sunflower. Mike, whose parents could barely afford to keep him in Wheaties, was getting a shot at college. Victor was headed for Brown, the crown jewel of Rhode Island's universities, and eventually he'd do post-graduate work at Harvard's Kennedy School of Government. Big dreams, big plans. Neither of them could have anticipated the outcome.

"I was injured my second season," he said before more questions could come. "I had to leave school." It was all so long ago that Mike couldn't get pissed about it anymore. But that didn't mean he wanted to talk about it.

"So what brings you back to town?"

"Divorce."

"Oh, Michael." Winifred patted his hand. "I'm sorry."

"Thanks." He fished in his pocket, slid a business card across the table. "I'm starting back in the construction business, but locally."

"Well," Winifred said, "it's a pleasure to welcome you back."

Okay, Mike thought. Out with it. Looking at a window displaying one of Victor's colored glass ornaments, he said, "I'm bidding on my first big job. A historical restoration in the area."

Winifred clasped her hands. "That's wonderful, Michael."

"I wanted to tell you because the house belongs to Victor's widow, Sandra."

A shadow swept over Winifred's thin, pretty face. "That run-down old place on Blue Moon Beach."

"I believe her plan is to restore the house, and then sell it. I just thought I should let you know. It's business," Mike said. "I need the work."

Ronald Winslow's eyes blazed. "If you choose to deal with that woman, we won't stop you, but you owe it to yourself to look at the facts—"

"Pardon me, sir. The fact is, she's in need of a contractor and I'm in need of work. I don't intend to get personally involved with her. Only her house."

Winifred covered her husband's hand. "I suppose we'd rather see Victor's money spent on you than on . . . the good Lord only knows what else that woman has in mind."

"We've never understood her," Ronald said, the fire in his eyes dimming.

"She was the one poor choice Victor made," Winifred said.

Mike tensed, trying to think of a polite way to leave. He'd said his piece, expressing condolences and explaining his situation. But before he could excuse himself, Winifred refilled his cup.

"He lost his very first election," Ronald said, his face softening with old memories. "So he decided to work on his image, and that meant getting married. Winky and I were delighted, of course, but we always assumed he'd choose someone he'd dated before, someone we knew."

"When he brought that woman home, she was already his fiancée," Winifred explained, drawing her mouth into a tight line of distaste. "We'd never heard of her, didn't know the family, didn't know a thing about her. But Victor seemed content. God knows she looked pretty enough on his arm. And he did win that next election."

Mike nodded, pretending not to pick up on their dislike of their daughter-in-law. "I always figured Vic would end up with a beautiful woman." He wasn't sure what made him say that. The fact was, he hadn't really thought about how Victor would end up, but it seemed the right thing to say to his folks.

"She was quiet, but had good manners. With a little coaching, she learned to dress and present herself at official functions. She and Victor seemed compatible—at first. But she always had a strange, secretive way about her." Winifred rubbed her thumb over one of the photographs on the table, a shot of Victor in a mortarboard, holding up a rolled diploma. "I know my son. He wasn't happy, and I suspect he stayed with her out of his natural sense of loyalty. Shortly before the accident, he admitted to me that she'd been pressuring him to have children." She held Mike's gaze with her own. "Believe me, I wanted grandchildren desperately, but not at the expense of my son's happiness."

"He wanted to wait until he was on firmer ground, politically," Ronald added.

That sounded odd to Mike. Other politicians had kids—look at the Kennedys.

"Winky and I believe that's what their quarrel was about the night of the accident," Ronald said, clasping hands with his wife.

"Look," said Mike, growing even more uncomfortable. "Don't feel you have to—"

"We were interviewed by dozens of crime investigators and the ME," Ronald said. "We can surely tell our story to one of Victor's old friends."

"That night, they were barely speaking," Winifred explained. "We were at a fund-raiser, and you could have cut the tension with a knife."

"At first," Ronald added, "we didn't want to believe Sandra was responsible. But as things came to light, we were forced to think the unthinkable."

"It made a sort of terrible sense," Winifred explained. "She was clearly unhappy. She stood to benefit from his life insurance policy." She exchanged an anguished glance with her husband.

Mike tried to understand their bitterness. What were they thinking? That Sandra had plunged Victor to his death because she wanted kids and he didn't? Because she wanted his money? Or did the Winslows simply need to find someone to blame, some way to make sense of the senseless?

"We don't know what was in her mind," Ronald said. "I don't think any of us ever really knew her."

"I always thought she resented Victor's success," Winifred said. "Everyone loved him, but she was a loner. Not cut out to be a politician's wife at all. They were having problems, but we respected their privacy. I think she wanted a divorce, but didn't want to let go of his money."

It all sounded pretty far-fetched to Mike. The woman would have to be off her rocker to stage an accident, risking herself as much as Victor. But he didn't say anything to Victor's parents.

"You're probably thinking we should let go of this," Winifred said. "That's what everyone else says. We should let go and move on."

"We can't," Ronald admitted. "We loved our son, Mike. You of all people should know that."

"I can't stand the thought that she took him from me, and she's getting away with it," Winifred said. "Be careful of her, Michael."

"Don't worry about me," he assured them, setting down his coffee cup. He flashed on an image of Sandra, saving the mouse in her woodpile. He made his escape, leaving the silent, elegant mansion so haunted by sadness. He respected the Winslows, but they were trapped by their grief, as trapped as Sandra was in her drafty old house on Blue Moon Beach.

He wished he could talk to Victor again, maybe shoot some baskets and hang out the way they used to, so long ago. What was Victor's side of the story? What had he been thinking, feeling? Was he scared? Had he suffered?

The questions would go forever unanswered. There was only one person alive who knew what had really happened.

Chapter 8

Ten Useful New Words

5. *Fungible—Freely exchangeable for another of like kind.*
6. *Elegiac—Of, relating to, or involving sorrow for that which is irrecoverably past.*
7. *Semiotic—Relating to signs or indications.*
8. *Caduceus—A winged staff with two serpents twined around it, carried by Hermes.*
9. *Euphonious—Pleasing or agreeable to the ear.*
10. *Defenestration—An act of throwing someone or something out of a window.*

Sandra drummed her fingers on her notebook, then set it aside in exasperation. On an empty Sunday afternoon, with the wind stirring whitecaps in the Sound, she wasn't getting much work done. Ordinarily, she did her best work during storms. She wasn't quite sure why, but there was something magical and evocative in the dark lash of wind and rain against the windows, the harsh voice of turbulence shouting from the sky.

At such times, as though infused with the energy of the storm, her favorite fountain pen often had a mind of its own, skating across the page, leaving a banner of peacock-blue writing in its wake. She didn't listen to her own words, but instead played the part of a medieval scribe taking dictation from a higher source.

But not today. She'd been so rattled by the encounter with Ronald and Winifred that she barely even remembered the drive home. The Winslows had cut her off as swiftly and cleanly as a field amputation. The searing contempt of Victor's parents had cauterized the wound.

The truth had finally struck her. The limb was gone. The identity she had made for herself—wife, daughter-in-law, community leader—had been excised. Could she have been more stupid, showing up at the church expecting . . . what? Redemption? Forgiveness? Understanding? She should have known better.

Simmering with anger, she shed the St. John's suit Winifred had helped her pick out last year, and put on her favorite old jeans and Victor's sweater—knowing it still smelled of him and would make her cry—and tried to get something productive done.

The blank screen of the computer resembled a gray, demonic eye stalking her, reminding her that she hadn't read her E-mail in a week, that there was a conspiracy to trash her books on an on-line book site, and that someone had set up an electronic newsgroup dedicated to proving that despite the ruling of the medical examiner, Victor Winslow's death had been caused by his wife. She was the woman on the grassy knoll.

Now, with her parents in crisis on top of everything else, the only thing she had left was her writing. At least that was still intact after the bizarre horror of the accident and investigation. Or maybe not. Hours after sitting down with her notebook, she glanced back through the scribbling, debating whether or not the pages were worth transcribing into manuscript form.

She used the old excuse of not turning on her computer during a storm. Like everyone else, she'd heard stories of people who ignored the warnings and worked at their computers with an electric storm raging outside. Such fools often came to a bad end—they were virtual lightning rods for disaster, anything from electrocution to having their hard drives reduced to burnt toast, taking all their life's work, their checking accounts and—horror of horrors—their E-mail into the digital ether, never to be recovered.

Computer-savvy people scoffed at such tales as urban legends, but Sandra couldn't afford to put it to the test. So when a storm rolled in—a frequent occurrence in the middle of winter—she kept her computer off.

Propping her chin in her hand, she stared out the window facing the sea and listened to the hiss and burble of the teakettle on the stove. The hundred-year-old timbers trembled; the wind found gaps in the old windows, rattling the glass and pervading the big house with a chill that no amount of heat would banish completely. The window caulking had crumbled years ago, and no one had ever bothered to fix it.

Her thoughts drifted to Mike Malloy, he of the big shoulders and battered pickup truck. If he hadn't shown up this morning, offered her a cup of coffee, she wasn't sure she would have made it home. He couldn't know how grateful she'd been for the company, and for his simple "who cares" attitude about the accident.

The accident. Finally, someone saw it for exactly what it had been—a horrible, disastrous accident, the sort of thing that happens on prime-time news shows.

Maybe it was just her imagination, but she felt a weird

connection with Malloy. She knew she shouldn't trust the dangerous warmth he stirred in her, but she wanted to. After the disaster with Victor, she wasn't even sure she understood the nature of love, of passion. Maybe she simply wasn't meant to. Maybe she was one of those strange creatures destined to live out her life alone, contenting herself with the quiet rewards of her small family and few friends.

If she knew what was good for her, she'd settle for that. Losing Victor—first to his secrets and lies, then to the murky currents that had swept him away—had created a hurt so intense she never wanted to feel it again. She didn't want to feel *any*thing again—not love, joy, grief, rage. . . . Because even joy had its price. She didn't want anyone to thaw the carefully crafted numbness that protected her heart.

Not even Mike Malloy.

She gave up trying to work and felt herself edging toward a decision. She needed a friend, someone who could pull her away from her world, just for a little while. It was a little humiliating to realize how much of her social life had revolved around his friends, his family, his agenda. Now the parties, the meetings, the convivial dinners and fund-raisers had fallen away, and she'd been left with only a couple of allies who cared about her rather than the man she'd married.

There was Joyce, her hairdresser, who owned the Twisted Scissors and listened with gum-cracking sympathy to Sandra's troubles, cheerfully dismissing the gossip about the accident. And then there was Barbara Dawson, who lived in nearby Wakefield.

As soon as the storm abated, Sandra drove to the small inland town and headed into a newish builder-designed community. She parked in front of her friend's house, wondering if she should have called first. Too late now. Shouldering a voluminous totebag, Sandra got out of the car. Despite the tract-home uniformity of the suburban neighborhood, the Dawson house stood out—a huge, half-finished monument to mediocrity. But there was nothing mediocre about the woman who lived here.

Stepping over a curb fringed by beaten-down weeds, Sandra made her way up a concrete path littered with a Big Wheel, a laser scooter, two soccer balls and a scrawled warning in rain-smeared chalk: *No Girls Alloud*. A minivan dusted with a cat's footprints sat in the side driveway.

When Sandra rang the bell, a chorus of "I'll get it" sounded, followed by the drum of running feet. The door opened wide, banging the much-abused wall of the foyer. Four identical pairs of brown eyes focused on her. Four grubby mouths, the degree of toothlessness varying with age, smiled in greeting.

"Hello, Aaron, Bart, Caleb and David," she said, naming them in order of height. "Can I come in, even though I'm a girl?"

"Yup." They shuffled aside to let her pass. She stepped into the colorful clutter of the Dawson house. Marred by the scuffs and smudges of the resident tribe, the house smelled of equal parts baking cookies and hamster cage. Aaron shouted, "Mo-om! Sandy's here!"

"Well, for heaven's sake." Propping a large, brown-eyed toddler with a runny nose on her hip, Barb walked into the foyer. "C'mon in, girlfriend."

"Can we go out now, Mom?" asked Bart. "It stopped raining, and we need to finish digging the foxhole."

His mother waved a weary hand in surrender. "I always dreamed of having trench wars in my backyard."

Emitting spontaneous machine-gun noises, the herd charged toward the rear of the house.

Barb stepped aside to let them pass. "Don't slam—"

The door banged shut.

"—the door."

Squawking in protest, baby Ethan squirmed free of his mother and waddled after his brothers, setting up a roar of protest until Barb hauled him in front of the TV, gave him a handful of dry Cheerios and turned on *Rugrats*.

"Just call me Mother of the Year," she said with a grin.

"Hello, Mother of the Year," Sandra said. "Is this a good time?"

"Let's see. Ralph's off in the wilderness on paintball maneuvers with his buddies, Ethan has an ear infection, I just cheated on my diet with half a bag of Doritos and my sons are destroying the neighborhood with entrenching tools. So, yeah. It's a perfect time." As cheerful and openly friendly as her boys, she clasped Sandra in a brief hug. "I'm glad you stopped by. I phoned after hearing the ruling, but you didn't answer. Let's make coffee."

Sandra took a seat at the boardinghouse-sized kitchen table while Barb bustled around. Creator of the wildly popular *Jessica and Stephanie* series of paperbacks for girls, she was one of the best-selling authors in the country. In her jeans, Keds and a sweatshirt smeared with jelly, she was as unpretentious as the mug of Sanka she made with instant hot tap water. Never mind that the mug had been imprinted to commemorate her first *New York Times* best-seller; it had a chipped rim, and the gold leaf lettering was flaking off.

The two had met at a meeting of the Society of Children's Book Writers and Illustrators, which convened four times a year at Newport's Redwood Library. On the surface, they had nothing in common—Sandra the quiet loner and Barb the soccer mom—but they shared one consuming passion that forged a sturdy bond: writing books for children. A few years ago, they'd begun reading each other's first drafts and talking shop. Barb was a consummate professional, and a godsend in the confusing and unpredictable world of publishing. Barb's life of yelling kids and madcap chaos contrasted wildly with Sandra's too-quiet existence.

She set her totebag on the table, a tacit indication that they would talk business. Although Barb had given Sandra sympathy and support from the very start of her troubles, Sandra didn't discuss the Victor issue much, not with Barb, not with anyone. "I have your manuscript," she said, taking it out. "Lady, you continue to amaze me. I wanted to stand up and cheer in the end, when Jessica and Stephanie rode through town on a pink parade float."

"Just like real life, eh?" Gesturing around the cluttered, male-dominated house, Barb added, "Can you blame me for writing idealized fantasies for girls? I finished reading your manuscript, too. Just a sec—I'll get it."

She hurried from the room, and Sandra sat listening to *Rugrats* and gazing fondly at Ethan, who had strewn Cheerios across the coffee table, then fallen asleep on the couch, clutching a black plastic Uzi. Barb's life with five rambunctious boys, her giant fireman of a husband and a hundred half-finished projects would make many women cringe, but when Sandra considered it, a powerful wave of yearning swept through her. What must it be like to have so many people depending on her, loving her, breaking her heart and making it whole again?

She was glad she'd come to see Barb today. She needed to get away for a while, to think about the one aspect of her life that hadn't deserted her—writing.

The publishing world knew her as Sandy Babcock, author of critically acclaimed children's novels. She felt safe in that skin. After marrying Victor, she'd kept her writing separate, walled off from her identity as his wife. She didn't ever want someone to buy her books because she was married to a public figure. Where was the sense in that? Besides, the material she tended to write about probably wouldn't endear her to his constituents. The fact that she published under her maiden name was no big secret, just something she never advertised.

Up until the accident, she'd had so much with Victor. A husband, a writing career, and all the subtle, understated luxuries the Winslow fortune could provide. She'd been lulled into believing she was a Winslow, too. Victor and his parents had made her feel a part of the family. But when disaster struck, all the support and belonging disappeared like a lost computer file.

"Got it," Barb said, returning to the kitchen with Sandra's manuscript, the pages now bleeding from copious—and probably richly warranted—red editing marks. "Congratulations on that write-up in the *New York Times*. I saved the clipping for you." Perching a pair of purple reading glasses on her nose, she said, "Here's the good part— 'a darkly beautiful addition to the canon of children's literature.'"

"That's code for calling me the Sylvia Plath of children's books. Sales on that novel were not exactly off the charts."

"Write something light," Barb advised her. "Think comical. Think commercial. Put a dog in it. Or a pet dragon. That's what kids want these days."

Sandra fiddled with her favorite fountain pen. Comical. Commercial. A dog. Maybe Charlotte, who was coping with her grandmother's descent into senility, could have a zany adventure with a basset hound.

"I just don't have those kinds of stories in me," she said. "My books always involve a struggle."

In each novel she wrote, she took her readers to dark

places where they were forced to confront fears, secrets, prejudices, injustice. Her stories depicted lonely kids with huge problems and narrow options. She loved to explore the shadowy roads those kids traveled—invariably alone—in order to find some sort of redemption. That was the beauty of fiction. When you closed the book, the trouble was gone.

"I know, sweetie. Just a thought. To be honest, you had me in tears by the end, when Charlotte tucks her grandmother in bed and kisses her good night. You must be really proud of this one."

Sandra nearly spit her Sanka. "I don't think proud quite says it. To be honest, I feel lucky my novels get published at all. And lately I've been wondering if maybe I should write horror. That way, my reputation would be an asset."

"Not funny."

"But true. Did I tell you Victor's family's filing a wrongful death suit against me?"

"No. Good God, what can they be thinking?"

"That they want someone to blame, I guess."

"So you're fighting it, right?"

"Yes. And then I'm selling my house and moving away."

Barb's misty blue-gray eyes widened. "No way. You love that place on Blue Moon Beach. It's so perfect—the perfect writer's retreat. I dream of having a place like that—something all to myself, where I can actually hear myself think." She gazed around the cluttered kitchen in frustration. "I'm weeks behind on my deadline, and Ralph and the boys don't give a hoot. I swear, sometimes I hate my life. I really do. I'd kill to have your life—oh, sorry."

Sandra forgave her with a wave of her hand. "Trust

me, you don't want my life. Sometimes *I'd* kill for a little of your noise and chaos."

Barb pushed aside her coffee mug and put her hand over Sandra's. The connection felt warm and good. "I worry about you, Sandy. You're too detached, alone." Barb held her gaze. "I'm speaking as your friend here. I was worried even before all this mess with Victor. I used to watch you at party functions and social events—you always seemed alone in a crowd, like a pleasant, uninvolved stranger who was just passing through."

Stung, Sandra withdrew her hand. "It's easy for you to sit here and say these things. You've got a houseful of guys who adore you, and your books are read by millions—"

"That's one way of looking at it. Another way is that I live in a house that's falling down before it's finished being built, the boys are a pack of hyenas and Ralph would rather think about his next chest-beating weekend with the guys than the fact that we've had three neighborhood guild warnings about the state of our yard. You think this has been easy street all these years?"

Her troubles sounded mundane and lovely, but Sandra understood that they were very real to Barb. She also realized that as wonderful as their friendship was, there were things about each other's lives they would never comprehend. "Got any tequila?" she asked, only half joking.

"I have something better." Barb got up from the table. Rummaging in the cluttered pantry, she moved aside boxes of Cap'n Crunch cereal and bags of Chee•tos held shut with clothespins. After a moment, she turned with a triumphant grin on her face and held out a gold box with a crushed Christmas bow stuck to the lid. "Godiva."

Chapter 9

T hat," Mike said, pushing back from the big kitchen table and grinning at Gloria Carmichael, "was the best thing that happened to me all week."

Wearing an old bib apron imprinted with a fish and the slogan "I Got Scrod In Paradise," Lenny's wife started clearing away the dishes. Round and soft as a ripe peach, she had crooked teeth and an honest smile. "Yeah? I thought the puttanesca sauce needed a little more anchovy."

"It was outstanding," Mike said, and he meant it. Lenny and Gloria invited him to dinner every other Sunday, when he didn't have the kids. They acted as though it was no big deal, but they had to know their gesture of friendship helped calm the loneliness howling inside him.

Gloria stopped behind his chair and planted a loud kiss on the top of his head. "Your mama raised you right."

"Don't go telling him that," Lenny warned. "He'll get all full of himself."

"Yeah?" Gloria scraped a plate into the trash. "You ought to try paying me a compliment sometime, pinhead."

"Don't believe her ribbing, Lenny," Mike said. "She's nuts about you." The earthy affection between the two of them was obvious to anyone with half a brain. This was what a marriage was supposed to be—love and laughter and being comfortable together.

"And she's taken," Lenny declared. "Hang in there, buddy. You'll find someone else."

"I'm not holding my breath."

Gloria patted him on the shoulder. "Angela really did a number on you, didn't she?"

That was putting it mildly. His ex-wife had ended up with the house and kids, and her father had taken over the business. Angela's father had bankrolled the company at the outset, and when the marriage ended, a very irate Rocky Meola seized control of the firm. Mike had ended up with a mountain of debts. Early on in the process his lawyer had suggested they could make an issue of Angela's affair, but Mike refused to do that. She was the mother of his children, and he wouldn't subject Kevin and Mary Margaret to a battle.

Lenny lifted a basket-clad bottle of Chianti. "Need a refill, Mike?"

"No, thanks. I've got to get up early—trying to round up subcontractor bids tomorrow."

Gloria paused on the way to the kitchen. "So you're going to be working for the Black Widow, Lenny tells me."

Mike stood to help with the dishes. "I'm putting in a bid to restore her house."

"I wish you wouldn't do that, Mikey. The woman's a

ghoul, if you ask me." She started rinsing plates and glasses, loading them into the dishwasher.

"How well do you know her?"

"Well enough. We use the same hairdresser, but she was always too stuck-up to give me the time of day. Her true colors showed when she drove her husband off that bridge."

"That's the part I don't get." Mike stood back while Gloria wiped down the counter. "If she's so clever, why the hell was she in that car, too?"

"One theory is that she got out of the car before it went over," Gloria suggested.

"Don't get her started," Lenny warned. "She'll bend your ear all night with this stuff."

"Maybe not all night." Gloria took off her apron and tossed it over the back of a chair. "Let me show you something."

"Aw, jeez." Lenny rolled his eyes. "My wife's a closet ambulance chaser, did I tell you that?"

She gave him a playful slap on the back of the head as she led Mike to the living room and selected a hand-labeled videotape from a big collection on a shelf. "Here's the special broadcast they did on *Evening Journal* last spring. Have a seat, Mike. Want me to fix some popcorn?"

"That's okay." Mike was curious as hell about the situation, but eating popcorn while watching a broadcast about a dead guy—especially a guy he used to know—didn't seem quite right. The accident had made headlines last year, and he remembered staring in shock at the front page news. But the fact was, he'd been dealing with the divorce, too caught up in his own business to pay much attention.

On the TV, a vaguely familiar blond reporter gazed into the camera, giving viewers a recap of the local scandal. Her breathy, urgent-sounding voice grated on Mike's nerves. With absurd gravity, she enumerated the salacious details of a fairy-tale marriage gone sour.

Victor Winslow.

Even after all these years, Mike felt a visceral sense of recognition. It was strange, hearing his friend's name on a newscast, stranger still seeing Victor's handsome, polished face smiling from the cover of *Rhode Island Monthly* that flashed on the screen when he'd been named the most eligible bachelor in the state.

He wondered how Victor had met his wife. Sandra looked a good ten years younger than Vic, mid-twenties, maybe. The scoop on the TV depicted her as a girl with an undistinguished past, a minor career in publishing and no identity outside of being chosen by Victor. These days, Mike figured, she probably wished she had been singled out by someone else. Hell, she probably wished she'd taken a job as a hatcheck girl.

A wire-service wedding picture appeared on the screen. Victor and his new bride stood in the arched doorway of Old Somerset Church. He wore a Brooks Brothers tux, his black silk bow tie flawlessly knotted. The bridal gown made Sandra look like a princess, her long-gloved hand tucked into the crook of his arm. She held her mouth in a stiff smile of terror. She was stunningly beautiful, as any Winslow bride was bound to be.

She looked radically different now. The hair, the clothes. Oh, but that face. Thinking about the first time he'd seen her, chopping wood on a cold day, he'd never forget it—those lost brown eyes, the set of her mouth. Though he ought to know better, her image was etched in his heart.

According to the report, Victor and Sandra Winslow had been the golden couple, youth and promise personified, capturing the public imagination. Their marriage had been a major social and media event, with Victor's own father, the venerable Reverend Ronald Winslow, presiding.

A montage of video clips flickered past. Victor and Sandra were as vibrant as a latter-day Jack and Jackie, waving farewell en route to their honeymoon, dancing at the swearing-in party after Victor's election, cutting the ceremonial ribbon at the opening of the new Sequonset Bridge, one of Victor's major legislative triumphs.

"Ironic, isn't it?" Gloria commented, sitting on the sofa next to Mike. "He supported the funding for that damned bridge."

"Should have got more funding," Lenny said. "Reinforced those rails."

Mike kept wondering what the hell had gone so wrong between Victor and his wife. But then, he reminded himself, every marriage was a mystery in its own way. Things might look fine on the outside, but a flawless facade might conceal irreparable cracks and fissures, dry rot and structural damage. He knew there had been plenty of headscratching over his and Angela's breakup, especially since they were both so crazy about the kids.

The video montage shifted to later scenes of the bridge, the rail ripped away, chunks of concrete dangling from torn and twisted rebar. No skid mark blackened the roadway.

Mike winced, thinking about that long fall into the murky water far below. What had Victor felt, flying through black night, the car making a nosedive into frigid seas? As kids, he and Vic had been fearless swimmers, daring each other to jump off the tall pier at Town Beach, racing each other from buoy to buoy. But that had been in summer, in broad daylight.

Mike could only imagine the icy sting of the water that

had engulfed Victor's car that night. Gloria shivered beside him, though Lenny swore she'd watched this broadcast over and over again.

"So did they ever figure out who called in the wreck?" Mike asked, his gaze glued morbidly to the images on the screen.

"Never," Gloria said. "The call came from an emergency phone box at the east end of the bridge. You know how it goes—everyone's got something to hide. No one wants to get involved. Happens more than you think. A guy sees something, uses the phone box and we never know who the good Samaritan was."

"Somebody not so good, maybe," Lenny suggested.

"You'd think they would have made more of the gun," Gloria said as the scene shifted to the chaos of the predawn search. Squad cars barricaded the bridge at both ends, helicopters buzzed and dipped through the winter sky, draglines dropped from open boats, divers in thermal suits plunged into the killingly cold water.

"No gun was ever found," Mike pointed out. "They just said so."

"At least two shots were fired from inside the car," Gloria said. "The windshield was smashed. Somewhere, there's a handgun lying around, and that woman pretends she doesn't know a thing about it."

There had been a thorough search for the weapon, although the thick sludge of mud and the strong sea currents made any discovery unlikely. All they'd caught in the draglines were some torn bits of clothing—the lab confirmed the fibers came from a wool tuxedo, the style Victor had been wearing the night of the accident. Investigators had combed the records for a gun registration. They'd come up with nothing. Without a gun, they couldn't prove

Sandra Winslow had shot her husband and let his body be sucked out to sea.

Still, that didn't stop everyone in the area from believing she had done just that. He thought of Sandra Winslow, alone now and practically in hiding, if the TV report was even half right.

The Black Widow of Blue Moon Beach.

". . . with only her conscience for company," the reporter chirped, the camera panning past the overgrown rose of Sharon hedge in front of the Babcock place, then zooming in on a crooked shutter and the sagging garage roof. Maybe Sandra hoped Thursday's ruling would change things, but glancing at Gloria's outraged expression, he doubted it. Folks around here wouldn't bail her out even if they had a life preserver in their hand.

Chapter 10

10 Things I Loved When I Was Little

1. *The smell of baking pizza.*
2. *Foreign currency, which I kept in a Dutch Masters cigar box.*
3. *My mother's handwriting.*
4. *Going to the library.*
5. *The sound of my father singing in the sho—*

"Working on your book?" Sandra's father asked, coming into the kitchen of the East Providence bungalow. Just out of the shower, he smelled the same way he had all Sandra's life. Irish Spring and Aqua Velva.

She flipped the notebook shut and capped her pen. "A few scribbles while I was waiting for you to get home. How was your round of golf?" She'd arrived just as he was returning home from his afternoon match. Since retiring, he played rain or shine, summer or winter, every weekday.

"Not so great. It's too damned cold to play. So how's the book coming?"

She watched him as though to reassure herself that this

was her father, not some stand-in planted by aliens while her real father, who would never let his wife leave him, was vacuumed into the cosmos. She wasn't sure what she was looking for—an apology for not returning her calls? An explanation about the breakup? Was he hiding some big secret? Holding something in? She couldn't be sure, because men didn't tell. It was as simple—and as frustrating—as that.

"To be honest, Dad," she said, "I haven't been able to concentrate on work."

He opened the fridge. It was the same refrigerator they'd always had, only now it was . . . different. Disorganized. Food was shoved in haphazardly—cheese and salami and canned drinks. No casseroles in covered, labeled dishes, no condiments lined up according to height, no dairy products organized in date order.

"You hungry? Thirsty?" her father asked.

"No, thanks." She waited while he found a can of beer and opened it.

"Why're you looking at me like that?" he asked, direct as always.

"Like what?"

"Like I got some disease or something."

"Excuse me, Dad, but last time I saw you, you were happily married to my mother." She knew it was stupid, but she half expected him to manifest literal evidence of the split—a gaping wound, a rash, an ugly growth. In the weeks following Victor's death, she had lost weight at an unhealthy rate. Her skin grew sallow, her nails brittle. Yet her father appeared unscathed. Something as monumental as the breakup of a thirty-six-year marriage should cause some obvious physical distress. How dare he look . . . normal?

He took a sip of his beer. "What, you expected to see a mushroom cloud coming out of my head?"

"Something like that."

"Sorry to disappoint you." He sat down at the kitchen table, moving aside a stack of unopened mail.

"That's not what's disappointing me, Dad. It's kind of scary, the way you're just—just . . . I don't know. Carrying on. As if nothing's really changed, except that Mom is gone."

He looked around the kitchen. The sideboard was littered with loose AA batteries, an oil-change funnel, a tire gauge and some lottery slips. Outdated newspapers lay on the counter next to his golf glove and hat. Sandra's mother always made him leave his stuff in the garage.

"She's not gone. She's everywhere in this house," he said. "She made the curtains. Put those little knickknacks on the shelves. Lined up all the stuff in the pantry." A small crack appeared in his facade. "So don't tell me I'm just carrying on. I'm thinking about her all the time."

"Then why don't you think up a solution?"

"We did. A separation. And then, I guess, a divorce."

"Is that what you want?"

"Jesus, honey, you know that's not the question."

"Then what is the question?"

He hesitated, pinching the bridge of his nose, his face anguished. "It's about what we don't want. As in, she doesn't want to play golf or fish. I don't want to take ballroom dancing lessons or travel. Or speak Eye-talian and learn to cook Chinese."

"Maybe you could do a little of each," she suggested.

He waved a hand with impatience. "That's what it says in all those 'How to Save Your Marriage' books."

"You've read books on how to save your marriage?"

"It's all a bunch of crap. How long would your mother last, pretending she likes golf? About as long as I'd last poking around the British Museum."

"Go somewhere you both like," Sandra suggested.

"Honey, your mother and I had this discussion. Over and over again. The fact is, I spent my whole career traveling, staying in hotels, meeting new people. And all I ever wanted was to stay close to home."

"All Mom ever wanted was to go somewhere new." Restless, Sandra got up from the table and went to the window, staring out at the postage-stamp backyard with its single apple tree and a row of peony bushes, sagging in the cold. She used to have a sandbox out there, a swing.

When she thought of her childhood, she remembered . . . silence. Her silent struggle with stuttering. Her parents' silent frustration with her problem. The silence of teachers, pediatricians, speech therapists, psychologists—all waiting for her to get the words out. Through no one's fault, hers had been a quiet childhood. She didn't have brothers or sisters to fight with, didn't have a bunch of relatives visiting on the weekends. And God knew, she didn't have legions of friends lining up to play with her.

She forced herself to think about her parents' marriage in objective terms, as an outsider might view them. Had she been the glue that held them together? No. Absolutely not. There was something between them, a subtle, smoldering fire, always present like embers banked for the morning chill. It was never obvious, particularly not to Sandra, who couldn't stand to think of her parents as lovers, but sometimes she'd catch herself reflecting on it.

"I wish you and Mom would work harder to sort things out," she said. Anger boiled through her, and she felt like ripping someone's heart out for examination. Her family was breaking apart—the three of them would never be together again. They'd cease to exist as a unit; the gestalt of her childhood was forever gone. Victor had failed her, and now her father was failing her, and suddenly she caught herself thinking of Malloy, who made her feel all sorts of things. She pushed that thought aside. "You're making yourselves miserable."

"We were pretty damned miserable before she left."

"Why?" She gestured around the kitchen in frustration. "You had a good life here."

"We had a life here. Whatever was good about it just . . . faded away, I guess."

She studied her father, trying to figure out what had changed. In his early sixties, he was a good-looking man, with clear eyes and a ready smile. He was tall enough for a woman to wear heels with, something her mother's bridge club regulars vocally admired about him. He was thickset but not overweight. His best feature was his abundant hair, which in recent years had turned to a dramatic sweep of pure white.

Her father's face had both character and kindness in it. And distance—something about the angle of his gaze, the set of his mouth. She wondered if this was new, or if she'd simply never noticed before. And for the first time, she wondered if she did the same thing—kept her distance, protected herself.

"Did you even try to get help, Dad? I don't mean reading a book. Did you go for counseling or to a—" The thought of sexual dysfunction crossed her mind, but wild horses couldn't make her go there, not with her own father. "I think you should try a marriage counselor."

"We did."

She lifted her eyebrows in surprise. "Yeah? And?"

"It was baloney. We were supposed to make lists about what we like about the other person, think up one compliment per day and go out on dates together, all that crap."

In spite of everything, she laughed a little. "Dates and compliments. Sounds tough."

"I'd've done it gladly, but that's all superficial stuff. Band-Aids. People drift apart—you know that. And your mother—" He broke off to finish his beer. "There are things about her that I've never understood—stuff she wanted, expected, dreamed about. I guess those things built up over the years, and it's too late to fix it now."

Sandra tried to conceive of her mother as a woman, but had trouble forming an image of Dorrie apart from wife and mother. She could picture her in that role clearly. Neat as a pin, the house spotless. Her favorite ashtray was on the back porch—since her husband had kicked the habit years before, she had taken her solitary vice outside. A knitting basket still rested beside her easy chair in the den, the skeins of yarn carefully balled and labeled with little tin tags.

Her favorite books were stacked on the coffee table, their spines lined up just so. Oh, she loved those books. Big album-sized tomes with glossy photographs of exotic places—Cadiz, Nepal, Tuscany, Tintagel. Sandra tried to imagine that her mother had led some sort of secret life, dreaming of far-off lands and dangerous strangers, but that was too preposterous to contemplate.

Or maybe not, she reflected, thinking of Victor. Some problems were buried too deep to fix. She'd discovered that the night of Victor's death.

"It's the retirement," she said at last. "Somehow, it didn't turn out the way you and Mom expected."

"Yep."

"Mom says you wouldn't help out. She wanted to retire, too."

"I tried to help but when I loaded the dishwasher, she rearranged it. When I dusted, she followed behind me, doing everything her way. And don't get me started on the vacuuming."

She shut her eyes guiltily. Perhaps with her problems,

she had unknowingly sucked away whatever patience and understanding her parents had for each other. "My troubles put a strain on everything. Losing Victor, the search for his body, the inquest—I've been a mess for months. No wonder Mom needed to get away for a while."

"Hey." Her father got up from the table and put his arm around her shoulders. "I don't want to hear another word of that. What happened with you and Victor is lousy enough without you thinking it caused your mother and me to split up."

Split up. Oh, those words hurt. In her novels, she had written about kids whose parents divorced. She thought she could imagine their confusion and fear, likening it to being dropped off a cliff in the dark, but now she knew she hadn't even come close. A free fall in the dark didn't begin to describe what it felt like to have her parents break up.

"Listen, can we talk about something else?" Her father's bushy brows knit as he studied her face.

She took a deep breath. "Actually, there is something I wanted to discuss other than Mom."

"What's that?"

"The deed to the house on Blue Moon Beach. Do you know where it is?"

"I think it's in the basement." Rifling through a drawer, he found a flashlight and took it into the hallway. "What do you need it for?"

Sandra cleared her throat. "I'm thinking of selling the house, Dad."

He paused at the top of the basement stairs. "Yeah?"

"Yes. I never thought I would, but . . ."

"Do you need money? Is that it?"

Her parents weren't well off; they weren't starving, either. But they sure hadn't factored bailing out their grown daughter into the budget.

"That's not why I want to sell the place. I want to get out of there, start fresh somewhere."

"I thought you liked the area."

She had never told her parents all the details of the petty vandalism, the phone calls in the middle of the night. The "Black Widow" stuff worried them enough.

"That doesn't matter," she said. "I've got plenty of time to figure out what to do next," she added, remembering Milton's advice. "The house needs to be fixed up. But I intend to sell it and get out."

"You're sure it's not the money."

"No, Dad. I'm okay."

"Scout's honor?" he asked.

"Scout's honor. In fact, there's a royalty check in the mail." She'd called her literary agent to explain about the one that had been destroyed. Her agent had been incredulous—*They blew up your mailbox? I thought you lived in Rhode Island, not Idaho.* "So is this a problem, Dad?"

"Your grandparents left the place to you. Selling it is your prerogative."

"But you don't approve."

"I don't have an opinion about it. Never much cared for the place myself. My folks used to drag the whole family down there every summer. I was always bored stiff. Couldn't even pick up Sox games on the radio."

The stairs creaked under his weight as he disappeared into the dark maw of the basement. She heard him bumping around, swearing as he smacked his head on a rafter. After a few minutes, he emerged with a fireproof box.

"Haven't looked through this stuff in years," he said. They sat together on the sofa, and he set the box on the coffee table, stringing the surface with cobwebs. Flipping open the lid, he revealed a collection of file folders, papers, little boxed objects.

He pulled out old photographs and stock certificates, school records, things that had once seemed important and no longer were—an instruction manual for a short-wave radio, the manufacturer's warranty on a typewriter, a Cracker Jack code ring, a clipped article about a neighbor's son making Eagle Scout.

Other things were so important that they seemed inordinately fragile, hard to hold—a lock of baby's hair, tied with a bit of white ribbon and tucked away in an envelope. Sandra's birth certificate. A child's drawing of a bird in a nest, the name Sandra B. printed carefully in the corner. A photograph of her great-grandparents, circa 1900. An emigration certificate from Ellis Island for someone named Nathaniel Babcock.

She picked up a yellowed, embossed document. "Your marriage certificate."

"Yep."

"What happens to this if you get a divorce?"

"Nothing. I suppose there's a new piece of paper dissolving the marriage, which trumps that one." He unfolded the certificate to find a small wedding photograph inside, paperclipped to the document.

Sandra studied the photograph, realizing with a jolt that in the picture, her parents were younger than she was now. In his early twenties, her father hadn't been her father yet. He was simply Louis Babcock, and he'd been flat-out handsome the way Stewart Granger or Gary Cooper was handsome.

And her mother, of course, was beautiful in the luminous, uncertain way of all brides.

Sandra knew she, too, had looked that way at her wedding to Victor. She knew, because the pictures had run in the papers.

She tried to read the smiling faces of her parents in the

old wedding portrait. Was there some clue, like a shadow hovering over them, that condemned their marriage to failure? Back in 1966, was there any indication at all that the union was only going to last thirty-six years? She wondered if the happiness of those young, naive people was worth the pain they were going through now. Some nights, lying awake, she wondered if she would have been better off never having met Victor at all. He'd changed her life in so many ways.

Her father's thumb lingered over his bride's signature, rendered in plump girlish script: "Dorothy Heloise Slocum." His face softened with remembrances she knew he wouldn't share.

"Dad," she said quietly, "I'm so sorry. I really do think you and Mom can fix this." She pointed to the photograph. "Look at you. There's so much love there. It's written all over your faces. You can't let it all break apart because you're having a tough time adjusting to retirement."

"It goes a lot deeper than that, honey."

"Then you'll have to dig deeper to fix it."

He pulled out a folded parchment document, tied around the middle with string. "Here it is," he said. "The original deed to Blue Moon Beach, the will and the transfer."

Opening the old papers, she read the terse legal definition of the property and ran her finger over the raised seals on the document. "Fair enough," she said. "I plan on getting the place sold by summer."

"And then what?" her father asked.

"And then—" A chill ran through her. She had no earthly idea how to start the rest of her life from here. "And then . . . I guess I'll see."

Chapter 11

Ten Lies I've Told My Therapist

8. *I never let my stutter define me.*
9. *I am fulfilled by my role as a daughter, wife, friend and writer.*
10. *I find sex enjoyable, rating it somewhere between "most of the time" and "always."*

No wonder she'd only managed to make it through two incredibly unproductive sessions, six months after marrying Victor. Even then, she'd sensed a problem—something her heart knew even as her common sense rejected it. But subconsciously, she probably hadn't wanted to explore the shadowy undercurrents pushing her and Victor apart, which was why she hadn't returned to the therapist.

Her stomach tightened into a hard ball of nerves when she heard the crunch of Mike Malloy's pickup truck coming up the drive. He made her edgy; she couldn't decide whether he was ally or adversary. Regardless, she knew she couldn't trust him.

Going to the front door, she absently ran a hand through her hair, and then felt a stab of surprise. She had dressed up for him, relatively speaking. Instead of donning her usual jeans and oversized sweatshirt, she'd put on khakis and clogs, an angora sweater with a silver cat brooch Victor had given her one Valentine's Day.

She looked good. Not politician's-wife good, but everyday good.

It was Victor who'd taught her to worry about her appearance. Until Victor, she never had, because she thought she was invisible. After the lonely experience of high school, she'd expected to settle into anonymity after college at URI. Her small, quiet life would have gone on undisturbed, except that one autumn night, her speech therapist had sent her to a support group meeting. She thought no one would notice the girl in the back of the room, scribbling in a yellow notebook. What she hadn't known was that she'd caught the eye of the local hero.

After that, everything, every moment of every day, had changed.

Watching through a front window, she observed that Malloy didn't seem to have much compunction about his appearance. Not that he needed it, she thought with a warm shiver she wasn't expecting to feel.

His dark, longish hair stuck out of a baseball cap. He had a face that looked lived-in and eyes the color of forget-me-nots. But on Malloy, the delicate blue wasn't a feminine attribute, and looked striking in contrast to his black hair. A thick athletic sweatshirt and an insulated vest exaggerated the breadth of his shoulders, and heavy gloves covered his hands. His Levi's were faded in all the right places, and his work boots added another couple of inches to his six-foot-plus height.

His rough but undeniable appeal drew a strange

visceral reaction from her. How could that be? She remembered how attracted she'd been to Victor's refined urbanity, his sophistication. Mike Malloy was a far cry from urbane and sophisticated. She didn't like his effect on her. She wasn't even sure she should have an opinion about him.

Then she saw something that surprised her. Two kids tumbled out of the passenger side of the pickup truck. The bigger one was a girl of about twelve or thirteen, wearing a pink ski jacket and matching hat and mittens. The boy was younger, clomping around in baggy jeans and unbuckled boots, with Malloy's scruffy dog tucked under his arm, wriggling and straining until the boy let him go.

When Mike spoke to the kids, he leaned down, resting his hands on his knees and making eye contact. As he talked to them, he pointed at the beach. The boy let out a whoop and ran up and over the dunes, the dog leaping along behind him. The girl stuffed her hands into her pockets and walked more slowly toward the water's edge.

When Sandra had first met Malloy, she hadn't been able to picture him as someone's dad. Someone's husband. Not that it mattered, she told herself. But as she watched him surveying the wind-carved dunes where the children played, and saw the expression on his face, she felt as though she had discovered a whole new side to him.

In the past couple of years, Sandra had found herself becoming increasingly preoccupied with kids. Sometimes when she saw people with children, she felt such an unholy envy that it burned like a fire in her heart. She felt that now, watching Mike Malloy. God, what she wouldn't give to have what he had, a couple of messy, loud, unpredictable kids. Someone to giggle with, to hold close at night, to love with every bit of her heart.

She recalled the first time she broached the topic of

having a baby with Victor. They'd been married a year; he was getting ready for opening session of the General Assembly. With the big-hearted charm that so endeared him to his constituents, Victor embraced the idea. He took her face between his hands, holding it delicately, as if it were something fragile and precious. "Oh, Sandra, yes," he said. "I want that, too."

She believed him. That was what made him such a good politician. Even his own wife, who knew him better than anyone else in the world, believed everything he said.

Composing herself, she opened the door for Mike Malloy. He grabbed a clipboard and a zippered leather portfolio from the truck and came up the walk toward her. She tried, without success, not to stare, but good Lord. The man turned a pair of old, faded jeans into living sculpture.

"Thanks for getting back to me so quickly," she said, hoping that sudden flush of warmth didn't show.

"No problem," he replied. His face was without expression, his eyes unreadable. He didn't appear to notice how neatly and carefully she was dressed.

Yet even indifference encouraged her. She'd learned to expect open dislike and suspicion from everyone, so this was new. "You brought company today," she said.

Neutrality changed instantly to defensiveness. "Is that a problem?"

She stepped back, holding her hands palms out. "Not at all. I like kids. I was just making conversation."

"I see. Sorry. I didn't mean to jump on you. I just picked them up from school."

"Let me take your coat."

Transferring the clipboard from one hand to the other, he slipped out of his vest and handed it over. Her fingers sank into the deep pile of the vest, where his body heat lingered. She resisted an absurd urge to press her face to the fabric before hanging it in the hall closet.

"If your kids get cold outside, they're welcome to come in."

He hesitated. She wondered if he'd heard any of the local gossip, or if he'd made inquiries after she told him about her troubles. Then he nodded and said, "Thanks." He inspected her then, his frank, assessing gaze taking in the angora sweater, the brooch. Then he removed his Red Sox cap, folding the bill and sticking it in his back pocket.

"I . . . guess we should have a seat." She walked over to the old piecrust table and moved the chairs around to face the bow-front window. From here, they could easily keep an eye on the kids. "How old are your children?"

"Mary Margaret turns thirteen in the spring, and Kevin's nine."

Resting her chin in her hand, Sandra watched them playing Frisbee while the dog ran frantically back and forth between them. "They look like a lot of fun."

"They are." He set some papers in front of her on the table, separating the pages into two piles. "Here's what I've done. I've worked up a bid for basic repairs. The other is for a full restoration. Why don't you look over them and I'll answer any questions you might have."

"Thanks. Um, would you like a cup of coffee or tea or something?" she asked, watching his big, squarish hands. "There are some snacks in the kitchen." She'd put out a plate of molasses cookies and a dish of cashew nuts. The simple act of readying herself for company had felt alien, reminding her of how long it had been since she'd entertained Victor's friends and associates at the house in town. She knew, of course, that this was not a social call, but in some ways, it felt like one. And it felt good. Almost . . . normal.

"No, thanks." He spoke fast, almost harshly. "I'm fine."

She ought to be smart enough to know a hired contractor wasn't going to fill the void in her life. Exasperated with herself, she gave her attention to the preliminary bids. His work, on crisp laser-printer paper, was clear and well organized, spelling out what each phase of the project would involve and the estimated costs in labor and materials. Computer-generated images of the house and grounds made the place look like a picture in a storybook.

She paged carefully through the first document, bracing herself for the bottom line on the last page. She stared at the number for a long time. Keeping a poker face, she turned her attention to the second proposal. This one was longer, more involved and detailed. As she read through it, she was able to picture what he had in mind. And it was a grand plan. The entire place, from the wild blueberry and rose hedges to the verdigris wind vane on the roof peak, would be transformed into a state of glory the old house had never enjoyed, not even when it was newly built.

She put her hands in her lap and looked from one page to the other. Six weeks or six months. Quick fix or full restoration. A hefty price versus a financial hemorrhage.

"Well," she said. "Well, thank you. You've given me a lot to think about."

"Don't you have any questions?" He folded his arms on the table and leaned forward. His stare was direct, unsettling, yet at the same time, she could look into his calm blue eyes without fear. A funny feeling came over her. He listened to her with a different quality than her folks did. For as long as she could remember, she felt their anxiety about her stutter. They didn't know it showed, but when she spoke, they were on the edge of their seats, straining with hope, and even as a child, she could feel that. Malloy simply listened, relaxed and confident. There was something rock solid about this man. For the first time in months, here was someone who knew exactly what he was about, who spoke plainly and honestly, who was entirely up-front.

Or so she thought. Maybe she shouldn't trust herself enough to conclude that he was all right. Events of the past year had proven her judgment dangerously flawed. Once again, she caught herself comparing Malloy to Victor. Her husband had been larger-than-life, whereas Malloy was just . . . large. Ordinary. Maybe that was why he appealed to her more than he should.

"These bids are clear. They say what each job entails, and approximately what it will cost. That's what I was hoping you'd tell me."

"Let me know what you decide, then."

Her heart sank at the finality in his voice, and the way he pushed back his chair. She'd cleaned the house for an hour this morning, expecting him.

He wasn't company, she reminded herself, repeating it like a litany. Still . . .

"You know," she said, "since I'm selling the place, I shouldn't care whether the house gets fixed up just enough to bring it up to code, or if it gets a full restoration."

"But?"

"The restoration is tempting."

"This is a special place," he said. "It's one of a kind. It would be a shame to see the house torn down or ruined by someone who doesn't know what he's doing."

"I agree. But why should I care?"

"Didn't you say the place is a family legacy?"

"Sure, but not after I sell it." She didn't consider herself a sentimental person, but when she thought of letting go of the house, she felt a lurch of her heart. This was her place, her sanctuary.

Ridiculous, she told herself. The sooner she got out, the better. Living in this old house, filled with family history and fond memories, didn't account for much when no one came to see you. Correction. No one but hired help.

"I'd better go with the lower bid, just the basics so it'll pass inspection."

"Have you calculated your asking price?"

"Um, not really." She hadn't been able to make herself go there. Somehow, disposing of the property seemed like a betrayal.

"I printed out some recent comparable sales in the area." Paging through the papers on his clipboard, he showed her the MLS listing on properties nearby. "Historically, in this area, a restored home sells for about twenty-five percent more than an unrestored home."

"This bid is a lot more than twenty-five percent higher than the other," she pointed out.

"I'm planning on doing a lot more than twenty-five percent more work. If I get the job," he added.

"Oh, you get the job, don't worry about that," she said. Realizing she sounded too easy, she added, "That is, if your references check out. You do have references, don't you?"

She expected him to get defensive. Instead, he took a stack of papers and a thick album from the zippered portfolio. "Of course," he said. "Help yourself. Feel free to call any of my former clients."

She opened the album and nearly choked. A Newport mansion shimmered on the page like something out of a dream. The ensuing layout showed gleaming floors, graceful staircases, soaring columns, polished woodwork. The album displayed house after house, letters of commendation from historical societies, even awards.

She lifted an eyebrow. There was more to this drive-by handyman than met the eye. "This is very impressive." Then she picked up a magazine. "*Architectural Digest*?"

"They've done a couple of features on my projects."

She located an article entitled "The Spirit of the Past." The photographs were stunning—Gilded Age and Colonial homes, lush gardens, storybook gazebos and beach cabanas. Scanning the captions under the spread, she read aloud, " 'Malloy is endowed with a shamanlike vision, a mystical gift for evoking the winsome charm of a forgotten age.' "

His face reddened and he shifted in his chair. "I didn't write it."

A smile tugged at her lips. "Shamanlike vision?"

"That's crap. The fact is, I do my research and work my tail off. I only deal with subcontractors who can do the job right."

Sandra sighed, studying a photo of a painted saltbox house in Sakonnet that might have passed for an Andrew Wyeth painting. "I have to be honest with you. I really can't afford to restore this place. I guess I'm not supposed to tell you that."

"Didn't you say you own it free and clear?"

"Yes."

"You'd qualify for a loan, no problem. The house is your collateral."

She pictured herself going to the local bank, applying for a loan, dealing with people who had known Victor for years. "It's not qualifying that worries me."

"Why do you say that?"

"You know, this thing about my husband."

"Banks are in business to make money. Not to listen to gossip."

She studied his rough-hewn face, his patient, blunt hands. He wore no wedding ring, but that didn't mean anything. He was a workingman; he'd probably left his jewelry at home. Maybe on the nightstand, next to his sleeping wife. Did he bend down to kiss her when he left in the morning? Did she inhale the scent of his pillow, feel his lingering warmth in the bedclothes?

Sandra swallowed hard, chagrined by the turn of her thoughts. "But my husband is . . . Victor was pretty well known around here."

"I don't know the finer points of the law, but it's illegal for a bank to discriminate."

She thought about what happened Sunday, the Winslows refusing her gift to the church, and the sting of that moment hardened into stubborn certainty. She couldn't recall the last time she had felt so decisive about something. But she wanted this. Wanted to transform the house on Blue Moon Beach into the beautiful home her great-grandfather had built for his family. It didn't seem to matter that she had to let it go once it was finished. The prospect of the building project itself had an elemental appeal. It was something constructive, something that had a beginning and an end. Maybe it would bring her life back into balance, at least for a while. "All right," she said. "Let's talk about the restoration."

They worked out a tentative plan, and he was more than reasonable, even agreeing to defer his own fee until the house sold. Enviably self-confident, Malloy led her through each step of the contracting process. Victor used to take charge, she recalled. But in a much different way. Victor had an agenda. Mike had a vision. They were two different things.

As they concluded their schedules and figures, the kids came back from the beach, running across the yard. Mike got up, his whole face softening at the sight of them. "I'll have them wait in the truck."

"Oh, no you won't," she said. "Not on a day like this. It's freezing outside. They're probably starving."

Doubt shadowed his face and her stomach plummeted. Maybe he wasn't immune to the gossip after all. Maybe he didn't want his kids in the house of a killer.

"They'll live," he said. "I don't like leaving them by themselves when I'm at work."

"You're a single dad?"

He nodded. "The kids live with my ex-wife in Newport."

"I see." So, he wasn't married after all. Suddenly, the world changed color. And her palms began to sweat. When she thought he was married, her interest in him had been like her interest in a Judith Lieber evening bag—something dazzling, but way out of her reach. The fact that he was single took away that safe distance.

"You seem to like having them with you," she said.

"It shows?"

She smiled. "In every breath you take. I really would like it if they'd come in and warm up."

"You asked for it." He studied her briefly, then went to the back door and held it open. "This way, you two," he said. "Leave your boots on the mat. Leave the dog out there too."

"But, Dad, Zeke is freezing his balls off," Kevin said. "His little furry balls."

"That's it. I'm leaving you on the porch," Mike said.

Kevin stared at the floor. "Sorry."

"Just leave your boots, okay?"

Trailing their jackets behind them and walking along

in stocking feet, Kevin and Mary Margaret came into the kitchen. They looked around, Hansel and Gretel with red cheeks and hungry eyes.

Sandra was suddenly grateful she'd made that batch of molasses cookies. "Hi," she said. "I'm Sandra. Would you like some cookies?"

"Sure, thanks." Kevin Malloy had round cheeks, lightly dusted with freckles, his father's petal-blue eyes and a grin that wouldn't quit. Just seeing it stretch across his face made Sandra smile, too. For that alone, she liked the kid immediately.

"What about you, Mary Margaret?"

The girl shrugged. "All right, I guess. Thanks."

There was nothing instantly likable about Mary Margaret. Sandra understood this as fully as a weather report. She noted the wariness in the girl's wind-chapped face and hooded eyes, and it was like gazing into a mirror through time. Mary Margaret was the same kind of child Sandra had once been—awkward, intelligent, emotional. Her sharp gaze never missed a thing.

"What about some hot spiced cider?" Sandra suggested. "It's from a mix, but it'll warm you up."

"Okay," said Kevin.

"Yes, please," Mary Margaret said. Without being told, she went to the sink to wash her hands, and motioned for her brother to do the same.

Pouring hot water from the kettle, Sandra mixed the spiced cider in thick china mugs. The kids sat at the table eating cookies, waiting for the cider to cool. Mary Margaret took a delicate sip. Almost crossing his eyes, Kevin blew on it with all his concentration. Sandra noticed Mike watching his son with a depth of affection so apparent and so private that she glanced away.

Mary Margaret tried to smooth down her fine, sandy

brown hair, staticky from the hood of her jacket. Her gaze wandered to the profusion of notes stuck to the refrigerator with cartoon-character magnets. Sandra's habit of making lists had long since gone beyond the notebook phase. Quickly, she scanned the notes to see if any of them would embarrass her. *Ten Things to Eat for Breakfast. Ten Things I Remember About Granddaddy Babcock. Ten Things to Say to a Phone Solicitor.*

"I keep a lot of lists," she explained, though no one asked. For some reason, she didn't feel at all silly—probably because they were kids. Children never made her uncomfortable. It was one of many things she liked about them.

"They all say 'Ten Things,'" Mary Margaret observed. "Why ten?"

"I'm not sure. I picked that number randomly, a long time ago, and now it's a habit. I suppose if you can't think of ten items for a list, then either you've picked the wrong topic, or you're not thinking hard enough."

Kevin made a loud slurping sound in his mug, then announced, "My dad's thirty-eight."

"Thanks, pal," Mike said, half smiling.

"Idiot," Mary Margaret muttered under her breath.

Kevin ignored her. "Did you know a horse's heart weighs nine pounds?"

"No, I didn't," said Sandra. "Did you know that a beaver can hold its breath for forty-five minutes?"

His eyes got big, and she could see him mentally filing the factoid away while Sandra did the same—assimilated the fact that Mike was the same age as Victor would be now, had he lived.

Kevin held out his wrist, showing off an oversized watch. "It's one A.M. in Italy right now. This thing's got three time zones."

Mary Margaret exhaled a long-suffering sigh at the ceiling. Malloy, who was scraping a cabinet with his penknife to see what was under the green paint, paused and turned to Kevin. "Where'd you get the watch, son?"

"Carmine. That's my stepdad," Kevin told Sandra.

She sensed a sudden chill in the room and changed the subject. "My dad spent all his summers here when he was a boy," she said. "He claims there's buried treasure in the yard, but he can't remember where."

Kevin asked, "Is this a haunted house?"

"I'm still checking on that. When I was little, I used to visit my grandparents here, and I thought it might be haunted."

"Really?" His blue eyes grew round with wonder.

"Yes, but I'd better not tell you about it, or you won't get to sleep at night."

"Ghosts don't scare me."

"See this?" She went to a square, shoulder-height door on the wall. "It's a dumbwaiter. Broken now, but it used to run between the kitchen and the root cellar. When he was a little boy, my grandfather used to hide in here. One day, when I was about your age, I noticed that it seemed to go up and down all by itself."

Kevin whistled between his teeth. "Cool. Does it still do that?"

"I'm not sure."

"But it might," he persisted.

"Maybe. This house is over a hundred years old— plenty of time to get infested by ghosts." Almost defiantly, she stole a glance at Mike to see if he disapproved of the conversation, but he seemed preoccupied with measuring the soffit space above the cabinets with a long metal tape measure.

"Why do you say maybe?" Mary Margaret asked. "Have you seen any evidence?"

"I haven't exactly seen anything. It's just a feeling I get sometimes. I might be staring at the fire in the wood-stove, and see something unusual in the flames."

"Do you get scared?" asked Kevin.

"No. A little sad, perhaps, because in most explanations of hauntings, the ghost suffered some sort of sadness or loss in the house. But my grandparents were nice people, so they'd probably turn into nice ghosts."

"I don't believe in ghosts," Mary Margaret said.

"Are you going to fix this place, Dad?" Kevin asked his father.

"You bet, sport."

"Good. It needs it."

"Kevin—"

"Sorry. Let me know if you spot a ghost."

Mike reeled in his tape measure with a metallic hiss. "Sure thing."

Chapter 12

They sure were happy to see you at the lumberyard," said Phil Downing, climbing into the passenger seat as Mike signed the invoices.

"Yeah, it's been a while." Mike started the engine, adjusted the mirror to check the load of lumber, plaster, concrete, nails and tools in the bed of the truck.

"Feels good to be working on something other than a leaky basement," Phil said. He was a plumbing and electrical contractor Mike had used in the past. Mike planned to subcontract for the painting, plaster and finish work, but not until the job was further along.

"Trust me, you'll find more than leaks at this place." The prospect of restoring the old beach house reminded him of the things he used to love about his work—probing the hidden mysteries of a hundred-year-old house, excavating the core layout, trying to see the building and landscape through the eyes of its original designer.

He'd spent days with the Babcock house in his head and on his computer screen, mentally and virtually weaving together history, symmetry, nature and architectural theory. He always liked this stage of the work, but it also brought on a bittersweet sense of regret. This was what he'd liked way back in his college days—this was what he was good at. Everyone had dismissed him as a jock, but his classes on architecture and design had set his brain on fire. Then the knee thing had happened, then Angela, and he'd had to leave in the middle of it all. Everyone said how great he'd done, the way he'd started his firm and made a big success of it—yet he'd always wished he could have stayed in school.

The current project couldn't compare to the work he used to do in Newport, when he'd hired crews of restoration specialists and handled seven-figure budgets for wealthy clients. All that had fallen away during the divorce and dissolution. Fifteen years of work and sweat. Maybe Mike would build back up to that point one day, maybe not. For now, he'd settle for a project with a scope and rhythm he could control.

He put the invoices in a folder and drove out of the parking lot. "This order is chickenfeed compared to our previous volume."

"One day at a time," Phil said, then chuckled at the look on Mike's face. In his late forties, a chain smoker in a knitted fisherman's cap, Phil was a quiet, deliberate type who did steady work and kept his promises. He had one other skill Mike found rather startling—Phil had become a sophisticated computer expert. His gift for ferreting out lost files and configuring systems had bailed Mike out more than once. Mike didn't know him well, but Phil was pretty open about the fact that he hadn't always been so reliable. He'd had a rough life. Years ago, he was held liable in an auto accident he hadn't caused. He started drinking, and his wife had taken their two boys out of state. Phil had hit bottom with a DUI, gone into court-ordered rehab and had been sober a good ten years.

He was like a ghost, sitting there—a sad, middle-aged guy, out of touch with his kids and ex-wife, subsisting on coffee and cigarettes and memories that grew dimmer every year.

Phil took out a Camel and turned it, unlit, over and over in his fingers. "That's pretty much the way to deal with any setback, I figure."

Highway 1 followed the curve of the Pettaquamscutt River, visible through the bare trees at the roadside. The sky was a sharp winter blue, so clear it made his eyes smart. If the weather held, he'd work on the old slate roof, a rare opportunity this time of year.

During the drive to the job site, he went over the work plan, while Phil studied computer-generated diagrams and elevations.

Paging through the printouts, Phil gave a low whistle. "You're looking at a tight work schedule."

"I'll finish on time and on budget. I promised."

"You'll have to practically live there."

"One thing I have plenty of these days is time," Mike said. "I only get my kids one weekday and every other weekend."

"Sorry to hear that."

"The arrangement's up for evaluation next summer. I intend to ask for a lot more time." He drummed his fingers on the steering wheel. "It sucks, after raising my kids for years, I suddenly have to prove to some social worker I can provide 'adequate and stable housing,' and a 'nurturing environment.' My lawyer's advising me to look for a house, but hell, my kids love Paradise. They're safe on the boat— they've spent practically every summer there."

"It's a damned funny thing—if the parents stay to- gether, they can do God-knows-what to their kids, raise 'em as idol worshipers or tattoo their behinds or whatever. But as soon as a judge gets involved, you're following someone else's orders. Buddy of mine who's Methodist has to take his kids to Catholic mass every other Sunday. By order of the judge, of course."

"Everything I've been ordered to do is reasonable," Mike said, "so far. I just don't like being ordered to do it, like I'm a moron or a deadbeat." The system seemed spe- cially designed to bring out the worst in everybody in- volved. He'd had to learn to let go of things even when every instinct told him to hold on with all his might. He'd had to change the whole focus of his life, and maybe that wasn't such a bad thing, but it sure as hell felt that way. He'd been cutting expenses every way he knew how, liv- ing on his boat while looking for the right house for his kids, putting something by for their education every month, no matter what, keeping up with child support pay- ments. Every spare dollar he earned went to savings—for the legal war chest he was amassing for the new custody evaluation, and for making a better life for Kevin and Mary Margaret.

"Hang in there," Phil said. "Things will settle down, you'll see."

Mike kept his eyes on the road. He was getting too used to the way things were. And he wasn't sure he wanted to get accustomed to living alone, to seeing his kids on a court-ordered schedule. What the hell kind of life was that?

Angela's husband, Carmine, had more money than time for a family, supplying ample quantities of designer toys while skimping on anything that resembled serious parenting. He liked the idea of having kids more than the reality of it. Mike tried to be thankful that Carmine was an okay guy—a business owner, volunteer fireman, seemed proud of the kids. He didn't care for Mike at all, of course, though he did a pretty good job of hiding that from Kevin and Mary Margaret. Mike wasn't crazy about the fact that Carmine doled out expensive gifts like candy on Halloween, but he never said a word, even though they always seemed to have something new from their stepfather.

Sometimes Mike tortured himself, wondering what it was doing to them to have their family split into two separate households. He'd watched Mary Margaret and Kevin stagger through the whole gamut of emotions from grief to remorse, insecurity to fury. The family counselor advised him and Angela to expect conflicts of loyalty, acting out, sliding grades in school.

What are we doing to our kids, Angela?

"Hey, slow down, pal," Phil cautioned. "Don't want to lose our load before we get there."

Mike glanced at the speedometer. Eighty-five. Jesus. "Sorry," he said and eased up on the accelerator. As they turned down the coast, the landscape grew wilder, more dramatic, the woods unkempt, the waves exploding against high, rocky banks. Mike could see the crooked wind vane of the old house poking above a thicket of mangled trees and overgrown bushes.

"There's one thing you ought to be aware of before we get started," Mike said. "The client is Sandra Winslow."

"Victor Winslow's widow?" The unlit cigarette twirled in Phil's hand. "You don't say."

"She wants to sell the family beach house."

"Doesn't surprise me. You can't get away with murder until you actually get . . . away."

"You think she did it?"

"Probably not," Phil said, "but where's the fun in that? So what's she like?"

Sad. Quiet. Nervous. Fragile. Mike wasn't sure how to describe her. He couldn't even figure out his complicated reaction to her. The fact that she was so alone reminded him of his own losses, bringing him face-to-face with a truth he didn't want to acknowledge. "She doesn't strike me as the type who would off her husband for the insurance," he said.

"You never really know about people, eh? But you're okay with her as a client?"

"I can't be choosy." In the past, his clients had reacted to his work with pride and wonder, but he didn't expect enthusiasm from Sandra Winslow. Impatience and irritation, maybe.

Mike pulled into the drive, parking behind her blue hatchback. Phil got out and lit up, pushing back his cap to look at the house.

"So this is it," Mike said. A hedge of mountain laurel bordered the yard, and Concord grapes, with last year's shriveled clusters still hanging on the vines, draped the rickety cedar fence on one side. Under a graceful sycamore tree stood a small bird feeder, and he was a little surprised to see that it was well stocked with seeds.

"This is some place," Phil said. "I don't blame you for wanting to restore it." He surveyed the long, curving porch and busy woodwork edging the roof. Like most Carpenter Gothics, the house had been drawn from the builder's own fanciful ideas rather than the plans of a trained architect. The ornate wooden detail was unique to this house alone, one of the factors that was going to make it a valuable piece of real estate.

A peculiar feeling came over Mike each time he studied the house. He felt a vague sense of recognition—not only because he was an expert on this sort of design, but because of the way the whole place was put together. It felt right, oriented perfectly to the ocean view, every line whimsical but balanced.

Sandra Winslow met them at the front door, and Phil ground out his cigarette on the brick walkway. She looked a little distracted, a pen tucked behind her ear, a tentative smile on her face. Today she wore dark slacks and a sweater, her hair pulled back. No makeup. Mike introduced them, explaining that Phil would be in charge of the electrical and plumbing work.

She held the door open wide to the formal vestibule. "There's coffee on in the kitchen. Help yourself."

"Thanks." Phil stepped into the entranceway, all business as he scanned the area from baseboards to tall ceilings. The house had a dining room adjacent to the broad front parlor, a library nook and a big country kitchen down the hall. Phil headed toward the kitchen, drawn by the sharp, rich aroma of coffee.

"Your copies of the contract." Mike handed her the stapled pages. "You'll want to take your time looking over that."

"Thanks." The softest of smiles touched her lips. "And I have something for you."

His mouth dried. *Damn.* What the hell was it about this woman? Just one look, a brief exchange of conversation, generated a swift, unexpected heat between them, and the reaction intensified each time he saw her. She wasn't beautiful the way Angela was, not in a head-turning, wolf-whistle way. Sandra had a subtle magnetism in the depths of her brown eyes, and there was something fresh and honest in her face. According to Ronald Winslow, that was how she'd beaten the rap during the medical examiner's investigation.

"So I'm supposed to guess?" he asked.

"You'd never guess." She led the way into the parlor, the most dramatic room in the house with its leaded bow-front window framing a view that dazzled today. The blue of the sky had the crispness found only in winter, imbuing the Atlantic with the deeper hue of sapphire. A pair of colored glass birds hanging from the window sash caught the light. He touched one with a finger, and color swept across the room.

"Victor made those," she said softly. "It was a hobby of his."

Mike turned away, making no comment. It was hard, seeing those little glass ornaments hanging in the sunlight, knowing Victor had made them. How much harder it must be for Sandra, his widow. He wondered how she could stand it.

She went over to the library alcove, which was littered with books, a desk with a computer and printer, stacking trays overflowing with letters and forms. He couldn't quite make out the text on the computer screen. Had she been surfing the Internet? Playing computer solitaire? Sending E-mail to a secret lover? Was her world inside that computer now that the locals shunned her?

He wanted to ask her, but he knew he wouldn't. Her invisible, self-protective shell set boundaries between them. At the same time, she moved him in a way he hadn't expected and didn't like. Her vulnerability made him sharply aware that he had numbed himself to emotion and had been doing so for too long. He wanted his family back, he missed them like hell, and for some reason, Sandra Winslow unearthed all that buried need in him.

"Here you go," she said, handing him a rolled document, yellowed with age and brittle at the edges. Just for a moment, her eyes shone with artless delight. He wondered if she'd been this way with Victor, unconsciously sexy, a little awkward, almost girlish in her appeal.

He unrolled the paper on the round table in front of the window. Sandra weighted the corners with a seashell, an ashtray filled with buttons, an empty soda bottle and a coaster from Schillers Bar. Mike stared in amazement at a well-preserved house plan, complete with detailed elevation drawings.

"Cool, huh?" she said, standing close enough to touch. "I found this at my father's, along with the deed."

"You're—" Mike broke off, unwilling to get too personal with this woman. "It's a rare document—pretty incredible. I'll have working copies made, and we can register the original with the historical society." For a second, a light glinted in her eyes, giving him a glimpse of a different woman beneath the somber facade. The unguarded moment revealed sensitivity, vulnerability, and those were things that shouldn't interest him at all. But the thought swept through him like a rogue wave—*I want you*—and somehow, she must have felt it, because she stepped back, as though from a too-hot stove.

"Fine with me." Even without moving, she seemed to withdraw.

"You're lucky. It's a hell of a find." Mike could tell he made her nervous, and he didn't know why. He thought about the way she'd been around his kids—far more relaxed and natural than she was with him. Kevin and Mary Margaret didn't have a clue about her troubles, and they accepted her at face value. In the truck on the way home, Kevin even declared that he liked her. Mary Margaret hadn't said much at all—Mike was never sure what was going on in his daughter's head these days.

"I'm going to start by pressure washing the roof while the weather holds," he said, warning himself not to speculate any further about this woman, especially with regard to his kids. She was a client, nothing more. "I don't think it needs replacing, but I'll know for sure once we get it cleared off."

"It's a bit cold to be working outside," she said.

"I'll live. Is there an outdoor spigot?"

"Yes."

"Good. I'll get started."

"Let me know if you need anything."

"Will do." He studied her for a moment—nervous hands, soft mouth, big eyes. She didn't look capable of helping with much. She looked troubled and complicated. An unfamiliar urge grabbed hold of him. It was weird to be thinking of a woman again, particularly this woman. He wanted to take her in his arms, hold her against his chest, smooth his hand over her glossy hair and—

"I need to get that sprayer rigged," he said. What he needed was to get outside, do a job involving cold water and high pressure. Maybe that would clear his head. Without another word, he turned and left her. A half hour later, he was standing on the peak of the roof, the hose connected to a roaring compressor on the ground far below.

Draped in cables and cords, Phil went back and forth between the house and power line, studying the antique knob-and-tube wiring scheme and scribbling notes.

Mike derived a distinct, primal satisfaction from the powerful gush of water pounding at the roof tiles, uprooting mosses and mildew, flaky lichen and the occasional dried weed sprouting between shingles of old slate. From his vantage point, he could see the traffic on the coastal road. In summer, the road would be crowded with SUVs, station wagons and open Jeeps with radios blaring. But in the dead of winter, the local traffic was sparse.

In the distance, he spotted a dark sedan gliding along in front of a white van with a bunch of equipment on its roof. He frowned when the sedan turned into the driveway, tires crunching over the crushed shell surface of the drive. The station logo for WRIQ News blazed from the windowless side of the van, and on its top was a small satellite dish. Two men jumped out and opened the back, reeling out heavy spools of thick cables.

Mike climbed down the ladder and turned off the pressure sprayer as a technician crossed the yard, a big camera mounted on one shoulder. Two men in dark suits exited the sedan.

"This is the home of Sandra Winslow, right?" one of them called.

"I'm just doing the roof," Mike said. Whatever was going on, he didn't want any part of it. He bent down to check a gauge on the compressor.

"And what are you doing, specifically, to the roof?" asked a female voice.

He straightened up to see a blond woman standing nearby. Polished nails, cherry-red lipstick, a stare that prodded, intruded. Recognition nagged at him, and after a few seconds, he placed her. Courtney Procter.

The TV newscaster was shorter than he'd imagined. Smaller waist. Bigger hair. Whiter teeth. Same outstanding tits. She wore a tight-fitting suit with wide, pointy shoulders that gave her the look of an executive dominatrix. A fancy scarf fluttered in the cold breeze, and her high heels dug into the crushed shells of the driveway. She'd done something to her hair so that it didn't move an inch no matter how hard the wind blew.

Grabbing a red bandanna from his back pocket, he wiped his hands clean. "Is that on or off the record?"

The genuine warmth and humor of her smile startled him. "Depends on your answer."

"I'm working on the roof." He indicated his rig. "Mike Malloy, of Paradise Construction."

"Courtney Procter," she said, "WRIQ News."

"I recognized you right away," he said.

"Of course you did." She laughed at his expression. "My ego thanks you." She studied him for a few moments, then said, "So you're a builder."

"A contractor. I specialize in historical restoration work."

"How well are you acquainted with Mrs. Winslow?"

"I know what you're asking, and the answer's not what you're looking for. I never met the woman until she hired me to renovate this house." He glanced over her shoulder to see the crew setting up. "Mind if I ask what's going on?"

"We're covering breaking news in an ongoing local story."

Every nerve ending came to attention inside Mike, but he pretended nonchalance, bending to tighten a connection on the sprayer. "Yeah?"

"She's being served a complaint in the wrongful death of her husband, Victor Winslow."

Mike didn't have to ask who was doing the complaining.

"Miss Procter," someone called. "We're ready."

Bars of white light flooded the area in front of a naked lilac bush. The garish lighting accentuated the shabby, weathered siding of the house, the peeling paint of the door frame and porch rails, the overgrown tangle of forsythia bushes with dead leaves still clinging to them. On TV, the place would resemble Ruby Ridge, or maybe one of those backwoods farms where Animal Control people seized starving livestock that had been standing in manure for a decade.

He wondered what Sandra was thinking right now, what she was feeling. She had to know she was trapped, and that the constable delivering the summons wasn't going to let her dodge process. And, of course, she realized the local news had come to record her shock and shame in high-definition color.

He fiddled with the valve on the compressor, letting out excess pressure with a wet hiss. The starter switch lay inches from his foot.

The van emitted a bunch of electronic noises, and its rooftop satellite swiveled in adjustment. Courtney Procter planted herself like an exotic orchid in front of the house. A woman in a logo windbreaker scurried forward, adjusted the fluttering scarf and brushed some powder over the ridge of the newscaster's small, straight nose.

The motor of the compressor made a knocking sound. One of the crewmen glared at Mike. The toe of his boot inched a little closer to the switch.

The suits from the constable's office shuffled some papers, and one of them took out a packet secured with a rubber band. He had a steely look in his eyes and cheeks chapped red from the cold. The sea wind plucked at his long black coat. He straightened it, clearly trying to look officious for the camera. The civil servant performing his duty. Your tax dollars at work.

". . . three . . . two . . . one," Courtney Procter said with practiced ease. "I'm standing here in front of the old beach house where Sandra Winslow has been in hiding since the disappearance and alleged death of her husband, State Senator Victor Winslow. Thursday's accident ruling by the medical examiner failed to end speculation about the mysterious circumstances of the February ninth tragedy.

"Witnesses who last saw Victor Winslow alive testified that the glamorous young couple left a Democratic Party function together, with Mrs. Winslow at the wheel of a late-model Cadillac. Though her blood alcohol level tested within legal limits, she reportedly drove erratically and with excessive speed . . ."

Courtney Procter summarized the known details of the accident while the process servers consulted each other over the hood of the car. A producer seemed to be mapping out the most advantageous shot of the front door.

". . . grieving parents have initiated a civil suit against Sandra Winslow," Procter stated, "charging her in the wrongful death of their son . . ."

The camera panned and tightened its focus on the constables crossing to the front of the house. In moments they would force their notification on Sandra.

Mike flashed on an image of his kids, sitting at her kitchen table and drinking spiced cider. Then he remembered the day he'd received the divorce summons and complaint. He'd just stepped out of the shower and stood on the doorstep wearing nothing but a towel, dripping water on the document and staring at it as though it were a package delivered in error. The shame and failure of that moment lived like a rock inside him, but at least he'd been the only witness to it.

A predatory sparkle flashed in Procter's eyes. One of the men pounded at the door.

It all happened in a matter of seconds. Mike held the nozzle in one hand as he flipped on the compressor with his foot. The machine roared to life and the hose bucked and stiffened. The wild stream struck the satellite dish on the van, knocking it to the ground. A fountain of sparks erupted, and the startled constables ducked low, yelling in confusion. He killed the compressor with a touch of his foot, just as the front door opened a crack. The stream of water died in a gradual arc, but not before spraying one of the cameramen. And Courtney Procter.

"Fuck," she said, dropping the mike.

Mike hurried forward. "Geez, ma'am, I'm sorry as I can be. I don't know how the heck that happened." He took out his bandanna and dabbed at her shoulder, her silk scarf. Half of her blond hair hung down as though it had melted.

"I hope to God you're bonded," she sputtered, grabbing the handkerchief from him and taking over. "Because you're about to get sued from here to kingdom come."

From the corner of his eye, he saw the front door open, heard the constable speak in a commanding voice and Sandra's halting reply. The envelope changed hands and the door closed. The moment was over almost before it had begun.

"It was an accident," Mike said.

Chapter 13

Ten Synonyms for Desperate

7. *hopeless*
8. *splenetic*
9. *woebegone*

In the hours following the visit from the process servers, Sandra remembered how she had felt, waking up in the CCU after the accident. She knew she was wounded, but a numbing cushion of shock kept the pain at bay—for a little while. Gradually, though, the cushion deflated until there was nothing but a bright window of pain. Milton had warned her this was coming and she'd braced herself, but she knew no preparation could keep her from feeling the broken shards of betrayal and disbelief.

She wondered if she should have—could have—handled the incident differently. It had all happened so fast. She'd taken a step back from the door, folding her arms in front of her, but the envelope had been pushed into her hand anyway. She didn't remember what the constable said, didn't recall her wooden-tongued response, but a few moments later, they'd left her holding the papers, her forehead pressed against the front door, while outside, Courtney Procter gave Mike Malloy a piece of her mind.

The summons now sat untouched on the hall table. She gave the manila packet a wide berth each time she passed it, as if it were a disgusting piece of taxidermy.

Wrongful death. Victor's parents were suing her for killing their son. *Loss of society, companionship, care, counsel . . . Negligent infliction of emotional distress . . .* The litany of damages read like second-rate free verse.

Calling on her well-developed talent for avoidance, she retreated to the study, closed her journal and read over the final chapter of her book, taking refuge in a fictional world far more hospitable than the real one. The story was a sanctuary, a place where she could make everything turn out all right. *Simple Gifts*, a novel of loss and redemption, was finally done. Charlotte, the main character, had come to accept her grandmother's irreversible senility, the grandchild becoming the old lady's caretaker in a role reversal that Sandra had wept through as she wrote it. With acceptance came healing, like a single trickle of sunlight through a midwinter day. On her friend Barb's advice, Sandra briefly considered letting poor Charlotte get a puppy in the end, maybe even a basset hound, but she couldn't bring herself to do it. The simple gifts of the title were much more subtle than that.

She used to have a ritual to celebrate the moment the final draft of a novel drifted out of her printer. She and Victor would share a bottle of champagne, indulged in only on special occasions. Tipsy after a glass and a half, she'd giggle through her acceptance speech for the prestigious Addie Award, doing a wicked imitation of Victor addressing the Daughters of the American Revolution.

She wasn't sure what to do now. How could she finish a novel without Victor around?

"You got any naval jelly?" called Phil Downing, the workman who had been banging around in the basement for most of the day.

A sense of the surreal passed through Sandra as she went to the top of the basement stairs. "What kind of jelly?"

"Naval. As in navy. Pink stuff that comes in a white container, for removing rust."

"Oh. It's possible. You could check the garage." When she was small, her grandfather used to putter each summer away in the old carriage house that smelled of motor oil and insecticide, pursuing his unfathomable passion for taking apart small motors. Fixing a lawn mower made life worth living for the old man, who had died so gently when Sandra was in college that she wasn't even certain how to grieve. He had left the old summer place to her—now she wondered if he had a sense of humor she was only just discovering.

"Help yourself to anything you need out there," she said to Phil as he passed through the kitchen. "Some of that stuff in the garage has been sitting around for half a century, though."

"Thanks. I'll take a look."

Phil clomped up the stairs, his tool vest clanking with wrenches and volt meters. He was the sort of person who didn't seem to want to take up much space—he held himself coiled inward and regarded the world with a tired wisdom in his eyes, lines of trouble around his mouth. There was a shiftiness about him Sandra didn't quite trust, but he worked quietly and steadily on the house, and unlike Mike Malloy, he didn't distract her.

Malloy was another issue altogether. She could see

him in the front hall, standing halfway up a ladder as he inspected the fanlight casement. Late-afternoon sunshine streamed over his long body, his dark hair, his muscular forearms. He had the flat stomach and narrow hips of a trained athlete, though he didn't strike her as the type to spend hours at the gym. There was no hint of classic refinement in his face; it was the sort of face you saw in war movies or outdoor-equipment catalogs.

But the attraction was more than physical. Beneath the tough-guy exterior, she had glimpsed a surprising, bright humanity; it was evident when he was with his kids, and again when he'd seen the original house plans. And maybe, just maybe when he fixed her blistered hands the first day she'd met him.

Or maybe not, she told herself. Maybe she was reading too much into a guy who simply intended to restore her house. Even so, she kept thinking about the way he watched his children, with love and pride and uncertainty. Or the way he drifted somewhere far away as he studied the antique blueprint. Or the way he touched her, with a gentleness that nearly made her cry, because it reminded her of how long it had been since any man had touched her.

She picked up her manuscript, fitting a long rubber band around the loose pages. With a Magic Marker, she addressed a big padded envelope to her agent. Though not a superstitious type, she didn't feel quite right about simply stuffing the two hundred eighty-four typed pages into the envelope and shipping it off without a second thought. This was Charlotte, after all. Charlotte, who had lived in her imagination for over a year, and who had been a part of Sandra for much longer.

Despite the fact that she was a fictional character, Charlotte was a powerful force. She'd been present, with her stringy hair and big uncomprehending eyes, all through the tragedy with Victor. She'd helped keep despair at bay even in the darkest moments of the night. She acted out a shining life on the page that was far nobler than any life in the real world.

For that, Sandra loved her in a strange, abstract way. Impulsively, she lifted the stack of pages and pressed her lips to it.

At the same moment, Mike Malloy walked through the door carrying a stepladder. The oddest expression came over his face as he set aside the ladder.

She froze. "I know how weird this must look."

"I've seen weirder."

"I was just about to mail in this book manuscript," she explained, fumbling with the envelope.

With unhurried deliberation, he took it from her, holding the edges open so she could drop in the pages. "What kind of book?"

"I write novels for children."

"Yeah?"

His closeness unsettled her, yet at the same time, she craved it. She became acutely aware of his body warmth, his smell, the way the worn denim work shirt lay across his shoulders. She could even hear him breathing, which should not have been a remarkable thing, but when was the last time she'd stood close enough to another person to hear him breathe? There was something else, too. That little shock of recognition a woman gets from knowing a man wants to touch her. Despite her lack of experience, Sandra felt that shock now and recognized it for what it was.

Flustered, she rummaged in a kitchen drawer for a stapler. "I studied writing in college and published my first book under my maiden name a few years ago."

"That's something. Really," he said. "I wonder if my kids have ever read any of your books."

"Mary Margaret might have. They're aimed at her age group."

"She's a big reader. Always bringing home stacks of books from the library." He gave her the envelope, and his hand brushed her forearm. An accidental touch, but a current of warmth ran through her.

She flashed a nervous smile even as she stepped away from him. "My kind of kid." With three quick squeezes, she stapled the package shut, eyeing him furtively the whole time. It had been so long since she'd had an ordinary, personal conversation with anyone. But more than that, she was drawn to other aspects of him, aspects that inappropriately fascinated her—the negligent way he stuck his thumb into the waistband of his jeans. The heat of his gaze lingering on her a heartbeat too long.

He didn't deliberately draw attention to himself, but her nerves hummed with awareness every second he was around. And against all logic and expectation, she caught herself thinking about the shape of his mouth, imagining the feel of it on hers, the caress of his hands, touching her in a way she hadn't been touched since . . . well, maybe never.

"So you've always been a writer?" he asked.

"Ever since I was old enough to hold a crayon. I never wanted to be anything else." She hesitated, pretending to check the address on the envelope. "Anyway, I wanted to thank you for what you did earlier. The thing with the news crew."

He positioned the stepladder under the trapdoor to a crawlspace above the kitchen, tilting his head back to see inside. "Purely an accident."

She pictured the stream of water taking out the satellite dish. Then she glanced at Malloy's hands. They were broad and strong, not the hands of a man who did things by accident.

"Either way," she said, "you spared me from being the lead story on the local news." She only wished he could have spared her from receiving the summons.

He climbed halfway up the ladder. "They'll still report it."

"But there won't be any film for people to slaver over."

"Is that what they do?" He raised his arms to dislodge the trapdoor. "Slaver?"

"That's what it feels like." She gave an involuntary shudder, envisioning the long envelope in the constable's black-gloved hand. She felt a wave of nausea, as if her body were rejecting what her mind knew to be true.

"You okay?" Malloy asked, frowning down at her.

"I can't believe they're actually doing it. I can't believe they're suing me. These people whose son I married."

He shuffled his feet on the stepladder. "Tough break."

What did she expect from him? He was a carpenter, not Sir Galahad. "I have to get this to the post office," she said.

"Okay." He climbed higher, so that only his lower half was visible through the trapdoor.

She stared at his faded Levi's, his thick-soled work boots. She thought of the big, squarish hands and the shaggy dark hair that needed cutting but probably wouldn't get it anytime soon. And she blushed at the high, unholy heat that burned inside her.

Every time she caught her thoughts wandering to that forbidden place, she tried to bring them back on track—to focus on practical matters rather than impossibilities. But she couldn't deny it—she needed warmth, connection, no matter how many times life had taught her that those were things she would have to do without. Usually she could control her blurry, unfocused yearning, deny the constant thud of need. But more and more frequently, in the middle of moments when she was supposed to be thinking of something else, she thought of this. Of skin pressing against skin, lips to lips, hands writing wordless poetry on her bare skin. There was something exquisitely ironic and painful in imagining something so vividly and knowing it was out of her reach.

Grabbing the summons and hurrying out, she decided to drive all the way to Newport to mail her package. She told herself it was because she had to meet with her attorney, but the real reason was that the local post office was run by one of Ronald's parishioners, who had known Victor since he was a boy.

Paradise was full of them—people who knew Victor. They all remembered him as a gifted, golden-haired lad, spit-polished in his Boy Scout uniform as he organized the annual paper drive, standing proud and tall to receive a Rotary Club honor, or grinning for the camera in front of the "Welcome to Paradise" sign that declared, "Home of Victor Winslow, 1982 State Wrestling Champion."

The whole town had always owned a piece of his triumph. People felt it gave them special access to him. It seemed only natural that after distinguishing himself at Brown and then at Harvard's Kennedy School, Victor would return home to run for public office.

To be elected by people who claimed they knew him, who had loved him, who mourned him.

Everyone, even those who didn't know Victor personally, felt diminished by his death and offended by the fact that she had survived.

Her palms grew sweaty as she drove onto the high, arching bridge that connected Conanicut Island to the mainland. The span seemed endlessly, torturously long, peaking in the middle, a dizzying height above the slate-gray waters of Narragansett Bay. Nausea churned in her gut. Keeping her gaze trained straight ahead, she gritted her teeth and counted slowly, telling herself she'd make it to the end. And she did at last, hounded by nightmare memories. The blinding jolt of headlights, reflected in the rearview mirror—they were being followed. *Objects in the mirror may be closer than they appear . . .*

Victor's shouting and then her own. The smell of rain-wet asphalt. The black lash of sleet on the windshield. The dull gleam of metal in his hand. The scream of the tires when she slammed on the brakes. She remembered thinking it couldn't be a gun. Victor had written the state's most recent handgun control legislation himself. He would never own a gun.

She could still feel the wallop of the car slamming against the bridge rail, breaking through, and then the powdery explosion of the airbag, forcing her hard against the seat.

Breathe, she told herself, her count winding down as she approached the end of the bridge. Just breathe. But at the other side of Conanicut lay another bridge, this one leading to Newport on Aquidneck Island, another few miles farther.

There was always another bridge to cross. She dragged herself through the ordeal again, forcing her mind to empty, her lips to count, her nerves to stop their silent shrieking until the gray steel naval yard on the west side of the island came into view. She turned gingerly to the right, where the city lay, postcard-pretty even in the dead of winter. Centuries-old brick walkways and buildings clustered around the pristine harbor, devoid now of the summer crowds.

After stopping at the post office, she found a parking space in front of her attorney's building on Thames Street. She and Victor used to love coming to Newport, with its rainwashed brick market, its cozy restaurants, busy nightlife and myriad shops. The little arts and crafts gallery near Bannister Wharf even carried his handmade suncatchers of colored glass—all profits to charity, of course. The gallery owner declared them best-sellers—everyone wanted to own a little piece of Victor Winslow, it seemed, even broken shards of colored glass.

Gathering up the summons and related documents, she hurried inside. The building dated from 1741, a narrow Colonial distinguished by clean red bricks, white-framed windows and a wrought-iron fence enclosing a highly disciplined collection of shrubberies.

Taking a deep breath, she entered the reception area. By now, of course, the staff here knew her.

"Good afternoon, Mrs. Winslow," the receptionist said. "You can go right up. I'll let Mr. Banks know you're here."

"Thanks." She climbed the stairs past mediocre portraits of the founding members of the firm, Claggett, Banks, Saunders & Lefkowitz. She knew them through Victor, of course. She knew a lot of lawyers through Victor. Soon after the accident, an investigator with the medical examiner's office had advised her to hire a lawyer.

She resisted at first, seeing the measure as an admission of guilt. She'd been so ignorant, she hadn't seen the point of having an attorney present during a death investigation. She remembered sitting in her hospital bed, her shock-numbed brain only dully aware of the images on TV—choppers and dive boats swarming over the bay, nets dragging and rescuers in survival suits diving in a desperate search for Victor. Dragged from the muddy depths, the car had looked obscene, unrecognizable—a death trap. As she watched, she'd had trouble breathing, even speaking, not because of her injuries, but because both hope and dread kept a chokehold on her.

After a day of searching, the slow strangulation of Sandra's hope reached an end. "Rescue" turned to "recovery." The water temperature was fifty-four degrees, survivable for a maximum of thirteen minutes, maybe less.

On the TV, the report came in that the team examining the bridge damage had found something unexpected—a bullet lodged in the steel cutwater at the base of a bridge pier. Not so unusual, given the habits of vandals and high school kids these days. What had been unusual was the bullet hole in the car of a high-profile elected official who made gun control a key issue.

The moment she heard about the discovery, Sandra went straight to the cabinet in her private hospital room, changed into the clothes her mother had brought her and walked out with the objections of the hospital staff echoing in her ears. A taxi dropped her off at the firm. She insisted on seeing Banks, because he was, Victor had once told her privately, a sleazebag. He had a talent for getting even the most obvious criminal off the hook with absolutely no regard for the defendant's guilt or innocence. With Milton Banks, it wasn't even about money, although he liked to charge a hefty fee. It was about the game, the manipulation of the rules, the verbal tricks and leaps of logic that swept the state's evidence into the dirt.

The first thing he'd said to her was, "Don't tell me a single thing more than I ask you. Don't tell me you're innocent—everybody is. Just give me the answers I ask for, keep it short and sweet, and I'll take care of the rest."

And he had. Sandra was grateful. The last thing she wanted was to be grilled into blurting out things she never should have known, things she wanted to forget, even now. She'd been questioned numerous times, and after the final polygraph test, the medical examiner concluded that Victor had been killed in a terrible accident. She hadn't needed defending after all. But she did now.

She knocked once on the office door and stepped inside. He sat at his painstakingly neat desk, waiting for her. Milton Banks never, ever appeared to be busy or harried. He reminded her of a lizard sunning itself on a rock. Then, with a motion so quick and deadly that you'd miss it if you blinked, he'd attack—the lizard's tongue flashing out and nailing a hapless fly.

That was Milton. A bald, middle-aged, thick-waisted, sloe-eyed lizard. With the same moral sense.

Sandra's hairdresser, Joyce, had met him once and declared him incredibly sexy. Sandra thought she was kidding—at first. Then, as she'd come to know Milton, she realized that his very coolness, his self-assurance and his aura of power worked magic on certain women.

Not on Sandra. At best, she found him off-putting, like a piece of fine art she didn't care for. At worst, he scared her.

He rose from his seat and shook her hand, knowing her well enough not to embrace her. That was another thing about Milton. He understood people, could read them based on a single meeting. Sometimes Sandra even thought he knew the secrets she held inside, but he was Milton Banks. He knew better than to pry.

She dropped the thick envelope on his desk. "Here it is, hand delivered."

He sent her an ironic grin. "We were expecting this."

She told him briefly about the news van showing up to film the whole thing, and how a workman had derailed it.

He chuckled appreciatively. Milton usually liked subtlety, but sometimes expressed a healthy admiration for the direct approach. Then he looked over the documents that had been served, his pale, manicured hands drifting down the long sheets as if to absorb their meaning. "Nothing special," he concluded after his inspection. "A civil suit. The complaint is that, through reckless driving, you caused the wrongful death of their son, Victor."

"It's insane."

"That's the beauty of it. A civil suit doesn't have to make sense. Doesn't even carry the same burden of proof as a criminal case—the law requires a 'preponderance of evidence' or fifty-one percent, compared to 'beyond a reasonable doubt' in a criminal trial."

"It was an accident. Why can't they see that? Why can't they let it go? I'm no more responsible for Victor's death than I am for the weather."

Milton said nothing.

"So what's going to happen?"

"They're seeking reparation."

"Money."

"Yeah. It's the old 'nothing can compensate us for the loss of our precious son so a big fat chunk of change will have to do' shtick."

"God. I should be used to you by now, but I'm not," Sandra said.

He wasn't even insulted. "Okay, look. Here's what you need to know right now. This is a civil matter. It doesn't involve jail time, regardless of the ruling—not that I'll let it get that far. If it does, though, the value of Victor's life is going to be determined by arbitration, or by the enlightened conscience of an impartial jury."

She shut her eyes, feeling the burn of tears. How much was a life worth? A life like Victor Winslow's? What was the value of his special smile, the cost of his hidden pain, the sum total of his complicated heart?

"You okay?"

She opened her eyes, forced herself to concentrate.

"The suit is seeking all the money and property he had at the time of his death—"

"Would that include his campaign debts?" she asked. "I'll gladly sign those over."

"—as well as compensation for the intangible factors— enjoyment of life, contribution to society, all that crap. You'll also be ordered to forfeit your claim to the insurance policy. But it's all moot, babe. Because even though they don't have the same burden of proof as a criminal case, they won't prove squat."

She hated it when he called her babe. "How long?" she asked.

He shrugged, flipping the papers with his thumb. "We've got twenty days to answer this. The plaintiffs will need a lot of time for discovery—but they're not going to discover diddly, are they?" He didn't let her answer. He didn't want to know. "This won't go to trial—I won't let it. But the Winslows being who they are, they could get a hearing fairly soon. My advice? Stick around. Go about your business. Don't sweat it. I'll handle the rest, and I'll be in touch."

She nodded as he dictated instructions to his assistant into a recording device on the desk. When he finished, she gripped the arms of her chair, preparing to leave. "My parents are getting a divorce," she blurted out, surprising herself even more than Milton.

"Say what?"

"They've been married thirty-six years, and now they're getting a divorce."

"You don't say."

Twisting her hands in her lap, she said, "It's not your problem, I know. I needed to tell someone because it's been bothering me."

"Do I look like an agony aunt?" he asked.

"No, I just—"

"Hire an analyst, honey, because I'm not your man. You don't want my take on your folks splitting up." He knew them only slightly. One of his assistants had interviewed them in the course of the death investigation. "You don't want to hear me say this happens more often than you think. A couple's together since dirt was brown, and then one day they up and call it quits. Big deal. The guy probably didn't even think about splitting up when he was working, and then he retires, and the wife's still doing all the cooking and cleaning, and she says hey, what about me? Where's my retirement? And the clod doesn't get it, so she takes off."

"Your sensitivity is astounding," Sandra said.

"You don't pay me to be sensitive."

She paused. "I'm fixing up my house."

"To sell."

"Yes."

"You have to think about how things will look."

"You mean, will it make me look guilty because I don't want to live among people who think I murdered my husband?"

"Will it?"

"I don't know."

"Do you have a buyer?"

"No. The house needs a lot of restoration work before I can even list it."

"The handyman, then," he said, putting two and two together. "The guy who took out the satellite dish."

"I hired him to fix things."

Milton grinned. "Honey, that's why you hired me."

Chapter 14

Mary Margaret's dad picked her up at the curb in front of the house as if he were a taxi driver or something. Even now that this was the usual routine, she felt funny walking out the front door, her backpack trailing its straps, her mother's watchful eyes boring into her so hard Mary Margaret swore she could feel it in her shoulder blades.

When the divorce had first come up, she hadn't worried too much. She figured it would go away, like a bad cold or a low grade on a spelling test. That's the way it always used to work when she was little, around Kevin's age. Her mom and dad would fight—not yelling or stomping around or anything. Their fights were like walking into the deep freeze at Carmine's restaurant—a chill that made you shiver inside and out. But after the freeze, there would be some quiet talking, and everything would be okay. For a while.

Then one day they used the word every kid on earth feared more than ghosts, more than booster shots, more than adults feared the word *cancer*.

Divorce.

The sound of the word was the wind rushing out of someone who had been punched in the stomach. At first it hurt so bad she couldn't move or breathe. And then when she started breathing again, it subsided to a dull ache that stayed with her all day, every day, and all night, every night, and she knew it would be there for the rest of her life.

Her dad got out of the pickup and gave her a hug. She inhaled his smell of lumber and truck and shaving stuff—the best smell in the world.

"Heya, Princess," he said, grabbing her backpack.

"Hi, Daddy-O."

As he shoved her backpack into the cab and held the door for her, she saw him looking sideways at the house. It was one of the nicest houses in the neighborhood—definitely nicer than Kandy Procter's, who drove Mary Margaret nuts because her aunt was on the TV news. The big yard sloped up toward the white porch, and the front door had fancy glass. The small upstairs dormer windows made the place look cozy and warm.

Her dad had restored the house; he'd even won an award from the historical society for it. Now he could barely set foot in it without her mom's permission and practically a signed order from a judge. Since her mom had married Carmine, they'd added a sunroom, all new furniture, everything they wanted, overnight.

When Dad was around, changes happened gradually—you got used to each little thing before moving on to the next. Now everything whizzed along like someone had hit the FAST FORWARD button.

Mary Margaret released a sigh as her dad shut the door and she fastened her seat belt. The weird thing was, as time went on, she found herself getting used to the way things had become. Her stepfather, Carmine, was actually an okay guy, even though his hair was oily and he smiled so hard you just knew he was faking it. But he made tons of money, bought Mary Margaret pretty much anything she wanted, treated her mom like a queen and kept her happy most of the time.

Getting used to the divorce was scary in its own way. What kind of person was she, getting used to something so horrible? It was like learning to eat raw oysters—what was the point?

Sometimes she wished she could be more like Kevin, who figured out a way to like everything.

The whole business confused Mary Margaret. When her dad first moved out, her mom took her to a therapist who told her to talk about her anger in terms of numbers. Was it a ten today? A seven? A four-point-five? Mary Margaret thought it was really dumb. She did want to sort out all her scrambled feelings, but not like that, with a woman who wore Birkenstocks with socks and had Yanni music playing in the background.

"How was school today?" Dad asked, pulling out onto Walnut Street. He balanced his wrist on the top of the steering wheel. Driving was the easiest thing in the world to him. Carmine always cussed at other drivers, shook his fist, gunned the engine, but Dad was always totally laid-back.

"Fine, I guess. Mrs. Geiger was in a bad mood, but I got an A on my math test." During PE, Mary Margaret had taken refuge in the nurse's office, something she did as often as she could, but she decided not to tell her dad that. He and her mom both worried when she said she despised PE with the heat of a thousand suns.

And actually, it wasn't the sports or the teacher she hated. It was the freaking locker room. She was practically the only one in her grade who hadn't started her period, the only one whose chest was still as flat as a waxed surfboard. Kandy Procter had already turned thirteen; she liked to prance around, showing off her cleavage in the lacy bras she shopped for with her famous Aunt Courtney. She also wore those butt-floss thongs for underwear. Privately, Mary Margaret thought half of Kandy's assets consisted of body fat—the girl ate like a cow—but everything seemed to settle in all the right places on her. Eighth-grade boys were already asking her out, and once she even sneaked into a high school dance.

"Good job on the test," Dad said. "You're awesome."

"Math is a cinch. They give you all the information, and you just have to organize it so the numbers all fit together." She liked it when there was only one possible answer in the universe, and you could check to see if you were right by plugging the solution in to the equation. It either worked, or it didn't.

Her dad checked his watch. "What time's the meeting at the Y?"

"Four-thirty. And Kevin's done with basketball practice at five-thirty."

"We've got a half hour to kill, then. I'd take you to Dairy Queen, but I don't want to spoil your dinner."

"Gee, I don't want that, either, Dad."

"Smart aleck." He grinned at her, then did a double-take. "Hey, when did you get your ears pierced?"

Her hand stole up and twiddled the gold post. "Monday."

His jaw worked, and he stared straight ahead at the road. "You'll get an infection."

She rolled her eyes. "Mom took me to the doctor to get it done. These are solid gold posts."

"Just what you need. Two extra holes in your head."

"Da-ad." Then Mary Margaret fell silent. She knew she shouldn't feel guilty, but she did.

He turned down Bellevue Avenue and pulled into the old Redwood Library and Atheneum. It had a wide portico with letters and Roman numerals over the door. Concrete urns and a storybook garden of gnarled trees surrounded the pathways. It was the oldest building on the street, with bare chestnut trees rising up and curving over it like giant claws. Two black crows perched in the upper branches. There was a sign in front with movable letters, and sometimes kids rearranged them to spell cuss words. Today the sign said, I CANNOT LIVE WITHOUT BOOKS.—Thomas Jefferson.

"You got your card with you?" her dad asked.

"You bet." Mary Margaret knew it was nerdy, but she liked carrying around the plastic card, tucked in her pocket with her lunch money and student ID. This was practically her favorite place in the whole universe. She loved to read and always had. When she was little, she used to follow people around with a book in her hand, quietly shadowing them until they broke down and read her a story.

It never took much to get her dad to read. Even though years had passed, she still remembered the way he got into the rhythm of *Mike Mulligan and His Steam Shovel*, or guffawed at *Babar and the Wulli Wulli* until he couldn't even read anymore.

Sometimes she wished she'd never learned to read, so her dad would always do it.

They went into the library together. He took off his

cap, folded the bill in half and stuck it in his back pocket. Miss Cavanaugh, who worked behind the main desk, looked up when they came in, and a huge smile lit her homely face. The fact was, practically all women loved Mary Margaret's dad. It was gross, the way they turned flirty whenever they saw him—grocery checkers at Stop & Shop, the pediatrician, even the teenager who worked at the video store and was only a few years older than Mary Margaret. As far as she could tell, he didn't encourage them on purpose. He was just a hunk. It wasn't his fault.

He nodded to greet the librarian, then whispered to Mary Margaret, "I need to look something up on the computer." She followed him over to one of the terminals, watching idly as he clicked to local news and did a search for a name—Victor somebody. Then she lost interest; her dad was always looking up names of dead architects and old buildings and stuff.

She wandered to the Middle Grade and Young Adult section. She was a good enough reader to read pretty much any book in the library, but adult books were strange, boring or depressing. Oprah could have them, and good riddance. Mary Margaret's favorite books were stories about girls her own age, maybe a little older, who had the same thoughts as Mary Margaret, the same problems, and they managed to work them out in the end. Jo in *Little Women*. *A Wrinkle in Time* with Meg, who had such a weird family. *Anne of Green Gables*, who suffered through every possible bad thing and still managed to find happiness as a teacher on a beautiful island.

She browsed through a few books, waiting for something to catch her interest. A few minutes later, her dad came over, standing in front of the shelves with his thumbs hooked into his back pockets.

She frowned. Now what? Had the stupid family court

judge thought up a new rule for him? Did he have to start reading children's books in order to prove he was fit to be a father?

"Are you looking for something special?" she asked.

"Maybe." He ran a finger through the As, then the Bs. "I need to ask the librarian about something."

She couldn't stand the suspense, so she followed him over to the desk. When she looked up, Miss Cavanaugh's cheeks got red. "May I help you?" she asked.

"I'm looking for some books by Sandy Babcock," Dad said.

Sandy Babcock? Mary Margaret had never heard of her.

Miss Cavanaugh was massively efficient, her fingers plinking rapidly over the keyboard. "Hm," she said. "We do have a few of her books in our collection. Children's novels. Is that what you were looking for?"

"Yeah, I think so. I didn't spot them on the shelf."

"They're available by special request."

"What's that mean?"

Miss Cavanaugh pushed a paper form across the desk to him. "You have to fill that out and sign it, and then I can get you the books."

"Why is that?" he asked.

Her face turned even redder. "Well, it looks as though these are disputed titles. A disputed title is one that a patron claims contains questionable or unsuitable material. A special request is required in order to access them."

"I thought censorship died out with the McCarthy era."

"I don't make the rules, Mr. Malloy. To be honest, I find this sort of thing appalling. But we're a public institution financed by public money and governed by a board of directors that answers to the taxpayers."

"Tell you what," he said, leaning his elbows on the counter, "why don't you track down these books and we'll see what kind of obscene material they contain."

Mary Margaret was starting to feel embarrassed for poor Miss Cavanaugh, who hurried to the shelves behind the desk, her rubber-soled shoes squishing quietly on the old wooden floor.

"What's up, Dad?" Mary Margaret asked.

"I'm curious about these books, is all."

"How did you even hear of them?"

Before he answered, Miss Cavanaugh came back with two books. Mary Margaret liked the look of them immediately—they were long. She loved long books. Her dad picked up one called *Beneath the Surface* and read the stuff on the inside of the book jacket. "Do you have some way of knowing why this was disputed?"

Miss Cavanaugh scanned the bar code and studied the computer screen. "Alternative religion is practiced, it encourages the breakup of the traditional nuclear family and there's a questionable scene with a mongoose."

Dad looked at Miss Cavanaugh. Miss Cavanaugh looked at her dad. At the exact same second, they both started laughing. Seeing them laughing together made Mary Margaret feel a little funny inside, not in a bad way, but not in a good way, either. Just . . . funny. The librarian had kind of a goofy smile, although she was a nice enough lady. But she worried Mary Margaret. All women making googoo eyes at her dad worried her. It was bad enough her mom had married Carmine only six months after her dad moved out. But for Dad to flirt with the librarian?

If he started dating, Mary Margaret would have no refuge at all. No parent who was hers and hers alone. She didn't know if she could stand that.

"What's the other one?" Dad asked.

"*Every Other Day*. The story of a girl in an alternative family situation."

"And the disputed parts?"

"The main character, uh, lives with two women." Now Miss Cavanaugh wasn't just red, but edging toward purple.

"You mean her mom's a lesbian." Mary Margaret couldn't help speaking up. It just popped out.

The librarian nodded. "Apparently so."

"Cool," Mary Margaret replied, feeling smug. She caught the look on her dad's face and said, "I don't think these books are going to harm me."

He grinned at the librarian. "Out of the mouths of babes . . ." Then he turned to Mary Margaret. "What do you think, Princess? Want to read either of these books, or do they sound too naughty for you?"

Was he kidding? The fact that someone had banned them, that an adult had to sign off on them, made them more interesting than Harry Potter's next adventure.

"Sure." She pulled out her card.

Miss Cavanaugh beamed at her dad as she processed the books and he signed the pink slip.

They got back in the truck and headed toward the Y on Bushnell Street. During the ride, Mary Margaret picked up one of the books. The cover of *Beneath the Surface* had a picture of a boy with swirling hot red-and-orange whorls and vaguely threatening tentacles reaching for him. It didn't look like the sort of book she usually chose, but she'd give it a try. Next, she read the summary on the book jacket flaps, and finally looked for the author's photograph and biographical information. To her surprise, there was no photo of Sandy Babcock. The bio read simply, "Critically acclaimed author Sandy Babcock lives in New England with her husband." That was it. Big deal. Either she had something to hide, or she had the face of a horse.

"What made you ask for these books, Dad?" she asked.

"Just curious."

She frowned. "How'd you even hear of them?"

"Actually, I met the author. You did, too."

"I don't remember meeting—oh. *Her*." She thought of the woman with the silky brown hair living in the rambling old beach house at the end of nowhere. A real-live writer. She always pictured them as magical creatures, different from regular people, living in faraway places, subsisting on misty air and dreams. The woman in the beach house seemed . . . ordinary. Funny and maybe a little sad. She was pretty, with large brown eyes and a face like a lady on a soap commercial, so Mary Margaret couldn't figure out why they didn't put her picture on her books. Maybe because they were the sort of books that got banned.

"So she's an author, huh?"

"Yep."

Mary Margaret stared down at the books. They felt weightier, somehow. She put them in her backpack as they drove up to the Y, just in time for the meeting.

She and her dad had started in Indian Princesses back when she was five. After fourth grade, they advanced to Fathers and Daughters. It was kind of dorky, but her dad seemed to like it. There were organized campouts, potluck dinners, community service and sports activities. It was pretty fun, being with other girls and their dads, learning to throw footballs and build fires. The campouts were the best. She loved the quiet of the woods, and the way her dad's face got all bristly because he said only wimps brought shaving kits on a campout.

On the way to the meeting hall, they peeked into the gym, where Kevin's basketball practice was going on. He was right in the middle of things as usual, racing up and down the court with shoelaces flapping.

Mary Margaret studied her dad as he watched Kevin. Dad had a strong face and gumball-blue eyes, and when he looked at Kevin, she could feel the love and pride coming from him like body heat. All of a sudden, she was consumed by a fierce wish that they could all be like a TV family, living in a house with cross-stitched sayings hanging on the walls, making each other laugh and fixing even the worst problem with heart-to-heart talks that ended in hugs.

In real life, it didn't work that way.

She tugged on his sleeve. "Let's go up to the meeting."

He nodded. "This is about that dance, isn't it?"

"The Valentine's Day dance." It was pretty dorky, too. Still, she liked the idea of getting dressed up, and her mom had said she could buy a new outfit for the occasion.

"I don't know how to dance," Dad said.

"I didn't think you did. Look, if you don't want to—"

"Are you kidding? Of course I want to, Princess."

Chapter 15

Journal Entry—February 1—Friday

Ten Places I'd Rather Be

1. The Rodin Museum, looking at "The Kiss."
2. On a cruise ship with my mother.
3. In Mike Malloy's arms—

Sandra hastily scratched out Item #3, then scratched it off again and again until the ink bled through the paper. Really, she ought to be working on the revisions for her novel, and having the house renovated was no excuse to stop. Ordinarily she would have sought total isolation in order to finish the rewrites. Since Victor's death, she'd found solace in the lonely boom and hiss of the surf and the disembodied howl of the winter wind. The brutal elements walled her off from the rest of the world, made her feel detached, no longer a part of things, so that she could concentrate on her writing.

But lately, isolation was in short supply around the place; it had been supplanted by the chaos of Malloy and his crew banging around. In addition to Phil Downing, he'd brought in two others, tall and thick-shouldered and so alike she could never remember their names, so she thought of them as Tweedledee and Tweedledum. Downing had actually made himself useful, fixing her old laptop after she'd given up hope of getting it to work again. She'd donated it to Phil—free to a good home—but now she wondered if she should have kept it, taking it to a quiet place where she could hear herself think.

These days, the atmosphere of the old house was charged with energy—busy, alive, productive. Her ears rang with the industrial rhythm of table saws and air hammers. The house smelled of fresh-cut lumber, oil-based paint, wet plaster—like something alive again. Malloy's scruffy, overly friendly dog had taken to sleeping on an old braided rug in front of the iron stove, and despite his size, he had a way of taking over a room.

The clamor of power tools drowned out her thoughts, mocking all attempts to weave a cocoon of numbness around herself. She craved that numbness, because it kept her safe from grief and regrets and confusion.

Malloy's presence changed all that. Rattled by the noise and activity, she gave herself over to worries about the looming civil action, moving away from Blue Moon Beach, her parents' separation. She caught herself going over and over her past with Victor. Then the anger would come—how could she have been so stupid?—and finally her thoughts would return to the lawsuit, and the next wave of worries would hit.

She was beginning to resent Malloy's intrusion. It wasn't simply his habit of standing on the beach in the morning, patiently throwing a stick for Zeke, again and again. It wasn't even that piercing sapphire stare, or the way he bent over a table to study the house plans, his angled body so close to hers that it felt like a long, quiet caress.

Surrounded by activity, she tried to sink into the strange music of the construction noise and delve into her book. She studied the opening page, but in the middle of the first paragraph, a series of hammer blows upstairs made her jump. Exasperated, she shoved her chair back from the desk and stomped upstairs.

Malloy stood in the middle of her bedroom, his imposing presence incongruous amid her dollhouse-sized furniture and frilly linens. A light dusting of plaster covered his baseball cap and the dark hair curling from the edges, and just for a moment she could picture him, old and still maddeningly handsome, like a latter-day Sean Connery. The image fueled her resentment—she didn't want to think about him getting old; she didn't want to think about him at all.

Perched on a ladder, he held a hammer in one hand and a long iron pry bar in the other, which he used to work the ruined plaster free to expose a plumbing leak. Spying her, he holstered the hammer and took off his safety glasses. "You need something?"

She felt stupid, standing there, seething, and that only made her madder. "A little peace and quiet might be in order," she said.

He laughed, completely unsympathetic. "A quiet house restoration. Hey, I'm good, but I'm not that good."

"I'm trying to work, and I can't hear myself think."

He shrugged unapologetically. "We'll be gone at six."

"That's six hours from now." A brilliant comment. What was the matter with her? Did staring at well-defined pectorals cause brain damage?

He came down from the ladder. His body moved like a sleek machine—there was nothing awkward about this guy. "Relax. Maybe you'll get used to the noise. While I've got you here, take a look at the paint for the upstairs."

Flipping open a binder crammed with invoices, work orders, and product sheets, he turned to a page of historic milk paint colors ranging from Wedgwood Blue to Clotted Cream. "I thought the green for the hall and—"

The sample was labeled Tavern Green. "I hate green."

"It was the preferred color in the 1880s, when the house was built."

"It's not my preferred color. What's wrong with Buttermilk?"

"It's bland. I like the green. Besides, why should you care? You're putting the place up for sale."

"Why should you?" she shot back.

"Because you hired me to do a historical restoration."

"It's my house until I sell it."

"Look, you've argued about details since I started the job. I'm just curious about why these things matter so much. You're investing a lot of energy in a house you intend to sell."

He was always doing that—always reminding her that she had the rest of her life staring her in the face. What was she going to do about it? Freedom was waiting around the corner, and maybe a part of her didn't want to step back into a normal life, because then she'd have to learn to feel again . . . to hurt again.

She bristled, trying to deny that she had a stake in this project. Was it because it had been in her family for generations? She glowered at Malloy—he didn't get it. Both of them seemed to care too much about this place, even though it wasn't really theirs to care about. "You're not the owner," she pointed out. Yet she could see him in a house like this, him and his kids and his dog . . .

She stuck her hands in her back pockets and paced, feeling his gaze stalking her. This was the source of her resentment. He and his dog and his workmen were intruding, disrupting her quiet melancholy. They were thawing out the numbness that had kept her from falling apart since Victor died, and that scared her. The numbness was her refuge, her sanctuary, and Malloy was taking a hammer and chisel to it. He was pulling down walls, altering the structure, changing the colors of the past.

"Whatever," she said at last. "The green's fine."

He blocked her exit from the bedroom, placing his long, bare arm across the door frame. "Is it?"

She could smell his scent of sweat and plaster and man. "You're the expert."

He grinned as though aware of his effect on her. "I am."

Ducking under his arm, she went back to work and somehow managed to get a few things done. At midday, the saws, drills and hammers stopped. Merciful silence. The crew was probably ready to take a breather. In the aftermath of the noise, Sandra could hear music from Malloy's paint-spattered radio drifting in from across the driveway. Feeling petty and mean after the exchange in the bedroom, she decided to hold out the olive branch.

Malloy had the radio set on a classic rock station that played the occasional fifties tune. Though she hadn't been around in the fifties, she felt wistful when she heard "Unchained Melody," as though the song were a part of her own past. Because of Victor's position in the General Assembly, their friends had tended to be older, many of them ten or twenty years her senior. Maybe that was why a wave of nostalgia engulfed her when she heard the mellow old song.

Zeke got up and stretched, then trotted through the kitchen to paw at the back door. Clicking SAVE on her computer, she went to let him out. It was lunchtime, judging by the open cooler and brown bags in the back of the painters' van. But Malloy wasn't eating lunch. In the windswept yard, he held a long-handled shovel in one hand and seemed to be dancing with it to the plaintive tune.

In his baseball cap, sweatshirt and tool belt, his movements clumsy and earnest, he looked absurd—and curiously appealing. An unbidden and rare laugh escaped her. Grabbing her jacket, she went outside. He didn't notice her at first, and she watched him, both baffled and fascinated. It felt good to smile again.

At a pause in the music, she cleared her throat to announce her presence.

He turned to her abruptly, his face beet-red.

She folded her arms in front of her. "I never pegged you as the type who had trouble getting dates, Malloy."

He sent her a sheepish grin. "At least my partner doesn't complain."

"Is this how you spend all your lunch hours?"

"I'd be better at it if I did." He propped the shovel against his truck. "I promised I'd take a very special lady dancing on Valentine's Day."

"Oh, th—" The rest stuck in Sandra's throat. She stood pinned to the spot while he watched her with mild curiosity that began to deepen into concern. The stutter possessed her, a force far more powerful than her own will. Years of therapy fell away; the stress increased and she felt the cords of her throat stiffening, standing out, betraying her helplessness. And all because he'd so casually revealed he had a woman in his life. As if it were any of her business. As if she should care. She made a sort of lame motion with her hand and walked back toward the house.

"Sandra."

She froze; it was the first time he had called her by name.

"I meant Mary Margaret."

Her throat and diaphragm relaxed as the stutter melted away and she turned to face him. "Pardon?"

"I'm taking Mary Margaret to a dance. It's a father and daughter thing we do through the Y. So I was just trying out a few moves, you know, to—well, you saw. I suck at it." He had an aw-shucks air about him that showed both the depth of his love for his daughter and a touching vulnerability. Interesting. Malloy was an expert at everything she'd seen him do. This uncertainty was new, and perversely, she liked it.

"Your daughter must be really excited," she said, praying her relief didn't show.

"Yeah, well, she hasn't seen me dance yet."

Dancing conjured up all sorts of memories of fear and shame and yearning. Oh, how she had wanted to go to a dance when she was Mary Margaret's age. But no one ever invited her, and wild horses couldn't have dragged her there alone. She would have loved it if her father had taken her dancing. Of course, it never would have occurred to him. He wasn't the type.

But Victor—now, Victor had been the dancing type. He more than made up for the lack in her earlier years. He taught her all the social graces, and dancing was near the top of the list.

Sandra hesitated. The music from the radio swelled to a crescendo, then echoed to a quiet finish. "Maybe you could use some pointers."

"You got any?"

She hesitated again. Then asked herself, where was the harm? "I do," she said.

"So you're a good dancer?"

"I've had a lot of practice," she said. "I was a politician's wife." Victor used to joke that his best move was the sidestep. All his moves had been good. She stepped a little closer to Malloy. Her stomach clenched, but she smiled up at him. "Are you up for a lesson?"

He slowly unbuckled his tool belt. Holding her gaze with his, he let it drop onto the tailgate of the truck. "Let's go for it."

The radio announcer was reading the weather: cloudy, small craft advisory in the coastal regions, winds up to twenty miles per hour. Cold.

"Don't worry about music for now," she said. "I'll show you the footwork. It's really simple. You're going to make a square, starting with your right foot." Standing beside him, she demonstrated.

He stepped forward.

"Good. Bring your left foot up to meet the right." Again, she showed him the move. "Now, half a step to the side—together. And the other side. Step—together. And back. See? It goes for eight counts."

Side by side, they practiced the footwork. The radio blared a song that worked all right for rhythm. His feet, in the well-worn boots, were huge. His hands were huge. Everything about him made her heartbeat speed up.

"You've almost got it," she said. "Just keep it up. Don't think about what your feet are doing."

"You sound like my old football coach."

"I should have guessed you were a football player. What position did you play?"

"It was so long ago, I barely remember."

"Quarterback, I bet."

When he said nothing, she knew she was right. There was something about him, something modest and circumspect, that made her want to ask him all sorts of things. "Where did you go to school?"

"URI. For a while. I didn't finish."

Ah, she thought, catching a note of regret in his voice. "Why not?"

"I can't learn to dance and tell you my life story at the same time, ma'am." He laughed, but the message was clear to Sandra. He didn't want to take her to that part of his life—to dreams and regrets and missed chances.

"Okay," she said. "If the next song's any good for dancing, we'll do it as a couple. Same footwork, but you'll have me blocking you." She positioned herself in front of him.

"Where do I put my hands?"

Reaching out, she took his left hand and placed it at the inward curve of her waist. "Here. Like this."

As soon as they touched, she felt an unexpected shock of awareness. Body heat gathered under his palm, so intense she wondered if he could feel it, too. The sensation of his hand circling her waist felt shamefully good. Flustered, she took his other hand in hers, cold fingers folding around his. "This is the general idea. Just relax—it should be a natural posture."

"Does this feel natural?"

His question evoked a wealth of responses that ran through her like chain lightning. He was tall and broad, a solid wall filling her field of vision.

"Y-you tell me," she said, then bit her lip, shaken by the ominous hesitation in her voice.

"Oh, yeah," he said, tugging her an inch closer. "It does."

"Um, maybe not so close. We're going to need a little room to maneuver."

"Like this?" His thigh brushed against hers, and his grin was a little wicked. "This, I can manage." The music changed again, this time to something old and bluesy.

"So far so good," she said. His hand was startlingly

rough. A workingman's hand. "Now. Listen for the beat. Then we'll move off with you stepping forward on your left foot."

He looked down.

"Don't look down," she said.

"But—"

"You know where your feet are, Malloy."

"Then where do I look?"

Again, she hesitated. "At your partner."

His gaze settled on her, ocean-blue eyes filled with unspoken inquiries. The air between them seemed heated by a languid, tropical breeze from a far-off place. She had no idea how he did it, but he managed to make her feel that stare all the way to her toes.

"Like this?" he asked again.

Agitated, she took a half step back. "The idea is to hold your partner where you can talk to her. It's a social thing."

"Sorry. They didn't teach us this stuff in work skills class."

She bit her lip. Now that he'd revealed his college failure, she understood why he was sensitive about that. "I didn't mean to sound condescending."

"But you were doing so well."

"Do you want to learn this or not, Malloy?"

"I do."

For no particular reason, that struck her as funny. "Then let's give it a try. Take one step forward."

His long stride nearly knocked her over.

"Maybe half a step," she amended, clutching him. His upper arm was solid iron.

He tried again. On the next upbeat, his left foot crushed down on her right.

Sandra emitted a yelp and jumped back. "Careful, Malloy. You don't want to cripple your partner for life."

"Maybe we'd better quit while you're still uninjured."

She gave her foot a shake. "I never pegged you for a quitter. Besides, better you make your mistakes on me, not Mary Margaret. Now, wait for the beat . . ."

They pushed off, and this time it started to work. To the tune of "Night and Day," they danced around the barren, windswept yard. The whole world felt different just for these few moments. The shadows lifted from her thoughts until she wasn't really thinking at all. She became aware of an overwhelming fullness of heart, growing from the long-buried need deep inside her. Oh, she had missed this. Closeness. Human contact. The simple act of dancing in a man's arms felt so good, and so right, and yet at the same time, it hurt and stung, like fingers thawing out after a long freeze. It had been ages since she'd actually been close to someone.

She stared at a point past his shoulder, hoping her feelings were not written all over her face.

"I thought you were supposed to look at your partner," he reminded her. His voice was tender, intimate. Close to her ear.

The song ended. She dropped her hands and pushed away from him, probably too quickly. "That's all there is to it," she said, flustered. "Eight counts, and you're Fred Astaire."

"The realization of a lifelong dream."

"You need to practice. A lot."

"Thanks. I sure as hell don't want to embarrass Mary Margaret."

"I think that starts with the teenage years," she said. "Right now, she worships you."

He put his tool belt back on, then opened a large metal

chest in the back of his truck. An array of round, steel-toothed saw blades gleamed from the box. "Yeah?"

"Most twelve-year-old girls do."

"She's almost thirteen. I better brace myself." He selected a blade and fitted it in the big power saw his crew had set up at the rear of the house.

Sandra felt relieved to see him going back to work—but a little bereft, too.

"By the way," he said over his shoulder, "I gave her two of your books to read."

Sandra felt a funny twist inside her. "Really?"

"Got them from the library. *Beneath the Surface* and *Every Other Day*. I had to ask the librarian for them. They weren't on the shelf."

Sandra flushed. "A lot of children's books get challenged at public libraries." She shook her head. "Right here in New England, the cradle of liberty." Though her editor often tried to console her, claiming she was in good company, with Mark Twain, Maya Angelou and Judy Blume, she hated the idea that her books weren't immediately accessible to the readers she wrote them for.

"So I imagine you howled good and loud when you learned they were banning your book." Mike twirled a wing nut on the saw.

She stared at his hands, his fingers. Large and capable, yet they'd felt so gentle when he'd held her. "I'm . . . I was a politician's wife. My job was to smooth things over, not make waves."

"Wait a minute. Your husband was a Democrat. The ACLU endorsed him. You're telling me he tolerated censorship of his wife's books in his own backyard?"

She let out a thin sigh and dropped her gaze. "Victor learned early on to pick his battles. He had to let go of a lot of things in order to get elected."

"Like the First Amendment?"

"You don't need to be sarcastic." She felt a bitter defensiveness and realized she hadn't even begun to deal with what happened to Victor.

"I'm no politician," Malloy said. "Still, I can't believe you'd let some fascist fringe group get away with this. Doesn't it make you crazy, knowing someone's censoring your work?"

She stuffed her hands into her jacket pockets. "Malloy, at this point in my life, pretty much everything makes me crazy. I've learned to pick my battles, too. Right now, book banning isn't one of them. And by the way, the books were challenged by law-abiding citizens, not fascists."

As she spoke, he measured and marked lumber, pausing every few seconds to consult a computer-generated diagram.

"I figured an author would make a priority of free speech and freedom of the press."

"Don't get me wrong, Malloy. I love my work. I love being an author. That means I have to protect myself. I don't want my personal problems to cast a shadow on my publishing career. In case you've forgotten, I'm in a bit of trouble here. The last thing I need is for WRIQ to do a feature on my controversial books. Haven't you ever had to go against your principles for the sake of being practical?"

"Yeah," he said, picking up a pair of safety glasses. "I guess."

"When Victor was alive, I kept the writing quiet for a totally different reason. Writing was my refuge, my safe and private place in a very public world. It worked for us, balancing his busy career with something that was mine alone." She picked up a stray nail from the driveway. "At first, I worried that his folks would have a problem with my books. They're—Ronald and Winifred Winslow—they're pretty conservative."

"So did they have a problem?"

She hunched her shoulders inside the jacket. "No. But only because they never read my work. To them, my writing was simply a little hobby, like doing needlework or collecting dessert plates. I think if they showed a deeper interest, they'd—" She stopped herself just in time. "Anyway, they were very proud of Victor, and regarded me as an adjunct to him. A wife, not a writer."

She tossed the nail into the trash container parked at the side of the house. "I wanted my books to stand or fail on their own merits rather than always wondering if my work was published because people were curious about Victor Winslow's wife. I didn't want to be regarded as the Marilyn Quayle of children's literature." She stared at a spot beyond the dunes, surprised at herself for speaking so frankly. "I was a writer before I was Victor's wife. Now I'm not his wife anymore, but I'm still a writer. To be honest, it's the only part of my life that makes sense right now."

"I guess I can understand that," he said.

"So how did Mary Margaret like the books?"

"I think she likes them a lot. I'll ask her tonight when we talk on the phone."

He probably called his kids all the time. What must it be like, having kids but not being there to tuck them into bed each night? She wanted to ask, but the dance of uncertainty between them stopped her. They weren't exactly friends. They were merely being cordial because they had a contract together.

"She was pretty impressed when she realized she'd met you," he commented.

"I was impressed with her, too." Sandra recognized a

kindred soul in Mary Margaret Malloy—the lonely intelligence in the girl's eyes, the serious set to her mouth, the watchful silence. The intensity of Mary Margaret's stare had hinted that she was the sort of girl who was always probing for things that weren't there. Not seeing the things that were. Oh, Mary Margaret, learn to look and see what is, Sandra thought. You'll spare yourself a lot of pain.

"If she has any questions about the books, or just wants to tell me what she thought, you could bring her by again. Or she could write me a note."

"She might like that." He stacked the lumber to be cut alongside the saw. In the front yard, the crew finished their lunch and rumbled back into action. The radio started playing "Stairway to Heaven."

"So I guess I'd better get back to work," Sandra said. "Holler if you need anything."

He lowered his safety goggles and bent from the waist, positioning a board in front of the saw blade, eyeballing it like a pool shark lining up a shot. "Will do. And thanks for the dancing lesson."

"Don't forget to practice tonight." She took a step backward, curiously reluctant to return to the house. "Every night."

"You got it." Flashing a reckless grin, he tripped the switch of the saw, and with a powerful roar and the reek of hot wood, sliced the board in half as though it were butter.

Chapter 16

S
o I see you were getting pretty cozy with the client," Phil said, ducking his head under the sloping attic roof. He didn't look at Mike but concentrated on tracking an electrical cable and checking it against the diagram on his chart.

"She was showing me how to dance," Mike said. If only that was all that was going on between them. He tried to think of her like any other client; restoring someone's house involved a certain level of intimacy that didn't happen under ordinary circumstances. Until today, it had been a forced closeness, an accidental touch, two strangers on a bus. Now the chemistry was different with Sandra. In bringing Mike into her house, she brought him too close for comfort. He saw the way she lived, the things she ate, smelled the light, soapy perfume that hung in the air of her bedroom. Each day, he delved deeper into restoring the old

Victorian beauty, and had to remind himself that this was about the house, not the owner. Yet he discovered layers and secrets within her, too.

"Dancing, huh?" Phil poked around a crate of old books.

Mike pried bits of ancient caulk from the ocean-view dormer windows. "Mary Margaret has a dance coming up and I don't want to embarrass her."

Phil cast a look over his shoulder. "You definitely need more practice."

"Thanks for the vote of confidence, pal." He went back to work, but kept thinking about Sandra. She'd felt like heaven in his arms, soft and warm, smelling of fresh air and clean skin. And holding her, he'd remembered how much he liked holding a woman close. Furtively, he had leaned down to let her hair blow across his lips.

After dancing with her, he'd been irritable and out of sorts, and work wasn't helping much, either. She'd unknowingly delivered a searing reminder that some needs couldn't be filled by work or by being a good father to his kids. She reminded him that there was only so much loneliness a person could bear. And there was only one way to scratch a certain itch.

He drew a bead of caulk along the edge of the windowpane. Why her? he wondered. She was Victor's widow, for chrissake, and plagued by troubles he didn't want to touch. She was the last woman in the world he should have the hots for.

Finishing the window, he cleaned off his putty knife and decided to inspect the long, hand-hewn rafter beam for signs of rot. The unfinished room held the cobwebby chill of long neglect, a virtual welcome wagon for squirrels or raccoons, particularly in winter. Taking out a flashlight, he navigated a path through the cast-off belongings of several generations: crates and boxes with hand-lettered labels, broken furniture, abandoned toys, a rotted beach umbrella, old lamps and appliances collecting dust. In one corner lay the scattered twigs and swatches and empty seed hulls of an abandoned squirrel's nest.

At the end of the attic, near the top of the narrow stairs, was a stack of recent arrivals—he could tell from the newness of the boxes. Some were mystery cartons, their contents unknown; others were identified in a hasty scrawl: "Old manuscripts." "Campaign '98." "Wedding gifts." "Personal corresp." "Misc."

The crates and luggage concealed a row of rafters and possibly another critter habitat. He moved the boxes one by one, realizing with a lurch of his gut that these were the souvenirs of Sandra's life. Her life with Victor.

Most were sealed with wide brown tape, though the "Wedding gifts" box contained some sort of knickknack in the shape of a circus tent, and the flaps didn't quite close over it. The box labeled "Misc." was unsealed, and by shining his light, he discovered a collection of plaques and framed certificates. "To Sandra Winslow, in appreciation of service . . ." Interesting. She had received commendations from Literacy International, the National AIDS Foundation, the Stuttering Foundation of America, Big Brothers and Sisters, a half-dozen others. He remembered, almost against his will, what Ronald Winslow had said about Sandra: "She's hiding something. She's always been secretive."

Restacking the boxes out of the way, Mike shook his head. "You're barking up the wrong tree, pal."

"How's that?" called Phil from the other end of the attic.

"Nothi—shit." As he lifted a large box marked "Old linens, etc.," the bottom dropped out of it. A collection of miscellany spilled across the floor—a cigar box held shut with a rubber band, a tackle box spattered with paint, a bunch of pillowcases and doilies, and an empty wheeled suitcase, carry-on size. When he picked it up, the top of the case flopped open. It was empty, but he could hear something sliding around inside. He hoped he hadn't broken anything.

He gave it a gentle shake, and a sheaf of papers and envelopes slipped out of the lining of the case, spilling across the floor. Cursing softly, he stooped to pick them up. Then it struck him—the case had a crudely homemade false compartment. Someone had slit the lining and then refastened it with a few staples.

"You need some help picking that stuff up?" asked Phil.

"Nope, I've got it." A chill slid across the back of Mike's neck. Turning the beam of the flashlight away, he told himself not to pry into this. But the watery winter light through the windows slanted across the papers like a spotlight. Letters, mostly. He didn't recognize the handwriting—even now, after all these years, he would know Victor's precise handwriting.

Phil got to work on the wiring, oblivious, whistling between his teeth.

Mike glanced down. Some of the letters were addressed to Victor at a post office drawer in Hillsgrove, near the airport, and had been postmarked in Florida, but it was too dim to read the city or date. Other letters were typed and addressed to "The Hon. Victor Winslow" at his State House office.

Mike had no idea what he was looking at. He just knew he didn't want to see any more. He scooped the papers together and stuffed them back into the lining of the case. He noticed a few receipts, too. And a computer disk with a lined label bearing one simple mark: *M*.

Mike wondered if this was something Victor had hidden away, or if it was Sandra's doing.

He stuck the suitcase back into the torn box. Everybody had secrets, he told himself. Everyone had things they hid—from family, friends, the world.

But not everyone was a murder suspect.

He thought about Victor's parents, filled with anguish and rage. The contents of the suitcase might be of great interest to them.

He shoved the box out of the way and got back to work.

Chapter 17

Ten Ways to Get Malloy in Bed

1. Tell him the roof's leaking over my bedroom.
2. Oversleep on purpose.
[Note to self—get hair done already!]

Sandra dreamed of being the president's date at a state dinner. But when she stepped into the East Room of the White House, she looked down to discover her bare feet—toenails disgracefully unpolished—sticking out from the hem of her gown. She fled, finding herself in the place all her nightmares took her—to a speeding car on a wet road . . .

She awakened still whimpering with horror, pushed aside the mound of afghans and stared at her feet. No polish.

Then she blinked at her journal, shoved it aside and pulled one of the blankets around her shoulders. The afghans, knitted by her mother, smelled faintly of Aqua Net and Kent Golden Lights.

"Miss you, Mom," she said aloud to the empty house.

She wondered what her mother was doing right now, what she was thinking. Was her cruise everything she'd dreamed it would be? Was she learning a foreign language, a new sport, a new definition of herself?

Running a hand through her tangled hair, Sandra yawned and blinked herself awake. Lord, dawn already. Saturday. She reached over and snapped off the little gooseneck reading lamp. The book she'd been reading— *Take Control of Your Life in Ten Days*—lay half-buried in the mound of blankets. She didn't remember getting past the first paragraph before setting it aside to scribble her futile fantasies about Malloy in her journal.

There was something supremely pathetic about falling asleep on the sofa in front of the stove. It meant you didn't go to bed because there wasn't anyone waiting for you there. No one to gently take the book out of your hands and turn off the light.

She went to the bathroom and brushed her teeth without looking in the mirror over the sink. She didn't want to see the hollow shadows under her eyes, bruised evidence of nightmares no amount of sleep could banish. She still suffered from them too often, was still visited by images of Victor turning into a stranger, a car careening out of control on a dark night. A terrible ringing in her ears. Water so cold that her brain shut down. An eerie sensation that as she lay on the beach after the accident, she was not alone.

There was a little bank calendar stuck into the frame of the mirror, and her gaze kept wandering to it. She didn't want to know the date. But even without the reminder, she would have known this day—it was burned into her heart.

Today was the anniversary of Victor's death.

Turning to the window, she raised the sash to let fresh air rush in at her. She scrubbed her face clean, ran a brush through her hair, wild with static and messier than usual.

The hairbrush slowed to thoughtful strokes as an idea came to her. The day was hers to spend as she saw fit. There was one person in Paradise who welcomed her no matter what, who didn't for a moment believe she'd hurt Victor. Sandra decided to pay her a visit.

She dressed in wool slacks and a burgundy Shetland sweater and drove into town, passing the landmarks of Main Street at a slow roll. Paradise was the sort of place that lived in the heart—a true hometown of tree-lined streets, a park with a pond, brick bike paths and hand-lettered signs over the storefronts. It was a place people brought their hopes and dreams, and sometimes even their sorrows.

She pulled up at the Twisted Scissors, the local beauty salon. A huge pair of mechanically improbable scissors hung in the window beside a sign that said "Open—Walk-ins Welcome." Sandra's heart lightened; how bad could things be when she was going to get her hair done?

"Hey, stranger." Joyce Carter greeted her with a grin and a wave. "It's about time you stopped by." Joyce was tall and boldly attractive, with bottle-red hair, long legs and a tight skirt. Even after the accident, her smile held a genuine warmth for Sandra.

"Can you handle a drop-in?" Sandra asked.

"You bet. Have a seat." Joyce draped a smock over Sandra's shoulders.

Robin, the nail tech, came in, all smiles until she spied Sandra. Robin was friends with Gloria Carmichael, the deli owner responsible for most of the conspiracy theories that swirled around Sandra. "Are we busy today?" she asked Joyce, looking straight past Sandra.

"You don't have a thing on the schedule until Linda Lipschitz's manicure at eleven," Joyce told her. "How about you get caught up on bookkeeping in the back."

"Good idea," Robin said, ducking into the office.

"Sorry about her." Joyce eased Sandra back to wash her hair with soothing, practiced strokes.

"Don't worry about it." She stared at the acoustical tiles on the ceiling. "I've decided to stop worrying," she added.

"Yeah? Glad to hear it."

"There's no point," Sandra said simply. "I want to get the house sold and get out of town."

Joyce worked in silence for a few minutes. "Are you sure about that?"

"I'm not sure about anything." Sandra shut her eyes. "I don't belong here anymore. I don't know where I belong."

"Oh, hell, you do too belong here, as much as anybody else. No one appointed the Winslows judge and jury."

"You'd be surprised," Sandra said.

Joyce shut off the water and scooped Sandra's hair into a towel, then marched her to a thronelike salon chair. "Okay, let's see what we've got here. Lordy, girl, this grows like corn in July. You need to come in more often."

"I was thinking of doing it myself. I'm a pretty good amateur barber."

"Do not try this at home." Joyce punctuated the words by stabbing the air with a pair of Swiss-made scissors. "So how's the renovation coming along?"

"It's fine. Malloy—the contractor . . . he's good."

Joyce studied Sandra's face in the mirror. "Look at you blush, hon. He's single, isn't he?"

Sandra nodded, and the telltale burn in her cheeks persisted.

"My God." Joyce grinned from ear to ear. "You're attracted to him."

"Maybe. I might be. It's pointless, though."

"Why? You're young, he's single and you've been alone too long." She combed and snipped with ruthless efficiency. "There's no law against finding someone else, Sandra. I bet after Victor, you thought you'd never feel that way again, but—"

"You don't understand," Sandra blurted out, "I have never felt this way. Ever."

"Whoa." She stopped working and folded her arms. "Maybe you'd better let this happen, then. This thing with—what's his name?—Malloy?"

"Mike Malloy. Why? I'm leaving when the house sells. So what's the point?"

Joyce started snipping again. "Hon, if I have to explain that to you, then you're really in trouble."

~~

Mike spent all day Saturday with his kids. He took them bowling and gave them pizza for lunch, then treated them to a mind-numbingly stupid movie. Although Kevin had giggled his way through it, Mary Margaret kept getting up to go to the concession stand or restroom. Mike had been restless, too. He'd always been crazy about Kevin and Mary Margaret, but since the divorce, his love for them had taken on an edge of desperation.

There was never enough time with them. Bit by bit, they were becoming strangers, taking on habits he had nothing to do with. And he was becoming a walking cliché—the single dad who wore himself out trying to show his kids a good time those few hours a week when they were his. Ordinarily they would have spent the night, but Angela wanted them back in Newport because Mary Margaret's Confirmation was tomorrow.

Mike hadn't been invited. Oh, he could have shown

up, and would have if Mary Margaret wanted that. But the fact was, Angela's side of the family specialized in over-the-top Italian celebrations of Catholic milestones. The Meolas had been known to party for two days in honor of a child's First Communion. It would have been awkward for Mary Margaret if Mike insisted on being there for her Confirmation, when she formally became a member of the church. Catholics weren't supposed to divorce, and his presence would remind everyone of that fact. So he bowed out and pretended not to notice his daughter's relief as he dropped them off at their mother's.

After a solitary drive to Paradise, he pulled into the dock parking lot and let Zeke out of the back of the truck. The dog stuck close, jumping up to sniff at the grocery bag Mike hefted in one arm. He'd stopped at Gloria's deli for half a roasted chicken, and the aroma had been driving the dog nuts for the last four miles.

The amber lights of the port picked out bobbing silhouettes of the fishing fleet, charters and lobstermen, the squat blocks of icehouses and packing plants. Stopping at a dilapidated bank of mailboxes, he pulled out a handful of envelopes. Bills, mostly.

"Mr. Malloy?" called an unfamiliar voice.

He stopped walking and waited for the stranger to catch up with him from the parking lot. The man was medium-sized, heavyset, wearing a denim jacket and jeans. Mike sifted through the various possibilities. Bill collector, social worker, attorney's assistant—a year ago, they had all been unknown to him. Nowadays, he never knew what to expect. "What can I do for you?"

The man held out a business card. "Lance Hedges, assistant news producer, WRIQ-TV."

A bad feeling infested Mike's mood as he took the

card. "Look, if this is about that problem with the satellite dish, I—"

"It's not about that. Not necessarily." The words slid from Hedges, oiled with suggestion.

"What can I do for you?"

"You're the contractor restoring Sandra Winslow's house," Hedges said.

"Uh-huh."

"I'll be straight with you. The murder of Victor Winslow—"

"The accident, you mean."

"The death of Senator Winslow is an ongoing story for us. Our researchers are gathering facts on the new investigation, and it occurred to us that you might have come across some information on the case. In the course of your work, that is."

Mike held his silence, listening to the quiet slap of the water against the hulls of the fishing fleet. He lifted the grocery bag. "I'd better go," he said with forced ease. "Dinner's getting cold."

"We have a generous budget for this type of thing," Hedges continued.

Mike thought about the bills clutched in his hand. "You want to pay me to snoop around her house for you."

"It's a baffling, high-profile case. Any information that throws some light on the facts would serve the public's need to know. Maybe your coworker—Mr. Downing, was it?—maybe he's come across something."

Shit, had this slimeball approached Phil? "He doesn't know any more than I do."

"Then if you'd consider—"

"I don't need to consider." Mike wished he'd never stumbled across those papers in the attic. "I'm a contractor. I work on old houses. I don't know anything, and if I did, I wouldn't hand it over to you."

"Mr. Malloy, you caused considerable damage to the equipment." Hedges held himself stiffly, and his voice chilled a few degrees. "We're prepared to absorb the loss, but only if you cooperate."

"I don't know a damned thing, and threats don't sit well with me," Mike said, swallowing the choice words he really wanted to utter.

"Is that your—"

"Final answer," Mike broke in. "Game over."

Chapter 18

Something was wrong. Suspicion nagged at Mike throughout the evening. It wasn't just the under-the-table offer from the news producer, nor was it just the hidden cache of papers he'd found in Sandra's attic. There was something off-kilter and incomplete, but at this point it was all so nebulous, he couldn't put his finger on the cause. Should he dig deeper or leave it alone? Tell Sandra? Tell her what? That he'd seen something he wasn't supposed to see? Warn her that the media was poking around? And why the hell should he care?

He glanced at the TV, a tiny black-and-white set bolted up under a shelf on the boat. The news was ending, with Courtney Procter staring earnestly out at her audience. "Finally," she said, "an update on a local tragedy. Today is the one-year anniversary of the death of local politician Victor Winslow, a rising star—"

Swearing under his breath, Mike grabbed his cell phone, dialed Sandra's number and got an incessant busy signal. Maybe she was on-line, or had the phone off the hook. He pictured her alone in the house at the edge of nowhere, reading or going over the restoration plans, maybe picking her next battle with him. But he knew she wasn't doing any of those things, because he knew about anniversaries. They turned an ordinary day into a dark monument of memories. The thought of Sandra alone bothered him more than it should have.

He wasn't her keeper. He'd never told her about his old friendship with her late husband. If he did so now, it would be awkward as hell. She didn't need to know about that, he told himself. It didn't matter. He didn't owe her a thing except to fix up her house. He was too emotionally bankrupt to do anything else for her.

Sifting through the papers on his desk, he found the perfect excuse to go to her. The county historical society had verified and catalogued her original house plans, and the place would qualify for a plaque and listing. He didn't really think about what to do next. He just acted. Got in his truck and drove to Blue Moon Beach. The night was black and empty, bitterly cold. He didn't pass anyone on the road. He'd just check on her, he told himself. Make sure she was okay. If she questioned him, he'd say he thought she'd want to know about the historical designation.

Leaving his truck running, he knocked at the front door and waited, but heard only the deep bass beat of the stereo.

He knocked again and waited, knowing she probably wouldn't hear him. Grumbling, he killed the engine of his truck and knocked a third time. An Eric Clapton song played loud enough to rattle the old windows. He recognized the tune "Forever Man." It had been a favorite of Victor's years ago.

After knocking a few more times, he used the key she'd given him and stepped inside.

"Sandra?" he called. "It's me . . . Mike Malloy." He passed through the vestibule, which already looked different from its former decrepit state. The walnut newel post stood straight again; the rails of the balustrade had been glued in place only today. "Sandra?" he said again, but the music was too loud. He knew she wouldn't hear.

She stood in the middle of the broad front room, holding a glass of wine and swaying to the rhythm of the music. Though she was facing him, her eyes were closed, her face soft with an expression so sad he couldn't look away.

He guessed she was thinking about the accident. Probably missing Victor like crazy.

Run away. The thought came fast, like a rush of adrenaline. He shouldn't be here, shouldn't interrupt an obviously private moment. He didn't need this solitary woman's troubles; he had enough of his own. But there was something about her. He'd noticed it right from the start. She called to him without words, drawing him toward the lonely places inside her. No matter what his brain was telling him, his heart made room for her.

At a pause in the music, he spoke her name again.

Her eyes flew open, and wine sloshed over the rim of the glass. Her cheeks turned a shade paler. "I didn't hear you come in." Furtively wiping the back of her wrist across her face, she hurried over to the stereo and turned the volume down. The song changed to a mournful, musical whisper.

"What are you doing here?" she asked.

Mike knew he should simply hand over the papers and hit the road. He also knew he wouldn't do that. He caught a whiff of the wine and glanced down at the half-empty bottle on the table.

"Drinking alone?" he asked. "I've heard that's not too good for you."

"Fine," she said. "You can join me."

Having a glass of wine with a woman was such an alien concept to Mike at this point in his life that for a moment he didn't know what to say. He didn't want to think about how long it had been since he had sat beside a woman, listening to music and drinking wine. "Thanks," he said. "I wouldn't mind a glass."

She looked so amazed that he nearly laughed. "Really?"

"I never saw anyone get that worked up over a beverage."

"It's been a long time since someone's wanted to have a glass of wine with me."

"It's been a long time since anyone has offered," he admitted, relaxing. "The certification papers came from the historical society. Your house qualifies for a special designation."

"Yeah? Then I guess we have something to drink to." She went to the dining room. Glass panes rattled as she opened the ancient buffet and took out a wineglass. She poured, then handed him the glass. It felt brittle and fragile in his hand. "Have a seat," she said, indicating the old sofa facing the hearth. She touched the rim of her glass to his. "What else shall we drink to?"

"You're the one with the imagination," he said. "You decide."

"To pressure washers," she said.

"You can do better than that."

"Not lately. You try it, Malloy." Keeping her eyes on him, she took a slow sip.

"To dancing lessons." He tasted his wine, liking it. Liking the feeling of sitting beside her.

The song changed, to one about losing a best friend.

He pretended not to notice the words, but it was hard to ignore the slow slide of the tune through the silence. He took a gulp of wine. Sandra, however, had a head start on him. She'd downed a third of the bottle.

"My parents are getting a divorce," she said, the statement seeming to come out of nowhere.

"What?"

"I said, my mom and dad are splitting up."

Whoa. Mike broke out in a nervous sweat. Why would she confess such a personal matter to him, of all people?

"Sorry to hear that," he said, feeling awkward. The emotions seemed to be spilling from her in invisible waves, and he knew he couldn't be the one to catch them, contain them. He offered the only honest statement he could think of. "I don't know what to say."

"I didn't mean to dump it on you." She turned to him on the sofa, tucking one leg beneath her.

"How long were they married?"

"Thirty-six years." She swirled her wineglass, watching the liquid slip around in a circle. "Seemed like forever to me." She sighed. "I keep asking myself how long they were unhappy, how long they carried on, day after day. And why didn't I know?"

"There are a lot of ways to hide unhappiness," he said.

She looked at him sharply, then said, "I know."

Mike was hardly an authority on marriage, but experience taught him more than he wished he knew. He'd never been able to pinpoint the precise moment it ended for him and Angela. It was a gradual thing, growing by subtle degrees. There had been no electric shock of horror and betrayal, only a dull sense of failure, its rusty edge roughened by the knowledge that only one of them would get the kids.

"With my ex-wife," he said, "I guess I saw it coming from a mile off. But as long as neither of us said a word, we didn't have to do anything about it."

"You could have gone on indefinitely that way," she said.

"An Irish divorce, my old Granny Malloy would have called it. Two strangers, living under the same roof, keeping up appearances for the sake of the neighbors and children." Forgetting caution, he took a healthy gulp of wine. "I was willing to do that for my kids, because I knew Angela would claim custody of them."

"So you would have stayed for the kids."

"Kevin and Mary Margaret would have preferred that," he said bluntly. "Kids always do."

She studied his face. "I don't know anything about your situation. But I do know that life is short, Malloy. You only get one shot at happiness. When you reach the place where my parents are, you don't want to look back and regret the previous ten or twenty or forty years. Your kids might not be able to see things that way right now, but they will. I guarantee they will."

Her words brought a rare ease to his chest, something he hadn't felt in a long time. "Either you're full of shit or full of wine," he said.

Sandra stared down into her glass. "Some of the former, a little of the latter." Lifting the bottle, she refreshed his glass.

"So what are you doing with your one shot?" he asked.

"What?"

"Your shot at happiness."

With exaggerated care, she set down the bottle. "Well.

I suppose I'd need to start by figuring out what would make me happy."

He became fascinated by the way moisture clung to her lips. He couldn't take his eyes off her mouth. "What would make you happy?"

She stared at him for a long time, the light from the stove fire flickering in the depths of her eyes. There was a whole world in there, he thought. A secret world. When it became clear she wasn't going to answer his question, he said, "I have a confession to make. I heard on the evening news that the accident happened a year ago today."

"And you came over to make sure I wasn't slitting my wrists."

"Something like that." He swirled the last of his wine in the glass. "So you weren't even close to . . . you know—"

"Suicide." She rescued him from having to say it. "No, Malloy. I have my idiosyncrasies, but being suicidal isn't one of them."

He cleared his throat. "Good to know. But I thought you might be . . . missing him."

"You thought right."

He thought about his discovery in the attic—the hidden letters and computer disk. He didn't know how it had been for the two of them, but he did know what it was like to be in a marriage full of secrets. "So you and your husband were happy."

Setting aside her glass, she crossed her feet at the ankles and propped them on the coffee table, clasping her hands behind her head. Staring up at a gaping hole in the ceiling plaster, where Phil had started a wiring repair, she said, "Did I think I was happy? Absolutely. Did I believe we had a good life together? Hell, yes. Did I love Victor?" She spoke with the unsettling cadence of a cross-examination. He remembered that she had just been through an inquest.

But did she love Victor? Mike was beginning to regret bringing it up. Yet he knew he wouldn't move a muscle until she gave her answer.

She dropped her hands to her lap, twisting her fingers together. "With every bit of my heart," she said, and he heard a disconcerting tremor in her voice. She cleared her throat. "Did Victor love me? Can you ever know what's in another person's heart? I used to think you could."

"What do you think now?"

"That I don't know a thing. You should know better than to have a serious conversation with a fiction writer who's been drinking."

He set both their glasses and the now-empty wine bottle at the far end of the coffee table. Then he studied her profile, the delicate lines of her features and the way the firelight shadowed her skin with amber and turned her eyes to coffee-brown. "You aren't speaking fiction."

"Whatever." She shrugged, staring straight ahead at the glass door of the woodstove.

He brushed a drifting lock of hair away from her cheek. He didn't think about it, simply did it. Just to see if it felt as silky as it looked. It did. "You cut your hair."

She gasped softly and pulled back. "Mike—"

"Shh," he said. "I won't hurt you."

"So you say." She studied him intently, considering. Her skin glowed from firelight and wine. "But I think it might not matter."

He leaned toward her again, lifting her chin with his knuckles. Her full lips were damp with wine, parted a little. Bending, he touched his mouth to hers. Just a touch. She let out a gasp of surprise, and a look of pure wonder suffused and softened her face. She leaned toward him in unstudied invitation. He sank his mouth deeper against hers, massaging her jaw with his thumb until her lips slackened and opened for him.

The taste of her made him higher than any wine could have. She held herself rigid at first, but after a few seconds the hands pressing against his chest changed to fists clutching into his shirt, drawing him closer. A sound came from deep in her throat, and he felt her yearning, an echo of his own. Her reactions had the intensity of new discovery; you'd think she'd never been kissed before. A second later, he wasn't thinking at all. He was simply holding her in his arms, kissing, tasting. She made the tension and desolate ache in his bones go away, and even if the feeling didn't last, he didn't care. It was as if the very muscles of his arms were starved for the shape and the texture and the essence of a woman. This woman.

She was pliant in his embrace, her lips yielding, her mouth warm. Heat and need built inside him, shot down his spine, and he moved his hands over her shoulders to the inward curve of her waist, feeling a ripple of response from her. With a little more pressure, he might be able to maneuver her to lie down on the sofa. With a seemingly accidental brush of his fingers, he could slip his hand under her sweater. And he sensed, with every nerve in his body, that she wouldn't resist.

Even as every impulse urged him to do it, Mike held back. He was no prince, but he knew there was something blatantly cruel about taking advantage of someone this fragile, this vulnerable, on the anniversary of the worst day of her life. Ignoring the fire inside him, he disciplined himself in a way he hadn't known he could, almost shaking with the effort. Finally, he made himself stop kissing her, pull back, get a grip.

She didn't move. She sat there with her eyes shut and her mouth softly molded by his, her face tilted up, looking wistful and sexy at the same time. He wasn't sure what to do. He cleared his throat.

Her eyes flew open. Almost as quickly, her cheeks flooded with color.

Mike couldn't help himself. He grinned. "Guess I was out of line."

"Probably."

"Should I apologize?"

She drew her fingertips across her lower lip as though to explore it for injuries. "For what?"

"For coming on to you."

"Is that what that was? A come-on?" She laughed. "If it was, you weren't very subtle. More like a full frontal attack."

She had no idea. What he'd done was mild compared to what he'd resisted doing. "It was only a kiss."

"Are you sorry you did it?"

"Hell, no." God, *yes*. He wouldn't sleep at all tonight.

"So much for the apology." She shifted away from him on the couch, pulling her knees up to her chest and draping her arms around them. In that moment, she didn't look like anyone's widow, least of all Victor Winslow's. The tabloids were wrong, Mike knew it. This woman hadn't killed anyone.

"Not only do you not get an apology," he said, "but I want to kiss you again."

"I'm not sure you should do that."

"There's one way to find out."

She moved back another inch, her eyes large in the firelight. "I've always heard it's a bad idea to get personally involved with someone you're doing business with."

"Yeah?"

"It might turn complicated."

"In what way?"

She laughed, flushing. "What if we get really intense, and then have a falling-out before you finish fixing up the place? I'd be left with a half-finished house and a broken heart, and you'd be too embarrassed or full of regrets or whatever to come back and finish the job."

Mike couldn't help himself. He threw back his head and laughed, long and loud. "No wonder you're a writer," he said. "You think too much."

"I'm simply going over the possibilities of the situation." She rested her chin on her drawn-up knees and glanced at her empty glass. "I think I need more wine."

"You want me to get you some?"

"There's another bottle in the kitchen."

He rose with care, with what he hoped was a natural, swift grace. In reality, he had an erection that didn't seem to know he wasn't seventeen years old anymore. He hoped like hell she hadn't noticed. He took his time opening the bottle with a corkscrew on his Swiss Army knife. Bringing the wine back, he poured her half a glass and set down the bottle. "I signed a contract, guaranteeing my work. Doesn't matter what happens between the two of us. I'll get this place fixed up."

She sipped her wine. "Good. I feel better now."

Mike didn't. She kindled a fire in him that wouldn't abate, no matter what. "I won't kid you," he said. "I find you attractive as hell. I can't help wanting you."

Her breath caught, and a startled look lit her face. "You mean it?"

"Is it so weird, me wanting you?"

"I have no idea. So what are we going to do about it? Have an affair?"

The direct question startled him, so he tossed back one of his own. "Do you want to?"

"I'm not really certain. I've never had one before, never been tempted."

He wasn't sure why, but he believed her. She and Victor had run with a crowd of beautiful people, powerful people, people whose well-groomed appearances in *Town and Country* and *Rhode Island Monthly* had kept them in the public eye. Surely he wasn't the first to find her attractive, the first to want her. The first to hit on her.

"Are you tempted now?" he asked.

She moved her gaze over him, its frankness unsettling. "Maybe. I might be."

He tried to think past the aggressive urges of his body, which refused to behave like it belonged to a responsible adult. He fought for common sense, and finally found it hanging by a thread. His custody lawyer had pounded the rule into his brain. Discreet dating was fine, even expected of the newly divorced. But his feelings were anything but discreet.

The most powerful objection of all came from deep inside Mike. Since the divorce, he'd gone out with women now and again, but Sandra was the first one to remind him of the things that really mattered. There was a huge hole in his life, and he wasn't ready to face that yet. He sure as hell didn't know how to fill it.

"You need a friend more than an affair," he forced himself to say. "You're alone too much of the time. It can't be good for you."

She drained her wineglass and set it aside. A flash of hurt glinted in her eyes; she had learned to be distrustful. "Why the heck do you think I'm so keen on selling this house? I need to be someplace where people don't hang garlic on their doors when they see me coming. Where I can go out in public and not worry about being called the Black Widow." She listened to the music for a moment, then gave a delicate shudder. "The fact is, I never had much of a social life. Victor was my first true friend."

He tried to picture a life without friends. What the hell kind of existence was that? He'd grown up carelessly, surrounded by friends, never questioning their presence, but always knowing he could pick up the phone, find someone who wanted to go for a beer and shoot pool. He couldn't imagine not having that.

"You know what Victor and I used to do sometimes, on stormy nights?" Sandra asked.

Mike didn't want to know. But he sure as hell knew what *he'd* do with her.

"We'd count our blessings," she said, "and for each one, we'd eat an M&M. It's true—we'd sit there and run through a whole list—everything from the fact that my tulip bulbs came up to his latest endorsement from the local union. That probably sounds silly to you."

"I'd put it more in the category of insane. If I had a beautiful woman alone on a stormy night, the last thing on my mind would be counting anything."

She laughed without humor, as though she didn't believe him. "I can't even remember what an M&M looks like."

"I'll make a note to get you some. They're not that hard to come by."

"It's not the M&M's, Malloy."

"I know."

"Does it bother you, my talking about my husband?"

"No," he lied. He knew he had to let her, tonight of all nights.

"We shared so much. Everything from our political views to our habit of doing the crossword in the Sunday *Times*. We ended up having to get two issues of the paper so we could each have our own puzzle."

He pictured her in the morning light, working the crossword. He wouldn't let her get past square one.

"We loved trying out new recipes and restaurants. We liked museums and concerts and playing tennis. Now that he's gone, I have all this stuff inside me, the kind of thing you share with someone, and it has no place to go." Her words moved like a slow, dark river, as though Mike wasn't even sitting there. Then she turned to him, and her eyes cleared as if she'd suddenly remembered his presence. "Does that make sense?"

"Yeah. I guess." He couldn't stand museums. He thought tennis was a bad joke. And crossword puzzles? He shouldn't be here at all—he couldn't be what she needed.

She tossed back the last of her wine. "I lost two people that night, a year ago. My husband, and my best friend." Lifting her hand, she shoved a thick lock of hair back from her face. "I don't think I'm ready for an affair yet. I may never be." She gave a crooked, borderline-drunk grin. "I like you too much as a person to have an affair with you."

"I see," he said, pretending to understand. But he still wanted to get her in bed.

Chapter 19

A late-model, dollar-green Lexus spat oyster-shell gravel as it wheeled into the drive in front of the house, taking the curve a little too fast, stopping a little too abruptly.

From the tasteful wood grain and leather interior of the car sprang a human dynamo, armed with a pocket digital camera, a pager and cell phone attached to her purse and a clipboard crammed with MLS printouts. Her suit was Armani, her pumps were Prada and her jewelry undoubtedly genuine.

Sandra stood at the front door, waiting to greet the real estate agent, but the visitor didn't come to the door. Instead, she assessed the property. Pacing back and forth in front of the house, she took a couple of snapshots, made some notes into a handheld tape recorder. She walked around to the other side of the driveway to inspect the view.

As she stepped out onto the front porch, Sandra wavered between admiration and aversion. She appreciated the woman's decisive demeanor even as she was put off by her brusque nosiness. "Hi," she said. "You must be Miss Witkowski."

"Sparky," the woman said, her gaze making a swift arc of the porch. "Call me Sparky. And you're Sandra Winslow."

"Please come in." Sandra wondered why on earth a grown woman would want to be called Sparky.

"My real name's Gertrude," she explained, reading Sandra's mind.

Milton Banks had recommended Miss Witkowski, who specialized in waterfront property. According to Milton, she had years of experience handling high-dollar estates. An aggressive deal maker, Sparky had far more interest in earning a commission than she did in the notoriety of the seller. Which made her a perfect match for Sandra.

But today, she discovered that she didn't want to think about the real estate agent. She wanted to think about Mike Malloy, kissing her. Giving herself a mental shake, she asked, "Can I get you a cup of tea? I have coffee, too, and soft drinks—"

"I'm fine." Sparky did a full turn around the foyer. "Trust me, I don't need coffee." She scarcely looked at Sandra, but continued her tour of the house, her darting eyes never at rest. "Here's the way I work. Let's do a quick walk-through so I can get a feel for the place. Then I'll put together a pricing scheme and marketing plan, and we'll go from there."

"Sounds reasonable." Sandra gestured around the foyer. The noise of pounding hammers and power tools echoed through the old house. "As you can see, I'm having some work done before I list it."

"Good. I was going to insist on it." Sparky scribbled something on her notepad. "How much work?"

"Quite a bit. The contractor says it's basically sound, but it's been neglected. It's listed as a historic building."

"That's a huge plus. *Huge.* Just make sure you run every alteration by me."

Sandra laughed briefly, but fell silent when she realized Sparky wasn't kidding. The historical society could dictate window sizes and paint color, but Sparky clearly knew what would sell a house. As the agent walked through the downstairs, she rattled off marching orders and opinions about color schemes and room arrangements, the strategic placement of potted plants, the hideousness of the cabbage rose drapes in the dining room, and the absolute, unadulterated perfection of the beach view to the east of the house. She tromped down to the basement, talked briefly and with startling authority to Phil about electrical matters, and then forged upstairs.

On the second floor, they encountered Mike Malloy repairing a wall. The plaster was torn away to reveal ancient, dark wood lathes, aligned like the ribs of a fossil. With the sleeves of his work shirt rolled back, a dust mask covering his nose and mouth, and a hammer and chisel in his hands, he resembled a crude surgeon. When he saw them coming, he removed the mask, letting it dangle around his neck.

Sparky stopped in her tracks. "Oh, my God, I can't believe it. I haven't seen you in ages, Mike."

Wiping his hand on a red bandanna, he held it out. "Hey, Sparky. Long time no see."

"So you're the one restoring this house," she said. "I think I'll increase the asking price by another forty grand."

"Don't get carried away."

"I always get carried away by you, Mike." She laughed and touched his arm with an easy familiarity.

Watching them, Sandra felt a taut chill in her stomach. She envied their ease with one another, and found their acquaintance oddly threatening.

Sparky turned to her and said, "He's won national awards for his restoration work, you know. He's been featured in *Architectural Digest*." She touched his arm again, her red-lacquered nails a bright contrast against his dusty skin. "You have a great reputation in Newport, my friend."

"Let's hope it holds up with the permits department." He disengaged his arm, glanced at his paint-spattered watch. "I've got to take some paperwork over there this afternoon," he said to Sandra, all business. "I'll be back in the morning, early."

As tongue-tied as a blind date, she managed to nod and say, "All right."

"See you around, Mike," Sparky said, her stare lingering on him. "Give me a call sometime."

"Will do." He headed down the stairs.

"You won't, but a girl can try," Sparky called after him, then turned to Sandra. "In Newport, people pay top dollar for a house that's been renovated by Malloy & Meola Restoration."

Sandra followed her into the master bedroom. Mike hadn't told her that. Not that he'd been obliged to, she reminded herself.

She had been avoiding him all day, but couldn't manage to keep her mind off him. She had forced herself to keep busy, phoning her agent, then her friend Barbara, who always knew the latest publishing gossip. She phoned her father, too, checking to see how he was getting along without her mother. Fine, he'd told her.

Liar, she'd thought.

And then she'd thought about Mike yet again—the strength in his arms, the lock of dark hair falling over his brow, the way his jeans were faded in all the right places, the startling softness of his mouth when he kissed her. A wet, messy kiss that made her melt inside. The swift heat of her reaction had taken her by surprise, and she wondered where all that passion had come from, how long it had been bottled up, waiting for escape. She'd been embarrassingly responsive to him. After their encounter the night before, she didn't know how to act around him. Should she go on as before, pretending nothing had happened? Or should she act like—so how did a woman act in front of a man who kissed her the way Mike had? How did she act when every single part of her wanted to say yes to him, except the part that knew it wasn't right?

"You're lucky to get him," Sparky said over her shoulder as they went up the creaky wooden stairs to the third floor. The attic was dim and chill, thick with the smell of old timber and dust.

"What?" Sandra felt a dull red stain creep into her cheeks. Was she that obvious?

Of course she was. When he'd kissed her, the whole world had shifted on its axis, and she couldn't blame the wine alone. Even now, latent spasms of yearning kept bringing her back to that moment.

Standing at one of the newly replaced windows, she and Sparky looked down into the yard. His old pickup truck pulled away, and despite the temperature, he drove off with one elbow sticking out the open window.

"Used to be a two-year waiting list for him when he was working in Newport," Sparky said. "He had a multi-million-dollar business."

Sandra let out a long, thin breath of relief. The real estate agent was talking about getting him as a *contractor*.

"That all ended when his wife divorced him." Sparky lowered her voice. "The settlement took just about everything he had. His father-in-law held the paper on the business, and called in everything when Mike and Angela split up." Sparky inspected the handrail where it had been fixed with new brass bolts, and nodded her approval. "So he's starting over. One good thing, though. At least he's single now."

"And that's a good thing?" Sandra dared to ask. She led the way past a tower of boxes.

"Are you kidding? You've seen him. The man is a living, breathing love god."

So it isn't just me, thought Sandra, ducking her head to hide a smile. The conversation reminded her of college dorm talk, when girlfriends bonded by comparing notes about guys. Sandra had never joined in, of course, but she could still remember the sometimes hilarious, sometimes brutal assessments women made about the men they met.

"I'm not surprised he came back to Paradise," Sparky said, checking out the new dormer windows.

Sandra frowned. "Back to Paradise? You mean he lived here in the past?"

"He grew up here. Didn't he tell you? Attic looks fine." Sparky turned on her heel and headed downstairs again for a closer inspection of the kitchen. She rattled off her opinion about the cabinetry and sunroom, completed her tour of the property, made a list of landscaping chores and promised to get back with Sandra soon.

Sandra didn't pay as close attention as she probably should have. She was too busy thinking about Sparky's remark that Mike Malloy had grown up here, in Paradise. He wasn't obligated to tell her that, of course, but the fact that he hadn't bothered her. A lot.

As she walked Sparky out to her car, the real estate agent turned to her. "There's a question I like to ask all my clients," she said. "You might think it's silly, but it's important."

"We're both on the same team here," Sandra said. "What can I do for you?"

"I need you to do something for me. I need you to visualize your ideal buyer. Not someone who can come up with the money, but someone you'd like to see living in this place that has been your home. I'm not exactly sure why this works—and of course, it doesn't always—but when the seller feels good about the buyer, the deal goes much more smoothly."

"I'll feel good about anyone who makes me a decent offer."

"Just give it a try, okay?"

"I'll think about it, but don't hold your breath. I'm sure you understand why I want to get this place sold. I don't expect to be picky about who decides to buy my house."

"You might be surprised. At the very least, your vision will help me with my marketing strategy. If I know you're picturing an older retired couple, I'll gear my marketing toward that. If you envision a thriving young family living here, that might slant the marketing in a different direction. See what I mean?"

"I'll give it some thought." *Ten Potential Buyers for My Home* . . . Sandra hated the idea. She was trying to detach herself from this place, yet now she was supposed to visualize who might live in the restored house. The idea of other people—strangers—moving in here created a heartache she hadn't expected.

She stood on the driveway as Sparky roared away in the Lexus, and watched until the car disappeared around a bend in the coastal road. But she didn't think about the task Sparky had assigned to her.

She thought about Malloy.

So he was a local boy. She already knew he was the same age Victor would have been, had he lived. Filled with apprehension, she hurried inside and went back up to the attic. She hadn't looked through her boxes of belongings since she'd flung everything together and moved out of the home she shared with Victor. There weren't a lot of crates to search through. She and Victor hadn't collected much in the way of personal history together.

Clicking on the overhead light, she inspected the stacked boxes containing the archives of her life with Victor. Just out of college, she'd owned a trunkload of clothes unbecoming to a congressman's wife, crates of books and manuscripts collected over the years, stacks of spiral-bound journals, a file crammed with rejection letters from magazines and book publishers. Until meeting Victor, she had led an undistinguished life, one that fit neatly into a few good-sized moving boxes.

Ten years her senior, Victor had far more to show for himself—and far more to hide. He'd been an overachiever, larger than life, probably since the day of his birth. How could he not be, with his war-hero father now a wheelchair-bound preacher, his mother a socialite whose fortune rivaled that of the Bouviers?

In a box labeled "1966 to 1982," he kept things from his childhood, lovingly collected by his mother and presented to him on the occasion of his marriage. His proud parents had marked each milestone with an appropriate gesture: his first lost tooth was enshrined in a sterling silver pillbox and engraved with the date of the blessed event. For each school year, they'd had his picture made at a professional portrait studio, eschewing the flat, cookie-cutter poses of the school photographer. There were mementos of his triumphs in swimming, wrestling, track, tennis and golf. Certificates honoring his achievements in scholarship. His

Eagle Scout pin hanging from a faded ribbon. There was even a framed photo of him at sixteen, shaking hands with President Jimmy Carter at a Rose Garden ceremony honoring outstanding high school students.

The whole box was about Victor, she realized. No friends or schoolmates, only Victor and his achievements. Victor and his public life. The things now rightfully belonged to her in-laws, Sandra thought. She hadn't even known him then. She'd have to ask Milton about handing it over to the Winslows.

Their trophy child. He had meant the world to them.

As she dusted off and uncovered the past, bringing old things into the light, she was seized by a strange sense of apprehension. Something was about to be unveiled, revealed. A terrible tension strained inside her. She felt a slow boil of emotion but tried to ignore it. Moving methodically through the labeled boxes, she forced herself to focus on her purpose—to find out if Mike Malloy had ever crossed paths with Victor. She didn't let herself think about anything else. It was too hard, even now. When she came across the box hastily scrawled with "Old linens, etc.," she thrust it out of the way, noticing a rip in the cardboard but hoping it would hold.

Finally she came to the one she sought, labeled in Victor's neat lettering: "Sports trophies, college & hs annuals."

Opening the cardboard box, she took out a variety of odd-shaped trophies in velour shrouds and then sorted through the books. Like all privileged New England boys, Victor had been expected to attend boarding school. She vaguely recalled something he'd once told her. He had, in fact, enrolled at the prestigious Brice Hall School in 1978, but withdrew after only a few weeks, returning home to attend the local high school. He never talked about the incident after that.

She found an annual from 1982, his senior year. A satin ribbon marked a page devoted to Victor and his achievements. Class president, Eagle Scout, varsity swimming, varsity wrestling, varsity everything . . . the list seemed endless. He'd led a varsity life.

Flipping back from the Ws to the Ms, she took only seconds to find a page for Malloy.

Shivers raced over her skin as she brought the annual to the window and sat down, with the late-afternoon light streaming onto the pages. Michael Patrick Malloy.

The simmering resentment inside her bubbled faster, higher. Why hadn't he told her?

She stared at the full-color photograph on the page. What was it Sparky had called him? A living, breathing love god. It was true now, and had been true twenty years ago. He looked like a young Tom Cruise, square-jawed, clean-cut, but blessed with a smoldering sensuality that made the difference between boy next door and boy most likely to break your heart. He was grinning into the camera as if the photographer were the head cheerleader and he'd just won the state championship. He wore a letter jacket, lived-in jeans and a smile that made her heart beat faster even though she realized she was looking at a teenage boy.

His high school career had not been as auspicious as Victor's, but then again, whose was? Still, Malloy posted an impressive roster of accomplishments: varsity football, swimming, membership in several clubs, community service for the Historical Preservation Society. His goals included becoming an architect.

She wracked her brain, trying to remember if Victor had ever mentioned Mike. He hadn't. Victor had been highly selective in speaking of the past. He told her only what he thought she should know.

She read what Malloy had written at the bottom of the

page in controlled, rectangular script. She recognized the penmanship from all the documents they'd pored over regarding the restoration: "Hey, Vic—I don't know what to say—that won't surprise you. You were the one who had a way with words, not me. Things to remember: Scarborough Beach, the blue Impala, sailing nationals, Linda Lipschitz, the old boathouse—violin music—You're the best, you'll always be the best . . . I wouldn't even be going off to college if it weren't for you, so stay cool and all that crap, man. Cowabunga, MM."

She slammed the book shut on the grinning, too-handsome teenager.

She felt like a prize idiot. She'd let him break through her aching loneliness. She'd let herself feel attracted to him, and the sting of lust had heightened her emotions, rubbing her nerve endings raw in places.

She ought to be grateful to Sparky, really. The woman had given her a reason to push him away just as she was about to trust him.

Shoving the old books back into the dusty box, she stomped down the stairs. Malloy had left before she could confront him. He wouldn't be back until morning.

The hell with that, she thought, hurrying to the bathroom to scrub the dust and cobwebs from her hands. This new information was burning a hole in her. She wasn't about to wait until morning.

Chapter 20

S o there was this talent show at the Y, right?" Kevin's voice streamed loudly through the receiver.

"I hear you, sport." Dripping from the shower, Mike slung a towel around his waist and ducked out of the minuscule bathroom. The phone had rung before he could dry himself off, and a chill crawled over his skin. He supposed he could have offered to call Kevin back, but the kid was talking a mile a minute.

"And most of the stuff was really lame, like Travis Gannon doing his duck calls, and Kandy Procter with this ballet dance that looked like a spazz attack. Then David Bates sits down at the piano on stage—one of those giant pianos with the curve in it."

"That would be a grand piano."

"Yeah, so he sits down, and he's looking kind of nervous and then all of a sudden he pukes."

"You're kidding."

"Nope, he yarked all over the piano keys. It was way cool. Mrs. Primosic said they'd have to hire some special company to take the keyboard apart and clean it all up. It was rad."

"I'll bet." Mike talked to his kids every night, and he never knew what he'd hear out of them. He didn't like the idea that he was getting good at picturing their faces as they told him about their day. But the fact was, he could conjure up a dead-on mental image of Kevin describing his four lay-ups in a basketball game, or Mary Margaret's dreamy expression as she told him about a field trip to the Breakers or the Gilbert Stuart birthplace.

Sometimes he wanted to hold them and touch them, smell their hair when they laid their heads next to his as he read to them at bedtime. Sometimes he wanted to feel their warmth so bad he ached.

"So anything else new and exciting in your life?" he asked.

"Guess not. If I think of something, I'll call you back. What're you doing, Dad?"

Mike stared down at his bare feet, rubbed his hand over the damp hair on his chest. "Just got out of the shower. I was going to open a can of tuna and do the bookkeeping on my computer."

"Bo-ring."

No shit, thought Mike. He'd give anything to spend the evening with his family, even if it was sitting around watching TV. Each day, it became clearer to him—he wasn't cut out for living alone.

"What's your sister up to?"

"Just a second, I'll put her on. Mary *Mar*garet, pick

up!" he hollered without bothering to hold the receiver away from his mouth. Mike winced, hearing a clunk, then a bobble as his daughter picked up an extension.

"Hi, Dad."

"Hi, sweetheart. Did you see the talent show, too?"

"Yeah. It was okay until that kid threw up."

"Kevin thought it was the best part."

"He would. Trust me, you didn't miss anything."

"I miss you, kiddo."

"Me, too." A smile softened her voice. "I got my dress, Dad. The one for the Valentine's dance."

In the background, Kevin made a gagging noise.

"Bug off, punk!" Mary Margaret yelled at him.

Mike held the phone away from his ear for a second. He heard footsteps as Mary Margaret carried the cordless phone to a more private place. He pictured her hunkering down in her favorite nook on the upstairs landing, holding the phone in one hand and twirling a lock of hair around her finger. His shy, pretty daughter, growing up so fast. "I bet it's a real nice dress," he said.

"It's pale green and has these really sheer sleeves. Mom and I went to Filene's, and she let me get shoes to match."

"Can't wait to see it," he said. Angela had always been a world-class shopper—he was still paying off her credit card debts. He didn't doubt the dress was great. "Hey, are you reading those books we got from the library?"

"I finished one, and I'm halfway through the other. They're awesome."

Mike thought so, too. He'd bought one the other day, curious about Sandra's work. The one he'd read was the story of a shy girl, thrown into impossible circumstances, who was forced to be brave and strong, and who rebelled in the end. Art imitating life? he wondered.

"I have to go, Dad. I promised I'd shoot baskets with Kevin and Carmine. He put floodlights in the driveway."

"Great." Resentment twisted inside Mike as he pictured the 1847 carriage house blazing with lights on aluminum posts. "I'll talk to you tomorrow."

"Love you, Dad."

"Love you, honey."

As he hung up, he tried to steady his nerves. Outside, the weather was kicking up, shoving at the boat. He told himself he should be getting used to the idea that some other guy lived in his house, slept with his ex-wife, played with his kids and tucked them in each night. There were a million single dads around these days, he told himself. Guys put up with this all the time.

But Mike couldn't seem to get used to it, no matter how much time passed.

To keep himself company while he got dressed, Mike flicked on the small black-and-white TV. Courtney Procter sat at the news desk looking cool and competent, buffed to a plastic sheen. Mike thought about her producer's proposition to him, turned the thing off and flipped on the radio instead, to a song by Aimee Mann.

A second later, he heard footsteps on the deck above. Zeke leaped into action, hurling himself at the glass saloon door. It was dark already, and the blinds were drawn. He slid open the door, feeling a rush of cold wind on his bare chest and legs. There, in the yellowish glow of the harbor lights, stood Sandra Winslow.

His reaction to the sight of her was instant and unrehearsed. Holding the towel around his waist, he grinned despite the raw wind streaming in through the open door. "Hey, stranger."

"You . . ." She paused, her mouth twisted, and then she spoke more loudly. "You can say that again." She didn't seem to notice he was practically naked, or that the dog went into a dance of joy at her feet. Without waiting to be invited, she grasped the rail and climbed aboard. She was wearing jeans—he'd always liked a woman in jeans— gloves that didn't match and an oversized parka.

"Say what again?" he asked, distracted by the shape of her thigh as she stepped into the saloon. He turned down the radio.

"Stranger. I thought we were getting over the 'stranger' stage, but apparently that was a little one-sided of me." The blustering storm slapped at the hull, and she steadied herself by clutching a handrail. Zeke gave up vying for attention and flopped down on his cushion.

"You'll have to explain." The wind shivered through the main saloon. It was a terrible night, with the promise of a storm heavy in the air, the wind whistling through the halyards, and Mike hurried to slide the door shut. "Just a second. I need to put something on before I freeze my n—before I freeze." He ducked into the stateroom and yanked on a pair of gray sweats. Pulling an old URI Rams sweatshirt over his head, he went back to the saloon. She was here. Sandra was here. He couldn't get over it.

What did she want? he wondered, haphazardly scrubbing his hair dry with the towel. A loud creak sounded as the boat strained at its moorings. What the hell was she doing on his boat, in his life? Neither of them was in a position to start anything. Neither wanted to feel the heat that stung the air around them each time they were together, but like the gale brewing outside, it couldn't be altered or ignored. Mike figured he'd have to ride it out, and hope it would blow over soon.

"Welcome aboard the *Fat Chance*," he said. "How'd you find me?"

"Your name and slip number are on the mailbox, and

the marina gate wasn't locked." She stood in the middle of the room and looked around. Mike felt her gaze assessing the place—business files crammed into every available shelf, navigation equipment and computer, pictures of the kids hanging crooked, Kevin's artwork and Mary Margaret's A papers adorning the little galley fridge. Though Sandra said nothing, he felt defensive. This is my life, he thought, and wondered what she was thinking, seeing it for the first time.

"What can I do for you?" he asked.

"Why didn't you tell me you used to be best friends with Victor?"

Whoa. He hadn't been expecting that. "Sparky said something." It wasn't a question.

"She didn't realize you were hiding it from me."

"Shoot, Sandra, I wasn't hiding anything. The fact that I used to know Victor . . . that's ancient history. I didn't think it mattered."

"Everything matters now. Don't pretend you don't know that."

"All right, I should have said something. I don't know what, though. We knew each other as kids, but after high school, we lost touch. I bet Victor never mentioned me."

"No, but—"

"It's no big deal."

"It was a lie. Okay, maybe a lie of omission, but why would you keep it from me?"

"Because I never know what the hell you're going to do," he snapped, surprising them both with a lash of temper. "Face it, Sandy, you're not the world's most predictable person. One minute you're in my face, arguing about paint color, and the next you're teaching me to dance. I didn't know if talking about Victor would make you laugh or cry."

A stricken look leached the color from her face.

"Sandra," he said, softening his voice. "Sit down."

She cast him a narrow-eyed glance, then yanked off her jacket and sat down. "So why didn't you tell me?"

His reasons were many and complex. And at the moment, not a single one of them made sense. "I'm not in the habit of sharing personal information with the people who contract for my services." He ran a hand through his damp hair. "Look, you don't tell your editors and publishing people about your personal life, do you?"

"What about after we started . . . whatever it was we're—we started?" Her voice shook, and he sensed the same fury he'd seen in her the first day they'd met. "Not that it matters now."

"Why not?"

"I was just beginning to trust you. I'll never learn."

Her words hit him like a slap to the face. A cold, hard feeling twisted in his gut as he realized her trust was important to him. "Look, I never meant—at first I never gave it much thought. In a small town, people's paths cross. And then after a while, bringing it up seemed awkward." And it raised questions for him, too, but he didn't mention that.

"Well, I've brought it up now."

"What is it you need to hear? That I'm sorry? That I should have told you my life story before fixing your house?" He studied the glow of her skin in the dim light, the way her bottom lip gleamed with moisture. Outside, the storm hurled itself in from the North Atlantic. "It's not like you've been a font of information about yourself, either."

Her accusatory stare burned into him. "Don't try that on me, Malloy. It won't work."

"Fine," he said. "What can I tell you? We met as little kids. Third grade, I think. You know how friendships are.

Kids just sort of fall into them, and then it becomes a habit to hang out."

"You did more than hang out. I read what you wrote in his senior yearbook. The two of you were best friends."

"Are you still in touch with *your* best friend from high school?"

She laughed without humor. "What makes you think I had one?"

"Everybody does."

"Right. So go on. You and Victor."

He hadn't touched the memories in a long time, and in his mind, they took on a peculiar glow of nostalgia. He could remember the laughter, the sea air, the racing around, the feeling that everything in the world was right.

"It's like I told you. We were kids. We lost touch."

"I came here for answers, Malloy, but you haven't told me anything yet."

"It's been years, Sandra. In all that time, I never saw him, never spoke to him. He didn't get in touch with me, either."

She pressed the palms of her hands on the table. He'd never seen a wedding ring on her delicate, ink-smudged hands, and now he wondered why. A widow in mourning wore her husband's ring for years after he was gone, didn't she? What keepsakes did Sandra cherish on empty nights—Victor's Eric Clapton recordings?

"I grew up here. I know most of the people in Paradise. I would have told you about Victor and me, but . . ." He paused. "To be honest, I'm a lot more interested in you. I figure that should be obvious by now."

"Nothing is obvious to me," she said. "Ever."

Watching her, he could see her anger running out of steam, and felt a deep relief at the prospect. "To tell you the truth, I didn't want to bring up the fact that I once knew

Victor. I thought any reminders of the past would make you sad."

"Is that what you thought? That your past with Victor would make me sad? You're so wrong. He was only mine for a few years. You knew him much longer than I did." She seemed to be on the verge of saying something. Her throat worked silently; then at last she said, "I wish you'd tell me more. Everything. All your memories of him, good and bad."

All right, he thought. She needed this. The missing past was something he could give her, though it wasn't much. Still, he couldn't help wondering—was it Victor she wanted to hear about, or Mike? "He was an only child and I had three older sisters. So we spent a lot of time to-gether—we had a teacher who called us Huck Finn and Tom Sawyer. We grew up running all over the place, riding bikes, hanging out at the beach every summer, the sledding hill or the skating pond in winter."

"What was he like as a boy?"

"He was a regular kid, I suppose. Smart, funny, good-looking. Everybody liked him—other kids, teachers, adults. And he liked everyone, too." Turning on the bench, Mike opened a sliding side cabinet and found one of the few framed photos he'd kept when he moved out of the house.

"This was taken at First Beach in Newport one sum-mer." He handed it to her across the table. "We'd just won the Junior Cup."

She studied the picture, its imperfect colors faded by the years. It showed the two of them aboard a small sail-boat. He still remembered the heat of the sun on his face and the heady feeling of triumph surging through him as their boat cleared the final buoys. In the photo, he and Vic-tor were shirtless, wearing matching surfer shorts Mrs.

Winslow had bought for them. They stood with their skinny chests puffed out, holding the shiny trophy between them, their free arms cocked up to show off stringy biceps. Both were grinning in the way boys did, heedless of vanity, pride radiating from every inch of them. Mike was bigger, his eyes very blue in his tanned face. Victor's hair was summer gold, his lean face bright with freckles.

Seeing the picture brought back a rush of sweetness Mike hadn't felt in a long, long time. The uncomplicated joys of a sunny summer afternoon, a winner's trophy and a best friend had filled his world back then.

"Malloy," Sandra said, eyeing him suspiciously. "What are you thinking?"

"I guess I'm thinking about the kids in the picture. Look at us—happy as clams."

"Why do people assume clams are happy? I've never understood that."

"It's just an expression. We were ignorant, closed up tight. Neither of us could have known what life had in store for us. Which was probably for the best. If people knew what the future held, they'd never keep going. You don't tell a kid, 'You're headed for a lousy marriage' or 'You're going to die before you're forty.' What would be the point of knowing?"

He caught her stricken expression. "Sorry. I'm rambling."

She traced her thumb over the old image of Victor. "His mother has a copy of this picture. It ran in the local paper, didn't it?"

"Yeah."

"I didn't realize the other boy was you, though. You were both so . . . beautiful." She handed it back to him, and her eyes were dangerously bright.

Don't cry, Mike wanted to beg her.

"Tell me more about these boys," she said.

"How much more?"

"Tell me everything."

Mike drummed his fingers on the table. "How long do you have?"

She paused, then said, "All night."

"I don't have any great revelations for you. We were just . . . two kids who were friends. Pretty boring."

"How can that be boring?" She smiled slightly.

"What's funny?" he asked, relieved but trying not to show it. At least she didn't seem to be angry, or on the verge of tears anymore.

"That's pretty much what all my books are about. Two kids who are friends. Maybe that's why they don't sell too well. Boring."

"A good writer can make white paint interesting. But I'm no writer."

She drummed her fingers on the table. "Come on, Malloy. I need this. I need to know what Victor was like."

"You were married to the guy."

"You were married, too. Can you ever really say you knew your wife?"

The waves heaved against the hull with a hollow thumping sound. He thought about Angela, and the first time he'd brought her aboard the boat. She'd spent most of the time out on deck, working on her tan and admiring the yachts headed toward Newport's Commercial Wharf. Even then, there were things about her he hadn't wanted to know or acknowledge.

"Maybe not," he admitted. "Things are a lot simpler for kids. Victor and I—the two of us seemed to fit. You wouldn't think so at first. He was rich, I was poor. He made good grades, I didn't. He had someone watching his every move and planning his every step. Nobody watched what I was doing, and that was fine with me. Still, we clicked. We went on campouts, hikes, all the stuff kids do. We built forts out of driftwood and had a hideout in an old boathouse on the south shore. We had an old dinghy we used to take on pirate raids—I bet it's still there."

He wondered if Victor had told her anything about Brice Hall. The year they'd started high school, Vic's parents sent him away to the boarding school attended by every Winslow male for the past umpteen generations. Six weeks later, Victor had shown up at Mike's house—he'd flunked out and hitchhiked to Paradise, and was afraid to go home in defeat to his parents. With rare understanding, Mike's dad counseled Victor to go home, convince his folks that he'd be better off in public school. Victor had done just that, and more. To make up for their disappointment in him, he became the best and the brightest at everything, and Brice Hall was forgotten. But for some reason, Mike remembered it now—and decided not to bring it up with Sandra.

"In high school, Victor joined everything—student council, debate team, sports, that sort of thing."

"And you?" she asked, watching him with a disconcerting stare. "What were you into?"

"Girls and cars."

He sent her a self-deprecating grin, but she didn't smile back. "Victor was the big planner, and I was doing well if I managed to find two matching socks. It was almost eerie, the way he figured out what he wanted to do and aimed himself at it like an arrow. He was only about thirteen when he decided to go into politics. I thought he was kidding, but it turned out he was serious. From that moment on, everything he did was calculated to get him there. The classes he took, the clubs he joined, even the friends he made. Except me. I wasn't what you'd call an influential friend. He kept me around because he liked me. People called us the odd couple."

"Really?"

"The jock and the brain. I don't recall that we ever bickered over anything. Well, maybe one thing."

"What was that?"

"A girl. What else?"

She leaned forward, her eyes keen and bright. "Really? Tell me about her."

"Linda Lipschitz," he said. "Curly black hair, huge tits and—sorry. She had a damned fine figure. We both wanted to take her to the senior prom. That was one of the few times I nearly punched him out."

"Why?"

"He was the one who always had everything, and now he was going to take away the one thing I wanted."

Finally, a smile. A wry one, though. "Did Linda Lipschitz have anything to say about this?"

"We were seventeen. Do you think we cared about some girl's opinion?"

"I can't believe you fought over a girl."

"Actually, we didn't have to. Everything turned out okay. We both took her. She got to be princess for a night, and we all had a great time. I talked her into sneaking away and parking with me later, but Victor forgave me."

"Of course he did," she said quietly.

"What's that supposed to mean?"

She hesitated. "Victor . . . was very forgiving."

Odd comment, he thought. But then, as little flickers of memory came back to him, he realized it was true. "Yeah, the only time he got truly pissed at me was when I didn't bother applying to college." He eyed Sandra. "Does any of this sound familiar to you? Does it sound like Victor?"

"Completely. He . . . liked to help people."

"He knew I wanted to go to college and knew my family couldn't afford to send me. He and his folks figured out a way for me to get a full ride at URI, and he kept after me until I went for it."

"The football scholarship."

"Yeah." He drummed his fingers on the table, picking through a minefield of memories. "It was my fault we lost touch. I wanted it that way."

"Why?"

"Because I left school before finishing. He would have been disappointed in me."

"You're not the type of guy to disappoint anybody. Isn't that obvious?"

Chapter 21

Sandra couldn't believe she'd just blurted that out. She should have known she'd regret coming here. She should have stayed home, making lists in her journal. *Ten Ways to Get Through the Day Without Speaking to Malloy* . . . But here she was, an uninvited guest in the place he called home. It was a strangely intimate intrusion—she discovered what he ate—a blue bowl of bananas and tangerines on the counter; what he read—histories of architecture, novels by David Malouf and Patrick O'Brian; what he stuck on his undersized refrigerator—Kevin's drawing of a T-Rex, Mary Margaret's perfect spelling test, this month's tide chart.

"I should go." She got up and reached for her jacket.

"You should stay." He took the jacket from her and dropped it on the chair behind him. The boat listed, straining at its moorings. She staggered with the motion, lurching into him. He grabbed her shoulders, then held on with firm insistence. Since he'd kissed her, they'd been tiptoe-ing around the issue, trying to keep each other at arm's length while they decided where to go from here. Judging by the heat in his gaze, she suspected he'd made up his mind. She had never thought of blue as a hot color before, but when she looked up into his eyes, she saw flames.

A moment ago, she'd found him hard to read. Now, watching him bracing for the storm, she had no trouble at all. With some ancient, embedded awareness, she sensed an invisible alchemy seething and bubbling between them, holding her spellbound.

You should stay. What a world of meaning she heard in those three little words. Her whole life had been about what she should and shouldn't do, and she'd never taken the path marked "shouldn't." Suddenly she wanted to, with every cell of her body.

"You impair my judgment, Malloy," she said, trying to drum up some of her old caution and timidity.

"Not on purpose." He touched her in that slow, delib-erate way of his, as though he couldn't *not* touch her. His hand slid down the side of her rib cage, settling at her waist and pulling her toward him. Outside, the storm sang through the staywires and rigging of the boats, its voice al-most human.

"I can't do this," she said, almost whispering in an at-tempt to get the words out. She leaned back to escape the suggestive touch of his hand.

"Stay with me. You're alone too much, Sandra."

She shifted a nervous glance at Zeke, who slept curled on a ratty-looking cushion in the corner. "So I'll get a dog."

"Not good enough." He trailed his finger down her upper arm. The light caress seemed almost casual, but she knew better. It was his way of reminding her that there was more going on here than this increasingly absurd conversation.

"Malloy—"

"Shh." He gripped her shoulders and drew her against him, ignoring her caution and hesitation. Her heart raced. A part of her that lay deeper than the fear wanted him, wanted his touch, wanted . . .

She clutched his sweatshirt. It felt old and soft against her fingers, fragrant with laundry soap and the warm smell of a man just out of the shower.

She reminded herself that he was a liar—that was why she'd come here. She should push him away, leave while she could still think straight, but against her will, she stayed, anchored by his immutable strength. She was like the moored boat—able to move and shift and strain, but unable to leave.

"This is not what I had in mind," she said, still trying to extricate herself from his arms, his boat, his life.

His hands closed around her upper arms; his touch held the heat of frustration. "What the hell do you need, then?"

Torn and shuddering with warring emotions, she couldn't answer. Everything inside her strained toward him, toward the simple promise in his eyes.

"I need—"

"I know." He didn't say anything else, and in a perverse way, she was grateful. Words were too easy to argue with or misunderstand. Malloy settled his mouth firmly over hers just as she was about to play her verbal trump card and declare the game over.

He slipped his arms around her, one across her upper back and one at her waist, shaping her against him, so close that she could feel . . . everything. The wall of his chest, his searching kiss, the press of his erection. He didn't seem either self-conscious or apologetic, but then, why would he? He was Malloy.

His hand skimmed downward as his tongue probed delicately into her mouth, and a shock of heat shuddered through her. Thoughts spun away, unformed, unimportant. He pressed her against the table, and she arched toward him to keep her balance, clinging, her fingers digging into his biceps. He whispered something into her mouth; she didn't hear the words but took the meaning of it deep into her heart. He robbed her of the ability to think . . . to object. She felt the strange power of a force stronger than reason, stronger than logic. Some ancient, long-buried call roared to life in a way she hadn't thought possible until she'd met him. It made her wild—knowing he wanted her, seeing it in his eyes.

He pressed her against the edge of the table, parting her legs, fitting himself there. He drew from her a smoldering compliance, made her step out of her tentative shyness and into a state of breath-held anticipation. She felt like water, like silk, some substance that had no shape or form of its own, spilling out into storms and whirlwinds.

His next kiss came with unhurried, inexorable deliberation, giving her time to anticipate the heat and the taste of him before she actually felt it. Their lips touched, the contact deepened; then he worked his mouth over hers in a slow exploration that sent searing waves through her in long, unstoppable ripples. She felt dizzy and lost, yet there was nowhere on earth she wanted to be—and that was her surrender.

She simply gave in to the tension and hunger that had been building for longer than she would admit. She moved her hands upward over his shoulders, tangling urgent fingers into the damp strands of hair that spilled over his collar. She felt free and fearless; his earthy openness invited her to explore him in any way she chose.

Except she didn't quite know how.

But her hands did. Her mouth did.

Someone who was not Sandra slipped audacious hands under the waistband of his sweatshirt. Someone who was braver, stronger, more intuitive than Sandra pressed her palms against his flesh, drew back momentarily in astonishment when she felt his ridged stomach, his broad chest, like seasoned oak, honed smooth.

Someone who was not Sandra lifted the edge of the old sweatshirt, then stepped back to pull it up and over his head.

Despite his height, he was oddly graceful as his arms brushed the low ceiling of the boat's saloon. Dropping the shirt, he held her with a look that was both frankly lustful and mildly bemused. She would die if he laughed at her, but she could tell he wasn't going to laugh. The radio played a slow, soft tune, but the thud and suck of the waves drowned out the melody. The constant motion created a cadence that was wholly unique, moving this moment ahead, stripping away layer after layer of resistance until she couldn't deny the stark truth even to herself. She wanted him, and she would not leave him tonight.

She pressed her mouth against his chest, right below the collarbone, inhaling his scent. Her hands slid across his shoulders and then lower, discovering the fascinating geography of his body.

A sound came from him, wordless but full of meaning, and those large, steady hands took hold of her, pushed her slightly away, not in refusal but in a silent invitation to go deeper, to do more. She understood the question in his eyes; he sensed the answer in hers.

Taking her by the hand, he led her through the narrow

galley, to the stateroom tucked into the bow of the boat. Louvered doors flanked the threshold of the room, and a polished wooden footlocker provided a step up to the bunk. A soft, diffuse heat blew gently through small vents overhead.

The wishbone-shaped bed dominated the room, sides curving like a welcoming embrace. A pair of sconces glimmered on opposite walls, creating waves of amber light and shadow over plain sheets and pillowcases, a thick tartan comforter.

A jolt of reality struck her, and she faltered, glancing backward through the door. But he stood blocking the way, challenging but not threatening her. She bit her lip, watching him—gray sweatpants slung low on his hips, bare chest and ridged stomach.

"Um," she finally said, speaking past a throat gone tight, "I'm not sure . . ." She kept staring; then, overwhelmed by impulse, she dragged her fingers along the bunched muscles of his arms and downward over his rib cage.

"Yes, you are," he pointed out in a taut, quiet voice. As he spoke, he unbuttoned her sweater—Victor's sweater—and dropped it on the floor. If she'd been a practiced seductress, she would have made certain that she wore a demi-bra of lace and gossamer satin, in some exotic color not found in nature. And under her jeans she'd have on a dainty thong that yielded under the pressure of the slightest touch.

No such luck, considering that her purpose in coming here tonight had been to yell at him. Under the sweater and jeans, which he removed with a slow, easy caress down her hips, she wore grape-colored long johns.

She tried to reassure herself—at least they were ladies' long johns, made of ribbed Thermasilk, a leftover from a disastrous ski vacation to Killington with the Winslows. A pity they were purple.

By the time she stepped out of the rumple of jeans on the floor, she began wishing she'd talked herself out of this.

"Now what's the matter?" he asked, moving the flat of his hand down her back, then over her hips. He bent to nuzzle her neck, and she yielded willingly, tilting her head to one side.

"I didn't say anything." The unrelenting gale battered at the boat, and she braced herself against the edge of the bed.

"You didn't have to. I can tell by the look on your face. You think too damned much. What were you thinking, just now?"

It was hard to keep things from him, she realized. "Skiing in Vermont," she said. "With the Winslows. I was the human bowling ball of the slopes."

"Your mind works," he said with a chuckle of affectionate amusement, "like a mouse in a maze. Quit thinking about the Winslows."

"But—"

"Don't think at all."

"I never planned to take my clothes off in front of you," she confessed. "If I had, I wouldn't have worn long underwear."

He slipped his hands down each side of her, shoulders, waist, hips, and up again. He moved so slowly, yet his touch had the impact of a shattering collision. He gave the waistband a gentle tug. "You look like a goddess in this, Sandy. I'm not kidding." He swirled his finger around her navel, lowered the elastic another notch. "Even so, I bet you look even better out of it."

The rhythm inside her echoed the frenzy of the storm.

Every word, every touch, every breath, sent little shocks through her. She was helpless, falling, burning out of control all at once. He didn't hurry, but there was no wasted movement as he finished undressing her, then rolled the sweatpants down his long, muscular legs. She'd always been taught that it was rude to stare, but she seemed to be breaking every possible rule tonight, and gladly left that one by the wayside.

"Come here," he said in a rough whisper, and took her in his arms. He thrust aside the covers and they fell together, facing each other, a clash of searching hands and mouths. His eagerness flattered her and she faltered, wondering if she could ever match his honest hunger.

"Now what?" he asked. "You're thinking again."

"I . . ." She made a halfhearted attempt to recall advice from the endless *Cosmo* articles she used to read with scholarly diligence—"How to Drive Him Wild (but Tame Him to Clean the Kitchen)." "How to Tell if He's Seeing Another Woman." "Tricks from the Hooker's Trade."

She couldn't remember anything. And judging by the harshness of his breathing and the way his body pressed deeply, aggressively against her, it didn't seem to matter. In the frenzied collision, her hands and heart had more sense than her brain on its best day.

His mouth covered her breast with frank possessiveness, and all her thoughts evaporated. The heady knowledge that he wanted her was intoxicating. Plain, uncomplicated lust had its own kind of purity. It was joyous, liberating, unself-conscious, like deep belly laughter. She didn't feel furtive or guilty as their bodies moved together in an unrehearsed dance that turned the night to pure magic. She was awash in sensation—the smell of the boat, his bed, *him*. Beneath her fingers, his chest thrummed with the heavy beat of his heart.

Her touch drew a groan of response from him. He caressed her with an intensity that was both deeply carnal and startlingly tender. He lifted her up, entered her with a swift movement that took her breath away. A feeling of total surprise took hold. This was so new, so different . . . Sensation flashed; she heard the roar of the storm and the slap of the waves, felt a lash of desire that stung and burned, as though the boat had caught fire. The moment swept her upward to a pinnacle of unbearable sensitivity.

With an inner sense of perfect rhythm, he seemed to know when to press forward and when to retreat; he could judge by the cadence of her breathing and the thud of her heartbeat the moment need consumed her entirely. She arched upward, crying out. His arms, braced on either side of her, trembled with restraint until she came with a shuddering, overwhelming sweep of intensity.

Astonished, she closed her eyes and saw colors fusing, melding, blurring before any image could form. It was the color of bliss, of surprise, of fulfillment. He wasn't far behind her, his surge powerful, her name on his lips. And then he lay covering her, his weight a welcome burden, his breath rasping in her ear.

Awash in wonder, she surrendered to the rocking motion of the boat and to his warm, fast breathing. Blinking her eyes open, she felt like Dorothy, stepping from her drab black-and-white world into a fantasy land of ecstatic, wild color.

"Are you a good witch," she whispered, "or a bad witch?"

With a reluctant movement, he pushed up and off, then lay at her side, his hand trailing over her with suggestive intent. "Beg pardon?"

"That's what they asked Dorothy when she landed in Oz."

"At least you're not thinking about a ski trip with the Winslows."

She looked him somberly in the eye. "I've gone somewhere better than that," she said. *To Oz. I've gone to Oz and I don't ever want to leave. Dorothy was a fool, a coward. She should have stayed there forever.*

"Yeah?" His hand kept up its evocative motion, and her limbs went slack as the surges and ripples started up again, gathering strength. He followed the motion of his hand with his mouth, tongue and teeth bringing every nerve ending to tingling life. Before she realized what was happening, they were making love again. It was different this time—the pace was elegiac, as though they were picking themselves up, exploring each other after the initial collision.

The sense of discovery yielded to an erotic bloom of awareness. They knew each other in a different way now. His heart was still uncharted territory, but his body was hers to explore. With a mysterious, inborn wisdom she caressed him, watching her hand trail over the contours of his body, which responded with gratifying ease. The leisurely heat rose again, more gradually. A sense of wonder gripped her. Could this really be happening? To *her?*

She could see the glint of lust in his eyes and his half smile. Noting the leap of his muscles beneath her searching hands, she felt a stunning, probably unwarranted sense of accomplishment. It was a revelation, heightening her own pleasure until she begged him for more. When he kissed her and turned her in his arms, when his hands found secret places and he whispered forbidden words in her ear, she forgot to feel bashful or awkward. A delicious tension built between them, built and crested and spilled down and over and through her in fiery trails of sensation that sweetly echoed the first shock of her initiation.

Afterward, feeling raw and exposed and confused, she wept, and he held her against his bare chest, damp with her tears. He never said a word, probably knowing she couldn't explain her feelings. Perhaps she cried because the intimacy was so deep. Or maybe she wept from the sheer joy of finding a hidden part of herself at last. Probably, though, she simply felt an overwhelming relief to find the warmth and familiarity of human contact again.

When the powerful waves of emotion dissipated, he propped himself up on one elbow and brushed at her tears with his thumb. He bent and kissed her cheeks, and then her mouth, her throat, her breasts, lower . . . She clung to him and answered each touch with one of her own, each kiss with one of her own, doing things she was pretty sure *Cosmo* had never published. Incredibly, they were making love a third time; she had no concept of time passing. She knew only the night and the storm-driven waves, the velvety cocoon of the stateroom and the dimly burning sconces throwing their moving silhouette against the hull.

Much later, they slept a little, but even so, she clung to him as though he were a life raft in a churning sea.

Chapter 22

I n the pearly predawn, Mike made love to her again, in a slow, comforting manner that didn't even wake her fully until she came. She blinked up at him, and her sweetly befuddled look made him smile.

"Hey, Brown Eyes," he whispered.

"My God. What happened?"

"It's a little late to explain the facts of life now."

She shifted away from him, tucking her elbow under her cheek, touching herself where he had touched her. Last night she'd arrived with guns blazing—so to speak—but this morning, she retreated into wary shyness again.

"I can't believe we did that."

He reached for her. "If you need further proof—"

"I'll take your word for it." She pressed her hand to his chest, holding him back.

Damn, she smelled good. Her touch felt like heaven.

For days, they'd been a fire waiting to be sparked, the embers banked with a coating of ashes, dim and miserly, but ultimately responsive to the coaxing breath of desire. His need for her had been unrelenting, something he had controlled with an iron will, but when he finally made love to her, he'd been beyond ready.

He kept trying to tell himself that the long absence of a woman from his life accounted for his intense, ravenous need for her. But the fact was, he had a special tenderness for her that grew and strengthened with each passing day. And he knew it wouldn't simply disappear when she sold her house and moved away.

"You hungry?" he asked.

"I could eat."

He rifled through a drawer at the end of the bed and produced a one-pound bag of M&Ms. "Actually, I bought these with you in mind. I was going to bring them over to the house."

"Not exactly breakfast material," she pointed out.

"I'll see what I can find." He slipped out of bed and pulled on his sweatpants.

Sandra sat up, moving a little gingerly.

It struck him then. He knew without a doubt that he was the first guy she'd slept with since Victor. Oh, man.

"Are you okay?" he asked.

She combed her fingers through her hair. "I guess."

He nodded; she probably wanted a few minutes to herself. "Bathroom's in there. Help yourself to whatever you need. I'll go put the coffee on."

He let Zeke out for his morning run and turned up the radio to listen to the weather while he fixed breakfast. The storm had passed through, but there was a high-wind advisory for the rest of the day. What the hell did she eat for breakfast? He kept a supply of Pop-Tarts on hand for the kids, but what adult ate Pop-Tarts? Wheaties would have to do. Who didn't like Wheaties?

As he poured the juice, he felt her presence and turned to see her standing there, wrapped in his terry-cloth robe and smelling of toothpaste. The robe all but swallowed her; it had been a Father's Day gift from Kevin and Mary Margaret.

The thought of his kids made him jumpy. They were so fragile right now. They needed him—all of him.

Then Mike grinned. He was getting way ahead of himself, and Sandra looked damned good in his robe. "Coffee?" he asked.

"Thanks." She sat down at the table. He pushed the milk and sugar toward her. She added milk, then a spoonful of sugar. Then another, and another. Glancing up, she saw him looking at her.

"You like it sweet," he commented. "I noticed that the first time I bought you a cup of coffee."

She nodded, then quickly lowered her gaze. "I remember."

"Hey." Reaching across the table, he lifted her chin. "Is this morning-after bashfulness, or is something wrong?"

She stirred her coffee. "Last night I came to talk about you and Victor, not—you know."

"But that worked out better. You know." Damn, he felt good. He hadn't felt this good in a long time. He knocked back a glass of orange juice and poured another.

She sipped her coffee from a spoon.

He poured Wheaties into a bowl and offered it to her.

She shook her head and perused the supplies on the counter. "Could I have a Pop-Tart?"

Amazing. She liked Pop-Tarts.

As he opened the package, she picked up the old photograph of him and Victor. "Do you have any others?"

"I do, but don't ask me where. I think I keep this one on the boat because it's a day I want to remember." The toaster released, and he tossed the Pop-Tart from hand to hand, then onto a plate.

"Thank you." She blew on the pastry to cool it. The sight of her puckered lips sparked a swift, erotic memory of the night before. Through the door to the stateroom, he could see the unmade bed.

He sat down across from her to drink his coffee. She glanced down at the photograph again and touched the image of Mike. She looked as though she might cry, and he silently begged her not to. It had been hard enough last night, feeling her tears on his naked flesh. Those tears didn't have anything to do with Victor, and Mike's wordless comfort had been enough. This morning was a different story—she seemed focused on that old photograph again.

"How old were you in this picture?"

"I'm not sure. Maybe twelve." He tried to think of a way to change the subject. Jesus, wasn't a night of great sex enough for this woman? Morning-after conversation was not supposed to be about the dead husband, was it? "So what were you up to, when you were twelve?"

She indicated the picture. "Not this." At his questioning glance, she added, "I didn't have many friends, growing up."

"Come on." He tried to picture her as a little girl. Big dark eyes, long dark hair, skinny legs. Partial to Pop-Tarts.

"Really, I didn't. And I didn't even think it was strange. I lost myself in books and hardly ever came up for air. I never had . . . what you and Victor had."

"Don't attach some deep meaning to it. We just hung out."

"All through your school years." She broke the pastry into smaller pieces, not seeming to notice she was crumbling it.

"Can we get off the topic of school?" he asked, putting the photograph aside.

"Fine. What about afterward?"

"I already told you that—didn't make it through college." He studied Sandra's face. What the hell was it with her? Something about the way she listened made him feel the need to explain himself. "I was sidelined by an injury and took to partying. Angela—my ex—was a cheerleader, but she quit the squad." The truth was, she'd been sidelined, too, by academic probation, and eventually she'd flunked out. "I left school, married her and started getting ready for the baby to come."

"Oh." Sandra's eyes grew intent as she put two and two together. But he knew she couldn't begin to imagine Angela's father, with his legendary Italian temper, his Old World values shaken to the core until Mike "did the right thing."

"So you have a grown child," Sandra concluded.

He stared down at his hands. He swallowed hard, remembering something he hadn't thought about in a long time. "Angela had a miscarriage."

The searing irony of it still stung. They'd married for the sake of the baby. In the sad aftermath of the loss, they'd probably both entertained the private, forbidden thought that their reason for staying together no longer existed. But they stuck it out, trying hard most of the time, neither of them admitting the slow erosion of their marriage had begun even before the miscarriage.

They should have listened to their hearts. But then there would have been no Mary Margaret, no Kevin.

Mike stared at the galley window, which framed a view of whitecaps out in the Sound. "After I quit school, we moved to Newport. Never sent a word to Victor, not even a wedding announcement. I knew he'd take my failure harder than I ever did."

"What failure? You settled down, had a couple of great kids. Look at all you've done. According to Sparky, your business was thriving, and you were winning national recognition for your work."

"I never got the degree."

"It's a piece of paper." She tucked a lock of hair behind her ear. "Trust me, it's no Holy Grail."

People with advanced degrees generally thought that way. They didn't know how many doors had been slammed shut in Mike's face because he lacked that key credential. He won admiration for starting up his own firm; no one seemed to realize he'd had no choice. He was forced to go hat-in-hand to his father-in-law and take out a loan.

Zeke scratched at the door, and Mike let him in. "Anyway," he said, sitting down again, "you asked about Victor, and here I am telling you all this stuff about me."

"I don't mind." She propped her chin in her hand, soft-eyed and dreamy. "He didn't talk about the past much. He said he had a happy childhood, that his folks spoiled him rotten and he tried not to let it show. Ronald and Winifred never had much to say to me."

We've never understood her . . . She was the one poor choice Victor made. Mike's last conversation with the Winslows echoed in his mind.

"They're nuts, then," he said. "You're beautiful. You're brilliant, and you have a big heart."

She regarded him as if he'd spoken in a foreign tongue. "Excuse me?"

"What more could they want in a daughter-in-law?" he asked.

"A pedigree." She spoke simply, with no surprise or outrage, just stating a simple fact. "Victor tried to warn me in advance, before he introduced us. He said his parents were 'very traditional' and 'filled with high-flown hopes' for him. That's code with the Winslows. Breeding matters."

He glanced at Zeke, who had flopped down on his favorite cushion to sleep off his morning run. "Right."

"Actually, I don't think it was so much a case of liking or disliking. I simply wasn't their choice."

"To marry Victor."

"Right."

"So did they have somebody else in mind?"

"Are you kidding? Ronald and Winifred? They probably started looking while Victor was a zygote." She turned her gaze to Mike. "I'll bet you know who she is."

"Know who?"

"The woman they wanted Victor to marry."

"Who is she?"

"Courtney Procter."

The local newshound—blond, driven and ambitious. "Yeah? Makes sense, I guess."

"She was this incredible debutante, attended Brown the same time Victor did. Her parents are friends of the Winslows. Victor took Courtney out a few times. Even after he married me, Winifred made a point of keeping a few photos around, showing them dressed in their formals, the happy couple ready to step out. But for once, maybe for the first time, he rebelled."

"Was that before or after he met you?"

She laughed. "What, you'd actually believe he'd throw her over for me?"

"Yes."

"Dream on." She seemed stubbornly incredulous that anyone might find her attractive. "He dumped Courtney long before he found me."

"How did you meet?"

"That's private," she said quickly, guardedly.

Mike leaned back against the hull, crossing his arms over his chest. "You're some piece of work, lady," he said.

"I don't know what you mean."

Mike was pissed, and he couldn't quite figure out why. Maybe after last night, he wanted her to trust him more. She'd slept with him, but she was still holding back, and it bugged the hell out of him. "You came barging in here, demanding to know why I kept something from you. So I tell you all this stuff I've never told anybody, and you can't even explain how you met your husband?" He leveled his gaze at her, and she stared implacably back. "Listen, maybe last night was a mistake. You're the client, I'm the contractor. Maybe we'd better keep it that way."

"You think?"

Don't go, he thought. Stay and talk to me. But he wanted the choice to be hers.

To his relief, she made no move to get up. She studied Mike for a long time, her gaze invasive, discomfiting. Then she drank her orange juice. "He changed my life."

It was the last thing Mike had expected to hear. "I don't get it."

"It's true. In a way." She splayed her hands on the table, her throat working in that strained way he'd noticed before. "To explain this, I have to go way back. You see, when I was little, I used to stutter."

He hid his surprise, and swiftly reviewed the concept.

Sure enough, he could recall a couple of times she'd stumbled over words, hesitated—but didn't everyone do that? "I understand lots of kids stutter at some time or other," he said.

"Not like I did. We're talking every word. Serious disability. My parents hired every sort of speech pathologist and child psychologist they could find. My dad worked overtime to pay for it all, and my mom drilled and sang and did everything she could think of. It . . . had a pretty powerful impact on my life."

He tried to imagine the teasing she'd endured as a kid, the frustration of having so much to say and no way to say it. No wonder she was a writer.

"Anyway," she went on, "I was writing books no one wanted to publish. No agent in the business wanted to represent me, and the best job offer I'd had was as an office assistant at the Trawlworks in Narragansett. My speech therapist had me going to a support group. I met Victor there. He was doing volunteer work."

That didn't surprise him. Community service was Victor's middle name.

"I could talk to him. Really talk. It's such a gift, to find someone who listens, who doesn't try to finish my sentences, prod me and put words in my mouth. I don't know why he took such an interest in me, but he did. I worked on his election campaign, wrote him a couple of speeches." She studied his expression. "I think he liked my loyalty. My . . . quietness."

"Trust me, he liked more than that." The oversized robe gave him a view of her cleavage, and Mike couldn't help staring at it.

She frowned as she clutched the robe tighter. "You don't know anything about us."

"Then tell me." He refilled their coffee cups.

"He invited me to the county fair—he had some official function that evening. We had our first fight over a carnival ride." The boat listed in the churning waters. "He wanted to go on the Ferris wheel, and I didn't. Victor practically forced me to go, even though he could tell I was terrified. Maybe that's why my memory of that day is so sharp. It was summer, and the air felt heavy and sticky with the smells of diesel exhaust and cotton candy. The Ferris wheel was the most popular ride of the night, and I was hoping it would be too crowded, and Victor would change his mind. But it was one of those moments when the universe conspires against you, and all the planets line up and launch you like a stone from a slingshot. The crowd parted, suddenly there was no line, and I stood at the gate with a cardboard ticket in my hand while Victor pushed me up the ramp." A faraway look of remembrance diffused her gaze. "I even remember the attendant—greasy blond hair, a muscle shirt over a dark tan. I was terrified to go on the ride, but even more terrified to make a scene. I think Victor always knew that about me. I'd rather die than make a scene."

A haunted smile touched her lips. "So I waited until we were airborne, and I let him have it. I was so angry, I didn't even stutter. And Victor just sat there beside me, listening. I don't remember how many times we took that ride, how many tickets he handed the attendant. We just kept going around and around, and I talked like I'd never talked to anyone before. It was like . . ." She paused, flashed a grin. "Like now, sort of. At one point, we got stuck at the top. That's when he asked me to marry him."

She folded her arms on the table. "Pretty romantic, isn't it?" Her voice was flat. He wondered what had soured the memory for her.

"And he made it happen, didn't he?"

"In a big way. We announced our engagement at the Providence Plantation Founders Ball three weeks later."

"Victor did everything in a big way."

"Yeah," she said, holding his gaze with hers. "Even die."

Chapter 23

*I*n the wake of her confession, Sandra wasn't sure what to say next. Waves struck the hull of the old trawler, thumping into the silence. The last words she'd spoken seemed to hang in the air, then dissipate like smoke on the wind. Maybe she'd said too much. People seldom wanted the unvarnished truth, even when they asked for it.

Malloy made an unlikely confidant, sitting there with his hair mussed and his eyes as clear as the sky after a storm, his hand covering hers. She tried to read his expression—a combination of incomprehension and regret that he'd broached the topic in the first place. Yet after last night, she wanted to open up to him. "Why do I feel like a waitress who just brought you a dish you didn't order?" she asked, pulling her hand away.

Leaning back, he absently scratched his bare chest.

The gesture, so alien, so *male,* drew her attention. "I guess I was expecting something—"

"Lighter. Cuter. Every couple has a fun story about the way they met. Getting their underwear tangled at the Laundromat. Falling in love in geometry class. With Victor and me, there was nothing fun about it. He helped me with a serious disability. Six months later, I was saying 'I do' in front of five hundred wedding guests. Actually, what I said was 'Yes, I do,' because I felt the stutter coming on." She shook her head. "I can't believe I told you that. I've never told anyone that story."

"Why not? It's a good story. Sounds like the two of you were a perfect match."

He was right, but not in the way he meant. Victor had needed her as much as she'd needed him; she hadn't realized it until the very end. He'd needed her unquestioning loyalty, her naiveté, her circumspection.

Malloy recaptured her hand. "I figured talking about it might make you feel better. But you look as though you—"

He broke off, but she filled in the blank. "Lost my best friend?" She'd thought so, but everything had changed the night of the accident. She questioned everything she thought she knew. What did she mourn? The life she used to share with Victor, or Victor himself?

"So he was the love of your life," Malloy said, misreading the look on her face.

"I . . . why would you say that?"

He hesitated, then said, "Because you can't move on. It's been a year since he died, and I get the sense that five years from now, you'll still be dwelling on this."

That stung. "Why do you care?"

"You know why." Standing up, he came around to her side of the table and pulled her up off the bench, into his arms. "Maybe I'm trying to figure out if there's room for someone else." He settled his mouth over hers and walked her backward through the galley, lifting her over the threshold to the bed. He tasted of oranges, and Sandra didn't think of resisting. His passion for her was utterly intoxicating and she wasn't about to deny him. For the first time in her life, she understood what it meant to be insatiable.

~~

Much later, when Sandra awakened, she discerned a golden thread of light around the forward hatch. Lord, what time was it?

Malloy was still there, asleep in the heavy, guiltless manner of a child—or a man with a clear conscience.

She hardly dared to breathe. What had she done?

All her life she'd tried to please everyone, even if it meant shortchanging herself in the process and relegating her adventurous nature to fictional characters. This was life, Malloy was all too real, as vital and powerful as a storm at sea. Last night, she threw the rules out the window. She'd been a stranger to herself. The boat had all but burst into flames.

Cradling her chin in her hand, she studied him. She had thought he was ordinary, a simple workingman, but that wasn't quite right. He was filled with an infinite variety of complexities she was only beginning to discover.

The handyman. He fixed broken things. In that way, he was exactly what she needed—someone to come into her life and bring her out into the world. Until now, she hadn't realized she'd been stuck in her own head, out of touch with her senses, for so long.

When he made love to her, she stopped thinking. In his

arms, she learned to explore sensation, instinct. It was not always comfortable, and sometimes it felt risky, but last night had been deeply fascinating in a way she hadn't anticipated.

She listened to the waves and the wind, watched the play of light through the hatch, inhaled the subtle, erotic scent of their lovemaking. Everything was heightened by the physical intimacy they'd shared. Even after exchanging their personal baggage, they were still attracted to each other.

But now what?

Apprehension coiled inside her. He was becoming dangerously important to her. Deeper commitments were impossible, even though her heart yearned for them. She couldn't let that happen, especially not now. She had to stay the course she'd charted for herself, and Malloy had to deal with the issues of his broken family. But Sandra knew their physical intimacy was going to make it harder for her to keep her secrets. She'd probably said far too much to him over breakfast.

She made an involuntary sound, trying to stave off another wave of tearful emotion. He opened his eyes, and his smile broke as slowly as the sunrise. They didn't kiss, didn't speak, didn't even bother with foreplay this time, but simply and wordlessly joined and spent themselves, all in the space of moments.

It wasn't nearly long enough. She came, but she wanted more, and gave a little grumble of protest as he moved away with a grin of sleepy satisfaction. He grabbed a water bottle from the shelf, took a swig and offered it to her. She dutifully took a sip. "That wasn't what I had in mind, Malloy."

He laughed. "Lady, you need an OFF switch."

She lay back against the bank of pillows, savoring the

gentle rocking motion of the boat. How had she lived so long without this? Lust and ecstasy had been foreign concepts to her, things that didn't exist except as vague abstractions. She always assumed passion was something unreachable, something that might happen in a fairy tale or a country-western song. An ideal, not something that could actually happen to a person like her. Now she knew the tenderness, the intimacy, the heat and energy, and her entire world had changed.

"You have the strangest look on your face," he said.

She took a hasty swig of water. "Do I? I came here last night to make a stand, and I wound up flat on my back without an argument."

He rested his hand easily on the sheet covering her breast. "I wasn't expecting it, either. Hoping, though." He rubbed her suggestively. "Still am."

An involuntary response shuddered through her. She wasn't sure Victor was as important as he'd seemed when she'd stormed onto the boat last night. "I think my circuits are overloading." She tucked the sheet under her arms. "What time is it, anyway?"

"Doesn't matter. It's Saturday." His hand stilled, and she felt his attention fixing on her. "You were a virgin when you married Victor."

Sandra froze. "Why would you say a thing like that?"

"An educated guess."

Humiliation burned through her. So he'd sensed her inexperience, her ineptitude. She'd thought, from his responses to her, that for once she was getting it right, but apparently not. "H-how did you know?"

He shrugged, laid an idle hand on her knee beneath the covers. "You never struck me as the party animal of Rhode Island."

"So I led a sheltered life," she said. "So sue me. You'll have to take a number."

He pulled back, eyebrows raised. "That wasn't a criticism. Christ, just the opposite."

"I don't know what you mean."

He pushed a hand through his thick hair. "I'm not like you, Sandy. Not good with words, so I'll probably say this wrong. Last night you were . . . a revelation. There's something incredibly sexy about total honesty."

Had she been honest? In a way, she thought. Her body, the things she had felt, couldn't lie. "Oh," she said.

The corner of his mouth slid upward in a half grin. "Now you're thinking too hard again. Say what you feel. Quit trying to analyze everything."

"All right. I never really knew sex could be like . . . like . . ."

"Like this?" His hand slipped upward from her knee, sending ripples along her nerve endings.

She gasped, forgot what she was thinking. Again.

"You and Victor weren't very physical," he remarked. It wasn't a question, rather a statement.

Discomfited, Sandra shifted away. "You have no way to judge that."

"I'm not judging you. Simply trying to get to know you."

"Suppose I did the same to you?" She drew her knees up to her chest. "Suppose I went poking into your past with your ex-wife?"

He spread his arms, and the sheet slipped below his waist, but he didn't seem to notice. "Be my guest. I've got nothing to hide. Do you?"

She knew without asking that sex had not been the problem between Mike and Angela. How could it have been, when he had that intent way of concentrating on pleasure, pushing everything else in the world away.

"You blush a lot," he said, studying her. "I like that."

She didn't know how to respond, so she fell silent, sifting through the past. She and Victor had shared the same bed. They danced together, walked hand in hand through the wet brick streets of Providence, gazed at each other across the linen-covered tables of exclusive restaurants, went on vacation together, spent holidays together.

With no basis for comparison, she used to think that was the essence of marriage. In one stormy night, Malloy had shown her a new world, a world filled with wonders she hadn't seen before, sensations she hadn't felt before.

He touched her shoulder, drew her around to face him, a question in his eyes.

She cleared her throat. "Victor and I—that is, we weren't . . . Our marriage was not centered on the—the bedroom."

"Was there another woman?"

She recoiled from that, pushing him away. "Not everyone is a sex maniac." She wanted to hide from his probing stare. He had been best friends with her husband for ten years, maybe more. He'd watched Victor grow from a boy into a man, had shared confidences only best friends ever share. Maybe he knew. Maybe he'd known all along. "Answer me, Malloy. What are you asking?"

"I thought I knew," he said, still looking at her oddly. "Did I ask the wrong question? Should I have asked if *you*'re okay?" He smiled, and she was amazed that a man with beard stubble and rumpled hair could look so charming. "After last night," he added, "I know the answer to that. So I wondered if Victor—I don't know—if there was some kind of problem with his . . . performance."

The irony of it struck her. His performance. He'd been a consummate performer.

As a new bride, she used to study self-help books that promised she could heat up her marriage by becoming the aggressor in the relationship. But each time she had tried to initiate lovemaking with Victor, he'd fallen back on the classic excuses. He was tired. He felt nauseous from overeating. He had a migraine. He stayed up so late at night that she often ended up falling asleep with the light still on and a book on her chest. Most mornings, he left the bed before she awakened. The one time she'd encouraged him to see a doctor had been one of only two times he ever lost his temper with her.

She used to worry that she wasn't glamorous enough, sophisticated enough, sexy enough. Sure, other men came on to her occasionally; her social life with Victor placed her in the public eye and she'd endured her share of propositions.

Of course, she had never once been tempted. When Victor had chosen her to be his wife, he had chosen wisely and well. Not because she was such a great catch, but because she had the one quality he needed above all others—she would never, ever breach his trust.

Not even after he was dead.

Chapter 24

The new floodlights looked like shit, Mike observed as he got out of the car in front of his house. Or not his house—what the hell should he call it? Ex-house? Step-house? Ordinarily, the sad implications of the term would bother him, but he had other things to think about these days.

A lot of other things.

He paused to check his reflection in the dark-tinted car window. For the Father and Daughter Dance, he'd borrowed the Carmichaels' Cutlass Supreme. His hair was too damned long; he couldn't recall the last time he'd been to the barber. But the fifteen-year-old tux still fit, and Mike had even managed to dig up a pair of cuff links, the ones he'd worn at his wedding. He hoped Mary Margaret wouldn't notice the bow tie was a clip-on. The only guy

Mike knew who actually tied them had been Victor Winslow, an expert at it by the age of ten.

Victor again. These days, he was never far from Mike's mind. Not just because Victor had been married to Sandy, but because something kept bugging Mike, something about the way Victor had died. He had a nagging feeling that something was missing from the accounts of that night, despite the persistence of the WRIQ news team. Mike had read and reread the reports. He'd even studied transcripts of the medical examiner's inquest, filed on the Internet under public records. Something didn't add up. He kept trying to think of a way to question Sandy, but he didn't want to push. Despite their new intimacy, certain boundaries stayed intact. She was touchy as an alley cat when it came to Vic. Mike would probably be better off if he left things alone—but he was quickly finding out that he couldn't leave her alone for a lot of reasons.

Running a finger around the stiff edge of his collar, he walked to the front door. Kevin's army of action figures posed at the edge of the walkway or crouched in tunnels dug in the flower beds, and the sight of them gave Mike a sharp pang. He missed the little stuff like this—seeing his son lost in a fantasy world, going about the serious business of play.

He rang the bell, noticing a new "No Solicitors" sign by the door.

"Just a sec." Angela's heels clicked on the wood floor, and then the door opened. She was in the midst of putting on an earring and held her head cocked to one side, her bright blond hair falling over her shoulder.

"Hey, Ange." Mike stepped inside.

She dropped the earring, and it pinged across the floor toward his feet. They both stooped to retrieve it, inadvertently bumping shoulders. "Sorry." Mike straightened up, handing her the little gold loop. "Here you go."

After a second, he realized she was staring at him. Her full lips were parted slightly, and her eyes were wide. He realized she hadn't seen him in a tux in years. "Thanks, Mike," she said at last.

"Is my best girl ready?"

She cast a glance at the stairs. "Almost."

He shifted from one foot to the other. He'd lived in this house for more than fifteen years, yet each time he came here, he barely recognized the place. Angela was always changing the decor. The house smelled different, too. Not bad, just . . . different. His ex-house, ex-wife. Ex-life.

"Where's Kevin?"

"He was driving Mary Margaret nuts all afternoon, so I had Carmine take him over to the restaurant. He likes doing his homework in the break room." She handed him a red paper heart from the hall table. "He made you a Valentine."

Mike unfolded it, and a smile tugged at his mouth. In careful lettering, his son had written: "Dad: Happy V.D."

Showing it to Angela, he said, "It's a keeper."

"I'll say." She laughed and shook her head. She was such a knockout, he thought. Always had been.

"So," he said. "I'll have her home by nine."

"Good. It's a school night." She gave a dry laugh. "What am I saying? You know that. She's really excited about going to a dance. Ah, Mike. She's growing up so fast." Angela looked up at him with such familiar, soft-eyed longing that for a moment he lost his bearings, forgot where he was. Ex-house, he reminded himself.

Rattled, he took a step back, spreading his arms. "How do I look?"

She eyed him from head to toe. "Not bad for a townie.

But your tie's crooked." She stepped forward, putting her hands up to adjust it.

Her nearness surrounded him, swallowed him up. He knew her with an intimacy wrought by years—knew every inch of her body, her perfume, the sound of her breathing. It was something that didn't go away when the divorce decree was delivered.

Her fingers trembled as she fixed his tie, and he realized she was probably thinking the same thing he was—he could see the pain and defeat in her eyes. When she finished the tie, she didn't step back, but rested the palms of her hands against him as though absorbing his heat through them.

A faint sigh slipped from her. "Sometimes I wish . . . God, Mike," she whispered, then stopped as tears filled her eyes.

He clenched his jaw, bracing himself, then said, "Ange. I wanted so much for us."

She tucked her fingers beneath his lapels and slid her hands downward, polished fingernails glittering. "I know, Michael." Her voice broke. "Why didn't we make it?"

"You know exactly why," he said, "but you're the mother of my children, and for their sake, I won't drag you down that path."

Angela's face turned pale, then hard. A footstep sounded on the stairs, and he looked up to see Mary Margaret on the shadowy landing, watching them. Jesus, how long had she been there?

He and Angela stepped apart. "My tie okay now?" he asked.

"Perfect," she said, blinking, swallowing.

"Ready, Princess?" he asked.

Mary Margaret hesitated, then came slowly down the stairs. As she stepped into the light of the foyer, Mike's heart seized with emotion. She looked incredible in a pretty green dress, her hair done, a glaze of pink lipstick on her mouth, her eyes shining. His little girl wasn't so little anymore.

"Sorry, ma'am," he said, forcing a grin. "I was just looking for my daughter."

She giggled. "Lame, Dad."

"You look absolutely beautiful," Angela said, holding the door for them. "Have a wonderful time. And spit out your bubble gum before you get on the dance floor, young lady."

Mike cocked out his arm. Mary Margaret didn't see it at first, so he nudged her with his elbow. She giggled again, then tucked her hand in and walked with him to the car.

She chattered like a magpie all the way to the Y, and Mike kept sneaking glances at her. Gone were the round baby cheeks, the chubby, dimpled hands. What a bundle of contradictions she was, blowing bubbles through her lipstick while admiring a fresh manicure.

He parked, and she forgot to wait for him to get the door for her. She spat her gum on the ground, then practically bounced with nervous excitement as they went inside to a candlelit room filled with giggling girls and their fathers, who'd skipped dinner to take them dancing and raise funds for the Y. Most of the men were busy helping themselves to little triangular sandwiches with the crusts trimmed off, heart-shaped cookies and paper cups of punch that turned everyone's teeth red. Paper hearts hung from the ceiling, and a mirrored ball spun like the slow blink of a lighthouse beam, casting diamonds across the milling crowd. A few brave pairs of dads and daughters were dancing to "Georgia on My Mind."

Mike and Mary Margaret stood at the edge of the room

for a minute, looking around. "That's Allie Monroe," she said, indicating a girl with curly hair. "She just got braces. And the one dancing right by the DJ is Kandy Procter. Her dad's related to that TV news lady. He's *bald*, isn't he?" Mary Margaret's face glowed, and she grabbed Mike's hand. "And everybody's checking you out. You're the bomb, Dad."

"You might change your mind after you see my dancing."

"We don't have to dance if you don't want to."

The music changed to "My Girl." Perfect. "Are you kidding?" he asked. "Come on, gorgeous. We're dancing."

Leading her out to the floor, he forced himself to remember the steps Sandy had taught him. Forward-left-back-right-forward. He hoped like hell he wouldn't blow it.

He didn't blow it. He and Mary Margaret danced as though they were old hands, never missing a beat. The way she looked up at him, with such wonder in her eyes, made him feel ten feet tall. He'd spent the past year nursing bitter regrets about all he'd lost; now it was time to move on. Moments like this reminded him that some things would always be a part of his heart, no matter what.

The song ended, and he twirled her under his arm like Sandy had shown him.

"I thought you said you didn't know how to dance," Mary Margaret said, grinning.

"Yeah, well, I took a few lessons."

"Really? From who?"

He could tell from the look on her face that she wished she hadn't asked. But she had. "From Sandra Winslow, as a matter of fact." He hesitated. "Do you have a problem with that?"

Mary Margaret hesitated, her face answering without

words. "I'm hungry, Dad." She headed for the refreshments table.

Fine, he thought, following her. She didn't want to hear it. She might have to one day, though. Since last weekend, when he and Sandy had all but ignited the boat, he'd thought a lot about what it would be like, having her as part of his life. He'd have to bring her together with his kids, and not just incidentally. He wondered if he could do that.

Chapter 25

On a blustery Saturday afternoon, Mary Margaret and Kevin scrambled out of the car at the Paradise docks. She almost forgot to say good-bye to her mother and Carmine as she grabbed her gear out of the trunk. It was a rare day of glorious sunshine, an unexpected gift in the middle of a drab winter. Her dad promised they could go boating if the weather held. She loved boating more than the Backstreet Boys, pepperoni pizza and field hockey combined.

Dad waited by the harbormaster's office. Zeke and Kevin raced across the parking lot toward each other and met in a joyous clash. Her mom went over to her dad and started talking while Carmine waited in the car, the engine running.

Mary Margaret could hear her mother rattling off the usual instructions. Make sure they wear their life jackets. Don't let Kevin drink anything with caffeine in it. They need to be home early tomorrow because both kids have homework. . . .

Mary Margaret thought about the way her parents had been the other day, when her dad came to pick her up for the Valentine's dance. Her heart had practically leaped out of her chest in wild, impossible hope. But the moment passed, and things went back to the way they were.

Her dad nodded his head and reassured her mom— they'd be fine, he wouldn't keep them too late tomorrow, he'd make sure they brushed their teeth. He always tried to be totally cooperative with her mom, because he didn't want to get a bad evaluation from the social worker who checked on them and wrote her stupid reports. Mary Margaret hated the fact that some custody evaluator kept tabs on them. It wasn't like they ever did anything wrong.

Mary Margaret remembered to turn and wave as her mother and Carmine drove away. Dad gave them both his special glad-to-see-you grin and said, "Ready, guys?"

"You betcha," Kevin yelled, and ran down the dock, his untied sneakers slapping on the planks. Zeke's toenails skittered on the wood as the dog kept pace.

Mary Margaret fell in step with her father. "Where are we going today?"

"I thought maybe the state park at Wetherill. What do you think?"

"Fine by me." She didn't really care. It was the getting there that mattered.

"We're having company today," he said, his voice very casual.

"What do you mean?"

"I've invited a friend along."

This was something new. Usually when her dad took them boating, it was just the three of them, motoring along through deep waters, exploring the islands and inlets of the coast. In summer, sometimes they'd go out as far as Block Island. But they'd never had company before. Back when her parents were together, her mother used to come along sometimes, making egg salad sandwiches in the galley and yelling at Kevin to keep his life jacket on.

"You mean someone else's going with us?"

"Yep. Grab that bag of ice, will you?"

She frowned, trying to figure out how big a deal this was to him. He was acting cool, but then, her dad always acted cool. They got to the *Fat Chance*. Mary Margaret froze when she saw who waited there, in the cockpit, holding on to an aluminum ladder.

"You guys remember Sandra Winslow," Dad said.

"Hiya." Kevin jumped into the boat. Zeke leaped in after him. Kevin grinned at Sandra, not at all bothered by her presence. Mary Margaret stared down at her hands. The Coral Candy polish from her Valentine's Day manicure was badly chipped. She should have rubbed it all off with nail polish remover.

"How are you, Kevin?" Sandra said. "This is my first time to go out on your dad's boat. You'll have to show me what to do."

"You need to wear a life jacket." Kevin puffed up with authority. "You have to keep it on at all times."

"I think I can handle that." She passed him a yellow life jacket from the stowage locker in the cockpit, and pulled out another for herself.

"That one's mine," Mary Margaret burst out, climbing into the boat. "I always wear that one."

"Liar," Kevin said. The traitor. "They're all the same."

"Shows how much you know," Mary Margaret said. "This is the one I always wear." She prepared herself for combat, but Sandra Winslow simply handed over the thick yellow jacket without saying a word.

"The straps are adjusted for her fat butt," Kevin said, doubling over with giggles.

Mary Margaret's temper seethed, but before she could react, Sandra grabbed Kevin by the vest and said, "So is this one adjusted for your big mouth?"

That made him giggle harder. Dad hadn't said a word, but she could feel him watching them. She couldn't tell what he was thinking.

Sandra put on a different vest, a mildewed one, clipping it over her green hooded sweatshirt. Dad paused to tighten the nylon belt around Sandra, and as he did, he leaned forward and murmured something in a low voice. When she looked up at him, there was no mistaking what was in her eyes. Mary Margaret had seen it a hundred times in a hundred other women—the librarian, the grocery checkout clerk, her earth science teacher . . . They all wanted her dad, and Sandra was now a member of that club.

Sandra stepped back and smiled, nice as you please. "It's good to see you again, Mary Margaret."

Mary Margaret didn't know what to say. Now she knew why Sandra was being so nice. It didn't have anything to do with her or Kevin, just her dad. She hated it when women were nice simply to impress him—it happened all the time. She was getting sick and tired of it.

She burned with resentment. This was her weekend with her dad. She didn't want to share him with anyone, even a famous writer.

"You want to help me fire up the engines?" he asked Kevin. Neither her dad nor her brother seemed to notice how quiet Mary Margaret was. She could feel Sandra watching her and wondered if *she* had noticed.

Dad went to the pilothouse and started the engines. They coughed to life, filling the air with diesel smoke. He acted like there was nothing unusual about having a stranger aboard. A stranger he called his friend. "We're ready to cast off," he said over the rumble of the engines. "Mary Margaret, can you get the bow lines?"

"Sure." She scrambled forward and untied the lines from the big cleats attached to the dock. She was an expert at this, and proud of it. She knew how to cast off and climb aboard without allowing the rope to foul or get wet. She did the port side first and then the starboard side, and finally the stern lines. Sandra stood there in the cockpit like useless ballast.

Within a few minutes, they were motoring through the narrow channel connecting Judith's Pond with the wide blue Atlantic. A fresh chill flavored the air. Kevin ran out of the pilothouse to wave at the fisherman monument, a ritual he'd followed since he was tiny. Dad remembered to sound the horn, another tradition. Zeke put his front feet on the gunwale and barked at the circling gulls.

They cleared the harbor and the land fell away behind them, the squat buildings turning Paradise into a toy town. When they got out into open seas, the boat picked up speed, slapping over the waves and leaving twin plumes of water in their wake. With the cold wind on her face and the sun in her eyes, Mary Margaret forgot her resentment for a few minutes. She loved being out on the water, looking back at the land, the trees and the tiny houses small and insignificant compared to the endless blue Atlantic.

Climbing to the foredeck, Kevin straddled the pulpit, his face pushed into the wind as he shouted random pirate phrases and lost himself in a world of make-believe. Sandra went into the pilothouse with Dad. They stood side by side, gazing out at the view ahead while her dad pointed at something on the horizon. They stood close together, their arms touching. Dad turned and bent his head to talk to

Sandra, and Mary Margaret didn't like the way it looked—private and intimate, a shared secret.

Turning her face into the sea breeze, she concentrated on the view of the lighthouse off the port side. The beacon bristled with antennas and radar equipment, but from a distance, it looked old-fashioned and postcard-pretty with a puffy bank of clouds behind it and the sun glaring on its polished windows.

Mary Margaret couldn't help spying on them. The next time she glanced at the pilothouse, she saw her dad take off his favorite cap and put it on Sandra's head, with the bill turned backward. They laughed together, and their hands brushed.

It was too much. As loudly as possible, Mary Margaret stomped along the deck and barged into the pilothouse. Kevin got cold, and took Zeke down the hatch to the saloon.

"Where are we going today, Dad?" she asked, her voice a little louder than normal.

"Lenny Carmichael put out a few traps at Purgatory Point. He said we could check them, help ourselves to whatever we find."

It felt cramped inside the pilothouse with the three of them there. But Mary Margaret refused to budge. "Good. Lenny's traps always have lobster in them. Lobster's my favorite food."

"We'll have it for supper if we're lucky."

"Can I steer?" she asked.

"Sure, Princess."

Stepping deliberately in between Dad and Sandra, she gripped the wheel. Sandra moved to the door. "I think I'll go inside and see what Kevin's up to."

She left in a cold swirl of wind. Mary Margaret was terrified her dad might leave, too. She was an experienced helmsmen and he often let her steer unsupervised. To her relief, he stayed by her side.

She didn't look at him, but kept her gaze fastened on the horizon. She scanned the waterway for any floating debris. Hitting a big log could be a disaster, and she had to make sure they didn't take a wave broadside.

"What's with the long face?" he asked.

So he'd noticed. Good. "It's the same face I always have."

He wasn't buying it. She knew that by the way he shook his head. "You're upset because Sandra's here."

"I thought it was going to be the three of us."

"I didn't think you'd mind."

Was he kidding? Of course she minded. But suddenly she felt selfish and petty admitting it. "Is she your girlfriend?"

Her dad was quiet for a long time. The motor burbled along at a steady clip. James Island rose to the north, a good distance away. The day was so clear she could see for miles.

"Well? Is she?" Mary Margaret prodded.

"Yeah, I guess she is. Does it bother you a lot?"

Of course it bothered her. A lot. It was bad enough her mother had Carmine; now her father had someone else as well. She should have known it was only a matter of time. Single dads dated. It was an ugly fact of life.

"Well?" he prodded.

Mary Margaret kept staring straight ahead. She nodded once, firmly.

"Sorry to hear that, Princess. It's pretty lonely out here for me and Zeke in between your visits. I like Sandra a lot, and I think she likes me." He stroked his hand down the back of her head, the way he'd done for as long as she could remember. "I like being with her. You know I love being with you. Let's just take it easy and see what happens."

He sounded so reasonable. *Too* reasonable. One thing about her dad—he took things seriously. She knew he wouldn't have brought Sandra if he didn't mean business.

Mary Margaret felt the surprise burn of tears. She hated the way everything kept changing. Nothing stayed the same. Until today, she'd been able to count on having Dad all to herself. Now that was over, too.

At least he didn't lecture her or advise her to be polite to Sandra. When her mother had introduced them to Carmine, she used to threaten Mary Margaret and Kevin, bribe them, warn them to be nice. Her dad did none of those things. He simply expected her to behave. She toyed with the idea of a low-grade tantrum. Maybe a bout of seasickness. But he'd see right through that, and no matter what she thought of Sandra, she couldn't stand disappointing her dad.

They didn't talk anymore, just motored along while the sun arched high overhead. The sea was a shifting mirror, mysterious and intensely dark blue, unusually calm for this time of year. After about half an hour, Dad pointed out the tagged markers of Lenny's lobster traps. There were three of them in a row, bobbing gently in the current.

"Go ahead and cut the engine," he instructed.

She did so, and in the sudden silence, could hear Kevin laughing in the salon below. The rat. He seemed to like Sandra just fine. The dork liked everybody. He was probably telling her all his favorite lame jokes, and she was probably forcing herself to laugh at them.

"Tell your brother and Sandra to come help with the traps," Dad said.

Mary Margaret clomped down to the cockpit and slid the door open. "Dad says come and help with the lobsters."

Without waiting for a reply, she turned away, leaving the door open. A moment later they both appeared, looking eager as kids on Christmas morning.

Dad dropped anchor and handed out thick rubber gloves. Mary Margaret grabbed the boat hook. Feeling superior because she had done this a hundred times, she snagged the bright orange buoy and dragged the trap toward the boat. She loved looking down into deep water. The rope seemed to disappear into dark eternity. When she tugged it upward, hand over hand, she savored the breathless anticipation of waiting to see what the trap held.

Working quickly and efficiently, she let the wet rope coil on the deck beside her. At last the igloo-shaped trap appeared, trailing seaweed and metal permit tags. Mary Margaret held her breath. Once the crate cleared the water, it grew heavy, but she wouldn't let the rope slip. Dad came and helped her haul it over the side. Eagerly, she flipped up the lid. Zeke went nuts, sniffing it.

The trap was empty, the bait reduced to broken skeletons of herring and beef spine. "Nothing."

"Can't win them all." Her dad opened a battered old ice chest. "Bait that trap again, and we'll lower it."

Mary Margaret hated baiting the trap. Chicken feet and old beef bones. It was completely disgusting. She turned to Sandra and spoke to her directly for the first time since they had pulled away from the dock. "You want to bait the trap?"

"Sure," Sandra said. "I've never done it before, so you'll have to show me."

"Easy as pie," Kevin piped up. "You just put some gross stuff from the bait bucket into the well of the trap."

Sandra eyed the bucket with suspicion. "Here goes nothing," she said, and flipped the lid. "You weren't kidding about how gross this is, Kevin."

Mary Margaret hoped she would act squeamish. Dad had no patience with squeamish people. Sandra didn't freak out, just kind of screwed up her face, reached her gloved hand in and grabbed some old bones and fish heads. Stuffing them into the bait well, she asked Mary Margaret, "Is this enough?"

"A little more," she couldn't help saying.

Sandra filled the well and Mary Margaret shoved the trap overboard. It made a big splash, then settled and sank into deep blue nothingness.

"That wasn't so bad," Sandra said. "Thanks for your help. You're a pro, Mary Margaret."

"Yeah, right," she muttered.

"You did a good job piloting the boat, too," Sandra added. "I've never gone out in a boat before."

"Really? That's pitiful."

"Never had the chance. I'm not a water person."

"I am," Mary Margaret said.

"I'm trying out for swim team this summer," Kevin piped up. "Do you like swimming?"

"Actually, I never learned how."

"You're kidding," Mary Margaret blurted out. Now that really *was* pitiful. She thought everyone knew how to swim. Her dad seemed as shocked as she felt. He stared at Sandra with narrowed eyes.

"I'll get the next trap." Kevin grabbed the hook. He took a long time reeling in the line.

This one was empty too, Mary Margaret saw with disappointment. They baited it again and sent it overboard.

"Let Sandra do the next one," Kevin said.

Mary Margaret sat back and watched with grim satisfaction as Sandra handled the rope clumsily, tangling it on the deck. It took her twice as long to bring the trap aboard, but when she set it down, they could hear the unmistakable clicking sound of a lobster. Zeke growled and shrank from the trap. Kevin jumped up and down in excitement. "Two of them," he yelled, punching the air. "Two great big ones. You caught two great big ones, Sandra."

"I take no credit for this," Sandra said, leaning down to peer into the trap. "They're pretty big, aren't they?"

"Did you know a one-pound lobster's seven years old?" Kevin said, going into his trivia-wonk mode.

"Did you know a female lobster can lay up to a hundred thousand eggs at a time?" Sandra asked.

How did she do that? Mary Margaret wondered. She must have a lint trap for a brain.

"Lobster for dinner," said Dad. "I was hoping for this."

Kevin was already playing his favorite game of holding the lobsters by their backs, stomping around the deck and making monster noises while the dog barked. He was such an idiot, but Sandra and Dad acted like he was hilarious.

Eventually, Kevin put a band around the crusher claw of each lobster so they wouldn't attack each other, and dumped them both into a big white plastic bucket.

"I'm cold," Mary Margaret said suddenly, tossing her wet gloves into the locker. "I'm going inside."

"How about you help me steer, buddy?" her dad asked Kevin, bringing up the anchor.

Sulking, Mary Margaret stood in the doorway of the stateroom she and Kevin shared when they stayed on the boat with their dad. The bunks were covered with Granny Malloy's quilts and a few stuffed animals, old and worn from years of loving. An overwhelming sadness swept through her. Since the divorce, she'd perfected the art of flinging herself on the bed. She could actually hover, suspended for a split second, before slamming facedown into a wailing pancake of despair.

Oh, she was tempted. But that would only make her look pathetic. Scowling, she went to the main saloon and flopped down in one of the cushioned chairs. Digging around her backpack, she took out the book she was reading. Then, to her horror, it dawned on her—she was reading a book by Sandy Babcock. She tried to hide it before Sandra saw, but she was too late. Sandra came in, slid the door shut and took off Dad's hat.

"So what do you think?"

"Don't know." Mary Margaret held the book at arm's length. "I just started reading this." Actually, she was nearly through, and really liked the book. She hated that she liked the book. She didn't want to like anything about Sandra Winslow.

The fact was, this one was her favorite so far, the story of a girl named Carly who had no father. She didn't even know who her father was. Carly's mother lived with another woman. They were lesbians, and the kids in school made Carly's life unbearable.

Mary Margaret was fascinated by the way Carly's feelings were described in the book—how scared she was sometimes; how embarrassed she got when people talked about her situation; how she was angry a lot of the time. How much she wanted to hate her mother's roommate, but ended up liking her instead.

Sandra was quiet as she fixed a pot of tea in the galley. When she came out, she had two mugs. "Your dad said you like cream and sugar."

Mary Margaret took a desultory sip of the tea, half wishing it didn't taste so good. Setting aside the cup, she picked at her nail polish, chipping a big section off her thumbnail. Then, even though she didn't want to speak to

Sandra, she said, "I don't understand how the girl in your story keeps going to school every day when the kids are so mean to her."

"It's not very fun for her, is it?"

"I don't see why you'd want to write a book about a girl everybody hates."

"If everyone loved her, it would be a pretty dull story, and I wouldn't be interested in telling it." She cradled her hands around her mug as if to warm them. "People with perfect lives are boring."

"But doesn't it get depressing to write about a girl going through all that?"

"Would you rather read about a perfect girl with a perfect life?" Sandra smiled at Mary Margaret's expression. "Trust me, that would be even *more* depressing."

"I hope her mom dumps the roommate and finds her real dad and marries him."

"Do you think that's going to happen?"

"That's what would happen if I had written this book."

"That's what's fun about writing. You can make things turn out any way you want. In my books, I always try to find the honest ending. The realistic one."

"You mean the depressing one."

"Sometimes. But there's always hope in the end. At least, I like to think there is."

Mary Margaret opened to a random page. It flipped her out to think that the words printed on this page had been written by somebody who was right in this room with her. She frowned. "How'd you think up all these words and paragraphs?"

Setting down her mug, Sandra rummaged around in a big tote bag and took out a dog-eared spiral notebook with an old-fashioned pen clipped to it. She opened the notebook to reveal page after page of cramped handwriting in turquoise ink. She showed Mary Margaret the pen, twirling it in her fingers. "That's a good question. Sometimes I think all the words and paragraphs are up inside this pen. And when I write, they just come out."

Mary Margaret's eyes widened. "I need to borrow that pen."

Sandra laughed. She had a nice laugh, and the silence that followed was a little more comfortable.

"So that's your next book?"

"Yep. Eventually I'll type it all up."

"So there's only that one copy? What if something happens to it?" Mary Margaret shuddered, thinking about the scene in *Little Women* when Amy burned Jo's manuscript. Never mind Beth dying; *that* was the scene that made Mary Margaret cry.

"Can you keep a secret?" asked Sandra. "I don't want people to know how weird I am."

Mary Margaret sat forward. "What do you mean?"

"Well, every night before I go to bed, I put the notebook in the freezer."

"The freezer?"

"So if the house burns down, the book won't be destroyed."

Weird times ten, thought Mary Margaret. "No wonder you don't want me to tell."

Sandra put away the pen and notebook and sat drinking her tea, watching the scenery go by out the window.

"I asked my dad if you were his girlfriend," Mary Margaret said, her mouth forgetting to clear things with her brain.

Sandra made a whooshing sound, as if she couldn't quite get the words out. "Who . . . who . . ." She cleared her throat, tried again. "And what did he say?"

So pathetic. She reminded Mary Margaret of a sixth-grade girl trying to find out if a certain boy liked her. Mary Margaret knew she had a chance to lie. She could say Dad had told her he didn't like Sandra at all. Mary Margaret could make her believe it, too. She could say he was only hanging out with Sandra because he needed that contract to work on her house. "What do you think he said?"

Once again, Sandra made that funny, breathy sound with her mouth, like she had to sneeze or something. Her face turned red, and the cords of her throat stood out.

"Are you okay?" Mary Margaret asked.

Sandra lowered her head and nodded. She stopped making the noise and took a few deep breaths. "Sorry about that," she said in her normal voice.

"Do you have, like, asthma or something?"

"Or something." A worried look must have crossed Mary Margaret's face because Sandra said, "I'm not sick. I have a stutter. Do you know what that is?"

Mary Margaret nodded, amazed. A stutter. Of course she knew what a stutter was. It was the most horrible of all speech impediments. The most noticeable. The easiest to make fun of. When she was in third grade, a boy named Peter had a stutter. Kids used to follow him around, chanting "Peter Peter P-p-pumpkin Eater," exaggerating the stutter until Peter started to cry. Mary Margaret tried to remember if she'd joined in the teasing.

"It doesn't happen too much anymore," Sandra said. "It was a pretty big problem when I was younger."

Mary Margaret kept thinking about Peter Peter Pumpkin Eater, and she could imagine just how big that problem had been. "So you're okay now."

"Most of the time. Sometimes I slip up and struggle with it, like I did a minute ago. When I get stressed out or nervous, I can get into trouble."

Mary Margaret felt sort of bad for making her nervous. It was weird, having an adult be so open about something as deathly humiliating as this. Most people would never admit to a kid that they were nervous. "How did you quit stuttering?"

"I never actually quit, just gained control. It took years of hard work and practice—mostly with my mom, and later with my—with other professionals. I had speech therapy and counseling. Growing older and gaining confidence helped. And I have a few strategies."

"What kind of strategies?"

"There's this thing I do with my diaphragm. And I use a lot of substitutions. For example, I can never pick up the phone and say, 'Hello.' That's one of my worst problem words."

Fascination tightened Mary Margaret's stomach, the way it did when she watched nature shows about snakes on the Learning Channel. "So what do you say?"

"Usually 'Yes, hello.' Or 'This is Sandra.' My therapist and I had to figure out where the problems were likely to come up, and how I could talk my way around them."

Mary Margaret was fascinated. It was like interviewing someone who had survived a plane crash or a tornado. It made her seem unique and strong. "Is that why you became a writer, because you didn't like to talk?"

"I'm sure it's a big part of it. I had plenty to say, but the stuttering blocked me from saying it. So I got into the habit of putting my thoughts and feelings on paper. You're pretty smart to make that connection."

"I'd like to write, someday," Mary Margaret said. The wish just popped out. As soon as it did, she wanted to reel the words back in, clap a hand over her mouth. It was the second-most private of all her yearnings, and she had confessed it to this person she wasn't even supposed to like. What was the matter with her?

"Why not today?" Sandra asked.

Mary Margaret shrugged uncomfortably. "I never know what to say. Or why I'm writing it down in the first place."

"Tell you what." She dug around in the totebag again. "Take this notebook—I always carry a spare." She passed it to Mary Margaret. "You can write anything in it you want."

The notebook felt unexpectedly weighty in Mary Margaret's hands. She opened it, smoothed her hands over the vast blank pages. "I wouldn't know what to write."

"Trust me, it'll come to you. When I don't know what to write, I make a list."

"A list of Ten Things." Mary Margaret remembered the notes stuck to her refrigerator.

Sandra paged through her own writings. "Ten Famous People I'd Love to Meet . . . Ten Signs of Agoraphobia . . ." Her face reddened.

"Ten Ways to Get Out of P.E. Class," Mary Margaret said.

"Exactly. You can share your writing with someone, like a letter, or keep it to yourself. Up to you. You might enjoy it. If you're lucky, you'll discover that you hate it." She grinned and winked. "Writers like to pretend they're deeply tortured at all times, but really, writing's great fun. I think, in my case, it kept me from going bonkers."

"It did?"

"Well, that and some intensive speech therapy."

Talking to Sandra wasn't like talking to a grown-up, but a regular person. Maybe that was why the next thing popped out: "I haven't started my period yet."

She wanted to die, completely die.

But Sandra didn't laugh or get embarrassed or anything. She said, "I bet a lot of your friends have started."

"All of them, I swear. Every single one."

"You probably feel as though they belong to some secret club you can't be part of."

"*Yes.*" How had she known?

"Trust me, I know the feeling. Mary Margaret, your
time will come. So far, no healthy, normal girl has escaped.
It's one of those things that happens in its own time. I
know that doesn't help, though."

But it did, sort of, the same way it seemed to help
when Sandra admitted the stuttering. "My mom says I
should be grateful, because getting your period is a pain."

"Your mom's right."

"I guess." She handed back the pen. "My mom and I
fight a lot, sometimes." As soon as she said the words, she
wished she could reel them back in. She shouldn't be talking about her mom behind her back.

Sandra simply nodded. "I used to argue with my mom,
too. Still do, sometimes, but we always forgive each
other." She hesitated, then said, "She and my dad split up
a few weeks ago."

Mary Margaret was stunned. "Really?"

"Uh-huh."

"Do you totally hate it?"

"I completely, totally hate it."

The connection between them strengthened. Then
Mary Margaret asked, "How would you feel if your dad
had a girlfriend?"

"It would drive me crazy. I'm supposed to say that it's
his life, and his happiness, but that's a lie. I want them to
be together." She sighed. "But it's not up to me."

They sat together in silence until Sandra buckled on
her life jacket. "I think I'll go outside and see the sights."

"Me, too."

The sun was high when they stepped out on deck.

Zeke balanced his front paws on the big locker, sniffing the air while the wind ran through his curly, dirty fur. Mary Margaret patted him on the head, and he squirmed and wagged his tail. "Did you know he's a real poodle?"

"I've heard that rumor."

"He's got papers and everything. But my dad never gives him a bath. I bet he'd look awesome with a poodle haircut."

"Maybe we could bathe him sometime."

"Okay. Could we—" Mary Margaret stopped talking.

Sandra stumbled back against the stern rail and was hanging on with both hands. Her face went completely white as she stared at a tall, arched highway bridge up ahead.

"Are you okay?" Mary Margaret asked. When Sandra didn't answer, Mary Margaret yelled, "Hey, Dad, I think Sandra's going to be sick!"

He cut the engine immediately. He and Kevin came out of the pilothouse. Bracing both arms on the ladder, he jumped down and asked her, "Are you all right?"

Sandra breathed hard and fast, not the way she did when she stuttered, but in a different, panicky way. "That bridge," she said. "The b-bridge up ahead. It's the Sequonset Bridge, isn't it?"

Dad started to say *shit* but he didn't say it all the way. "Sandy, I'm sorry," he said. "I didn't think."

Mary Margaret was confused. Why were they so upset about a bridge?

Dad put his arm around Sandra.

"I'll be all right," she said. "I have to drive across the bridge a lot. But I've never seen it from this perspective."

"What happened?" Kevin asked.

"Don't be nosy," Dad said.

Sandra sent him an unreadable look, then turned to

Kevin. "About a year ago, I had a bad accident on the bridge. The car I was driving went over it, into the water. My husband was with me, and he was killed in the crash."

"Whoa," Kevin said under his breath. Mary Margaret rarely agreed with her brother, but she did now. *Whoa*. Then she couldn't help herself. She grabbed Sandra's hand and squeezed it hard.

"Mary Margaret, how about you steer for a while," Dad said. "We should be heading back to port pretty soon, anyway."

She restarted the engine and turned west, then south, watching their position in the GPS. Her dad kept his arm around Sandra, and she leaned against him, looking tired. Mary Margaret thought about the accident on the bridge. How weird to think that Sandra had been involved in such a horrible thing.

"Hey, Dad," Kevin said. "Show us some places where you used to play when you were our age." He seemed desperate to put the bridge behind him, and hearing about when their dad was little was one of Kevin's favorite things. Since Dad had moved back to Paradise, he kept remembering funny stories to tell them.

"See that little cove?" Dad pointed at the shore, where it was fringed with bracken between jutting rocks. "My friends and I used to have a hideout there. It's an old abandoned boathouse."

"Can we go see it?" Kevin asked, bouncing up and down. "Can we, Dad? Please."

Dad glanced down at Sandra, who nodded. "I guess we have time," he said. "It could be gone now. It's been years."

They anchored the boat and lowered the dory. All four of them crammed in, and Zeke leaped into Sandra's lap. Mary Margaret and Kevin each took an oar and rowed to shore. Stirred by the waves, the loose rocks on the beach made a sound like beads poured out of a bag. Dad showed them where to tie up. The boathouse was still standing, its roof sagging and covered with green moss, abandoned and gloomy as a haunted mansion.

"This is so cool," Mary Margaret said, trying to picture her dad as a kid, messing around in this very spot.

"It's still in good shape," her dad said. "It's a pretty protected cove."

The boat ramp had collapsed, and the storm cloth covering the opening hung down, torn and tattered and green with slime.

"Can we get out and look around?" Kevin asked.

"Sure. If you don't mind getting your feet wet."

Mary Margaret and Kevin both stripped off their shoes and socks and rolled up their pant legs.

"Geez! It's freezing!" Kevin howled as he stepped into the water. He wasn't kidding. Mary Margaret felt her feet turning blue as she staggered up the beach. Zeke barked his head off, finally hit the water with a splat and scrambled up to shore. He immediately shook off, lifted his leg, then started running around, sniffing like crazy.

"Come on, Dad," Kevin hollered, stuffing his feet back into his sneakers. "Come on, Sandra!"

Dad didn't look too happy about wading through the frigid water, but he and Sandra came ashore, holding hands.

"So this is where you and your friends used to hang out," she said.

He got a faraway look in his eyes as he regarded the boathouse. "Sometimes," he said. "Last time I came here was prom night, 1982."

"Why would anyone come here on prom night?" Kevin asked.

"You'll figure it out when you get older."

"What did you use to do?" Kevin said. "I bet you did bad stuff!"

Her dad grinned. "Stupid stuff."

"Did you smoke cigarettes and drink beer?" Kevin wanted to know. "Did you bring girls here?"

"That's for me to know and you to find out." Dad and Sandra looked at each other, their mouths tight like they were trying not to laugh.

Zeke went inside first, skittering around, sniffing like a professional hound dog. He gave a couple of short, loud barks.

Kevin ran after him, thumping around in the creaky wooden structure. "Yech," he called. "Spiderwebs."

The barnacle-crusted wood felt rotten and squishy beneath their feet as they stepped into gloomy emptiness. Zeke scrabbled around, growling. The fur on the back of his neck bristled, and Mary Margaret figured he'd sniffed out a critter of some sort.

She tried to picture her dad here, hanging out with his friends. She'd seen pictures of him from high school—he'd been a jock with big shoulders and a friendly smile, the kind who walked through the halls without a care in the world, while every dork and dweeb in the school wondered how to be exactly like him. She knew, because things in school never really changed. She knew, because she was one of those dorks, wishing she could be like the popular kids.

She wondered why she never seemed to fit into the "in" crowd, and did her dad know? Was he ashamed of her because she wasn't popular and good at sports? Oh, how she wanted to be. All the cool girls played tennis or became cheerleaders. The jocks all seemed to go everywhere together in a big, giggling nebula. Sometimes, she imagined herself a part of them, and it was like being in a movie—glorious, fun, with a theme song playing in the background.

"Look at all this stuff carved in the wall." Kevin poked a finger at a crude heart surrounding the initials "*LC + GV*" and the message, "*2-nite and 4-ever.*" "What's that supposed to mean?"

Mary Margaret had a pretty good idea, but she pretended she didn't.

"Hey, *MPM*—is that you, Dad?" Kevin demanded. He didn't seem to notice that no one had answered his previous question.

Dad got a faraway look in his eyes. "I think it probably was, a long time ago." He wobbled an old wooden railing with his hand. "There used to be a fishing dory in here. Nobody knew who it belonged to, so my friends and I named it the *Robert Chance*, and we'd take it out sometimes. We almost drowned in a storm once."

"Why the *Robert Chance*?" asked Mary Margaret.

"He was a local fisherman from down at the Galilee docks in the thirties, right after the Great Depression. They say he went out for bluefish one day, and was never seen again, so everyone assumed he drowned. The name became famous because, years after he was gone, locals kept hearing about Robert Chance popping up all over the world—on Prince Edward Isle, in Chicago, California . . . but no one ever actually saw him again."

Sandra winced, like someone had poked her.

"Anyway, it's just a story. We'd better weigh anchor," Dad said after a few minutes. "We've got fresh lobster to fix for dinner."

They left the boathouse. Mary Margaret couldn't help noticing that her dad stayed back for a minute, studying the carvings on the wall.

Journal Entry—February 16—Saturday

Ten Things I Worry About

1. Finishing my History Day project.
2. Getting fat on lobster with butter sauce.
3. The pimple on my forehead.
4. Getting my period during school.
5. Getting my period in the middle of the night.
6. Getting my period when I'm staying with Dad.
7. Not getting my period, ever—

"Almost time for lights-out, Princess," Dad whispered from the doorway.

With a guilty start, Mary Margaret slid her new notebook under the quilt of the upper bunk. "It's the weekend," she whispered back, propping herself on her elbow. In the snug stateroom, her head nearly touched the ceiling. "Lights-out doesn't apply."

"Yeah?" He leaned his shoulder against the edge of the door. "Since when?"

Since Mom and Carmine said I was big enough to choose my own bedtime. She bit her lip, refusing to say it aloud. The family counselor said it was a bad idea to compare house rules, and sometimes Ms. Birkenstocks-and-Yanni was right.

"Since I'm almost thirteen," she said.

He shook his head. "When'd that happen? Seems like I was just reading you Babar books yesterday." Ducking his head, he stepped into the room and bent low, gently disengaging Kevin's hands from the latest Harry Potter adventure. Her brother stayed fast asleep, his arm encircling a blissful Zeke.

"Okay, so try to get some sleep," he said, cupping his

hand over her head in a way that made her inexplicably sad. "Your mom wants you home early tomorrow."

"All right. Can I just finish my book?"

"Sandy's book."

"Uh-huh."

"So what do you think? Of her, not the book."

Mary Margaret twirled a finger in her hair. "She's okay, I guess." Even though she had a million other thoughts about Sandra, she refused to say another word. But her father kept watching her, waiting, so she finally said, "I can't like somebody just because she's your girl-friend, Dad."

A look of hurt shadowed his face, and Mary Margaret wanted to cry. She hated it that her father could be hurt. She wanted him to be invincible. Taking a deep breath, she said, "She writes good books, and she's sort of weird, and I guess I like her okay."

He bent down, kissed her forehead. "You're sort of weird yourself," he whispered. "But I like you okay."

"Night, Daddy-O."

"Night, Princess. I love you."

He let her keep the dim reading light on, and she opened Sandra's book. She could hear her father in the saloon, his computer modem crackling as he went on-line. Before falling asleep, she wondered what he was searching for.

Chapter 26

On Sunday evening, Mike went to the house on Blue Moon Beach. By now, the work on the old place had progressed far enough to be obvious even to the untrained eye. The dormers and sagging porch were now as straight as the horizon; a landscaping crew had begun cleaning out and pruning the beds. Shutters had been carted off for refinishing; the ghastly corrugated tin carport was gone. The house resembled an accident victim who was halfway on the mend.

As he got out of the truck, holding the door for Zeke, he wondered who would live here when Sandra was gone. A young family, kids running around in the yard and leaping over the dunes? An older couple, wearing knitted mufflers, walking arm in arm on the beach? A pair of yuppies, installing a Sub-Zero fridge and Viking range to fix gourmet meals for their dinner parties?

He adjusted the bill of his cap, trying not to think so hard. He concentrated on checking the property lines, comparing the tiny flag markers with the plat information on his clipboard. Nothing seemed to match, but that didn't surprise him. The shifting dunes and wild vegetation had a will of their own. No one had bothered with the boundaries here since a survey done in the 1920s.

Sandra wasn't expecting him; they hadn't learned the rhythms and patterns of each other's lives—not yet. He didn't know how he fit into her life, or she into his. He didn't even know if "fitting together" was what they were after. Every time one of them drew a line, the other seemed to push at it until it was in a different place.

Initially, their functional working relationship had been clear—he was the contractor; she was the client. But their lives kept interweaving back and forth across the lines. She had vaulted over it completely when she'd barged into his boat . . . and then into his arms.

He'd loved every single moment of that.

He kept trying to tell himself that the long absence of a woman from his life accounted for his intense, ravenous need for her. But the fact was, his feelings grew and strengthened with each passing day. And he knew those feelings wouldn't simply disappear when she left Paradise. It was a little scary, finding out at this stage of his life that he could love with such abandon. He'd always blamed Angela for the divorce, but maybe she hadn't been the only problem. With Angela, he had never felt the things he felt for Sandra, the fierce passion, the consuming tenderness, the mind-blowing lust.

Angela, with uncanny instinct, already knew something was going on, something was different; she'd said nothing when she picked up the kids, but he'd read it in her face. His ex-wife saw something powerful happening, and he could tell it bothered her. She didn't want him to have anyone else, and it would make her insane to realize how hard he'd fallen for Sandra—it scared her, somehow.

He didn't give a shit about Ange's opinion, but he'd been nervous about bringing Sandy together with his kids. Still was. Mary Margaret and Kevin owned his heart, and he wasn't sure how a woman fit into the picture. He tried to pretend it wasn't a crucial issue for him. But it was. It would kill him to lose Sandy now, but he had to face facts. She was set on leaving, and he had to stay close to his kids.

Despite their new intimacy, some boundaries remained intact. It went without saying that Sandra would not stay on the boat when Mike's kids were there. Nor had she gone with him to drive Mary Margaret and Kevin back to their mother in Newport. There was an unwritten code about this sort of thing. Even Carmine respected the invisible borders when it came to the kids. He knew Mike would break his face if he messed with them.

Mike made some notes for the survey crew that was scheduled to come in the morning, then went and knocked at the door. He was about to push past another barrier. She would resist, of course. She might even tell him to get lost. But then again, she might draw even closer to him.

She didn't answer the door. He swore under his breath and dug in his pocket for his key. Zeke let out a bark. At the edge of the dunes, he imitated an experienced pointer, one paw raised, nose and tail aimed like the ends of a weather vane.

Mike never knew whether or not to trust the mutt's instincts. He was as likely to unearth a dead scrod as a lost child.

He went around to the beach side of the house, shading his eyes against the glare of sunset reflected on the water. With the light behind him, his shadow fell long across the rustling yellow salt grass.

He spotted Sandra walking along the beach in the distance. She made a solitary figure on the wide stretch of sand littered with wrack and debris, her slender silhouette black against a brilliant sky. She couldn't know it, but the picture she made, so small against an overpowering backdrop of nature, etched itself on his soul—Sandy against the world. All alone, not an ally in sight. He wondered how she'd managed to survive a whole year of being thrust away to this remote spot. No matter what else happened, he would always remember her like this—isolated, her shadow covering the path in front of her.

The beach smelled of salt and rot and air so cold it cut the lungs. Zeke's sharp bark alerted her, and she stopped walking while Mike jogged to catch up. She didn't smile, didn't speak. He couldn't tell why. Maybe she sensed he was going to a place in her life where he was not welcome, a place she kept walled off and wholly to herself.

She looked lonely and filled with pain and still so beautiful it made his heart hurt to look at her. He didn't say anything, but took her by the shoulders and kissed her— harder and with more possession than he'd intended. She surrendered to him with a shudder that ran the entire length of her body. She fit against him as though molded by nature to occupy that space as a permanent resident.

He curved his hand over her head, stroking her cold, smooth hair. "Hey," he said, "I got worried when you didn't answer the door."

"I missed you," she said.

"Ditto." Since Thursday night, they had only been apart maybe sixteen hours, but it felt ten times that long. His bunk on the boat already held her shape and her scent. The pillow had a hollow in it where her head had lain.

"I didn't know whether to call you or not," she said, shivering. "So I didn't."

"You should have." He bent and gathered a fistful of driftwood. It was easy to find this time of year, when the beaches were deserted and undisturbed by foraging tourists. The smooth pieces were bleached by the cleansing sea, dried by the steadily blowing wind. He arranged the firewood in the lee of an old log, then searched his jacket pockets for a book of matches. "I never have a match on me since I quit smoking," he said.

"When did you ever smoke, Malloy?"

"Truth?"

"Truth."

"In 1980. Same year I learned to drink beer. The habit didn't stick with me, though."

"Why not?"

His search finally yielded a bent cardboard matchbook from Gloria Carmichael's Shrimp Shack. "Blame it on a woman."

"Linda Lipschitz."

He grinned, surprised she remembered that conversation. "She couldn't stand the smell, so I gave it up."

He went down on one knee and struck a match, cupping his hand around it, touching the flame to a crumpled bit of paper, then nurturing it along until the twigs caught and snapped. Within a few minutes, a good blaze took hold.

Sandra sat cross-legged on the sand, stretching her hands out to the fire. The orange flames painted her face with mysterious color.

"Impressive, Malloy," she said. "I should award you a merit badge or something."

He sat next to her and slid his hand inside her jacket. Her yielding flesh was warm and vital beneath a soft sweater. "I've got a better idea," he said, and whispered an explicit suggestion in her ear.

She nestled her head on his shoulder. "That's supposed to cheer me up?"

"It cheers *me* up." But he was here to talk, not seduce her, and so he kissed the top of her head and removed his hand from her jacket.

Her hand went inside his pocket and found his. "I had a good time with your kids."

"Yeah? I was a little worried about Mary Margaret—she acted sort of prickly."

"This surprises you?"

"Hell, yes. The kid has her moods, but I never saw her act rude before. I wasn't sure whether I should ignore her or yell at her."

"Did you ever bring a woman out on the boat with you before?"

"Other than Angela, no."

"As Mary Margaret would say—*duh*. You're her hero. She's used to having you all to herself. What's she going to think when you bring a stranger onto her turf?"

"Sounds like you know her better than I do."

"No, I see her more clearly. She's a great kid, but she can't be great all the time."

"Kevin is. He's great all the time. It worries me."

"Wait a minute. You're worried because your kid is great?"

"He's too good to be true. I keep thinking that he's holding in his true feelings, and one day his head will explode."

"You're a good dad, Malloy. I like the way you worry."

"You give strange compliments."

She lifted her head from his shoulder. "I'm a strange person."

"Mary Margaret seemed a lot more friendly in the afternoon. Whatever you said made her warm up to you."

"You think?"

"Yeah. So what did you say?"

She hesitated. "We talked about my books. Writing. A few other things."

"What—"

"Female things. And if you keep pushing me for specifics, I swear I will tell you, word for word, exactly what was said." She took her hand out of his pocket.

Mike knew a warning when he heard one. "Yeah, okay." He fed another stick to the fire. Twilight had turned the sky deep purple, and the flames from the driftwood spread a soft fall of firelight on the sand. The heat formed a cocoon without walls, enclosing them in gold and shadow.

"Sandy, there's something I have to ask you," he said, pushing the words out.

She straddled the log to face him. Her eyes grew wide and wary in the fluttering light. "Why did I just feel the whole world shift?"

"You've got good instincts, maybe." It was true. There had always been subtext between them, from the first moment he'd seen her. Beneath the words they spoke ran a separate current of meaning. The current was strong now. She picked it up like a radar receiver. Moving away from him, she looped her arms around her drawn-up knees.

He turned to face her directly. "I want you to tell me what happened the night Victor died."

"No." Her reply was as swift and vicious as a slap.

Mike had been slapped before. So he simply sat and watched her. "Sandy," he said at length. "Talk to me."

"Christ, Malloy, do you have something against my feeling happy? I actually had a good day."

"Right up until you saw the bridge and had a panic attack."

Her look was poison. "Maybe it's your job to make sure my misery index didn't fall too low."

"You know better than that." All day long he'd been debating with himself about how to approach this. He couldn't say he had a hunch—she'd never buy it. He wasn't even sure he bought it. But in the boathouse yesterday, the weirdest feeling had swept over him, as insubstantial as cobwebs, but he couldn't stop thinking about it. This was hard, but he needed to do it, to uncover the past and convince her it was all right to stay in Paradise.

He knew in his gut that Sandra's story of that night was incomplete. She hadn't lied, but her monosyllabic replies to the death investigator's interrogations hid much more than they revealed. "I know you've been over this before, but I want you to tell me what happened," he said.

"I don't talk about it, Malloy. Not even to you."

"Why not?"

"Because it won't change anything."

"He used to be my best friend. I want to know what happened. Especially since I've gone crazy for you—"

"You have?"

He spread his hands. "What, you didn't notice?"

She slipped her arms around his neck. "That's the sweetest thing anyone's ever said to me."

"You need to meet more people, then."

"Crazy for me," she repeated, sitting back to study him. "Really?"

He thought of the things they had done in the bow of the boat, the ways he'd touched her, the places she'd taken his heart. "Hell, yes. That's why I want you to talk about the accident. That night changed your life."

"Weren't you listening at all? I don't talk about it. To anyone. Ever."

"Maybe you should." He caught her face in both his hands. "Please."

She blinked fast, as if she had sand in her eye. "I don't see the point."

He lowered his hands to capture hers and tucked them deep into her jacket pockets. "Tell me, Sandy. Tell me about that night."

"Why is this so important to you?"

It was a question he'd asked himself dozens of times. "Because *you're* important to me. I need to know because what happened that night is part of you."

She inhaled deeply, a diver about to take the plunge. "It was a black tie gala at the Newport Marina," she said. "A political fund-raiser, what else?"

"You and Victor attended a lot of those." This was nothing new, but he would let her start slowly, build to the critical point.

"He spent more time raising money than he did drafting legislation. It's the name of the game in politics. He who has the biggest war chest wins. Anyway, this was a major party bash. The Winslows attended, of course—they sponsored a table for ex-POWs and one for breast cancer survivors. We could always count on Victor's folks to make an appearance and bring in heavy donors. They were a big part of his success. He was a wonderful politician but I won't pretend his charisma alone could have carried him.

"That night, he drank more than usual." She flashed Mike a look. "The stress of the job, the pressure to raise funds for the next campaign, his mother's health. There was plenty for him to worry about."

"Everybody has worries about work and family. It doesn't drive us all to drink. Why Victor? And why that moment?"

"His drinking wasn't obvious. He made it through the speech just fine."

Mike noticed that she hadn't addressed his question.

"Afterward," she said, "he seemed tense, short-tempered. I asked him to dance. He relaxed, made a joke. Then I said something stupid, and it set him off."

Interesting choice of words, thought Mike. *Set him off.* "What did you say?"

"A throwaway remark. I don't even remember it. I'd been pretty up front about wanting kids, and he seemed on board with the idea. So I said something about getting busy in that department. I wanted a baby so badly, and I was out of patience. My mistake was in discussing it when he obviously had other matters on his mind. But that night I—I brought up the subject in a way I never had before. I don't know, maybe I gave him an ultimatum, I don't really remember. He . . . sort of made a scene. It was so strange, so unlike him. He walked away from me on the dance floor. I was totally humiliated. Not our finest moment."

She poked a dry stick into the heart of the fire, letting blue flames curl around the end. "It was so public. And he was always painfully conscious of appearances. But that night he was—I don't know—wild. Everyone was staring at me. I didn't know what to do. So I left. I intended to drive myself home." She pulled the stick from the fire, the flaming tip vivid against the gathering night. "He followed me out to the parking lot and . . ." She hesitated.

Mike waited, not sure whether she was sorting out her thoughts or hesitating over one of her "problem" words. Maybe it was all in his head, but he sensed some indefinable difference in the quality of her brief silence. Weightiness. Calculation, maybe.

"He got in the car with me."

"And you let him."

"I was furious. Con-confused. But what else could I have done? He was my husband, and he needed to get home, too." She paused as if to gather her thoughts. "I live through that accident a dozen times a day, and in my nightmares when I sleep. It was sleeting that night. Windy. The anemometer at the bridge recorded gusts of up to forty miles per hour. Victor and I were still . . . arguing in the car."

"Arguing about what?"

She was silent for a long time. Inside her pockets, he gently squeezed her hands. She looked at him, and her eyes were drenched in despair. Then she dropped her head to stare at the fire. "The storm grew worse, and Victor didn't seem to pay attention or care that my driving was erratic, dangerous. On the bridge, I lost control."

"Why?"

She watched a spark drift upward from the heart of the fire. "I don't know. It was icy. Black ice."

He tried to picture the scene—were they yelling? Did Victor grab for her? Christ, did he strike her? "Were you drunk?"

"No. I'd had a glass of champagne at the party. That's it. Do you need to see my blood alcohol test from that night? There is one, I assure you. They did every possible test on me."

"You're an experienced driver. You know that road. I'm trying to figure out what made you go off the bridge."

"I was distracted by the quarrel, the car hit a slippery patch on the bridge. It smashed right through the rail." Finally she looked back at him with tortured eyes. "The airbag went off. I remember the noise it made, a popping sound, like a firecracker, followed by a loud hiss. It was huge, and sort of blasted me against the seat. I remember a spray of white powder—and then, nothing. The car went into the water, but I have no memory of that. The next thing I remember was waking up in the hospital."

"The emergency medical service found you on the shore."

Suspicion flashed in her eyes. "You've been doing your homework."

"You don't recall escaping the car."

"The doctor who examined me said people who suffer trauma frequently have gaps in their memory. Sometimes the truth never does fill in the blanks. According to the death investigator, I exited the car via the windshield and made it to shore."

"Wearing an evening gown, a long coat and high heels."

"My shoes were off. And no, I don't recall taking them off. They've never been found. But I'm sure you know that, since you obviously researched this."

"What was Victor wearing?"

"A tux."

"What did he carry in his pockets?"

"Back off, Malloy. This is absurd."

He ignored her resentment and changed tack. "Did you tell anyone you can't swim?"

Her expression didn't change. "Nobody asked."

"And you didn't think to point it out?"

"It was one of those adrenaline-induced feats of desperation. People can do the impossible when it's a matter of life and death."

"Even survive in frigid water."

"Yes."

"Amazing."

"But not unheard of. The crime investigators explained that. Under the circumstances, swimming wasn't an option even for an expert. If you had read the reports, you would understand."

"Victor's blood was found on your clothes."

"Traces of it. The assumption being that he was injured in the crash, and bloodstains don't necessarily wash out in seawater."

"And the bullet holes?"

"An unsolved mystery. N-neither Victor nor I owned a gun."

He noticed something about her. Sometimes she stammered over her words when she lied. She had stammered twice during this conversation. Once when she described their quarrel, and just now, about the gun.

Chapter 27

Ten Places to Go After I Sell the House

~~*1. Manhattan*~~
~~*2. Big Sur*~~
~~*3. Cape Cod*~~
~~*4. The Caribbean*~~

Sandra gave up. She wanted to leave, but realized she couldn't escape herself. Some days, she woke up, unsure even of who she was, unable to decide what she wanted to do. Deep in her heart, she knew she and Mike were headed for trouble. Raging hormones could only take them so far. At some point, they'd have to engage on a deeper level—or disengage.

But she could never quite seem to make herself do it. At first, she'd tried to ignore the strange electricity leaping between them, but finally gave in to the attraction. She had been giving in ever since that first stormy night aboard his boat. His unconscious, primal magnetism overrode her will every time. Her need for him turned into a force more pow-

erful than common sense or fear or even the implacable re-
luctance of her own uncertain heart.

As time passed, she felt more tightly bound to the
house on Blue Moon Beach when she should be letting go.
Despite her determination to move away, she sensed the
tug of a place she wanted to call home. Walking through
the freshly plastered front parlor, she chafed with irritation.
Maybe he didn't mean to, maybe he did, but Mike Malloy
opened her eyes to what she wanted—and she wasn't particularly happy to know that she secretly yearned to stay.

But her whole world was at stake—her life, her future.
Even as she clung to Mike, everything seemed to be slipping away or gone. Home, community, her parents' marriage, the life she thought she'd had with Victor. Stinging
flashes of guilt warned her that the illicit affair with Malloy was wrong and no doubt headed for disaster. He
seemed too interested in the past, and all she wanted was
to leave it behind.

On impulse, she drove to Providence to see her father.
Since her mother had left, she'd hardly heard a word out of
him; he'd never been big on sharing his feelings. It was
impossible to gauge how he was handling the breakup with
her mother. Perhaps it was like grieving for a death. Someone who had been with him for years was suddenly gone to
a place where he couldn't see her, touch her, hear her
singing in the shower, ask her where the coffee filters
were.

And would he talk to his daughter about it? He'd always been emotionally stiff, though his love for her had
run like a steady stream through her life. She had vivid
memories of him sitting with her when she was very small,
practicing the breathing exercises her speech therapist recommended. He made a game of the tedious process, re-
warding progress with M&M's and gold stars on a chart. In

the spring when she was five, he'd put her on a brand-new bike, pretending not to hear her sputters of apprehension. He kept his hand at the back of her bike seat, trotting along beside her as she learned to ride the two-wheeler. At some point, he let go, but stayed next to her so she wouldn't realize she was on her own.

When she went away to college, he had been quietly bereft but encouraging. And when she married Victor, he'd had little to say. "He'll look after you," her father had said, but she wondered if it was hope rather than certainty. After the accident, he and her mother had sat vigil at her hospital bed. Somehow, he'd always been *there,* but he was not always present in the way she needed him to be. Not that it was his fault. She didn't know what she needed; why should he?

She parked in front of the little bungalow on the street where she'd lived until she was eighteen. It was a small, unassuming neighborhood of arching trees whose roots had heaved up the sidewalks, brick houses hunched atop postage-stamp yards, cars that didn't fit into one-car garages built in the forties.

The front steps of her father's house needed sweeping, and the mailbox overflowed with catalogs, flyers, a bill or two. She grabbed the mail and knocked at the door. No answer. Maybe she should have called first. But his car was in the driveway, and he never walked anywhere.

What if he'd fallen? she thought in sudden panic. What if he was sick? Her hand shaking, she took out the house key she had carried since she'd turned ten years old and was deemed responsible enough to have a key of her own. She used to wear it on a string around her neck.

She let herself in and stood in the dim living room. The blinds were drawn, and a faint musty smell of neglect hung like dust motes in the air.

"Dad?" she called. "Dad, it's me." She set the mail on the hall table and headed toward the back of the house. Maybe he was in the shop attached to the garage where he often went to tinker with his golf clubs or fishing lures.

"Dad," she called again.

Then she heard his voice in the study upstairs. Exhaling a sigh of relief, she went to find him. The door was ajar, and she saw him wearing headphones and sitting at the computer, his back to her.

Curious, she watched him for a moment. A picture of a tapestry suitcase appeared on the screen, and her father said, "*La maleta.*" A pause. The picture changed to an umbrella and he said, "*Un paraguas.*"

Sandra's heart melted. His accent was terrible, but he held himself with such tense concentration and spoke so earnestly that she couldn't help smiling. Ah, Dad, she thought. I hope it's not too late for you.

Finally, when the picture changed to a passenger train, she stepped into the room and touched his shoulder. "Hey, Dad—"

He jumped violently, nearly falling out of the chair. "Jesus, Sandra." He ripped off the headphones. "You almost gave me a heart attack."

"Sorry." She squeezed his shoulder and kissed his cheek, its rough familiarity comforting her. "I rang the bell, and I was calling for you, but I guess you didn't hear." She picked up the illustrated book he had propped open in front of him. "Spanish lessons?"

His color deepened a shade. "A new computer program. I was just fooling around with it."

"*Le admiro,*" she said, drawing a phrase from her college Spanish courses.

"*Gracias,*" he said. "*Puedo conseguirle algo beber?*"

She laughed, impressed. "I'd love a cup of tea." She

could tell from his expression the idea of actually having to make tea intimidated him, so she said, "Actually, I'd prefer a soda."

They went down to the kitchen and he took a ginger ale from a fridge that looked even more toxic than it had the last time she had visited. Her mother would have a fit when she saw it. But maybe she'd never see it. She might never come back here again.

Sandra noticed a business card stuck to the fridge with a magnet. "An audiologist?" she asked, turning to her father.

"I've got an appointment to get my hearing checked." He shuffled his feet, even more chagrined than he'd been about the Spanish lessons.

She set down the ginger ale and hugged him. "Aw, Dad. That's great."

He shrugged. "Your mother was always nagging me to get it checked."

"She'll be so glad," Sandra said.

"Who knows?" He moved a stack of newspapers and motioned for her to sit down.

"How are you doing?" Sandra asked.

"Fine."

"How can you be fine?"

"Golf and fishing whenever I want, nobody telling me to wipe my feet or to quit using so much salt."

She studied his kind, ruddy face, trying to see past the studied nonchalance. "I think you're lonely."

"Never been busier. I have my pals at the golf course. I joined a poker group on Thursday nights."

"Lonely for Mom," she amended. She touched his hand. They'd never been a demonstrative family, and she found herself wishing they had been. Mike had shown her the power of a human touch, the way it could reach a level of unspoken intimacy she had never known before.

"It's all right to say you miss her," she said. "What good does it do to pretend you don't?"

"You think I'm pretending?"

"Yeah. I do, and it's no good, Dad." Had she been pretending about Victor? And if someone had pointed it out, would it have made a difference?

Her father stared down at their joined hands. "Okay. I guess I've had plenty of time to think."

"About what?"

He scowled. "I guess I like being with her. I like her cooking. I like sitting with her in the evening, reading the paper or watching the tube. Hell, I even like her nagging." He shook his head. "I don't think I ever told her those things."

"It's not too late," Sandra said with sudden urgency. "When she gets back from her trip, you can ask her to come home."

He took his hand away and shoved it through his hair, which was getting too long. "I was a jerk for a lot of years. Hearing aids and Spanish lessons aren't going to erase all that."

He had to be wrong. She thought of the way her parents used to be—her mother matching his socks and scheduling his haircuts, her father checking the tires on the car and phoning home twice a day, no matter where he was. They were always thinking of each other even when they didn't realize it.

"Dad, it's not the hearing aids and Spanish lessons per se. It's the idea behind it. Convince her that if she comes back, things will be different. And then make sure they *are* different."

"I'm working on it." He looked glumly around the

cluttered kitchen. "I'll work harder. So have you heard from her?"

"She's been sending postcards. Says the cruise is great but the stop-smoking seminars are boring—"

He shifted in his chair. "She's quitting smoking?"

"Sounds like she's trying. It's called a Cruise to a New You. Self-improvement of all sorts. You didn't know?"

An endearing, lopsided grin lit his face. "You don't say."

"I do say. Another postcard said she'd moved up to the advanced tai chi class. And she caught a trophy-size marlin."

"Yeah? So your mother's fishing?"

Sandra finished her ginger ale. "I don't think she's ready to write off your marriage either, Dad."

"Then why did she up and leave?"

"Because you weren't listening."

There was a brightness in his eyes that hadn't been there a few moments ago. *Hope*. He put his hand on her cheek, a rare gesture of affection. "So how you doing, anyway?"

Driving up here, she had made up her mind to keep things to herself, but she hadn't expected to find her father speaking so openly or listening so well. She had always adored him, but with the remote, filial love expected of a daughter. Now she knew their relationship went much deeper.

"There's an evidentiary hearing scheduled. Milton thinks the judge will throw out the suit."

"That's good."

"If he rules in my favor," she said.

"Why wouldn't he?"

"The Winslows' team is trying to dig up new evidence."

"They won't find anything." He paused. "Will they?"

"I don't have a crystal ball."

He got up, paced the kitchen. "What the hell are the Winslows thinking? Christ, they don't need your money."

"You know it's not about the money, Dad. They just— I don't know—they want to believe I took Victor from them. I'll always be seen as the person who caused their son to die. It was such a meaningless death. Maybe this is their way of finding meaning in it."

He stopped pacing and gripped the back of a chair. "Why are you so understanding of these people?"

If only he knew how tempted she'd been to voice the nightmare inside her. But she didn't. She never would. She could never do that. It wasn't understanding at all, but the lowest, most cowardly form of self-preservation there was. She wasn't protecting the Winslows.

She was protecting herself.

"They're not bad people," she said, "they're just . . . in pain."

"And hurting you will help?"

"I don't know, Dad. I'll be all right. Milton doesn't think they can win this."

"They can't, for Christ's sake."

She didn't want him getting all worked up over it. "The renovation on the house is coming along fine," she said to change the subject.

"Yeah? That's good."

"I hired a real estate agent named Sparky."

"Sounds like he's a used car salesman."

"It's a she. Milton says she's the best in the area. She thinks the house is worth a fortune."

"Good. Location like that, it ought to be. So how come you don't look so happy about selling the place?"

She hadn't realized her doubts showed on her face.

Before the accident, she and Victor used to talk about fixing up Blue Moon Beach, turning it into a summer retreat. They used to picture themselves old and settled, looking out to sea as they rocked on the porch each evening. Even then, Victor must have known they'd never make it to that point—but Sandra had believed they would, with all her heart.

"It's the uncertainty, I suppose," she told her father. "I can't imagine where I'll end up."

"Sure you can, honey. After you sell, you can drive up to the Cape, maybe even go down south or something—didn't Victor used to talk about Florida all the time?"

She swallowed a knot of panic. "We never had the chance to go there."

"Maybe now's the chance you've been waiting for. Take your time, find the place you want to be."

But Florida had been Victor's dream, not hers. She'd always been content in aptly named Paradise. She knew there would never be another Blue Moon Beach, no matter how far she traveled or how much money she spent. She would never find a place that filled her with an almost childlike sense of wonder, an elusive awe that nourished her spirit. The beach had a special atmosphere filled with the sounds of foghorn and hissing surf, a quality of light that made the air glow, the grass and hedges intense with color, the sea an endless expanse beneath an endless sky. Each day, letting go seemed more impossible—and more inevitable.

"Besides, those people down in Paradise have been giving you crap. You don't want to hang around there any longer than you have to—"

"I've met someone." She hadn't planned on saying anything, but it came out, startling them both.

Her father lifted a bushy eyebrow. "Yeah?"

"He's, um, actually he's the contractor working on the house."

He sat down again, watching her closely. "Somebody Malloy. You mentioned him before."

"Mike. I—I wasn't expecting this. God knows I haven't been thinking about meeting anyone, but we, Mike and I—" How had it happened? And what, exactly, was going on between them? She honestly didn't know. Yet from the first moment she'd seen him, even through a blur of frustrated tears, the world had looked different— brighter, safer . . . more honest. She couldn't explain it to herself, let alone her father.

"At first, we were cordial—I guess that's how you'd describe it. I hired him because he promised to fix what was wrong."

"With your house."

"Yes. Didn't I say that?" She frowned, then went on. "Obviously, we saw a lot of each other because of the house, but lately we've been getting closer." She didn't elaborate and knew her father wouldn't ask more than he could bear to hear.

Her father sat forward. "So what kind of guy is he?" A few years ago, he'd asked the same thing about Victor.

Her answer had been naively sincere. "He's perfect," she had said. "Absolutely perfect."

She would never say that of Malloy. She was older now, smarter. Sadder. Wise enough to know Mike wasn't perfect. But he was . . . everything else. Caring. Strong and tender. Indecently sexy. And steady, an anchor in a stormy sea. "You'd like him, Dad. He's a guy's guy. He used to run a historical restoration company in Newport, and now he's starting up in Paradise. He's a single dad, with a boy who's nine and a girl who just turned thirteen."

"So is this serious?"

"I have no idea." She knew she was hedging. The truth was, she got chills every time she thought of Mike, and one long, smoldering look from him made her heart soar. This was a conversation she should be having with Joyce or Barb, yet here she was, talking it all out with her father. Amazing. Maybe he really had changed. "There's something you should know. He and Victor were friends when they were kids."

"What?"

"He grew up in Paradise. He knows a lot of the locals."

"Sandra, have you explained this to your lawyer?"

"Why should I?"

"The guy might be taking you for a ride. You got him tearing your house apart, poking around in everything. What if he's looking for evidence against you?"

"That's a bit melodramatic, Dad. Besides, I have nothing to h-hide." As she spoke, she nearly choked on her own words.

"Be careful," her father cautioned. "You're in a tricky spot, with this lawsuit coming up. Don't let the guy take advantage of you."

"He would never do that," she said, her confidence shaken.

But her father's suspicions haunted her on the drive home. She'd gone to him, desperate for hope that her parents would reconcile and for assurance that her relationship with Mike wasn't doomed. But instead of quelling her fears about getting involved with Mike, her father had raised more questions.

Chapter 28

As soon as she got back to the house, she went looking for Mike. The crew had left for the day, but he was still there, with Springsteen playing on the radio as he put the finishing touches on a cornice of the dining room.

Watching him work would never get old for her. There was something mysteriously evocative about his manner, the way he held himself. She couldn't pinpoint what caught and held her attention, exactly. But each move he made touched a chord deep inside her—the deft motions of his hands. The angle of his hip, jammed against the top rung of the ladder. The set of his jaw and his intent stare as he studied a carpenter's level and made a mark with a flat blue pencil. These were routine, probably tedious chores, but he did them with such . . . skill. Maybe that was the word for it.

It was compelling in a way she couldn't explain to herself.

Everything about him was exciting to her. She hadn't expected to discover that about him. Especially because from all outward appearances, she had been married to a man the whole world considered exciting. When Victor had first been elected to the state legislature, he'd been—much to his chagrin—profiled as *Cosmo*'s bachelor of the month. There was even a Web site put up by fans enthralled by his looks and charisma, and each week, that site had generated everything from borderline illegal sexual favors to offers of vacation homes on Maui. The site might have solicited more than that, she thought with a grim chill.

Bringing her wandering thoughts back to Mike, she tried to imagine him being underhanded enough to spy on her. To search her home and provide information to the Winslows' investigators. The image was simply ludicrous, a portrait in garish paint colors. He would never do that. She felt stupid, paranoid, bringing up those accusations.

Zeke woke from a nap on the window seat and trotted over to greet her, alerting Malloy. He relegated the level and hammer to his tool belt while turning to her. That was another thing she found so sexy about him. In the blink of an eye, he gave her his whole attention, his whole self, making her the center of the world.

"Hey," he said, climbing down the ladder. "I didn't hear you come in."

Grabbing her by the waist, he kissed her energetically. Her body flared to life like a struck match. Every time he touched her, the intimate sensations felt brand-new. She was unexplored territory, and his frank, gentle caresses mapped her most secret places, claiming her for his own. He kissed her breathless, and when she finally pulled away, she tried to remember what she had meant to say to him. Instead, she could only find a whisper: "I missed you today."

"Oh, baby," he said, tugging her tightly against him, "I missed you, too." Dropping the tool belt, he kissed her again, walking her backward across the foyer, never letting up until he steered her to the stairs. God, she loved this— loved the way he wanted her. The way he forgot everything else in the world but her. The way he made her forget . . .

Upstairs, they fell back on the bed together, causing the ancient springs to creak. She kissed him hungrily, wanting to pull all of him close. There was so much of him—broad shoulders and big hands and a mouth that moved over hers with unexpected tenderness.

He smelled of sweat and industrial adhesive as he crushed down on her, caressing and searching. She still had her purse hanging from her shoulder, and when he reached up to unbutton her blouse, his hand tangled in the strap.

"Let's get organized here," he said, pulling back.

She laughed. "I hadn't planned on being seduced." Now, she reminded herself. Ask him now.

"Unplanned seduction is the best kind." He stood, pulling her up beside him. He set down her purse and lifted the blouse over her head.

Her doubts floated away, helium balloons released to the sky. She couldn't catch them back, didn't even want to. She unbuttoned his blue denim work shirt, parting it to bare his chest. It was still light outside, and weak sunshine through the window illuminated the contours of his body. There was something wicked and delicious about doing this in broad daylight.

"I need a shower," he said as she tugged his shirttail from his jeans.

"Now?"

He skimmed her panty hose down, pausing to kiss the inside of her knee. Several times, lightly. "Yeah. Now."

"But—"

Standing, he unhooked her bra and stepped back to look at her. "Now," he repeated, then pressed one finger to her lips. Taking her hand, he led her into the adjoining bathroom.

It was as old-fashioned as the rest of the summer place, with black and white hexagonal tile and a huge, claw-footed iron tub clad in white porcelain. The brass shower head snaked to life when he turned on the water, letting it run while he shucked off the rest of his clothes. Hot billows of steam filled the room, and he grinned at her through the whitish mist. In a curiously formal gesture, he took her hand and motioned for her to step into the tub. The spray beat down on them as they kissed, and then he put a bar of soap into her hands.

She turned it over and over, letting it slip through her fingers. He leaned down and whispered in her ear. "Quit thinking so hard."

"I'm not—"

"I can see it in your face."

She took a deep breath, drawing moisture and heat into her lungs and focusing on Mike—his body, the smoothness of his skin, the taste of his mouth on hers. Her hand came up, tentative, exploring, sliding over his chest and across his collarbone, leaving a wake of soapsuds. His eyes lowered to half mast, and the sound he made in his throat told her she was on the right track. She went up on tiptoe and kissed him, then slid her hand downward, the warm rain and steam washing over them. He touched her everywhere with his hands and mouth, and she finally stopped thinking about everything except the falling water and the heat of need slipping through her. Under the steady flow of the shower, their bodies slid together, melding and searching, until she grew dizzy with need. Winding her arms around his waist, she put her mouth next to his ear. "Now," she said. "Please."

"Whatever the lady wants."

Wet and dripping, half-dazed, she shut off the taps, hurrying to the bed where she welcomed him with a sigh.

They made a mess of the bedclothes, something neither of them noticed until much, much later. Sandra lent him her pink chenille robe, laughing when he put it on. Wrapping herself in a bath towel, she stripped off the damp sheets and gave him detailed instructions as he helped her remake the bed with dry linens. After they tugged the coverlet into place, he captured her around the waist and tackled her again. "That was just what I needed," he said, nuzzling her neck.

"A shower?"

"Great sex."

"Is it?" she asked. "Is it great?"

"What do you think?"

Her smile disappeared. She couldn't lie or bluff about this. "It's heaven. I never thought I—" Though it seemed absurd under the circumstances, she felt awkward even after all they had shared. Sobered by conflicting sentiments, she extricated herself from his embrace. "You're very skilled."

He laughed and sat up, sloppily tying the robe closed. It barely went around him. "Honey, skill has nothing to do with it." His eyes grew dark, hooded. "It's the way I feel about you."

"Mike—"

"Don't you get it?"

"Get what?"

Leaning down, he cupped her cheek in his hand. "I'm falling in love with you. Fast. And hard."

She stared at him in devastated shock. But she didn't say a word. She had no idea how to respond to him. Hurrying from the bed, she pulled on leggings and an over-sized sweatshirt, wanting to hide.

He watched her with an unsettling stare. "This is where you're supposed to say, 'Really? That's good. I feel the same way.'"

"But I'm not falling in love," she finally whispered, and was shocked to feel a burn of tears in her throat. "I'm already there."

Chapter 29

They ate scrambled eggs for dinner with Natalie Cole crooning on the stereo. Afterward, they let Zeke out for a run. Sandra sat on the sofa, looking out at the gathering twilight, a deep indigo sweep of sky, a scattering of stars. They didn't talk about the words they'd spoken upstairs, but new feelings swirled like a mist in the air. Mike made a fire in the stove, and Sandra reveled in the chance to sit back while someone else warmed the house.

The pink bathrobe—which most men would regard as an abomination—did nothing to detract from his looks. She had never known anyone who could be so comfortable with himself. She envied that. Then she realized she was comfortable when she was with him. The doubts that had plagued her earlier vanished. Suspicion seemed preposterous in the wake of what they'd just shared, what they'd said to each other.

He fixed things: her house, her life, her broken heart . . . He had found her at her lowest moment, and bit by bit, he'd been lifting her up, showing her what love could be. She felt an aching surge of affection, watching the way his big shoulders strained the seams of the robe as he stacked more wood in the bin, his thick hair spilling over his collar. What she felt when she looked at him was so intense that it hurt. He was an expert at taking care of things. But who took care of him?

"I've got an idea," she said with sudden inspiration. She grabbed his hand and led him into the kitchen. Setting a three-legged stool under the hanging light, she said, "You need a haircut."

He put his hand on the back of his neck. "Yeah? You think?"

"Definitely." She got the Fiskars from a drawer.

With a shrug of nonchalance, he took a seat on the stool. "Okay."

Putting a dish towel around his neck, she took a comb from her purse and positioned herself in front of him, using the comb on his thick, soft hair, still damp from the shower. "I can't believe you're letting me do this."

"I trust you," he said easily.

"I've always liked cutting hair," she confessed. "No credentials in the field, but I have a knack for it. Do you think that's weird?"

"Different strokes," he said. "It's probably Freudian. Or biblical, like Samson and Delilah."

"I used to practice on dolls when I was little," she told him, snipping and shaping the thick, dark locks. "Every doll I had wound up with a haircut. When I was six, I gave myself a Mohawk long before Mohawks were popular."

"I bet that was a sight."

"It's one of the few times I ever saw my mother cry. I think I wore a hat or scarf to school for six weeks."

"You were probably a great kid."

"You lose, Malloy. I was a mess." She didn't like to think about those long-ago, lost years. Even so, she still remembered how the words used to lock in her throat, then emerge as mangled bursts of nonsense; she could still hear the hushed whispers of adults, the open jeers of the other kids. She was Sandy Bab-bab-babblecock, the girl who stuttered.

"But maybe if I hadn't been such a mess, I wouldn't have started writing," she added. She used to write with an anger and eloquence far beyond her years. "In my stories, I was always the big star. The prima ballerina, the doctor curing cancer, the heroine saving a town from a flood. I was larger than life in my imagination. Maybe that's why I'm such a Walter Mitty in reality."

As she circled around to check the front, he grabbed her and held her still. "Not in my reality." He kissed her briefly and hard.

"Quit distracting me, Malloy. I'm almost finished."

A few minutes later, dark curls littered the newly refinished floor. She dusted his neck with a towel and stood back to admire her work.

"Damn, I'm good," she said. "You're Russell Crowe."

"Who's Russell Crowe?"

"Duh. Didn't you see *Gladiator?*"

"Nope."

"Well, you should. You look like him. Sparky was so right about you."

"What did Sparky say about me?"

"She called you a living, breathing love god."

He hooted. "Yeah, right. So I'm done?" He reached up

and ran a hand through his hair. "Thanks." He went and got a dustpan and swept up.

"Don't you want to check yourself out in a mirror?" Sandra asked.

He dumped the clippings into a paper bag. "Does it look okay to you?"

"Living, breathing love god," she reminded him.

"Okay by me." He put the broom away, stuffed the bag in the trash and opened the back door. Zeke came in from his run and flopped down on the hearth.

Mike led her upstairs and they made love again, slowly, with a lingering ecstasy she found so moving that she felt like a different person. She found a new side of herself, and it was like finding a secret door in the old house, stepping through to discover another world, a place she had never been before and had never quite believed in, Neverland or Oz. The journey back was gentle and leisurely; she was reluctant to leave, to let go.

Quite late, he kissed her and slipped out of bed, groping for his jeans. "Got to go," he whispered.

"Don't," she whispered back. "Stay with me."

He hesitated.

"Please, Mike."

"Okay." He got back under the covers and she snuggled up against him, and happiness shimmered through her. "But why are we whispering?" he asked.

She didn't answer; she was filled to overflowing. She understood completely what she had with him, what could be lost, and beneath her cautious joy lay a stark fear.

Chapter 30

*I*t felt so damned good to wake up with a woman in his arms that Mike didn't move a muscle other than opening one eye at six A.M. He had never needed an alarm clock—he naturally awoke at the same time each day.

Here in this isolated house, there was no need to draw the drapes for privacy, and the big picture window framed a stunning view of the sea. The sun hadn't risen, but its silver gleam lifted the sky above the horizon and sent a bloom of light across the quiet bedroom.

Carefully propping himself on one elbow, he watched Sandra sleep for a while. Just the sight of her moved him. Smooth skin and untroubled brow, silky hair fanning out across the pillow, full lips slightly parted, colored like the heart of a rose. He was glad he had stayed, though he understood it changed things between them. He might be forced to put a name to this, something he had deliberately avoided doing.

There were all kinds of useful phrases—they were "seeing each other." "In a relationship," whatever the hell that meant. The trouble was, none of those fit anymore.

All he knew was that she filled the places inside him that had been empty for so long, and he didn't want to let her go. But her secrets ran deep, and she held them away from him. He wondered if she would ever let him know her completely.

He touched his lips to her temple, affection radiating through him. She was like the faceted glass that edged the antique windows of the bedroom—finely wrought, ever-changing, switching from sunshine to darkness at a shift in the light.

From the very start he'd sensed that she held a part of herself back, even as she surrendered her body to him and offered the broken, whispered confession that she loved him. She had not given him everything; he knew that. She kept some of her facets hidden.

Right on cue, Zeke awakened at six-thirty and scratched at the door. Grumbling softly, Mike got up, ignoring the sleepy, pitiful protest that issued from the tangled covers. Promising he'd be back, he pulled on his jeans and went to let the dog out.

It was so cold in the house he could almost see his breath. He didn't like to think of Sandra here, day after day, waking up alone to an uncertain future. He stoked the stove and put on the coffee, and the morning routine felt as natural and right as breathing.

While the coffee brewed, he watched Zeke scramble across the dunes on his way to the beach. The ocean was flat and impenetrable, the rising sun dimmed by clouds the color of gunmetal. The harsh beauty of the shore called to him as it always did, raw and elemental.

Leaning against the window frame, he stared out at the view. He felt a rare and deep sense of connection to this place; this was the landscape of his boyhood, where he had learned the secrets of the coves and marshes, the sounds of crying gulls and ships' whistles, the ways of the sea. In a strange way, he had fallen for the house as well as the owner.

Zeke sent a flock of sandpipers scattering across the wet sand, and Mike grinned at the dog's exuberance. The coffeemaker hissed to a stop, and he wandered into the kitchen. He fixed two mugs and took them upstairs. She was sitting up in bed, her hair tousled, a slow smile unfurling on her lips. "Bless you," she said, reaching for the mug he offered. "When I smelled coffee, I thought I was dreaming." She took a sip, then frowned at something on the floor. "What's that?"

With his thumb and forefinger, he picked up a tattered brown object. "Oops," he said. "It's that old teddy bear you kept on the bed. Zeke must've gotten it." Rotten stuffing dripped from the mess.

"Victor won that thing in a ring toss the night he proposed." She paused, then added, "Put it in the trash."

"Sorry," he muttered, and carried the ruined toy to the bathroom. When he returned, she cradled the mug between her hands and regarded him with such intensity that he turned away, pretending interest in the recently rebuilt bay window. On her house, at least, he was doing a hell of a job. The enduring lines of the architecture and the matchless view each window commanded gave the place a powerful appeal. As the renovation continued, the house was turning out as fine as the place on earth it occupied.

His phone rang, and he pawed through his pile of

clothes to find it clipped to the waistband of his jeans. "Mike Malloy."

"It's Angela."

"Angela." From the corner of his eye, he saw Sandra stiffen and draw up the covers. "Are the kids okay?"

"Absolutely. Listen, I need a favor. School's been canceled today—some kind of central power outage again. I've got to go up to Providence. Can you take the kids?"

"Of course. I'll be over in half an hour."

"Thanks, Mike."

He explained the situation to Sandra as he got dressed. "Can you tell Phil to call me when he gets in? We've got another electrical inspection today. I wanted to be here for that, but I'll have the kids with me, so I'll have to cancel."

"Bring them along," she said reasonably.

He rubbed a hand over his stubbled chin. Another new turn in the road. Putting her together with his kids for a boat ride was one thing. Having them spend the day at her home was another; he wasn't sure how he felt about it. "I can't ask you to—"

"Malloy. I like your kids. I'd love to hang out with them today." She handed him a pink disposable Lady Schick. "You'd better shave."

～～

Sandra moved through the morning in a haze of happiness. The presence of Malloy and his kids brought the world into balance. Everything seemed brand-new and magical, painted in brighter colors, with sharper clarity. She fixed blueberry muffins from a mix, and was rewarded by a look of pure bliss on Kevin's face when he walked into the kitchen and smelled the aroma from the oven.

After he and his sister devoured several muffins, Sandra played half a dozen games of checkers with him. He showed no mercy, trouncing her five times. She gave Mary Margaret the pen and notebook she'd promised, and the girl spent an hour bent over the book, writing until her fingers cramped. Sandra asked Mary Margaret if she would like to read *Simple Gifts* in manuscript form, and the girl jumped at the chance. She sat at Sandra's desk in the library nook, absorbed in reading the crisp, typed pages, turning them with painstaking reverence.

"What if you spelled something wrong?" she asked.

Sandra gave her a pad of Post-it notes. "Stick one of those to it and I'll fix it."

"Really?"

"Sure. I'll put your name on the acknowledgments page."

"Cool." Tucking a stray lock of hair behind her ear, she started reading again with diligent concentration, and was soon oblivious to the parade of workmen passing through the room.

Kevin was distracted by a lumber delivery, so his dad gave him a hard hat and let him tag along while the crew sorted and stacked the new wood.

Having the kids around made the day feel like a holiday. Sandra wondered what they thought of her relationship with Mike. By now, Mary Margaret probably understood they were more than friends, but Sandra hoped the girl hadn't guessed how much more. Their tentative approval could chill if they saw her as a threat, competing for their father's affection.

After lunch—fried baloney sandwiches that made Kevin wild with delight—she took them out to the beach, with Zeke in the lead. He raced ahead, barked at the chasing waves, took off after scolding gulls. Kevin was nearly as frisky, running along with his jacket and shoelaces loose, making jet engine noises as he dive-bombed imaginary targets.

Mary Margaret walked in a meandering path, picking up shells and bits of colored sea glass and putting them in her pocket. "Charlotte's grandmother isn't going to get better, is she? In your book."

"No." Sandra wasn't going to be coy with this kid, tell her she'd have to read the book to find out. Mary Margaret was a girl who liked honesty and could spot a phony a mile off. "No, the grandmother won't get better. But Charlotte will change."

"She sure has a lot of troubles. Failing in school, her mom working all the time, her grandma getting worse and worse every day."

"That's the way fiction works. My fiction, anyway. Sometimes the character finds out there's no perfect solution, but she goes on anyway, and she's better off for it."

"Oh, gross!" Kevin yelled out, running toward them, Zeke at his heels.

"What's the matter?" Sandra asked.

"Zeke found something rank, and he rolled in it. Gross! Gross! Gross!" Kevin made a gagging sound and pretended to retch in the sand.

Sandra and Mary Margaret recoiled from the dog. Some sort of dead matter, fishy and harsh, clung to his coat as he skittered in a circle around them, certain this was a new game to play.

"Ew, that reeks," Mary Margaret said.

"We're going to have to bathe him," Sandra said, wrinkling her nose.

"No way! I'm not—"

"We'll all pitch in." Sandra whistled for the dog, patted her thigh and led the way back to the house. In the garage, she found an old picnic tablecloth and wrapped

Zeke in it, tucking the foul thing under her arm and marching upstairs to the bathroom.

"Fill the tub with lukewarm water," she said to Kevin.

"What's lukewarm?" he asked.

Mary Margaret rolled her eyes. "I'll let you know."

Sandra made a quick, furtive assessment of the bathroom, praying they'd notice no trace of Mike here. The pink plastic razor beside the sink looked innocent enough, she hoped. She tried not to think about the unspeakable pleasures she'd experienced here the night before, but her body remembered with a warm spasm of pleasure. She didn't want his kids to know he'd spent the night with her. She wasn't ready for that yet. She was pretty sure they weren't, either.

"Do you have dog shampoo?" asked Kevin, his question banishing any lingering traces of lust.

"She doesn't have a dog, moron," his sister said, and he stuck his tongue out at her.

"Use that stuff in the blue bottle." It was French organic shampoo from Bergdorf Goodman in New York City.

Mary Margaret dumped in about half the bottle.

Sandra wiped off the worst of the muck with the tablecloth, then lowered the dog into the tub, mounded high with white suds. Zeke panicked, paddling wildly and trying to shake himself off. Kevin shrieked with glee as he and Mary Margaret took turns soothing the woebegone, trembling dog and scrubbing him with a loofa sponge Sandra knew she would never use again.

"Look how scrawny he is," Kevin said, lifting the dog to show off his undersized physique.

While her brother guffawed, Mary Margaret kept scrubbing. "Hey, check it out," she said. "His fur is actually white. I always thought he was gray."

Sandra finally took pity on Zeke. She drained the tub,

then held him under the shower while he howled in misery. Shutting off the shower, she wrapped the dog in a thick Egyptian cotton bath towel. It had been a wedding gift from Victor's great aunt, a dozen of them delivered in a shiny red Macy's box.

Zeke shivered uncontrollably, whining like an infant.

"What if he catches cold?" Mary Margaret bit her lip.

"Hand me that blow dryer," Sandra said, pointing. "And the brush," she added.

"Isn't that your hairbrush?" asked Mary Margaret.

"I'll buy another," Sandra said, resigned.

Zeke actually liked that part—the blow drying and brushing. Kevin thought it was hilarious, the way the dog pushed his nose into the hot stream of air, as if he stood in a wind tunnel. Mary Margaret was enchanted. "He's pretty," she said. "He almost looks like a real poodle. But his face is disappearing into all that fluff. He probably can't even see. I think he needs a haircut."

"You just said the magic words, Mary Margaret." Sandra became a woman on a mission. She sent Kevin to get the scissors—the same ones she had used on Mike the night before. Grooming a dog was a new challenge. She stood Zeke on the linen cabinet by the window, directing Kevin to keep hold of him. Both kids offered advice and opinions while she snipped away. "Make a puffball on his tail, like they have at dog shows." "Can we put these barrettes here?" "What about a bow?" "Let's paint his nails!"

An hour later, Zeke looked as perfectly groomed as a Purina dog chow label. The three of them stood back in awe.

"He's perfect," Mary Margaret whispered.

The dog jumped down from the cabinet and pranced around, delighted by all the attention.

"Think he knows?" Kevin wondered.

"Hard to say." Sandra surveyed the bathroom—a wasteland of wet towels and white dog hair.

"Let's go show Dad." Kevin burst out into the hallway, Mary Margaret and Zeke at his heels. Sandra followed more slowly, thinking about how much fun these kids were, wishing the day would never end.

As she watched the kids, she felt a stirring inside her. She used to believe in the impossibility of a perfect love, but this felt as close to perfect as she'd ever come. A rare contentment took hold. The possibility, the promise of happiness with Mike and his kids dangled in front of her, tantalizing. Today, they'd felt like a family, they'd functioned like one. Whether they'd planned it or not, she and Malloy had opened the door to a new kind of intimacy, deeper and truer—maybe even stronger.

Yet as she descended the stairs, she felt the old currents of fear traveling through her, the ominous sense of calm before a storm.

In the downstairs parlor, Mike stood talking to Phil and the crew. They looked up when his kids and dog pounded down the stairs. Mike gaped at the white powder puff trotting across the foyer toward him. "Jesus H. Christ," he muttered, dropping a pencil on the floor.

The other guys shuffled their feet and elbowed each other.

"Zeke," said Mike. "Zeke, buddy. Oh, man, what did they do to you?"

"Isn't he adorable?" Mary Margaret cooed. She scooped up the dog and presented him like a gift to her father. "Isn't he just the cutest thing?"

"Nice poodle, Malloy," said Phil. "I guess we'd better be going." The three slipped out while Mike shook his head in chagrin.

He held the dog out at arm's length. Zeke squirmed with delight and strained toward him, licking his face.

Only Sandra heard the slam of a car door. Through the sidelight, she noticed a burgundy Volvo parked in the drive, and a tall, attractive woman walking to the door.

There was no mistaking the visitor's identity because of the striking resemblance to Mary Margaret. Swallowing a knot of nervousness in her throat, Sandra composed herself and opened the front door for Malloy's ex-wife.

"H—" The word stopped, severed at the throat. God, not now.

Recognition—and then suspicion—dawned on the woman's face.

"H—yes, hello," Sandra finally managed with a burst of air.

"Hiya, Mom." Kevin sped out onto the porch. "Check it out—we gave Zeke a haircut."

"That's nice, sweetie." At close range, Angela was more than attractive. She was quite beautiful in a polished, honey-haired fashion. She wore a dark cashmere coat and thin leather gloves the color of butter.

Sandra tried not to think about her own appearance— an old sweatshirt and jeans, soiled from the dog's bath. "How do you do," she said. "I'm Sandra Winslow."

"Angela Falco." The words were clipped off, just short of rude. She looked past Sandra. "Mike?"

"Hey, Angela. What are you doing here?"

"The meeting ended early, so I thought I'd pick up the kids, save you a trip to Newport. I stopped at the harbor, and someone said you were here." She said *here* as though it were one of the inner rings of Dante's inferno. "Come on, kiddos. Get your coats and let's go." She turned to Sandra. "Good to meet you."

Both kids thanked Sandra without being prompted and

waved good-bye. Mike walked them out to the car, kissing them both, then giving Kevin a high-five. He and Angela spoke briefly while Sandra watched from the doorway with Zeke tucked under her arm.

She studied the way Angela looked up at Mike and leaned in close, putting her hand on his forearm, the gesture both possessive and intimate. Sandra wondered if it was her imagination, or if some sort of sexual energy leaped between them. The two of them had been married a long time. Even divorced, they probably still remembered their private lovers' shorthand, the unspoken communication that passed between long-married couples.

After they drove away, Mike returned, glancing at Zeke and shaking his head. "He doesn't even look like himself."

Sandra set down the dog and shut the door. "That was awkward," she said.

He took one look at her face and pulled her into his arms. "Don't sweat it."

"I can't help it, Mike. I'm no good at this." Her words were muffled against his shoulder.

He pulled back. "At what?"

"At—I don't know. Whatever *this* is. Dating. Is this dating?"

"Oh, yeah."

"You have this whole other life on another planet, at least that's how it seems. Your ex, the kids, your friends and family. I have no idea how to be in your life."

"We'll figure it out."

"Will we?" She paused, running her hand down the hard length of his arm as though to erase Angela's touch. "Should we?"

"Why not?"

"There are a million reasons. You're living on a boat.

I'm moving as soon as the house sells. You can't leave Paradise and I—I can't stay."

"Why not? Because of the lawsuit?"

"Because of a lot of things." She pressed her forehead against his chest, listening to the gentle thud of his heart.

He tilted her face up to look at him. "You love this house, this place."

And you. She didn't say it aloud. Their love was as uncertain and new as a flash of sunlight on quicksilver ice. Maybe that was why she couldn't settle on exactly where she would go, once she was free to leave. "It's only a place to live. I'm just passing through."

"You could choose to stay. Or is that too hard for you?"

She pulled back, challenged by his question and posing one of her own. "Is that what you want? Are you asking me to stay?"

He hesitated. In that hesitation, she tasted defeat. He knew the score as well as she did.

"What if I did?" he said.

"I don't know, Malloy. I don't know a damned thing anymore."

Chapter 31

"Are you nuts, Malloy?" Loretta Schott's voice shrilled through the cell phone and he held it away from his ear. "Have you absolutely lost your mind?"

Sitting in his boat, drumming his fingers on the table, Mike said, "What have you heard?"

His lawyer took an audibly deep breath. "That you're letting your kids hang around with a murderer. It'll look so impressive on your next custody evaluation."

Damn Angela, he thought. She must have gone straight home with the kids and called her attorney. And it had been such a good day. He'd liked seeing his kids running around Blue Moon Beach, hanging out with Sandra. It all seemed so right at the time. He'd loved seeing the kids chasing the dog, Sandra fixing them lunch and catching his eye from time to time, the look on her face a sweet reminder of the night before. The memory caused his heart to constrict with a deep knowledge of what he needed, a feeling of longing.

"First of all," he said, "Angela asked me to take them for an unscheduled day. I was more than happy to do it, but I'm in the middle of a big project. Second of all, Sandra Winslow is not a murderer. She is the victim of an accident, and I'm sick of hearing otherwise."

"That doesn't matter. She's poison—she's facing a wrongful death suit, and I guarantee that's not going to endear her to the custody evaluator. And what's this about these controversial books she writes? Angela said Mary Margaret has been reading them, and they're so full of inappropriate material that the library keeps them behind the counter."

"They're stories for kids. Even the librarian was embarrassed to admit they were challenged."

"For God's sake, Malloy, give the kid *Pollyanna* to read. You've got to play it safe, my friend, or you'll have your visitation rights cut back faster than you can say *family values*."

"Damn it, Loretta—"

"Don't damn-it-Loretta me. So what are you, dating the woman, banging her?"

"Don't go there, Counsel." His voice was low, calm and deadly serious.

"Then don't you go where I think you're headed. If you need to get laid, maybe you should steer clear of accused murderers. Judges tend to frown on people like that."

He clenched his jaw until it hurt. Goddamn Angela. She couldn't let him go. She was terrified he would love someone more than he'd ever loved her. He ought to call her bluff, expose the affair—but then he thought of the kids, and knew he'd never do that.

Every cell of his body screamed for him to break something—and to fire the bitch on the other end of the phone. But he focused on the photograph propped by the computer—a shot of him and the kids laughing together, his arms draped around them. For their sake, he had to keep his temper in check.

He took a deep, steadying breath. "Look, Loretta. Your job is to make me look like Captain Kangaroo for the family court."

"Then quit making my job impossible. At least be discreet until the next evaluation. Don't give Angela any more ammunition, okay? Make sure they see your mug in church every Sunday. Get yourself a nice house, something with a nice yard, maybe even a white picket fence. It'll be one fewer issue for Angela to raise. Have you found a place yet?"

"I'm working on it."

"Work harder."

"Ditto, Loretta."

He hung up and raked a hand through his hair. He didn't understand why Angela was trying to stir up trouble for him. Or maybe he did understand. She was a good mother, but apparently she wasn't above using the kids to jerk him around. He was out of her control now, but she'd found a way to manipulate him.

Maybe.

Angela objected to Sandra's reputation; she didn't want the children under the cloud of suspicion that shadowed her. And Mike kept thinking maybe, just maybe that suspicion was misplaced.

He made a couple of phone calls, then changed out of his work clothes. This was not the way he had planned on spending his evening, but a nagging pressure had been building inside him for a long time now. He'd been doing a lot of research, trying to fill in the blanks about the accident. His hunches were starting to harden into reality, and to dovetail with his suspicions. Sandra might hate him for it, but he knew he wouldn't rest until he probed into her secrets.

~~

He pulled up at the county annex just as twilight was coming on. The cramped and sleepy front office huddled at the end of Bay Street. Its single storefront window had the blinds pulled halfway down like a large eye in the middle of a blink. In a place where two panty thefts from a clothesline constituted a crime wave, there was not a lot of activity for the local law enforcement agency.

Mike hesitated before stepping inside. This was the only way to put his questions to rest—or to find the answers he needed. Stepping inside, he found himself at a reception counter littered with forms. Beyond that was a workstation with two desks facing each other. At one, a woman in a khaki uniform was talking on the phone and playing computer solitaire. At the other sat Stan Shea, whose father had run the icehouse at the docks when they were boys.

Stocky, balding and cheerful, Stan stood up. "Mike Malloy. Jesus, it's been a coon's age. I'm glad you called. So what's up? You got trouble?"

"Some questions, like I said on the phone. About Victor Winslow's accident."

Stan folded his beefy arms on the counter. "Hell of a thing, wasn't it?"

"I want to take a look at the case file." He'd already

read or viewed all the newscasts, articles and documents archived on the Web, but they raised more questions than they answered.

Stan shrugged. "It's a public document. I pulled the stuff from the files after you called." He led Mike down the hall to a room filled with files and forms. Dragging open a heavy drawer, he lifted out a stack of thick files. Finally, he gave Mike a disclosure form to sign. "Mind if I ask why the interest?"

"It's been nagging at me. Vic and I go way back."

"I remember that. The two of you were like Mutt and Jeff." He shook his head. "Hell of a thing," he said again.

Mike hoped Stan wouldn't probe further. Rules required that he stay in the room, but he was a quiet sort, working a crossword puzzle in a chair by the door. Mike felt out of his depth, paging through reports, statements, diagrams and official forms—this was not his line of work. The stark photographs touched his nerves with ice. There was the bridge, its railing ripped away at the point of impact. The car, with its mangled front end and smashed mosaic windshield, had been dragged up from the bay a few hours after the incident.

Each object in the vehicle and trunk had been tagged and catalogued: tire iron and spare, a box of Kleenex, *Phantom of the Opera* in the CD player, two pairs of sunglasses, papers from the glove box, a map of Rhode Island, a Boston city map and one of South Florida. The usual items commonly found in anyone's car. Except this one had belonged to Victor and Sandra.

He came across photos and medical assessments of Sandra, and his heart skipped a beat. The unforgiving black-and-white photographs portrayed a woman pasty with shock, her eyes dark and huge in her bloodless face.

Medical jargon and shorthand covered the papers—everything had been screened, scanned, scrutinized.

There were close-up shots: a hole in the dashboard, the shattered windshield, the driver-side airbag a limp, mud-stained object wadded on the seat, a woman's stained winter coat.

He must have made some involuntary sound, because Stan looked at him. "Hard to believe they couldn't make a case, eh? Her lawyer made it out like Victor was wounded in the accident and then was sucked out to sea. While she swam to safety."

But she can't swim. She had disclosed that fact the day they'd gone cruising on the *Fat Chance*. Sandra couldn't swim. But Victor had once been a distance champion in the eight-hundred-meter freestyle.

Mike said nothing to Stan. He needed to do some serious thinking. "She was unconscious when they found her," he said, reading from a transcript he'd already viewed a hundred times on the Internet. "And no one followed up on the witness who called in the wreck."

"Nothing to follow up. The transcript of the call's there."

Mike had already read the brief exchange. *A car just went over the bridge . . . Yeah, the Sequonset Bridge. It was headed west . . . Jesus, just send someone—he's going to drown—* The dispatch operator, who logged the call into the police computer, reported that the exchange, with an adult male, had ended abruptly. The first emergency vehicle arrived thirteen minutes after the call came in.

"Why do you suppose the caller said *he*'s going to drown? Why not *she* or *they*?"

Stan spread his hands, palms out. "Who can say? *He* might be a generic term. Or the guy might've been confused. A wreck like that—it's not something you see every day, eh?"

"Where's the car now?" he asked.

"In the boneyard over on Yancy."

"Mind if I have a look?"

"Fine with me." Stan told the clerk he was stepping out and they walked together across a nearly empty parking lot to a fenced yard littered with vehicles in various stages of disrepair. A fine, cold rain hissed from brooding skies.

The Winslows' Cadillac STS hunched amid the rusty ruins, a sad, crumpled monument to the tragedy, splotched with neon orange paint from the investigation. Bracing one arm on the roof, Mike peered inside at the broken steering wheel, the buckled dashboard, airbag, and seat belts lying stiff and twisted on the seats. The liner hung from the warped ceiling, caked with silt and salt.

He spent a long time going over the car, hating every minute of it as he pictured Sandy at the wheel, Vic uncharacteristically drunk, yelling at her. Yelling what? He tried to see what they'd seen that night, even tried to feel what they'd felt at the point of impact.

He sat in the ruined leather seat, stiff with ancient salty sand and sludge. Tiny darts of sleet pelted him through the empty hole where the windshield had been. Old houses had a way of talking to him, revealing the past with coy whispers, elusive clues. But the car seemed impenetrable; the ghosts that haunted it guarded their secrets.

As he got out, he glanced at the dome light, then did a double take. The battery was long dead, of course, but the light switch on the passenger side was in the ON position.

"Hey, Stan," he said. "Why do you suppose this was switched on?"

Stan stuck his head through the window. "Beats me.

Could've been tripped during the wreck, or maybe during the investigation. Whole team swarmed over it." ·

As he drove back to Paradise, Mike kept playing the scenario over and over in his mind; he imagined the car breaking through the high bridge, tried to feel the jarring impact when the car hit the water. On a dark winter night, with the vehicle sinking fast, would he have reached up to turn on the light?

The detail was insignificant—the investigators had noted and dismissed it. But Mike was pretty sure they didn't know about the things hidden in Sandra's attic.

Chapter 32

Ten Signs of Spring

8. *Mom and Carmine send away for summer-camp brochures.*
9. *Kandy Procter goes on a pineapple diet so she can fit into her bikini.*
10. *Kevin (aka Barnacle Brain) starts Little League— finally!*

Bored with watching his sister writing in her journal, Kevin snatched the notebook away and held it high over his head. "I saw that," he said.

Zeke woke up from sleeping in the sun at the end of the dock. The dog yawned, then settled his chin between his paws.

"Give it back." Mary Margaret jumped up and lunged at Kevin. "I'll break your face."

He wasn't scared. She was a big old klutz anyway, always keeping secrets from him. He didn't give a hoot what was in her stupid notebook, but it was important to her, so that made it worth stealing.

"I bet this thing is full of love poems to Billy Lawton," he said, grinning when her face turned red as a tomato.

"You weasel," she yelled. "You worm."

He held the book out over the dark, clear water surrounding the dock where his dad's boat was moored. He let it dangle from two fingers. It would serve her right if he dropped it. Mary Margaret was so freaky these days. Maybe now she'd finally pay attention to him.

She did. Darting out her fist, she grabbed the front of his hooded sweatshirt and twisted, hard. Instead of hauling him toward her, she gave him a shove. He teetered on the edge of the dock, and below him the clear water shimmered like a sheet of ice.

"Hey!" Kevin wheeled his arms to regain his balance. Ready for action, Zeke began to bark. Mary Margaret snatched the book from one flailing hand, then let him go. He saved himself by grabbing a tarred pylon. "You almost drowned me, you maniac."

"I should have." Making a face like a wounded martyr in his catechism workbook, she tucked her precious notebook into her school backpack.

She wasn't even much fun to pick a fight with anymore. Kevin grabbed a stick and poked it at a cluster of anemones clinging to the sharp underwater rocks below the dock. "You're always writing stuff," he complained. "Just because Sandra writes, you have to."

"That's not why," she snapped. "I write for myself."

She sounded so freaking holy. She was totally in love with the stupid notebook because it was college-ruled and had a fancy cover, and the pen had liquid ink instead of regular ink. Big fat hairy deal.

"You idolize Sandra," he accused.

"You don't even know what that means, moron."

"You worship her big toe. You're trying to be exactly like her."

"Am not."

"Are so."

"Am—" Mary Margaret snapped her mouth shut like a frog catching a fly. Looking over Kevin's shoulder, she said, "Oh. Hi."

"Don't let me interrupt." Sandra stepped onto the dock, a large pizza box balanced in her hands. "The two of you were bickering so well."

Kevin wiped his tarry fingers on his jeans. "Hi, Sandra."

"I thought you two might like some lunch."

He grabbed the dog while Mary Margaret picked up her backpack. "I'm starving," he said.

"Where's your dad?"

"He's at the harbormaster's, talking to some guy." Mary Margaret jerked her thumb toward the cluster of buildings at the head of the dock. "We're waiting for our mom to pick us up."

Dad had been having all kinds of meetings lately. Maybe it was about a job. Dad was always fixing things. In the old days, when they'd all been together in Newport, he used to fix fancy mansions and historical buildings. Everything was different now. Dad wasn't surrounded by secretaries and assistants and subcontractors. He didn't have a phone glued to his ear and meetings scheduled morning, noon, and night. Nowadays, he had more time to spend with Kevin. The trouble was, Kevin didn't seem to have as much time for Dad. He visited only on assigned days, and there never seemed to be enough of them.

"More pizza for us, then," Sandra said. "Let's eat outside. It's the most gorgeous day we've had all year."

"I'll set up the folding table," Mary Margaret offered, scrambling to the deck of the *Fat Chance*.

"Go wash your hands, okay, Kevin?" Sandra said. "You might need the mineral spirits to get that tar off."

He clomped into the boat. Sandra sounded kind of like a mom, and he wasn't sure how he felt about that. But most of the time, she was pretty nice, friendly and never fake. She was more fun than most grown-ups Kevin knew. She actually seemed to like hanging out with kids rather than putting up with them because she thought she had to. Sometimes Kevin got that feeling about Carmine. They'd be right in the middle of shooting hoops or something, and Carmine would get a call on his cell phone, and that would be that. When he cut a game short, he'd slip Kevin a five-dollar bill, which was way cool. But sometimes Kevin would rather have the game.

He figured he was lucky. At least Carmine didn't pretend to be his father, like other stepdads seemed to do. Kevin had never met a kid so stupid he couldn't tell the difference.

While he scrubbed away at his hands, he wondered if Sandra might become his stepmom one day. She and Dad never did any lovey-dovey stuff around him, but sometimes he saw them looking at each other in a special way that made him a little nervous.

Outside, the three of them ate the steaming, gooey pizza, throwing the crusts to circling gulls while Zeke barked his head off. Afterward, Mary Margaret decided she wanted her hair done in fancy braids, so Sandra got a comb and went to work. Bored, Kevin found a net and fished off the dock for a while. He got a crab, and Zeke went nuts barking at it before it scuttled off the dock and dropped into the water. While they were all laughing and talking, his mom showed up.

When she saw Sandra doing Mary Margaret's hair, Mom got a hard look on her face. "Where's your father?" she asked.

"Harbormaster's office," Kevin said.

Sandra finished the braids, her hands quick, all of a sudden.

"Go get your stuff," said Mom. "We need to get home."

Kevin and Mary Margaret went down to their stateroom to shove everything into duffel bags. It was weird, packing for a trip every time they went to visit their dad. He was getting used to it. But he wasn't sure he liked it.

"Hey," he said to his sister. "Where's my Gameboy?"

"Shh." Mary Margaret stood still, her head cocked as she listened to Mom and Sandra talking abovedecks.

". . . could lose his visitation privileges," Mom was saying.

A pause. Then Sandra said, "You'd do that?"

"It's up to the custody evaluator. I didn't make the rules. I'm looking out for my kids. That's what's important." It was the voice she used when she went to school to complain about a teacher. She tried to sound really nice, but sharp underneath.

Sandra said something else, but it was too soft to hear.

". . . or this will show up on the next custody evaluation. Your choice," Mom said.

Kevin frowned. "What are they—"

"Shh," Mary Margaret said again. She nibbled at her bottom lip, the way she did when she was thinking hard.

". . . force him to choose," Sandra said.

"Look, it's one thing for him to work for you," Mom said. "But another . . . Hey, life's full of hard choices, isn't it?"

"Mom's mad about something. What's she got against Sandra?" Kevin whispered.

Mary Margaret shrugged. "She doesn't like him dating, is what I think."

"He's not dating," Kevin said. "Is he?"

"God, you *are* a moron." She tossed him his Gameboy.

They finished packing and took their stuff to shore. Mom waited by the car, the lid of the trunk up. Sandra carried the empty pizza box to the trash. Her face was white and real serious when she said good-bye. Kevin felt a squirmy sensation in his stomach. He had never liked good-byes.

Chapter 33

Sandra drove home from Newport, knowing she ought to concentrate on the meeting with Milton Banks. He had been coaching her about the upcoming hearing—how to act, what to wear, what to say, and most importantly of all, what *not* to say. But she couldn't focus on that; instead, even though the lawsuit loomed like a bank of heavy clouds, she thought about Mike.

She'd found a glimpse of happiness with him. She could admit that now, though only to herself, no matter how great the temptation to confess it to him. The idea of letting him go hurt so much. It meant letting go of all the hopes and dreams she had built in such a short time. It meant forcing herself to forget him, the kids, all the impossible things she wanted and should have been smart enough to know she could never have.

She tried to imagine what it would be like, never again to feel his arms around her, never to hear the easy rumble of his laughter, never to know the soaring ecstasy of making love with him. But she had to end this. She had no choice. Angela had made it clear that Sandra was poison. She declared her kids off-limits.

Angela Falco wasn't a bad person. She actually seemed to be a pretty good mother—with a mother's very real concern for the people in her children's lives. She'd do what it took to keep Sandra away from Kevin and Mary Margaret. And from Mike. If Sandra insisted on staying with him, he'd be forced to choose between her and his kids. And for a man like Mike, that was no choice at all.

How to tell him? She couldn't explain that she was afraid he'd lose his kids because of her; he wouldn't stand for that from his ex-wife.

The temptation to draw the lines of battle burned as intensely as the afternoon sunshine breaking through the clouds. She gripped the steering wheel and grimly shut down the impulse. She could never do that to Kevin and Mary Margaret.

She braked and pulled her car over to the mailbox— the first thing Mike had fixed at Blue Moon Beach. Near the base, a trio of daffodils nodded in the breeze. When had those come up? she wondered.

Putting off the confrontation a few moments longer, she sifted through the mail—catalogs and coupons, credit card solicitations and grocery circulars. Tossing them onto the seat of the car, she turned into the driveway.

The crew had finished the porch. The ornate white railing circled the house like spun-sugar icing. Solid, symmetrical steps led to the front door and the entranceway, now as handsome and welcoming as it must have been the day the first Babcock had brought his new bride here for a summer-long honeymoon more than a hundred years before.

She stepped out of the car and blinked, feeling as though she was coming out of hibernation. Malloy had done it. He'd taken the broken wreckage of a neglected house and restored it to the private retreat envisioned by the original builder. The improvements had been gradual, but until today, in the dazzling sunshine ripe with the warm promise of spring, she hadn't realized how dramatic the changes were.

Over the weekend, she and Mike had worked side by side with a yard crew, cleaning out beds, pruning lilac bushes and wild roses, trimming the edges of the walkways. Coaxed by the sweet, inexorable breath of spring, crocuses pushed up their purple bell-shaped heads; daffodils and early tulips splashed color through the garden.

The world was bright and brand-new, clean and promising as an unwritten page. But with her usual caution, she reminded herself that springtime was an uncertain prospect in Paradise. The season of storms wasn't over yet; the weather of coastal Rhode Island could never be counted on.

Two workmen stood on ladders, stripped to their undershirts today as they installed newly repaired and painted antique shutters. One of them waved at her. "There's a delivery for you on the porch," he called.

At the door, she noticed a lavish flower arrangement beside a FedEx envelope. Her heart lurched. Who would be sending her flowers? Frowning, she plucked out the card and read the message, "Marvelous! Good luck!" Her editor's name had been signed to it. Confused now, she opened the envelope to find a certificate from the National Library Society, announcing that *Every Other Day* had been short-listed for the Addie Award.

She let out a gasp. The Addie was the Holy Grail of prizes for children's literature. It belonged to writers she had admired all her life—Beverly Cleary, Madeleine L'Engle, Lois Lowry—and represented a validation by the booksellers of America. Winning it meant her publisher would sell more copies of her book, bringing that many more readers to her. And that, she concluded, was the whole reason she wrote—in order to touch readers' hearts.

She ran her thumb over the embossed letterhead of the stationery. Slowly, she picked up the big glass vase. For a fleeting moment, she savored the beauty of the flowers, the house and the satisfaction of her news. One thing was missing. Someone to share her joy. She wanted to race inside, fling her arms around Mike and babble the news to him. But she couldn't, not now.

In the old days, she would have gone running to Victor. He would have hugged her, kissed her, taken her somewhere exclusive for dinner and ordered a bottle of Cristal.

She went in through the warm sunroom in the back, setting her purse on the kitchen table. "Mike?" she called out. "Hey, Malloy!"

"In the study."

She expected to find him caulking a window, installing crown molding or changing the hardware on the cabinets. Instead, he sat at the desk where she usually worked.

When he saw her, he got up and walked around the desk. "Sandy—"

"Mike." She interrupted him, trying to figure out how to tell him about her decision. "I have to talk to you."

Her tone made him frown. "What's with the flowers?"

She set down the vase. "My book is up for an Addie Award—big prize for a children's book." Chickening out, she went on, "I won't win, of course. I'm listed with the best writers working today." She heard herself babbling, but couldn't help it. "Anyway, thanks for asking."

"Congratulations." He offered the small dish of M&M's he'd kept filled on her desk ever since she had told him the M&M's story.

She helped herself to a few, nervousness itching through her, turning—irrationally—to irritation. "Mike—"

"Look, Sandy, I need to talk to you about something, too."

She studied his face and realized with a start that he was deadly serious, and had been since she'd barged into the study. Maybe his ex-wife had given him an ultimatum, too. Maybe he was going to do the breaking up.

"What's the matter?"

"Have a seat."

Eyeing him warily, she sank down on the wooden chair beside the desk. "Did you find termites? Is the house falling down?"

"It's about Victor." He propped a hip on the desk and regarded her in a way that made her deeply uncomfortable—as if, for the first time, he didn't trust her. "I want you to tell me the truth about you and Victor."

It was the last thing she expected, and she felt unbalanced by the abrupt demand. She'd spent half the day being grilled by her lawyer; now Mike?

Studying his troubled blue eyes, she tried to figure out what he wanted from her. What was he digging for? Her father's warning rang in her ears. Life had taught her to distrust everyone, even the people she loved. Did she love him enough to trust him?

"I don't want to talk about it anymore."

He slammed his fist on the desk. She'd never seen him like this—edgy, threatening. It occurred to her that she had never seen him angry. Could you ever really know a person until he got angry with you?

"I won't let you do this anymore," he said, his voice quiet yet somehow ominous. "I won't let you hold back."

"I never—"

"It's time you told me the truth about your marriage."

Her marriage.

"I've already done that. We were married, and then he died in an accident." She thought about the way she and Victor had been together. About the things he'd said to her in the car that night. The things she'd said to him. *Victor*. She loved him. She hated him. She wanted just five more minutes with him.

"What in the world is your point?" she demanded.

He narrowed his eyes until they glinted like ice. "You haven't leveled with me from the start. Were you ever planning on doing that?" When she didn't reply, his stare drilled deeper. "How long did you know he was gay?"

Everything stopped—breath, heartbeat, the waves on the sand, the world on its axis. Instantly she thought, He's bluffing. He can't know. But Mike Malloy never lied, never bluffed. That much she knew about him. Her throat froze, trapping denial in a vise. Her mouth worked, but only silence hung in the room, as though someone had just breathed his last breath.

So this was it, then, the moment she'd dreaded, the moment she'd prayed would never come. This was what she'd been afraid of all along. This was why loving Mike was so foolish, so futile. As foolish, in its way, as loving Victor had been.

She crossed her arms in front of her and bent forward as though shielding herself from a blow. But it was too late. She should have known from the start that a man like Mike would keep delving deep into her life, that he would finally succeed in opening secrets she'd kept bottled up. The moment confirmed what she had known all along— that although it hurt to hold her secrets in, it hurt even more to give them up.

Shame, guilt, and inadequacy lashed at her from a past that would never really go away. She wanted to retreat back into her frozen state, to keep her anguish private, for it was as much a part of her as her soul. Now, with one simple question, he'd taken the shadowy truth from her. He held it up, forcing her to face it.

She stood and walked away from him, toward the window. For one terrible moment, she felt a soaring relief— maybe she could confide in someone at last. Then she hesitated, watching one of Victor's suncatchers spin slowly, a dolphin of blue and green glass turning the sunlight to the deep and mysterious colors found at the heart of a flame, and she felt hostility, not gratitude. "D-damn you, Malloy," she said in a tortured whisper.

"No," he said, and his hand closed on her arm as he pulled her around to face him. "Damn *you*, Sandy. Why the hell didn't you say anything?"

"I would never do that," she said, dragging conviction from her well of pain. She yanked her arm away from him. "It's none of your business—or anyone else's. Why would I tell you? So you can accuse me of killing your best friend because he was gay?"

For a moment, incomprehension suffused his expression. Then he gave a humorless bark of laughter. "Why the hell would I do that?"

"Anyone who finds out is going to assume it."

"So you haven't told anyone."

"Can you blame me?"

"Yes. You withheld information from a formal investigation—"

"Information that would only cause more hurt, and it wouldn't change a thing. It would only get me in deeper trouble and damage more lives."

"It's already damaged your life."

"I'm dealing with it."

"You're running from it. Again—I think this is a habit with you. You've always held part of yourself back from me. From everyone. From life. You're using this as an excuse."

It was an effort just to breathe. "I think you should leave, Malloy."

"And make it easy for you? Hell, no, I won't. Not until I get some answers. Did you know when you married him? Christ, is that *why* you married him, so you wouldn't have to endure the mess of actually loving someone? So you could hold him at arm's length and keep your heart walled off?" His face was hard, uncompromising, and he made a visible effort to take hold of his temper, inhaling slowly and deeply. "Why couldn't you trust me with the truth?"

"You have it so wrong. It's not about trusting you." *It's not even about the truth.*

"Sit back down, Sandy. You might as well, because I'm not leaving."

Defeat shuddered through her. Or was it surrender? She couldn't tell. Her stomach twisted, and she sat down on the cushioned window seat. Outside, the wind picked up, and an arching branch of forsythia scratched across the antique glass pane. Plump yellow buds clung to the branch where, just a few weeks before, the bushes had appeared naked and dead.

Sitting beside her, he took both her hands in his, rubbing them, trying to warm them. "Talk to me, Sandy. I want to understand."

"You could never understand. We were happy, Malloy.

364 / Susan Wiggs

We liked being together. We shared things, but . . . there was this other side to him."

"The fact that he was gay." He planted his elbows on his knees, his eyes filled with lost incredulity. "I can't believe I didn't figure it out."

"For all I know, you did," she shot at him. "You were his best friend."

"You were his wife, and he had you fooled. So which one of us is the bigger idiot?" Agitated, he got up and paced the room, which suddenly seemed too small for him. For the first time, she realized that he was dealing with this, too. What sort of earthquake was it to learn that your best friend, the person closest to your heart while growing up, was not the person you thought he was? It must be a real shock, particularly for someone like Mike, who hid nothing.

"He was good, Malloy. You don't know how good."

"I should have guessed, but, Jesus, it was Victor. Your mind just didn't go there." He stopped pacing to study the photograph on the desk—a smiling Victor, his arm around Sandra, laughing out at the camera. Mike's eyes were awash with torment. "Maybe he tried to tell me, and I never took the hint. And then maybe he quit dropping hints."

She could relate to his guilt, though it didn't ease her resentment of his prying. But she felt guilty, too, and stupid and blind. Right under her nose, her husband had been fighting to deny his sexuality, to beat it out of himself, to smother it. And he'd used her as his means of self-flagellation.

"He did everything in his power to hide it," she said, then added bitterly, "and that's where I came in." She felt a familiar sting of anger. Victor's love and friendship had been secondary to his need to use her as a smoke screen.

"What better way for a gay man to hide his preference than to marry a woman? And to make that marriage look as blissful as a fairy tale?"

She focused on the suncatcher again, letting time fall away, taking herself back to summer days of innocence, of ignorance. From the start, from the first turn of that Ferris wheel, she'd believed Victor loved her as much as she loved him. Until that final argument, she never knew that making love to her was a form of penance for him. She was the scourge with which Victor flayed himself every day of their marriage.

She glanced away from the glittering, translucent ornament and shuddered. "You know what his family is like—the pride, the expectations. He struggled all his life to live up to that. He gave everything he had to being someone he could never be. He knew that if this came to light, he'd have to give up the love and esteem of his parents, his community and his career in politics, everything he'd worked for all his life. I believe he thought he was prepared to make the sacrifice."

She pressed her hands together in her lap, trying as she had so many times in the past year to imagine the things that went on inside him. All his shining achievements had not been able to compensate for surrendering the defining element of who he was. "But as time went on, he became increasingly distracted, unhappy and . . . lost, I guess. He claimed he was physically faithful to me, but now I realize he was becoming consumed by frustration. And fear, too," she added, thinking of that last night, the last terrible words they'd spoken. "I unknowingly made matters worse by pressuring him to have a child. I wanted kids so badly, sometimes I ached with it."

She shut her eyes, fighting for control, then made herself look at Mike again. "I used to wonder why I'm not angrier at Victor, why I don't feel more betrayed. The fact is, maybe he wasn't my dream lover, but he was someone special and rare—he was my friend. That's pretty hard to come by."

He shot to his feet so fast that she flinched. "Quit being so fucking understanding," he said. "Don't you see what he did to you?"

"He was good to me—"

"Oh, yeah? How was your sex life, Sandy? Answer me that." He grabbed her aggressively, pulling her to her feet, putting his mouth very close to hers. "Was it like ours?"

She said nothing; he knew the answer to that. He'd been a revelation to her. She'd never known passion until him. But Mike was wrong about one thing—she was angry, sometimes so angry she couldn't see straight. All during her marriage she'd felt inadequate, unattractive, thinking she was at fault. And Victor had let her believe that, let her suffer. What she'd found in Mike's arms—Victor had deprived her of those things. She didn't think she could ever forgive him, and that was a problem, because now he was dead and she could never confront him.

"There's simply no point in being bitter now," she said.

"I don't get it, Sandy. What holds you so tight that you'd go through a lawsuit, ruination, maybe bankruptcy when you hold the truth in your hands?"

"What, you think telling the world my husband was gay is going to exonerate me?" She shook her head. "Don't be naive. What good would it do to tell people now? In the first place, no one would believe me, and in the second place, they'd say that finding out his sexual preference gave me a stronger motive to do him in. They'll call me a liar, an opportunist, smearing the reputation of a good man to save my skin."

"You're still hiding behind Victor."

She stood and began putting books up in the newly refinished shelves, aligning the spines with obsessive precision. "How can I hide behind a ghost?"

"You're some piece of work, you know that? You pretend it's noble to hide the truth, but in fact, you don't want to save yourself. You'd rather keep yourself in seclusion, hiding from the world. You'd rather play the martyr, letting the town force you to leave. If you had to stay, you'd actually have to live a life outside your books. You'd have to give yourself over to loving a man in a way you've never dared. You're afraid of taking a risk. And you're probably afraid of looking stupid, too—isn't that right? Married to a man you didn't know was gay?"

She felt as though he'd slapped her. Worse, he held up a mirror, showing her the selfishness in her anguish over Victor. Malloy was forcing her to face the fact that she'd never had a successful romantic relationship in her life. She thought she had that with Victor, but on the last day of his life, she discovered that she was wrong. Now she felt safer alone, cocooned by her own fictional world, apart from those who found love and meaning with their families and friends. She didn't want anyone to reach her, to touch her, to make her feel again. And here was Mike, forcing her out of her numb state, making her feel the fire and tingle and searing agony of yearning.

"I really need you to leave." Her quiet plea struck the silence from the room. "Please, just . . . just leave."

"I can't do that, Sandy." He walked over to the desk, pulled open the top drawer and grabbed a handful of letters. A labeled computer disk dropped from the pile. "Do you recognize any of this?"

At first glance, it resembled anyone's old mail. But every single letter was addressed to Victor.

Her throat tightened. She couldn't breathe.

"Wh . . ." The failed word aspirated from her as the crippling strangulation seized her vocal cords again. Everything she felt stayed locked inside, burning to escape. Yet the harder she tried to speak, the tighter her muscles grew.

Mike waited, calm and patient. Most people took pity on her when she struggled with her stutter; some tried to finish her thoughts for her. He merely stood by the desk. Deadly serious. Waiting.

She willed the words to emerge. Summoning all her strength, she pushed out a question. "Wh-where did you get that?"

"It was in the attic, hidden in a box. An old suitcase, actually. I came across it by accident."

A slow burn of anger curled through every fiber of her body, all the way to the bone. Suddenly the man to whom she'd given her heart, her body, had become a stranger. The stutter melted away. "And you've made it your business to read private letters? Hidden letters?" Her voice was low and husky, wavering over the words.

"No," he said. "Not when I first came across them. But the more I thought about the accident, the more I realized I couldn't leave it alone."

"You can now," she said. "You can leave me alone—my life, my house, everything."

"These letters, the data on this disk—they could explain so much. But they pose a lot of new questions, too."

"Damn it, Malloy." She shot to her feet. "It's not your place to ask anything."

"Somebody has to. God knows, the investigators wrote him off fast enough."

"They didn't write him off. There was a ruling of death."

"Don't you think that was a bit premature?"

A wave of nausea swept through her. She glared at Malloy as though he were a stranger. Her resentment curled in on itself like a withered autumn leaf. "Oh, for God's sake, are you working for the tabloids now? I'm supposed to be the one with the wild imagination. Every expert in the state worked on this. They didn't overlook anything."

"But they didn't know Victor the way I did. Or the way you did."

Against all good sense, she felt a leap of hope in her chest. *Alive. Victor, alive after all.* Then cold reality crushed down as she pictured the mangled, muddy car, the hopeless faces of the recovery crew.

Roused by Mike's shocking suggestion, nightmare memories swept over her, and once again, she was in the driver's seat, racing through the icy winter night. Disjointed impressions bombarded her. The car racing up behind them. Victor's voice rising in hysteria. Her own panicked pleas. The feeling that someone had ripped away the steering wheel, a carnival-ride sensation as the car spun out of control. The stunning impact of the car striking the rail. The explosive hiss of the airbag, and then . . . nothing. Until the glare of the ER, and the devastating report that Victor was missing, presumed dead.

After the accident, everyone had prayed he'd somehow survived. His mother clung to her wild hopes for an unhealthy length of time. Winifred fled to the hospital chapel, beseeching God on her knees until she fainted from exhaustion. She refused to believe her son was dead. Even when her husband had explained that a person couldn't have survived the frigid waters for more than a few minutes. Even when the police reported evidence of gunshot. It was only when the bizarre twist of the investigation pointed suspicion at Sandra that Winifred finally understood that her son was dead.

"I'm begging you, Malloy," Sandra said, dragging the words from an icy hollow of terror and grief, "don't bring this all up again."

"I have to."

"Why?"

"Because I'm right."

"So are Elvis's fans," she said. "And Jimmy Hoffa's family."

"The investigation didn't go far enough." He picked up the framed photograph of her and Victor, standing in front of the white-domed State House. They smiled with a unity of purpose that had held their marriage together far longer than it should have. "I've been doing some checking."

Her gut twisted as she pictured him pawing through the evidence file—reports, statements, photographs, sealed bags containing the flotsam and jetsam of their last moments together. Everyone's pain and confusion had been reduced to bald statements on public documents. "You're a carpenter, Malloy," she snapped, "not an investigator. They did their job."

"But they didn't remove every shadow of doubt. That's why the Winslows are suing you."

"That's my problem."

"It's mine, too, now."

"Why?"

"Because I care, God damn, it." In two strides he crossed the room, gripped her upper arms and drew her to him. "Look, I studied all the conclusions, all the different theories. But I have one advantage over the medical examiner's staff. I know you. And I know Victor. He didn't die,

Sandy. He wouldn't. He rescued you from the car. Then he disappeared."

"That's insane." She drew back, but he kept a firm hold on her. Despite her denial, her heart sped up. "They searched every rock on the shore, every square inch of the marsh, every blade of grass on both sides of the bridge."

"He took off."

"Just walked away."

"Or ran. Took a bus, a train. Caught a ride with a stranger."

"So he walked away from his home, his family, his flourishing political career."

"Yeah, he did."

"So where did he go?"

He searched her eyes, and she forced her gaze not to waver. She didn't want him to know how much he was scaring her. Finally he broke away and stood. He scooped the letters from the desk drawer and dropped them on the table next to her. "Maybe this will explain it."

Her heart lurched to her throat. "Your job is to renovate my house, not pry into personal affairs."

"It is personal." He reached for her, and just for a moment, for a heartbeat, she wanted his touch so badly it created a physical ache.

She stepped back toward the door, eluding him. "I hired you to fix things, not foul things up. God, don't you think I wanted to find him? Don't you think we considered the possibility that he was disoriented or had amnesia after the crash? The best investigators in the state found no trace of him. What makes you think you can?"

He gestured at the letters. "I can read between the lines."

"Don't you think if Victor were alive, he would have contacted me? He wouldn't do this to me."

He stared at her in disbelief. "He did it to you all through your marriage."

She stared back. "You know, in a way, it's a good thing we're having this conversation now. Otherwise, I might have gone on indefinitely, not knowing what a son of a bitch you are." She slammed her hand on the door frame so hard that her fingers went numb. "I want you out of here, Malloy. Now. Out of my house, out of my life. Let your crew stay and finish, send me a bill for the final payment, but I don't want to see you again. Ever."

She tried not to glimpse in his face all the things she had come to love—the passion, the tenderness, the strength. She didn't want to see those things now, because she couldn't trust them. She wondered if he knew that until this moment, she had thought of him as her refuge, her one safe place in a world where she didn't belong.

That was over. Their time together had the phantom allure of cotton candy from an itinerant carnival. Unbelievably sweet at first taste, but ultimately it disappeared, insubstantial as mist.

"Get out," she said, forcing herself to let go of all the foolish things she'd wanted—for herself, for Mike, for *them*. "Or I swear I'll call the police." She waited for him to call her bluff, to see what the local police would do for the Black Widow of Blue Moon Beach.

Instead, he studied her a moment longer, then went to the door. "To hell with it." His anger was new and startling to her. "I'm out of here. When you're ready to listen to reason, call me."

She bit her lip to keep from calling him back, begging him to stay. In fact, she ought to feel relieved. She'd fretted all day about how to break it off with Mike, to give him back to his kids and to the new life he was building for them. He just handed her the perfect excuse.

Chapter 34

Dorrie Babcock drummed her fingers on the armrest of the car door. She wanted a cigarette in the worst way, and alone in the back of the taxi, there was no one to stop her. The taxi driver was obviously a kindred spirit, with a brown-tipped Camel tucked between his nicotine-stained fingers. The acrid odor of stale cigarettes haunted the interior of the car, tantalizing and mocking her.

Forcing herself to sit up straight, she went through the litany of exercises she had learned in the stop-smoking seminar—self-talk, a visualization exercise, a piece of gum from her pocketbook. If all those failed, she had her prescription tablet.

The driver flicked his half-smoked Camel through the vent, right past the "Thank You for Not Smoking" sign. Dorrie turned her gaze out the window to watch the landscape swish past. After such a long absence, it felt strange to be back. Strange to be home. She had left in the bitter cold of bleak midwinter; now she was returning to burgeoning spring. The budding lilacs would soon burst into fragrant flowers; a rush of late winter storms had scoured the streets and sidewalks clean. Schoolchildren walked home with their jackets tied around their waists and their faces lifted to the sun.

Dorrie's journey had taken her beyond simple time or distance. She had gone back into herself, excavating the person she'd been when she still remembered how to dream. Somewhere along the way, that person had been lost, but in the warm breezes of the tropics, wearing resort clothes and socializing with people she'd never met before, Dorrie had found herself again. To her relief, she discovered that she still liked that person.

She'd learned to dance, play blackjack and swallow tequila slammers. She'd posed beside a trophy fish, her sunbaked arm raised in victory. Foreign phrases rolled off her tongue. So many ways to say please, thank you, where is the bathroom . . .

But at night, while lying in her small, nondescript stateroom, she dreaded the deep ache of loneliness; the consequence of her decision to leave her husband.

True, she had relearned the art of dreaming. But the startling truth was, her dreams had always included Lou.

She missed him. She missed the crackle of his newspaper as they sat together on quiet evenings, missed his comforting presence in bed beside her at night. She missed his smell, and the way he stared at her, his face a picture of wonder and delight, when she got out of the shower. And not just when she was young and firm, but always.

She even missed his clumsy, earnest attempts to help

with the housework, cringing as she recalled her reaction—he wasn't doing it "right."

As if there was a "right" way to Windex the kitchen.

Floating upon the turquoise sea had a dramatic effect on her. When she stood at the rail of the *Artemisia*, the vastness of the ocean and sky swept over her, putting everything—including household chores—in perspective.

The craving for a cigarette passed, as she knew it would. Each day was a little easier than the last. How many times had Lou begged her to quit, crazy with worry about her health? She'd clung stubbornly to the habit, even when the rest of the world stopped smoking.

Now, finally, Dorrie Babcock was a nonsmoker. She applied that obstinate will and used it to stay smoke-free. Did he still want her to quit, or did he no longer care?

The taxi turned down Sycamore Street and a wave of nostalgia engulfed her. For nearly forty years, this neighborhood had been her whole world—a quiet, unassuming street of bungalows from bygone days, filled with the sound of children's laughter, the smells of simmering soup or baking bread in the air. She had been one of those slender young mothers strolling along the sidewalk or sitting in a webbed lawn chair watching her little girl play in the yard. She used to sing along with the radio as she fixed dinner, and when she heard Lou's fin-backed Chrysler pull up, it never failed. Her heart skipped a beat—as it did now.

Somewhere out there on the endless azure sea, she'd found that youthful, soft-hearted woman again. That woman was still inside her, all but buried in the small, meaningless worries accumulated over the years. It was called living, she had discovered. No one so far had ever escaped it, though plenty—Dorrie included—had tried. During her time away, she managed to excavate a woman who loved her husband and wanted to spend the rest of her life with him.

She felt dizzy with apprehension as the taxi drew alongside the curb in front of the house. She paid the driver, and he took her bags to the door. The house looked the same as it did every spring. Half asleep, the hedges and yard still dormant, the bulbs pushing up through the loamy ground.

Home. Standing in the driveway, she held herself very still, torn between terror and gladness. The voyage had brought her to the last place she expected to wind up, to the only destination her heart desired. Home.

But there was one thing she wasn't sure of. She had no idea what she would find here.

This might have been a time of discovery for Lou as well. And he might have discovered that he still wanted a divorce.

Before her courage evaporated, she walked through the back door and into the mudroom. A golf bag leaned against the wall, spiked shoes set on a newspaper beside it. Standing in front of the kitchen door, she hesitated, then finally let herself in.

The kitchen smelled funny.

But the place wasn't a disaster. The counters were wiped and relatively uncluttered. The coffee canister lid was ajar; she resisted the urge to straighten it. The picture window over the sink framed a familiar view of the gnarled apple tree, decked in tightly folded buds that would soon burst into pale blossoms.

Oh, she hoped she would be here to see the apple blossoms come out.

On a knickknack shelf over the sink were the usual things: a Niagara Falls toothpick dispenser. The one good vase she owned. Her demitasse from Wanda's trip to Florence. Dorrie used to joke that the tiny gold-leafed espresso cup was as close as she would ever get to visiting Italy.

There was a new addition to the shelf—a framed photograph. With a lurch of her heart, she recognized Lou's favorite shot of her and Sandra, one he'd kept on his desk at work for years. In the backyard, Sandra, about eight, hung upside down from her knees in the old apple tree as Dorrie stood nearby. Mother and daughter smiled—unretouched, ordinary folks. What did Lou see in the photograph?

In the den at the other end of the house, the TV burbled softly. Hope built in Dorrie's chest as she left the kitchen. "Hello?" she called. "Lou?"

He must have heard a noise, for when she stepped into the living room, he was already on his feet.

Dorrie looked across the room at him and saw everything that he was, everything her heart desired. She saw the bridegroom who had pledged his life to her, the proud father holding his baby daughter for the first time, the endlessly patient, steady man who went to work to support his family, day in and day out. Year in and year out. The man who, a few months ago, had looked at her with his heart in his eyes and said, "Please don't go."

"I'm home," she said, her statement foolish, unnecessary.

He stood very still for a moment. She was about to repeat the statement in case he hadn't heard, but he held out his hand, palm up. "I'm . . . glad," he said, his voice quieter than she remembered.

Her pocketbook dropped to the floor but she didn't even look to see where it landed. "Are you?"

"Yes."

"You moved the easy chair," she observed, burning inside with fear and hope.

"Didn't like being so close to the TV," he explained. "If you want me to put it back, I—"

"No, Lou." She began to cry, the tears pouring down her face. "I want you to put *me* back." She took a step toward him. "Will you? Please?"

He didn't speak, didn't seem able to. Her heart dropped. He hadn't heard her.

She took a deep breath. "I said—"

"I heard what you said."

She remembered about the hearing aids. Sandra had told her in a letter. Dorrie had pestered him for years about it, and finally he'd seen an audiologist.

He crossed the room and took her in his arms. His familiar embrace surrounded her. Holding her close and tight, he buried his face in her hair. "I've been waiting so long, Dor," he murmured. "I could never stop loving you." He kissed the tears from her cheeks and then her mouth, and when she shut her eyes, the years fell away, and they were everything they'd set out to be—full of hope, full of love, full of dreams. She knew the solid core of their love would never change; time had only deepened the bond.

She pulled back, resting her fingers on his shoulders. "I sailed five thousand miles on that boat," she said. "But the only place I wanted to be was here. Here in your arms."

He kissed her again, then said something in her ear.

She frowned. "What was that?"

"It was Spanish for—" He bent and translated in a wicked whisper. An incredulous laugh escaped her. A blush seared her cheeks, her ears.

"I've been studying Spanish. It's not so hard, now that I can hear." He kissed her again, then took her by the hand and led her up the stairs.

Chapter 35

Journal Entry—April 9—Tuesday

Ten Things My Mother Taught Me

6. *The world's best donut recipe.*
7. *The fact that each donut contains more fat than a pound of bacon.*
8. *No hole or run in your panty hose is ever invisible.*
9. *If you want to know a boy's true character, look at his father.*
10. *Nobody ever said marriage was easy, but it's easier than the alternative.*

"Check out your mom and dad," Joyce said, elbowing Sandra. "They look like a damned Viagra commercial."

Sandra stopped in the middle of the courthouse parking lot. Joyce pointed at the Babcocks' Grand Marquis, parked in the shade of a budding dogwood tree. Her father held the car door for his wife, then rested his hand solicitously at her waist. Walking beside him, Dorrie pressed close as though she couldn't bear to be separated from him. She wore a new cherry-red coat, and their faces glowed, and it wasn't the spring sunshine alone that gave them such color and life.

"See what I mean?" Joyce said, elbowing her again.

"They're my parents, for Pete's sake."

Joyce turned toward the wide concrete steps of the courthouse. "So I'll see you inside, okay? Good luck."

"Thanks. I'll need all the support I can get in there." When Joyce was gone, Sandra hurried across the parking lot. "Mom!"

A second later she found herself embraced by both of them. For a moment, she felt totally safe and cocooned by their steady love. For a moment, she forgot that she was about to face the Winslows.

"Welcome back," she said to her mother. Her face was a bit plumper, her skin touched with gold from the tropical sun. "I missed you so much."

"I missed you, too." Her eyes shining with tear-bright emotion, Dorrie clung to both daughter and husband.

Warmth and gratitude wrapped around Sandra. Two days earlier, her mother had phoned to say she was back, and the news was better than Sandra could have hoped for—her mother was home, and the divorce was off. She held tight to both of them, afraid she might melt into a puddle of relief. She wasn't all that surprised, though, because any fool could see that their love was real, and always had been. The reconciliation was the one bright spot in an otherwise bleak period for Sandra. She hadn't seen Mike since she'd banished him from her house, from her life. Not that he seemed to be fighting the banishment. He'd taken off, exactly as she ordered, leaving the crew to finish the work on the house.

"Doesn't she look great?" her father asked.

"You both do." Sandra blushed, remembering Joyce's remark.

"We've worked out a compromise," her mother said with a wink. "I'm going to play golf, but only on foreign soil. And your father will poke around antique shops and museums with me." She tucked her hand into the crook of her husband's arm. "Scuba diving and skydiving are still under negotiation."

Sandra's heart soared and broke at the same time. Her parents' bond was even more durable now, strengthened by the fibrous cords of healed scar tissue. Why did they succeed where so many, Sandra included, had failed? It came down to bravery, she realized. Her parents were brave enough to fight for their love and brave enough to change in order to make it last.

Studying her mother's delicate, age-spotted hands and her father's round, mild face, she wondered where they found that sort of courage. She kept urging herself to be that brave, that strong, but every time she reached for the phone or drove past the Paradise docks, she chickened out. Nothing could compare to the emotional pain she'd felt after telling Mike to leave. Nothing—except the joy of being with him. She acknowledged that she had been motivated by fear. As long as she didn't give her heart over to him and his kids and even his annoying dog, she didn't risk herself.

"I'm proud of you both," she said. "I know what you went through wasn't easy."

"Holding together through the tough times—that's the real test," her mother said, sobering. "There's really no limit to how idiotic two people in love can be, is there? We made the mistake of thinking retirement would be perfection—we'd reached our life goals. Instead, we have to find new roads to travel, new discoveries to make about each other and about us, together."

"I'm glad," said Sandra. "Because I'm going to be needing you."

They went into the courthouse through a side entry and made their way to a conference room with a brass plaque on the door. Milton and his two associates were there already, going over notes and procedures. The lawyers barely acknowledged them as they arrived, except to inspect Sandra's clothing.

"You look good," he pronounced, checking out her navy-blue suit. "Conservative, not too flashy." He waved at Sandra's parents. "Don't want the judge to think she's out shopping with the ill-gotten gains." He studied them. "So are you still getting a divorce? Sandra said you were going to call it quits."

"We changed our minds," Lou stated.

"Yeah, at our age, it's probably better to stick with the devil you know."

"Yes," Sandra said to her parents' unspoken question. "He's always this obnoxious. I'll see you in the hearing room, okay?"

"What's the media doing here?" her father asked, scowling at the crowd in the hallway. "It's only a hearing. You'd think somebody called them all."

Courtney Procter? Sandra wondered. No, she'd want an exclusive. But judging by the crammed foyer, bristling with microphones, she'd been scooped. It was odd, though. Sandra's case was old news, yet the press was acting as though this were a breaking story.

"Don't say a word to the Winslows, the press, the spectators," Milton cautioned. "I can only help your daughter if I have complete control over what goes on during the hearing."

"Trust him," Sandra said. "He's all I've got."

"And the best there is," he added.

"Everything is going to be fine," her mother promised. They each hugged her and went to the door. Their departure left a hollow inside her, raw and sensitive.

She prayed Milton would be good enough now. Returning to the conference room, she thought, as she often did, about Mike. She struggled to see herself as part of a loving relationship with him instead of accepting solitude for the rest of her life.

Though she'd only known him a short time, she was different because of him. She'd never look at life the same way. How could she have known she could live so fully, with such joy? Before, she'd been half-alive, never knowing the peaks and valleys of the roller-coaster ride, never realizing what she could be with a man who loved her.

But this insanity, the wild things he believed about Victor, his futile obsession with finding him, erected a barrier. She told herself Mike was doing her a favor, staying away. In time, she might be able to get back to that numb state she'd lived in for so long—safe from love, safe from harm.

It was true that her life had changed because of Victor. But Mike had affected her more profoundly than that. He'd changed the landscape of her heart.

But that fragile geography had not been tested and tempered by time, and she was haunted by the possibility that had been ripped from her grasp.

A part of her wanted him to come crawling back, swearing he'd made a terrible mistake, begging her forgiveness.

But another part acknowledged the reality that he was, first and foremost, a single dad struggling to stay in his kids' lives. He had no choice about that, and she wasn't about to put his relationship with his kids at risk.

He was gone from her life. Kevin and Mary Margaret

were gone. Angela had seen to that. Soon, Sandra herself would be gone from Paradise.

"You ready?" Milton asked, gathering up his notes.

She walked to the door. "Oh, I can hardly wait."

He paused to grin at her.

"What?" she demanded.

"You're different."

"Yeah? I had my hair layered—"

"Not like that, I mean really different." He stood back, narrowed his eyes. "You used to be afraid of your own shadow. Now you're tougher. Ready to kick some butt."

"I take it that's a compliment."

"You bet your ass it is."

A gauntlet of reporters and photographers lined the corridor. As she and the attorneys walked to the courtroom, flashes shot off like fireworks; shouted questions peppered and bounced off her. She reminded herself of something Mike had nearly seduced her into forgetting: she was the girl on the Ferris wheel. Around and around and around. Nothing could touch her. Nothing could stop her or slow her down.

From the corner of her eye, she spotted a familiar blond head, glossy red-lined lips, a threadlike mike wire tucked into the collar of an Armani blazer. Courtney Procter. She was shoving a WRIQ mike forward.

"Mrs. Winslow, how do you plan to answer the charge that you engineered this whole thing for money?"

"Actually, Ms. Procter, I have a question for you. Are you ever going to get over the fact that I stole your boyfriend?" Sandra said as she walked past. "Better yet, try reporting the truth this time."

Milton gave a low whistle.

"I can't believe I just said that." She entered the creaky wooden quiet of the courtroom. Milton reminded her not to look left or right. But she couldn't keep from seeing the faces there. Ronald's parishioners jammed the benches, stabbing her with accusing glares. There was Gloria Carmichael from the deli, wearing a sweatshirt that announced, "99 Percent of Lawyers Give the Rest a Bad Name." Her parents and Joyce sat behind the bar of the defendant's table. She was startled to see Malloy's work crew, almost unrecognizable without their paint-spattered coveralls. They had their hair slicked back, work-worn hands balled into nervous fists on their knees. Oddly enough, Phil Downing sat near the Carmichaels, behind the plaintiffs' table. She wondered fleetingly if spectators were physically divided down the aisle—Friend of the Groom, Enemy of the Bride. The ushers at her wedding to Victor had been instructed to seat people evenly behind both sides of the aisle—no one gave a reason, but she always knew it was to conceal the fact that her friends and family could be counted on the fingers of one hand.

She was even more surprised to see Sparky Witkowski in a cobalt blue power suit, cell phone glued to her ear. Catching her eye across the room, Sparky stabbed the air with a stiletto fingernail and mouthed the words, *I need to talk to you.*

Not a good day to discuss real estate, Sandra thought, passing through the low swinging gate and taking a seat at the long Formica table. She didn't look at the Winslows but could feel their presence, a phantom chill as though someone had left an unseen window open.

She encased herself in numbing armor as Judge Santucci entered and everyone stood. Looking like a Tony Bennett clone, he settled at the bench, then motioned for everyone to be seated. He perched a pair of reading glasses on his nose, peered over the rims and addressed the attorneys, reminding them they were still bound by the instructions he had delineated in the previous days of the hearing.

She tried to find something to do with her hands. She picked up a pen and wrote on a yellow legal pad. *"Ten things nobody knows about me . . ."*

Every item on the list reminded her of Malloy. Riding into her life in a rusty old pickup truck, he'd found her at her most despairing moment. Instead of turning his back on her, he calmly went about the business of bandaging her hurts, repairing her house, her heart, filling her life. Making her laugh for the first time in months. Making her love him in a long, dizzying leap that explained why the term *falling* was so apt.

It was not just him that she loved, but everything he represented—the small, everyday miracles that made life worth living. She adored his kids, even liked his dog. She liked that Mike was ordinary, not famous. Good with his hands. Calm and strong, he was the fulfillment of a dream she didn't know she had until she saw him. He embodied the promise of security, a cushion, a flotation device.

But now she felt as though she were drowning as she walked to the witness stand, raised her hand, swore to tell the truth.

Whose truth? Her own? Or Victor's?

Milton had coached her to keep her eyes on him throughout the questioning, even when the plaintiffs' attorney addressed her. She concentrated on Milton, watching for clues. He did his lizard on a rock imitation, sitting statue still.

As expected, the Winslows' attorney began with benign, polite questions—a bit about where she grew up, went to school. The idea was to lead up to a vivid picture of a desperate woman greedy for her husband's money.

"Mrs. Winslow, how would you characterize your marriage to Victor Winslow?"

"We were happy together." She didn't elaborate. Milton forbade it. Besides, it wasn't quite a lie. They had been happy, although as time went on, Victor grew increasingly distracted, short-tempered and lost. She'd worried about him, but all she'd known, back then, was that there were moments when he seemed a complete stranger to her.

"We understand you have a career in publishing."

This was something new. She looked at Milton, who scowled, then shrugged.

"That's correct."

"To be exact, you've published five novels under an assumed name."

"Under my maiden name," she stated.

"Most people think authors are rich. Tell the court, have you gotten rich off your books?"

"You'll have to define rich."

"Do you make a living wage?"

"Objection," Milton said, the word flicking out like a snake's tongue. "This line of questioning is going nowhere."

"Your Honor, our purpose is to show that Mrs. Winslow is incapable of supporting herself through publishing alone."

"Counsel, please confine your questions to the circumstances surrounding the incident."

"This goes to motive, Your Honor. Other than your negligible earnings from failed books, Mrs. Winslow, what was your means of support during your marriage?"

"My husband's salary as a state senator. His earnings are—were—a matter of public record."

"Why would he carry such a hefty life insurance policy?"

"He was a young, healthy man. The premiums were small."

"How perfect for you."

"Objection," Milton zapped out.

"Sustained. Curb the editorializing, Counsel."

The lawyer pressed the tips of his fingers together and bowed his head, a prayerful man bracing himself to face the devil. "Mrs. Winslow, take us back to the night of February ninth. Please tell us in your own words what happened."

Milton had anticipated this, and she'd rehearsed her response for days. Still, she wasn't prepared for the icy current of dread that slipped through her as she leaned toward the microphone. Nor was she prepared for the almost overwhelming urge to blurt out the truth Malloy had forced from her on their last day together.

"We—Victor and I—attended a formal dinner at the Newport Marina that night. It was a fund-raiser. . . ." She recited the facts, much as she had for Malloy when he demanded to hear her version of that night. She described Victor's brief address. She admitted that he drank too much, and recounted her humiliation when he walked away from her on the dance floor. At that moment, she hadn't understood his rage, but she did now. Something snapped that night. Victor had felt shackled by his own life, and she was part of that trap. But she wasn't the trigger.

She described her swift departure, her intention to drive home. She didn't mention the man who had approached her as she started the car. She'd never mentioned him. Not even to Mike.

Tell your husband he forgot our meeting tonight. Tell him Max asked you to pass that on.

The stranger called Max had melted into the dreary

night, leaving her baffled and unsettled. Victor had left the building a moment later and Max intercepted him. Even though he and Max had stood apart like opponents in a duel, she'd sensed a strange, silent electricity between them. She never heard what they said, but she saw Max step forward, take hold of Victor's arm. Victor threw off his hand and strode to the car, his slender form gilded by the sodium vapor lights of the parking lot.

Reporters and photographers rushed out of the building with cameras raised, and Victor jumped into the passenger side of the car. Without thinking, Sandra accelerated, the Cadillac fishtailing as she drove into the winter night. She went too fast, hoping to avoid the press, while beside her, Victor turned into a stranger.

Even then, she hadn't fully understood. That would come in the moments that followed, when they realized Max's car was tailing them. Victor fell apart then, filling the dark car with revelations about his secret life, his private struggle, the unbearable pressure finally exploding with a passion for Max that had raged out of control.

Recounting the now-familiar story of the accident, she could still picture the dismal night, the howling wind, the road slick with oily rain. She described the wreck, the detonating airbag, the eruption that left a terrible ringing in her ears. Even now, even knowing what she knew, she wept as she spoke, pausing to take a sip of water and get her bearings.

She never knew what became of Max that night. He was probably the one who had phoned for help, but she didn't want him to be found because of what he would reveal about Victor. He might even accuse her of causing the wreck deliberately.

The Winslows' attorney did not ask what made her

lose control of the car on the bridge. No one had asked that.

"Mrs. Winslow," he asked when she had finished, "were you proud of your husband's work in the State House?"

"Of course."

"What about HR 728? Tell us about that, if you will."

Her insides turned to ice. "It's a gun control bill."

"And you supported that?"

"I certainly did."

She tried to keep to her vow to look at Milton, but a movement in the back of the courtroom distracted her. A constable spoke to someone at the door. She saw folded notes sliding across the long tables to Milton and to the plaintiffs' second chair.

"If that's the case, Mrs. Winslow, can you tell me why, on January fifth of last year, you bought a handgun via the Internet? Specifically"—he consulted his notes—"a Cobray semiautomatic nine-millimeter Luger with a five-inch barrel and a ten-round magazine. The pre-ban model with the threaded barrel."

A collective shock froze everyone in the courtroom, Sandra included. Then the room erupted with spectators discussing the revelation, reporters and sketch artists attempting to capture the moment. Santucci's gavel cleaved through the noise until a heavy, waiting silence took hold again. Milton didn't move a muscle, but she saw the jolt of alarm in his eyes. He hadn't been expecting this.

Shock trapped her reaction deep inside, and she said nothing.

"Mrs. Winslow, do you need me to repeat the question?"

She shook her head as her lips made the shape of a word, but still, no sound came out.

"Please answer the question," the judge instructed.

Her tongue atrophied. Her throat locked. Wordless air rushed out of her, nothing more. She felt her eyes bulge as though she were choking.

"It's a simple enough question," the attorney said. "Did you or did you not buy a handgun from Gunexchange.com?"

She tried to speak, to protest, to explain. Nothing came out. She was Sandy Bab-bab-babblecock. She could not utter a word even though her life depended on it.

More commotion stirred in the back of the room, adding to her confusion.

Her parents leaned forward, spoke to Milton's associates.

Milton surged to his feet. "Your Honor, may I—"

"Please direct your answer to me, Mrs. Winslow," the judge advised.

What could she say? Her panicked gaze glanced off Phil Downing. She'd given him her old laptop, free to a good home . . .

"A simple yes or no, please. We have the data from the transaction. The number of a credit card issued in your maiden name. Verification of delivery to a post office box registered to you under your assumed name, Sandy Babcock. Tell us about buying the gun."

"She didn't buy the gun," said a voice from the back of the room.

Santucci's gavel slammed down again. "Order!"

"I bought the gun."

A man in a dark suit stepped through the doorway and stood next to a uniformed cop.

Sandra couldn't move. The blood dropped from her face.

His hair was blond now, cut short. He'd been in a

fight, apparently—his jaw looked bruised and swollen, and he had a split lip, the dark laceration healing now. Still, his tanned face was lean and more handsome than ever, his compelling eyes solemn and intense. He was still a dynamic presence. He still had the power to fill a whole room with his peculiar, unforgettable energy. Like the wind blowing through a field of wheat, whispers rustled through the crowd, gathering force. People twisted around in their seats to stare.

Winifred Winslow moaned and grabbed for her husband.

And at last, Sandra's throat unlocked and she was able to speak. The single word she uttered through the microphone caused the entire room to explode in chaos.

"Victor."

Chapter 36

Victor Winslow did what he did best—he held a press conference. Preparing himself for the onslaught of questions, he felt a surprising—but undeniable—surge of adrenaline. He'd missed this.

Alerting the media had been his idea, even though he knew it would be painful. Since leaving Paradise, Victor had learned much about pain, and he'd learned that there were worse things than feeling hurt.

Hurting someone else, for example. Hurting someone who had done nothing wrong, except love him.

Sandra's suffering had been a matter of public record. Therefore, he intended to set the record straight in the most public manner possible. His return needed to be as dramatic as his disappearance had been.

He had only a moment to locate his parents at the plaintiffs' table, but it only took a moment to discern the shock etched on their faces. Their stunned expressions of burgeoning joy and relief reminded him of the reason he'd worked so long and hard to protect them.

Why couldn't you leave well enough alone? Ironically, they'd made it impossible for him to keep up the charade. If they'd left Sandra in peace, he never would have had to come back. In a moment, a new sort of suffering would take hold, sharpened by betrayal and disgust. But at least the lies and hiding would be over.

Exiting the courtroom, he and Sandra were swept along like leaves in a gushing stream. As the press jostled for position in the lobby of the courthouse, he moved to the stairs that would serve as a makeshift podium, and reached for Sandra's hand. Icy cold.

"Don't touch me," she whispered, pulling away. She looked around in panic, but spectators clogged all escape routes, so she had no choice but to stand at his side. Just as she had during their marriage.

How could he have known what this would do to her? When he and Max had driven away that night, it had all seemed so simple. *Ah, Sandra. Everything went so wrong.*

Under the hot glare of lights, microphones bristled from a battalion of cameras and correspondents. He hoped they wouldn't make too much of the cuts and bruises he'd sustained in the fight yesterday—that was another story. He orchestrated the events with his old easy command. Reaching into his pocket, he took out a prepared statement. He'd worked on it all during the flight to Providence. It was filled with his trademark sincerity and artful phrasing, but no amount of clever wording would change his fundamental message.

"Ladies and gentlemen, this is a story about courage— not my own. God knows, my lack in that area will be clear enough in a moment. I never thought I'd return, never thought I'd ever stand next to Sandra again, but I've come back to face up to my mistakes and to set the record straight."

Shouts and camera flashes erupted. Sandra flinched. Victor held up his hand, looking out into the blurred sea of faces until the flurry of questions abated. "My wife did nothing wrong," he stated. "Her only mistake was keeping silent."

"Are you saying Mrs. Winslow colluded with you to fake your own death?" a woman in the crowd demanded.

Courtney Procter. He had a few choice words for her, but that would have to wait. "Was it her intention to defraud the insurance company?" Procter persisted before he could speak again.

"Are you here to get the facts or to start rumors?" Victor snapped. He took a perverse pleasure in reducing the aggressive journalist to blushing and stammering. Back in his days in the State House, he couldn't afford to tick off reporters; now he no longer had to pretend to be gracious. "Until a moment ago, my wife believed that I'd died. I didn't plan to disappear the night of February ninth. But under the circumstances, it became my only option, or so I thought.

"The fact is, this whole tragedy started many years before I ever met Sandra. I bought the gun in order to deal with someone from my past—my ex-lover, a man named Max Henshaw."

He paused to let that sink in, then waited as the predictable questions erupted. "You had a male lover?" "Are you a homosexual?" "Who is Max Henshaw?"

He could feel Sandra's mortified presence at his side, but he didn't look at her. He wanted all the attention focused on him. "Mr. Henshaw and I were lovers in 1992. I always thought that incident was buried in the past, but of course, the fact that I'm standing before you today proves the old adage—nothing stays buried forever. Years after we parted, he wanted to see me again, even though I made it clear that I intended to stay loyal to my wife. His demands became . . . aggressive. I dealt with them on my own for as long as I could, but eventually, the situation slipped from my control. I got the credit card under my wife's maiden name. I acquired the gun, using an Internet dealer that didn't ask questions, not because I could ever imagine using it, but to try to frighten him, convince him to back off. On the night of the accident, Mr. Henshaw tried to confront me, which is why I left the marina in such haste."

He permitted himself a fleeting glance at Sandra. She stood frozen, unable to escape. "The accident in question occurred exactly as my wife described it—we quarreled, and she lost control of the car. There is one fact she didn't mention—we were being followed that night, by Mr. Henshaw in a rental car. He was the one who phoned for help from the bridge. The car went into the water and the electric windows failed. My wife was unconscious, and I shot out the windshield in order to escape. Mr. Henshaw helped us ashore. What I did next was unplanned, an impulse. Maybe I wasn't thinking straight because of shock and hypothermia, I don't know. No matter—I take full responsibility now. I drove away with Max Henshaw." He paused, watching the words sink in. He had them—they were more fascinated by him now than ever. His mother dropped her face into her hands while his father sat unmoving, like a granite war memorial statue.

"I was raised to believe homosexuality is morally wrong. I prayed for strength every day of my life, keeping my struggle hidden from my parents, my friends, my wife, my God. Everyone but myself. Being true to myself meant losing the love and esteem of my family, my community and my career in public service. I believed I was prepared to make the sacrifice. And for a long time, I succeeded. But ultimately, the price was too high. Some things are more powerful than a man's will. I'm not ashamed of who I am anymore, only that I took the wrong way out. I will, of course, take full responsibility for the laws that were broken."

He paused, then added, "I'll answer your questions later today. Right now, you'll understand, I have something more important to do."

Courthouse security guards escorted him and Sandra, along with his parents, through the press of reporters and photographers to a private conference room. Flashbulbs popped, questions battered him, but he ignored them. Sandra looked shell-shocked as she was borne along behind him, and he wondered if that was how things had always been for them—he leading, she following, buffeted by the wreckage he left in his wake.

When the door to the conference room closed, his mother stepped toward him, then hesitated, her eyes filled with yearning and shock. His father didn't hesitate at all; with a low, electric whir, the chair glided to the far end of the conference table and swung around.

Victor's heart constricted, but his resolve never wavered. If he'd learned anything in this ordeal, it was that his parents were wrong to despise what he was. Never again would he try to hide his true self just to spare them pain and preserve the Winslow reputation.

Sandra perched on the edge of the chair nearest the door as though poised to flee. "I-I assume you have a few things to tell me," she said.

He could see the cords straining in her throat, and felt a flood of tenderness. She still struggled with her stuttering. The valiance of that struggle was one of the things that had endeared her to him in the first place. She might curse the day they met, but he knew he'd never regret it. "Bear with me," he said, knowing how ironic that must sound to her. She'd borne with him far too long.

Sitting down across from her, he started to speak, taking himself back through the events that had led to the accident, bringing Sandra and his parents with him into the world he'd kept secret. He remembered when the first phone call had come. After all this time, Max was contacting him again, and deep down, Victor knew why.

The wild sexiness that had attracted him to Max in the first place had grown dark, unpredictable and more compelling than ever. He knew he and Max would destroy each other. And they had, almost.

Letters had come through the mail, over the Internet, to Victor's office, crushing him into a place from which there was no escape. The cold terror of disclosure and his never-to-be-forgotten passion had changed to desperation. Operating out of sheer panic, he acquired a handgun. He couldn't imagine actually using it, but neither could he imagine giving up the life he'd built—his work in the State House, his reputation. Most of all, he couldn't imagine the shock and disgust of his father if the truth was ever revealed. The moment Max approached him in the parking lot, Victor's life spun out of control as surely as the car itself did later, on the bridge.

He remembered the stunning impact of the sedan hitting the bridge rail, breaking through. The car smacked hard on the surface of the water. His teeth jarred together with the impact. He recalled the thick hot trickle of blood down his chin as he sat immobile, curiously detached and unconcerned as the car slowly and clumsily sank, trunk first, ghostly white headlamps pointed at the sky. Twisting around, he could see the submerged taillights, luminous pools of blood shimmering beneath the surface.

The idea of dying held no terror for him. Given the way he'd forced himself to live, it was almost a relief. His parents and community would mourn, but his death would be a far kinder blow than having them find out what their son really was. An abomination, according to his father's teachings. Victor himself had believed that, too.

A dreamlike calmness filled him. The gun felt cold and heavy in his hand. Max's secrets would cease to matter now. It was perfect . . . almost.

But something buzzed through the haze of confusion. Some impulse made him reach up, turn on the map light. Sandra. She lay half-buried by the airbag, the seeping water nearly covering her. He touched her face, moved by the lingering warmth in her cheek. Sandra. She was guilty of nothing except wanting him to be someone he was incapable of being. A husband, a lover, the father of her children. She'd done nothing but love him with a loyalty he didn't deserve.

He had to get her out of there. On a narcotic surge of adrenaline, he unfastened her seat belt. She flopped like a rag doll in his arms, and he didn't know if she was dead or alive.

The electric windows failed. Even pushing with all his might, he couldn't open the door. For the first time, he felt true panic. He picked up the gun, feeling its solid, lethal weight, and pulled the trigger.

The earsplitting shot went awry. Shaking, he tried again. The windshield imploded, crushed under the pressure of the water. Bits of glass scraped his face, his hands. A gush of cold seawater slammed him inward, plastering him back against the seat. The air bag created an awkward pocket of buoyancy. Convulsions started in his air-starved chest, and he almost lost his grip on Sandra. But Victor had grown up beside the water, and he'd always been a strong swimmer. He managed to keep hold, to escape through the ruined window as though pushing through a birth canal.

Fighting the swift currents, he swam for shore. Max had already waded out to help him. The car's headlights still wavered eerily, deep beneath the surface. Neither said a word as they dragged Sandra to the rocky beach. White foam bubbled from her nose and mouth. She choked, then gasped for breath.

He stood shivering, wave-washed rocks rattling under his feet. The onset of hypothermia imbued him with a strange sense of freedom and detachment. He had defied death. He had saved Sandra's life.

Sandra, who finally knew the truth.

"I called for an ambulance." Max took Victor's arm. "Are you hurt?"

"No."

A distant keening sound filled the dark, wet air. A siren.

Max fell absolutely still, his grip hot and strong. "Come with me."

"What? That's crazy, that's—"

"Don't you get it, Victor? Your life here is over. After this, nothing will be the same—you'll have to resign from office, your wife will divorce you. God knows what your parents will do. Is that what you want?"

"No, but—"

"We'll go to my place in Florida. Now, tonight. Before anyone comes. They'll find the woman here—but not you."

He felt light-headed. He was shivering, drifting. "Jesus, Max."

"This moment is a gift, an opportunity we'll never have again."

Victor shuddered with icy excitement. He'd been baptized by the brutal sea and had emerged a new person. He knew what he was giving up. He could never look back, never come back. He could never contact the people he loved or comfort his grieving family.

How strange that it should all end in this place, where he used to design elaborate hideouts in the dense, sucking marshes or borrow a fisherman's dory and take to the sea for an afternoon's adventure. Few knew the secrets of this geography better than Victor. A boy could disappear for days and never be found.

In the terrible cold night, he'd said Sandra's name, but she didn't hear. "I love you," he said, his voice all but drowned by the wind and waves and the oncoming siren, "but I can't do this anymore." He kissed her once, on the forehead. It was too dark to see traces of his own blood sinking into her wet coat. And then he made his truly terrible and unforgivable choice—he got into Max's car and they drove off, leaving Sandra unconscious, to be found by the rescuers.

Within a week, they arrived in Miami, then headed for the ends of the earth—Key West. Staying at Max's bungalow in Sugarhouse Row, Victor completely reinvented himself, acquiring a new identity with ridiculous ease via the Internet. He chose the name Robert Chance—almost no one would understand the significance of that. At Max's busy gallery in a historic waterfront icehouse, he sold his jewel-colored suncatchers to tourists.

It was the life he'd always dreamed of having. He became someone so different from Victor Winslow that sometimes he forgot his former life.

But not entirely. Via news links on the Internet, he

learned of the dark turn the death investigation had taken. Many times, he'd been tempted to intervene, but Max always convinced him to wait, to see how things turned out. When the accident ruling came down, he believed it was an affirmation that he'd done the right thing. But the latest development—his parents' civil suit—had taken him completely by surprise.

He liked to think he would have come forward on his own, but would he?

Hollow silence echoed in the wake of his story. He pulled in a deep, unsteady breath, pressed his sweating palms down on the tabletop and looked at Sandra. He wanted to touch her but didn't dare. She seemed so different now. She was still beautiful; she always had been, with her dark hair, haunted eyes and her unique combination of fragility and resilience. But now, subtle changes strengthened her posture, her demeanor. The way she sat so near his parents and refused to flinch was new to him. Yet her poise was hard-won; he could see the whiteness of her knuckles as she held her hands in her lap.

"I couldn't have known what would happen," he told her. "I thought that by disappearing, I'd be giving you the shot you deserved. Life insurance fraud seemed the least of my sins, because I convinced myself *that* person was dead, and you'd be free to start a new life for yourself—"

"Don't expect me to swallow that," she stated in a tone he'd never heard from her before. "You can't just walk away and pretend you did it for me. What do you suppose it was like, losing you, grieving for you, putting up with the accusations and hatred while you went to Key West with your boyfriend?"

"I never could have predicted that everyone would hold you responsible."

"Sandra, we're so sorry," his mother said. "If only we'd understood—"

"You didn't want to understand," Sandra stated calmly, addressing her directly for the first time since they'd entered the room. His father glanced at Sandra and then, with a twist of guilt on his face, stared down at his knees.

Ronald Winslow's head was not bowed in prayer. Victor knew what prayer looked like. He used to pray on his knees for hours, begging God to make him straight.

When his father finally looked up at him, there was agony—but no forgiveness—in his eyes. "Why did you come back?" he asked. Ignoring his wife's gasp of horror, he added, "Why did you even bother?"

Victor surged to his feet. "You brought me back, you with your idiotic lawsuit. I left because I couldn't be who you wanted me to be. You'd rather see me dead than have a son who is gay. So I gave you that. I died. You should have left it that way."

Without a word, Sandra went to the door, but he stopped her, blocking the way. "Wait."

"Just let me go," she said.

"I will. I know I have to." Voices drifted from the wide hallway outside. "It's a different world for you, out there," he said.

"Yes."

Watching her, he realized she wasn't afraid—this woman who used to quail at the prospect of facing the press. She was no longer the passive bystander he'd married; she was strong, sure of herself. She could walk away from him and his parents because they were part of an old life, old concerns that no longer affected her.

"Please believe that I never meant for you to suffer,"

he said. "I honestly thought it was the best solution, until Mike—"

"Mike?" Shock swept visibly through her, leaching the color from her cheeks.

"Malloy."

Understanding dawned on her face as she studied the fresh bruise on his jaw. His split lip stung as he tried for some semblance of his old grin. "He brought me back, Sandra. There will be charges against me and I'll face them. I'm here to pick up the pieces, pay whatever this cost you in legal fees, deal with the insurance company, clean up the mess I made of everything."

"Even my life?"

"Whatever it takes. Anything, I swear."

"I only want one thing from you, Victor."

"What's that?"

"A divorce."

Chapter 37

M ike lifted the plastic bag of frozen peas from his eye and leaned toward the mirror. The swelling had gone down some, but the bruise was turning dark. He was tempted to tell himself Victor had gotten in a lucky punch, but that wasn't the case. Mike was out of practice. It had been a long time since he'd beaten the crap out of anyone.

He checked his paint-spattered watch, certain it was broken, because the hands hadn't moved. Briefly, he considered checking the local news on the TV or radio, but dismissed the idea. That would only make him more crazy. Restless, he left the *Fat Chance* to pace up and down in the boatyard parking lot, debating whether or not to drive over to the courthouse.

Victor had warned of a media circus, and Mike knew his own presence would only add to the confusion and possibly raise even more questions. His lawyer would have a cow. The last thing he needed was for his kids to see him, with a black eye, on the evening news as part of a story about a gay fugitive. So Vic was probably right in advising him to keep a low profile, but that didn't make the waiting any easier.

Hooking his thumbs into the back pockets of his jeans, Mike stared out at the water, glinting with the hardness of late-afternoon sunlight. The reunion with Victor had been surreal, almost. When he'd finally arrived in Key West, Mike had been dog-tired, pissed off and out of patience. He found his way to Henshaw's house, but no one was home. A neighbor directed him to a gallery in the waterfront area. Amid the heat and hustle of Mallory Square, he entered a world of tourists and beach bums, gay couples and honeymooners, starving artists, street entertainers and serious students—a transient, relaxed population moving through a sea of anonymity.

From a cantina painted Pepto-Bismol pink, he watched strangers strolling past, sometimes stopping for a drink beneath the Campari sun umbrellas. In the arts and crafts gallery across the way, tropical sunlight flashed through dozens of handcrafted suncatchers hanging in the display window. People wandered in and out, and then at closing time, a tall man had locked up with an electronic security keypad.

Mike hadn't recognized Victor at first—yellow hair, cutoffs, sandals, a muscle shirt revealing glossy, tanned shoulders. But that long-legged, easy gait and that confident manner had been instantly familiar.

Mike registered only one emotion—rage. He stalked across the street and shoved him up against the seawall, gouged and pitted from centuries of battering storms. "Hey, Victor. Long time no see."

The suntan had paled. "*Mike?* Mike, Jesus, is that you? What do you want with me?"

"Oh, I think you know, Vic."

Victor's fist exploded outward, catching Mike in the left eye. Seeing stars, he grabbed Victor, spun him around and drove his fist at his best friend's face. The impact split his knuckles and snapped Victor's head sideways. He staggered back against the wall, sinking slowly. Then he pulled himself up again to flee.

Mike's second punch drew blood, and a crowd as well. Onlookers gathered in a murmuring clot. Mike didn't give a shit. "Pack it in now, Victor. Or are you going to make me drag you by the short hairs to the airport?"

Victor brought his knee up, forcing Mike to feint to one side. "I'm not going anywhere—"

"Wrong answer. You're going back to get your wife out of trouble."

"She doesn't need me, Mike. Everything's going to be fine, you'll see."

He twisted his fist into the bloodstained shirt. "I'll pretend you never said that. You married her knowing you'd never make her happy, and then you disappeared, you fucking coward."

"I did it for Sandra," Victor protested, ducking Mike's fist. "She wanted—"

Mike threw him to the pavement, hearing the wind rush from his lungs. "She wanted a goddamned husband. She wanted kids, you son of a bitch."

Victor crabwalked backward. "I never meant to hurt her. I thought she was . . . perfect for me."

"She was safe. You used her." Some latent sense of fair play caused Mike to allow him to climb to his feet again. The fascinated tourists fell back, expanding their circle. "Were you perfect for her?" he demanded. "Or did you even bother to think of that?"

"I honestly believed I was. She was so innocent, so lonely. She . . . moved me."

Mike's next blow had swung wild, missing its mark. "She could move a rock," he said. "She could move a dead man. Didn't you see what you were doing to her? She thought *she* was the problem."

"That's why disappearing was the answer."

"Ever heard of divorce, Vic? Handy thing, and it's completely legal in this country." Mike pushed him up against the wall again, this time with his forearm across Victor's throat. They both reeked of sweat and rage, and the crimson trickle of blood from Victor's lip gleamed grotesquely in the sunlight.

"No Winslow's ever been divorced. But plenty of us have died young." He swallowed hard against Mike's pressing arm. His face turned dark; his breath became an air-starved wheeze, and the fight drained out of him.

As Mike eased his grip, the adrenaline haze slowly cleared. He felt the curiosity of the onlookers, the heat of the South Florida sun on his back. "We need to talk," he said.

Victor warily sidestepped him. "Show's over, folks," he said. The tourists dispersed, shuffling away, casting dubious glances over their shoulders. Victor studied the palms of his hands, scraped and livid. "I had no idea everything would blow up in her face," he admitted. "I just didn't think—and when I did, I wanted this new life and didn't know how to give it up."

Now that Mike could relate to. He had a hard time giving things up himself.

Victor stood quietly for a long time, studying the glitter of sunlight on the water, oblivious to the drying ribbon of blood down his chin. "Okay," he said. "Let's go."

During the flight home, Victor told Mike everything— the secret affair, his vow to live "straight" in order to honor his family and focus on his political goals, the reappearance of Max, the constant terror of discovery and the opportunity that had been given to Victor the night of the accident. "I thought a second chance was what she needed," he said.

"Sandy doesn't need a second chance," Mike said. "She needs you." Everything Mike thought he knew about his best friend had been turned on its ear. And yet, for the first time, Victor finally made sense in a way he never had before. Mike couldn't keep from asking the question that had nagged at him ever since he found out. "When did you know?"

Some of Victor's old humor had glinted in his eyes. "You mean, did I get turned on at our campouts or sleepovers? Hell, Mike, it wasn't some big epiphany. I guess I sort of always knew, but I trained myself to ignore it— even after Brice Hall. I never told you what happened there, did I?"

"I figured you didn't want to talk about it. I was a dumbshit growing up, Vic, but even I'd heard about the weird things at all-boy boarding schools. I thought they only happened in English novels."

"I thought it was a case of adolescent experimentation. Denial's the Winslow way, you know. I really thought I could live straight. God knows I tried. But in my family, when you're torn between duty and desire, you choose duty every time, hands down. I never even knew I had a choice."

"You made a lot of choices," Mike snapped. "Sandy

was one of those choices. Christ, you almost destroyed her."

Victor had settled into a thoughtful silence. Then he said, "You love her—that's what this is all about, isn't it?"

"You fucked up any chance I might've had with her."

"Oh, no, Mikey." Victor's old aplomb shone through. "I'm guilty of a lot of things, but not that. I'll shoulder the blame for my screwed-up relationships, but not yours."

The words lingered in his mind even now, as the light deepened with the end of day and an evening chill sharpened the air. Mike turned up the collar of his jacket. By now, Victor would have made his appearance, his public statement. Had Mike done the right thing by forcing the confrontation, or had he blown it?

All he could do was wait and hope. He thought about the house, and the past they'd never shared, the dreams that hadn't had a chance to come true for them. He'd gone into his relationship with Sandra the way a hiker goes into a pristine forest—he wasn't sure what he was looking for or even if he'd find anything, and he risked getting hopelessly lost. But he went forward anyway.

Quietly, maybe without meaning to, Sandra showed him the way back to love. But even though falling for her was the most powerful thing that had ever happened to him, it was fragile. Mike knew he needed to protect his love for Sandra in a way he never felt compelled to do with his wife. He used to think that working hard and getting ahead proved his commitment to Angela. With Sandra, he realized commitment meant risking the deepest part of himself—and damn the consequences.

Putting his fingers to his lips, he whistled for Zeke. The dog, still a little too well groomed for his taste, raced across the parking lot and leaped into the truck.

Chapter 38

Journal Entry—April 9—Tuesday

Ten Things to Do with the Rest of My Life

1. Think up ten tortures for Victor Winslow.
2. Take up a career in public speaking.
3. Write a tell-all memoir and go on the talk-show circuit.
4. Stop at the pharmacy and buy a home-pregnancy test.

It took a long time for Sandra to extricate herself from the chaos of the courthouse. Despite all that had happened, some things never changed. Being around Victor was like being a groupie to a rock star. Everyone was eclipsed by his burning, almost manic energy. Even as he bared his soul to the press, he had a way of sucking up all the attention.

Except today, the focus had shifted to her. Everyone wanted to talk to her—Victor, his parents, her lawyer, Sparky, the press. She felt half-drowned in the attention, battered by questions. She managed to telegraph a look of desperation to her parents. Joyce shoved her into the ladies' room and stood guard at the door. She and Sandra switched hats and coats, then kept their shades on and heads down as they left the building through a rear exit.

Her parents traded cars, driving away with Joyce in tow. The news vans followed them while Sandra took the Grand Marquis and quietly and anonymously made her way back to Blue Moon Beach.

She wept as she drove home; her tears expressed neither grief nor joy, but simply a shattering relief. She felt empty, scoured clean.

It was late afternoon by the time she walked into the now-beautiful house. Isolated and lovely, it reminded her of a single perfect seashell left on a deserted beach.

The phone rang incessantly; instead of answering, she unplugged all the extensions. In the creaky silence of the old house, she could hear the rhythm of her own heart. Dropping her borrowed coat and hat on the window seat, she looked out the big picture window, unsure of what to do with herself next.

Her life had taken a left turn again. She was no longer a murderous wife, but the victim of a troubled man whose worst crime was loving too passionately and being afraid of who he really was. She supposed she would forgive him one day . . . not today, though. Today, she simply had to get used to the idea that the nightmare of the past year was finally over.

But she was still Sandy Babcock, who wrote controversial books and sometimes stammered when she spoke.

Her gaze fell on the fax machine. The thing had disgorged a long, unbroken banner of thermal paper that hung down the side of the desk. Idly, she scanned the first page.

Her book had won the Addie Award. Although the honor represented the highest level of achievement in her career, the news echoed hollowly through her. That's what she was—hollow, with nothing inside that knew how to savor her blessings. She helped herself to a few M&M's from the bowl on the desk. Perhaps she should call her folks, share the good news with them, but . . . Victor's dramatic resurrection made everything else seem trivial. And the fact that it had been Mike who'd made him come forward—with cuts and bruises that implied a struggle—trumped everything else in the world.

The other pages of the fax were unrelated to the award. They were preceded by a scrawled message on Sparky's letterhead. "I couldn't get near you today. Join the living and get an answering machine. News! I found you a buyer. Coming out to meet with you at six P.M. You're going to *love* this. Offer to follow. Suggest you accept, contingency and all."

Sandra checked the clock. Almost six P.M. Damn. She didn't want to see anyone, not now. She tugged on a jacket and hurried outside, crossing the yard and forging over the dunes. Loose sand poured into her good shoes, but she didn't care. She also didn't care that she was running away again—avoiding her problems rather than facing them.

On the beach, she stood at the water's edge, feeling the breeze pass over her and listening to the hush of the waves. A sweep of clouds reflecting the color of sunset crowned the horizon. Everything was happening so fast, yet the unhurried rhythm of the changeless sea calmed her with its never-ceasing heartbeat.

Selling the house, moving away, had been her goal, yet achieving it was a bittersweet victory. What now? she wondered. Manhattan? Mendocino? Athens, Hong Kong, Copenhagen?

She wondered who would live here after she was gone. A happy couple just starting out, a young family seeking a storybook setting for their kids. A pair of cheerful retirees, perhaps, who would sit on the porch together each morning and watch the sun come up. Now that the offer had actually come in, she felt an overwhelming sadness. It was going to be so hard to let go after all the time she'd spent here, all the energy she'd put into restoring the dilapidated old house, all the arguing she'd done with Mike over light fixtures and door hinges, all the time they'd spent making love in the tall-ceilinged bedroom overlooking the endless sea. Without meaning to, she'd filled the place with memories, and now she didn't want to let go.

Her chest hurt with the effort to contain her emotions. This was the plan, she told herself. But deep down, she knew what was wrong. She'd reached a point in her life where she could go anywhere—but the only place she wanted to be was here, right here in Paradise.

A light evening breeze, with the faintest hint of summer borne on it, sifted through the top layer of sand. Restless memories stirred inside her. She thought of Mary Margaret and Kevin and how they loved to come here even in winter, playing and shouting, running from the waves and throwing sticks for the dog. She remembered how she'd felt the first time Mike took her in his arms, even though it was for a dance lesson, and she thought of the day he built a fire on the beach for her and warmed her hands in his. Maybe then, she thought. Maybe that was the day she'd started to love him.

He had taken her empty, broken-down wreck and made it into a home. Blue Moon Beach was a part of her, perhaps the best part, but coming to love this place hadn't been in her plan.

Falling in love with Mike hadn't been in her plan, either. She'd let him into her house, into her life, and he'd found the way into her heart.

At the faint sound of an engine, she hunched her shoulders, hoping Sparky and the buyer wouldn't see her out here. Maybe they would just go away. For the time being, she wanted the whole world to go away.

A sharp bark sounded above the dunes, startling her. Seconds later, Zeke bounded down the sandy slope, a whitish streak with tongue lolling. Her heart took a sudden leap. But everything inside her froze the moment she saw Mike. Lit from behind by the evening sun, he seemed to emerge from a nimbus of red and gold while she squinted and shaded her eyes.

The heat of tears filled her throat. She had missed him, everything about him—she missed looking across the room to find him watching her with a smile in his eyes, the way he whistled through his teeth as he worked, the smell of his pillow after he left the bed in the morning, the moments of intimacy so deep and true that she found a new person inside her. He had cracked through her wall of ice, and she would never be the same.

But she didn't know what to say after all that had happened. She didn't know how to begin again.

"Hello, Malloy." Amazing. She'd said her problem word—*hello*—without hesitation. "Or should I say Detective Malloy?"

"Not a bad piece of work for a handyman."

A faint tan—a Florida tan—made him look more rugged, a little exotic, somehow. She noticed that his left eye was swollen, ringed by a darkening bruise. "You've been busy."

"I had to find something to do with myself after you fired me." He shifted his hip to one side, hooked a thumb into the waistband of his jeans. For the first time, she realized he was nervous. "So did it work out okay?" he asked. "At the courthouse, I mean."

"Everything works out okay for Victor, even a public confession. He actually had reporters in tears. He made all sorts of promises—he'll give me a divorce immediately, sort out the mess of our finances, deal with the charges of insurance fraud, cover all the legal fees. When all is said and done, he's still Victor, still good at taking charge."

"No surprise there."

"So . . . what are you doing here?" she made herself ask.

"I left something behind."

"What?" she asked, speculating. Maybe he'd left some tool, a loose wire, his toothbrush in her bathroom, some small part of himself that he needed to go on.

He hesitated, took a deep breath. "My heart."

She shoved her hands in her pockets and stepped back. "God, Malloy. You always do this."

"Do what?"

"Make me . . ." *Make me want you more than I want the next breath of air.* Blinking fast, she realized she was inches from falling apart. "We have a lot to discuss, but this isn't a good time. Someone is coming."

"I know." He took a step toward her. The breeze plucked at his dark hair, and sunlight glinted in his smile. She kept staring at that black eye; it made her feel shaken by wonderment. No one had ever fought for her before.

"Sparky is bringing a buyer for the house." Finally a tear escaped, and she brushed it away with the back of her hand, but another one quickly followed.

"I know that, too." With infinite delicacy, he touched his thumb to her cheek, catching the tear.

His caress nearly undid her. "How?"

"Sandy." He held her shoulders, steadying her.

She wanted to sink against him, disappear into him, somehow, but apprehension held her rigid. "What?"

"The offer is from me."

"What?"

"I'm offering to buy the house."

"Malloy . . . *Mike*."

"I know you planned on leaving Paradise, but everything's different. People around here will forgive Victor—or not, that's up to them. He did exonerate you, and there's no reason for you to leave now."

She listened to the waves running up on shore, the plaintive cry of a curlew high above. Then she took a deep breath and asked, "Is there a reason to stay?"

He held her hand, chilly fingers holding fast. When he smiled down at her, she held her breath. "Did Sparky explain the contract? There's a contingency."

"Which is?"

"Well, I didn't exactly put it in the contract. It's a marriage proposal."

A sudden pounding in her ears drowned out the roar of the waves, the wind, everything. She couldn't hear a sound except the echo of his words, filling her with wonder and magic. After a while, she found her voice. "Mike. Oh, God."

"I love you, Sandy. The kids and I—we all love you. Stay here and marry me. Marry *us*. We'll finish the house together. We'll fight about paint and plaster and cabinet hardware . . . I've seen the look on your face when you walk through that house with me. It's what you want, Sandy."

"It won't work. How can it, when Angela—"

"Don't worry about her." He spoke with a brusque decisiveness that startled her.

"She's the mother of your children. She'll always be a part of your life, Mike. A powerful part. And she doesn't want me anywhere near the kids."

"This is not about what she wants. After a while, she'll get used to the idea—I'm not giving her a choice. She just wasn't expecting me to find anyone else." The wind blew a strand of hair across her cheek, and he brushed it away with his hand. "She never knew . . . I could love like this, and I think it scared her."

His words struck Sandra like velvet blows. She wasn't used to the sort of passion he ignited—fiery comets and unstoppable whirlwinds that left her tender and exhausted and filled with a dangerous, fragile bliss. Loving him consumed and frightened her, and she found herself bracing for loss even before she flung herself fully into the relationship.

"I'm afraid, too," she blurted out in a burst of honesty. "What I feel for you is so . . . big, so out of control. I'd risk anything, Mike, commit any crime. It can't be healthy. Loving this intensely is a destructive thing. It's dark and frightening. Look what it did to Victor."

"Lying to himself did that to Vic. You don't have to do crazy things like he did. There are actually legal ways to deal with true love." He slid his hands down her arms, twined his fingers with hers in her pockets. "He never put you first, and I will. You were convenient for him. That's not how it is with me. I love you and to be honest"—he grinned a little—"you don't always make it convenient to do that. But that only makes me love you more. Every day."

She remembered the Ferris wheel and how frightened she'd been—but she'd done it anyway. She thought about her parents and realized love was never meant to be perfect. "I'm still afraid," she said.

"I know. Aw, honey, I know. We all are. People really do let the love of their life walk away because they're scared to show how much they want or need. But you're not like that anymore."

She was struck, as she so often was, by his plain-spoken wisdom. She never expected a man like him to have such insights into the human heart, into *her* heart, but he did. Only a few moments ago, being with him had seemed impossible but it was really so simple.

He mistook her hesitation for doubt, and drew her closer. "You can't turn away from life, and I can't protect you from everything bad." Pulling back, he offered a half smile. "I don't need to, and you don't want me to."

He was so right. Life as it unfolded, day by day, was just too rich. She wanted it all—the gladness and pain and laughter and tears. And she wanted it with him.

"We'll finish the house together," he said. "Maybe we'll make a baby or two—" He wiped her tears with a bandanna from his back pocket, and then he kissed her forehead, cheeks, mouth, all the while whispering, "Please. I love you. Please."

That was it, then. The real deal. The scariest, most exhilarating ride of all.

"Say yes," he whispered in her ear. "Whatever you want. I'll give you whatever you want."

She discovered that happiness could hurt—it was a piercing joy, the sweetest sensation she'd ever felt, rushing through every part of her, rushing out to meet him. "You already have."

Slipping his arms around her, he brought her close against him, sheltering her from the cold sea wind.

Acknowledgments

Thanks as always to the real Barb and Joyce; to Alicia, who is always so good at brainstorming; and to the Port Orchard gang: Anjali, Kate, Janine, Lois, Rose Marie, and PJ. My agent, Meg Ruley, and her associate, Annelise Robey, read and commented with insight and tact. Maggie Crawford was there at the beginning, and the superior editorial skills of Beth de Guzman guided the final revisions. Special thanks to Harry Helm for reading an early draft and adding his insights.

Thanks also to: Lisa Baumgartner for helping with local color, the resources of Newport's Redwood Library, the Stuttering Foundation of America for providing insights and awareness, Officer Joseph Cabaza for answering endless queries about the sad business of death investigation, and the amazing artsy attorney, Sandra McDowd, for providing legal advice to fictional characters.

Reading Group Guide

Discussion Topics

1. The town of Paradise holds different meanings for Sandra Winslow and Mike Malloy. What are these meanings? What would you define as "paradise" for each of these characters? How would you describe your perfect paradise?

2. In the first scene of the book, we see Sandra making a list about a TV reporter and chopping firewood. What do these two things tell us about her character? What would you say are her strengths and her weaknesses? Do you think her decision to sell her house and leave town is courageous? Are there other options she could have considered?

3. The tragedy of Victor Winslow's disappearance is officially ruled an accident, yet the locals persist in believing that Sandra murdered her husband. Why? Does the strength of their belief in Sandra's guilt justify their actions toward her? How far would you go to right a wrong that you think has been committed?

4. Mike Malloy doesn't know what to expect when he meets his high school buddy's widow, Sandra. What is his first impression of her? How does this impression change over the course of the book? If Mike didn't need work so badly, do you think he would have declined the job of restoring Sandra's house?

5. At one point Mike describes Lenny and Gloria as having "what a marriage should be." Why does Mike say this? What happened to him in his marriage? Many times in the story the idea of the "perfect marriage" arises. What is the

perfect marriage? How does Sandra feel after hearing her parents may divorce? Do you think her mother has good enough reasons to leave her husband?

6. Sandra's books are available by request only at the library due to questionable material in her books. What is the "questionable material"? Did it bother Mike's daughter, Mary Margaret? Do you think the material warrants censorship? How do you feel about Sandra's attitude about the censorship of her books?

7. Mike conducts a secret investigation into the night of Victor's disappearance. Why? What role do his feelings for Sandra play? Do those feelings warrant his going behind her back? When is "I'm doing it for your own good" not an acceptable reason for taking a particular course of action?

8. Mike's ex-wife, Angela, is still a part of Mike's life. In what way do they remain connected? When Angela confronts Sandra, what does Sandra do? What explanation does Mike have for Angela's behavior? If she is happy with her new marriage, why does she act this way?

9. When Victor reveals the truth about himself, his parents reject him. How would you react to such a revelation from your child or someone close to you? Do you think Victor's parents' standing in the community will be affected? His father tells him, "You should never have come back." Is there ever a situation when not knowing the truth is better?

10. Characters in the book make sacrifices and changes in the name of love: Sandra hides Victor's secret, Mike doesn't attend his daughter's confirmation, Sandra's father learns Spanish. What are you willing to do for love?